Also by John Updike

POEMS

The Carpentered Hen (1958) • *Telephone Poles* (1963) • *Midpoint* (1969) • *Tossing and Turning* (1977) • *Facing Nature* (1985) • *Collected Poems 1953–1993*

NOVELS

The Poorhouse Fair (1959) • *Rabbit, Run* (1960) • *The Centaur* (1963) • *Of the Farm* (1965) • *Couples* (1968) • *Rabbit Redux* (1971) • *A Month of Sundays* (1975) • *Marry Me* (1976) • *The Coup* (1978) • *Rabbit Is Rich* (1981) • *The Witches of Eastwick* (1984) • *Roger's Version* (1986) • *S.* (1988) • *Rabbit at Rest* (1990) • *Memories of the Ford Administration* (1992) • *Brazil* (1994) • *In the Beauty of the Lilies* (1996)

SHORT STORIES

The Same Door (1959) • *Pigeon Feathers* (1962) • *Olinger Stories* (a selection, 1964) • *The Music School* (1966) • *Bech: A Book* (1970) • *Museums and Women* (1972) • *Problems and Other Stories* (1979) • *Too Far to Go* (a selection, 1979) • *Bech Is Back* (1982) • *Trust Me* (1987) • *The Afterlife and Other Stories* (1994)

ESSAYS AND CRITICISM

Assorted Prose (1965) • *Picked-Up Pieces* (1975) • *Hugging the Shore* (1983) • *Just Looking* (1989) • *Odd Jobs* (1991) • *Golf Dreams: Writings on Golf* (1996)

PLAY

Buchanan Dying (1974)

MEMOIRS

Self-Consciousness (1989)

CHILDREN'S BOOKS

The Magic Flute (1962) • *The Ring* (1964) • *A Child's Calendar* (1965) • *Bottom's Dream* (1969) • *A Helpful Alphabet of Friendly Objects* (1996)

TOWARD
THE END
OF TIME

John Updike

TOWARD THE END OF TIME

Alfred A. Knopf   New York

1997

THIS IS A BORZOI BOOK
PUBLISHED BY ALFRED A. KNOPF, INC.

Grateful acknowledgment is made to Harvard University Press for permission to reprint poem #812 from *The Poems of Emily Dickinson*, edited by Thomas H. Johnson (Cambridge, Mass.: The Belknap Press of Harvard University Press), copyright 1951, © 1955, 1979, 1983 by the President and Fellows of Harvard College. Reprinted by permission of the publishers and the Trustees of Amherst College.

The account of the contracting universe in Chapter 5 is based on that of Paul Davies in *The Last Three Minutes*, Chapter 9. The poem approximated on page 85 is by Emily Dickinson, "A Light Exists in Spring."

Library of Congress Cataloging-in-Publication Data

Updike, John.
 Toward the end of time / by John Updike.—1st ed.
  p.   cm
  ISBN 0-375-40006-0 (cloth)
  I. Title.
813'.54—dc21   97-5167
                                                   CIP

Manufactured in the United States of America
Published September 9, 1997
Second Printing, September 19, 1997

> *familiar only with God,*
> *We yearn to be pierced by that*
> *Occasional void through which the supernatural flows.*
>
> —CHARLES WRIGHT,
> "Lives of the Saints"

> *We cannot tell that we are constantly splitting into duplicate selves because our consciousness rides smoothly along only one path in the endlessly forking chains.*
>
> —MARTIN GARDNER,
> "Wap, Sap, Pap, and Fap"

Chapters

TOWARD
THE END
OF TIME

i. *The Deer*

FIRST SNOW: it came this year late in November. Gloria and I awoke to see a fragile white inch on the oak branches outside the bathroom windows, and on the curving driveway below, and on the circle of lawn the driveway encloses—the leaves still unraked, the grass still green. I looked into myself for a trace of childhood exhilaration at the sight and found none, just a quickened awareness of being behind in my chores and an unfocused dread of time itself, time that churns the seasons and that had brought me this new offering, this heavy new radiant day like a fresh meal brightly served in a hospital to a patient with a dwindling appetite.

And yet does the appetite for new days ever really cease? An hour later, I *was* exhilarated, clearing my porch and its single long granite step with my new orange plastic shovel, bought cheap and shaped like a scoop and much more silkily serviceable than the cumbersome metal snow shovels of my childhood, with their sticky surfaces and noisy bent edges. Plastic shovels are an improvement—can you believe it? The world does not only get worse. Lightweight, the

shovel hurled flakes sparkling into the still air, onto the bobbing leucothoë in the border bed. There had been bloated
yews there, planted by the previous owner beneath the win-
dowsills and over the years grown to eclipse the windows
and darken the living room. My wife, the dynamic Gloria,
commanded men to come and tear them out and plant little
bushes that in turn are getting increasingly shaggy. Nature
refuses to rest.

The transient sparkles seemed for a microsecond engraved upon the air. The weathervane on the garage, a copper mallard in the act of landing—wings lifted, webbed feet
spread—pointed west, into a wind too faint to be felt. The
snow was too early and light to summon the plowing service (our garden-and-lawn service in its winter guise), and I
hadn't even planted the reflector stakes around the driveway; but that inch evidently intimidated the FedEx truck
driver, for at some point in the quiet morning a stiff purple,
orange, and white FedEx envelope appeared between the
storm door and the front door without the truck's making its
way up the driveway. How did the envelope—containing
some bond slips I was in no hurry for—get there? By the
time I walked, in mid-afternoon, down to the mailbox, a
number of trucks and cars, including one cautiously driven
by my wife, had passed up and down. It was only when walking back up the hill that I was struck by—between the two
broad grooves worn by tire treads—the footprints.

They were not mine. My boots have a distinctive sole, a
mix of arcs and horizontals like the longitude and latitude
lines on a globe. Nor could I match my stride to the other
footprints—they were too far apart, though I am not short-
legged, or unvigorous. But, stretch my legs as I would, I
could not place my boots in the oblongs left by this other's
passing. Had a giant invaded my terrain? An angel dropped

down from Heaven? The solution eventually came to me: the FedEx driver this morning, not wishing to trust his (or her; a number are women, in their policelike uniforms of gray-blue) wide truck to the upward twists of our driveway, had dismounted and raced up and back. He—no woman could have run uphill with such a stride—had cruelly felt the pressure of time.

Yet, though I had solved the mystery, the idea of a visitation by a supernatural being stayed with me, as I clumped into the house and spread the mail, the main spiritual meal of my day, upon the kitchen table. Perhaps the word is not "spiritual" but "social" or "contactual"—since my retirement from the Boston financial world I go for days without talking to anyone but my wife. I have kept a few old clients, and transactions for them and my own portfolio are frequently handled by FedEx. I once enjoyed the resources of faxing and e-mail, but when I retired I cut the wires, so to speak. I wanted to get back to nature and my own human basics before saying good-bye to everything.

My premonition of the FedEx driver as a supernatural creature was not merely an aging man's mirage: creatures other than ourselves do exist, some of them quite large. Whales, elephants, rhinoceri, Bengal tigers, not quite extinct, though the last Siberian tigers perished in the recent war. Giraffes and moose, those towering creations, even flourish. Deer haunt our property here. Walking on our driveway, I sometimes see an especially bold doe in the woods—a big haunchy animal the dull dun color of a rabbit, holding motionless as if to blend into the shadows of the trees. The doe stares at me with a directness I might think was insolence instead of an alert wariness. Her heart must be racing. Mine is. When I say a word or make as if to fling a stone, she wheels and flees. The amount of white tail she shows is startling. Startling also are the white edges of her large round ears, which swivel like dish antennae, above the black, globular, wet eyes.

Gloria does not share my enchantment, so I do not tell her of these surreptitious encounters. She rants against these poor deer, who ate her tulip shoots in the spring and trimmed her rosebush of blooms in September. Who would imagine that deer would eat roses? My wife wants the deer killed. She gets on the telephone, searching for men with rifles or bows and arrows and an atavistic hunger for venison and the patience to stand for hours on a platform they will build in the trees; she has heard rumors of such men. So much projected effort makes me weary. My wife is a killer. She dreams at night of my death, and when she awakens, in her guilty consciousness she gives my body a hug that shatters my own desirous dreams. By daylight she pumps me full of vitamins and advice as if to prolong my life but I know her dreams' truth: she wants me and the deer both dead.

More snow, in early December. This morning, as I dressed to the shimmering, straining (what are they aspiring to? what Heaven awaits at the edge of their resolved harmonies?) violins of Vivaldi's *Four Seasons*, I saw a deer, looking like a large dark dog, curled up on the flagpole platform at the front of the lawn, toward the sea, with its snow-dusted islands. We have a majestic view, south and southwest across Massachusetts Bay, and the sight of the reposing deer was also majestic. I must have thought I was married to some other wife, to judge from the innocent enthusiasm with which I called the deer to the attention of my own. She became galvanized, rapidly dressing and urging me to follow her downstairs while still in my pajamas. "Just put on boots and a coat," she commanded.

Obedient, I yet thought of my years, my heart. Gloria makes my heart race, once with appetite, now with fear.

She raced to the closet under the stairs and from its hiding place there she brought her basket of my old golf balls. She keeps them to throw at the deer. When I had first protested against this waste she cited an article she had read, to the effect that golf balls lose compression within a few months of being unsealed, and balls over a year old are basically worthless. Outside we went, she in her righteous fury and shimmering mink coat, me in my pajamas and boots and old parka spouting goose down through its broken seams; but by the time we had trudged through the crusty snow around the side porch the deer, hearing us close the front door, had disappeared. "Look!" said my wife, the basket under her arm giving her the burdened, innocent air of a primitive gatherer. "Its tracks go everywhere!"

And it was true, one could see how the hungry animal, its innocence burdened only by the needs of its own sizable body, had gone from the yew bush by the rose bed to the box bush on the other side, from the box to the privet ball by the birdbath, and from the birdbath to the euonymus over by the driveway, not so far from our front door.

Among my minor conflicts with Gloria is an inability to agree which is the front of the house and which is the back: she thinks the side facing the sea should be considered the front, and I the other side, where the people park their cars and enter from the driveway. Perhaps the house has no back, but two fronts. It does not turn its back upon either visitors or the ocean breezes.

The poor graceful, bulky creature had nibbled only the merest bit from each bush, like a dieting banqueter sampling each course. I must have smiled slightly to myself—a mistake. "You don't give a *damn*," my wife told me, "but each bush would cost *hun*dreds of dollars to replace." Like many of us past a certain age, she says "dollars" when she means "welders," the Massachusetts unit of currency named after a fabled pre-war governor, a rare Republican. She corrected herself. "This deer will do fifty *thou*sand welders' worth of damage—then see how funny you think it all is." Whenever Gloria feels me balking, she pulls out the whip of money, knowing me to have been a poor boy, and in my well-padded retirement still tender with financial anxiety.

"Do I think it's funny?" I asked. I doubted it. Rapacity, competition, desperation, death to other living things: the forces that make the world go around. The euonymus bush once had some powder-blue irises beneath it, but its spreading green growth, insufficiently pruned, had smothered them, even as their roots crept forward, damaging the lawn.

"Look how he kept shitting everywhere! Little puddles of shit!"

"Can't you say something other than 'shit'?" In our courting days I had been attracted to her way of saying "fuck" instead of a softer expression. "With deer, I think you can say 'scat,'" I suggested. "Or 'spoor.'"

Scornfully Gloria stared at me, not even granting me a moment's incredulous amusement. Her face was pink in the morning cold, her ice-blue eyes vibrant beneath a bushy wool hat that, set square on her head like the hat of a wooden soldier, is oddly flattering. Symmetry, fine white teeth, and monomaniacal insistence upon her own concept of order mark her impress upon the world. Hunting and tracking and plotting an enemy's death become her, like fur at her throat. Before we were married I, still married to another, bought her a black cashmere coat trimmed in bushy gray fox at the collar. The middle-aged saleswoman exclaimed, "How great that looks on her!"—sublimating her hope of making the sale into the simple rapture of a shared vision. It was a blessing of sorts; she connived in our adultery. I yielded up fifteen hundred dollars as painlessly as emitting a sigh.

Gloria asked sharply, "Can you tell by the tracks which way he went?"

The deer had seemed to me clearly a large doe, but to my wife, in her animus, the creature was a "he."

For my own sanity I had to resist this inexorable, deer-pitched tilt the universe was taking on. "What does it matter? Into the woods one way or another," I said. Some of the woods were ours, and some belonged to our neighbors.

"It's important to *know*," Gloria said. Her pale, nearly white eyes narrowed; her killer instincts widened like nostrils to include me in her suspicions of a pervasive evil. "If he had been still there, shitting all over our hedge, would you have helped me throw golf balls?"

"Probably not," I admitted. My time on Earth is getting too short, gradually, for lies.

"*Oh!*" Her disgust couldn't have been more physical if I had held one of my turds—a sample of my own scat—up to her fair pink face. "You *want* him to destroy everything. Just to get at *me*."

"Not at all," I protested, yet so feebly the possible truth of her assertion would continue to gall her.

"If we got a gun, would you shoot it then?"

The cold air was sifting through my pajamas. The morning *Globe* was down by the mailbox, waiting to be retrieved. "Probably not." Yet I wasn't sure. In my youth in the Berkshires, those erosion-diminished, tourist-ridden green hills,

I had handled a .22 owned by a friend less impoverished than I. There had been a thrill to it—the slender weight, the acrid whiff, the long-distance effect.

She sensed this uncertainty, and pried into it the wedge of her voice. "The homeowner *can*, you know. Out of season or anything, as long as it's on his property. Shoot any pest. That's the law."

"I'd be scared," I told her, knowing it would sting, "to shoot a neighbor. Talk about money, honey—what a lawsuit!"

———

That night, we planned to go to bed *de bonne heure*, to make love. In our old age we had to carefully schedule copulations that once had occurred spontaneously, without forethought or foreboding. Before heading upstairs, she said, "Let's look out the window, to see if the deer has come back."

The yard was dark, with the thinnest kind of cloud-veiled moonlight. My wife saw nothing and turned to go up to bed. Once I would have given all my assets, including my body's health and my children's happiness, to go to bed with her, and even now it was a pleasant prospect. But, damn my eyes, I saw a black hump sticking up from the curved euonymus hedge, whose top was crusted with hardened snow. The black shadow moved—changed shape like an amoeba in the dirty water of the dark, or like some ectoplasmic visitation from a former inhabitant of our venerable house. "Honey, he's eating the hedge," I said softly.

My wife screamed, "He *is! Do* something! *Damn* you, don't just stand there smiling!"

How could she know I was smiling? The living room was as dark as the front lawn with its ghostly herbivore.

"I'm calling the Pientas! It's not too late! It's not even eight-thirty! I'm going to borrow Charlie's gun! We've got to do something, and you won't do *any*thing!"

The Pientas live fifteen minutes away. Louise is a Garden Club friend of Gloria's; Charlie has that Old World–peasant mentality which loves the American right to bear arms. He owns several shotguns, for ducks mostly, and my wife, having hurled herself and her teal-blue Japanese station wagon into the dark, brought one of Charlie's guns back with her, with a cardboard box half full of ammunition. The church bell down in the village was tolling nine. "I'll prop it right here behind the armchair," she said, "and we'll keep the bullets—"

"Shells."

"—shells on the bench in the upstairs hall. Charlie does that to keep children from putting them together."

We were in too jangled a mood to attempt love; we read instead, and then kept waking each other up, going to the bathroom in the middle of the night. Though she is younger, her bladder is graciously weakening along with mine. It was still dark when she woke me in a voice between a tender sexual whisper and the whimper of a terrified child. "*Ben!* He's eating the euonymus again! *Hurry!* I've assembled your socks and boots and overcoat."

I had been dreaming of photographs, of life-moments that were photographs and had been placed in a marketing brochure for a mutual fund that called for them to be reduced to the size of postage stamps, though they were in full color. I couldn't quite make them out. My children by my former marriage? *Their* children? I was a grandfather ten times over. I wondered about the printing costs and determined to report my reservations to Firman Frothingham, then one of my colleagues at Sibbes, Dudley, and Wise given to such unseemly wooing of the general public. As Gloria insistently woke me I realized, with a twist in my stomach, that I was retired and this brochure was not my problem. I said, hoping to smuggle out my truth-telling wrapped in a blanket of sleepiness, "I don't want to shoot any fucking deer."

"Not *shoot* him," she pleaded, "shoot over his head, so he gets the idea we hate him. Oh *please*, darling, *hurry!*"

She rarely asked anything so heartfelt of me, not since we had managed, twenty years ago, amid many social impedimenta, to marry. With much of me still immersed in my warm, puzzling dream, I found myself outdoors in the pre-dawn murk, holding the shotgun, which I had with difficulty, drawing upon ancient boyhood memories, broken open and loaded with a Remington shell.

But by the time I got around the house, the front (or back) door opening noisily and the snow crunching at every step, the deer had vanished. A pile of fresh scat made a dark round spot on the snow by the euonymus hedge. Inside the house, her voice pathetically muffled and dwindled by the double glass of window and storm window, my wife was rapping the glass and shouting, "Shoot! Shoot!" It was like the voice of a cartoon mouse in a bell jar. Involuntarily a smile of sadistic pleasure creased my face. The peace of the gray morning— dawn just a sliver of salmon color above the lefthand, east- ward side of the sea's horizon, beneath a leaning moon—was something sacred I didn't want to mar. And I didn't want to shock my sleeping neighbors. We own eleven acres but from the house the land stretches in only two directions. The Kellys live just a wedge shot away, on the other side of a wide-branching beech, and the Dunhams a solid three-iron down through the woods toward the railroad tracks, and Mrs. Lubbetts in the other direction, a good drive and then perhaps a five-iron drilled straight toward the sea. I trudged around, willing to shoot over her head if the doe showed herself; but the 360-degree panorama was virginally quiet, except for the pathetic racket my wife was making inside the house, trapped and muffled in her fury of frustration. If I by some mad quantum leap of impulse wheeled and fired at the living-room window, there would have been a mess of broken glass and splintered sash but likely no clean fatality.

"You bastardly coward," she said when I went back inside. "You didn't do *any*thing."

"I didn't want to wake up the neighbors."

I noticed, uttering this remark, a certain oddity within myself, a displacement of empathy: I could empathize with the sleeping neighbors and the starving deer but not with my frantic wife and her helpless hedge. "That euonymus hedge," she amplified when I voiced this perception by way of apology, "can't run or hide; it can only stand there and be eaten."

Just as she, I thought, was helpless to do anything but attempt to direct and motivate me: ferocious female nagging is the price men pay for our much-lamented prerogatives, the power and the mobility and the penis.

———

Julian Jaynes thinks that until about three thousand years ago men went about in a trance, taking orders direct from the gods. After my wife went off to work—she still works, in a gift shop of which she owns a third, while I languish about the house, writing these paragraphs now and then as if by dictation—I did dutifully keep a lookout for the deer. She didn't show all day, beneath a dull sky lackadaisically spitting snow. But at dusk, walking down to the mailbox, I saw her—

up by the flagpole, in the corner of my eye, the shadow of
a ducking head. Did I see or imagine her alert sensitive
ears and questioning stare? I scrambled up the path by the
rock-face and saw her bounding away in that unhurried,
possessive way that animals have, leaping to lift her legs
from the crusty snow, down past the garage into the woods
on this side of the railroad tracks. I write "possessive" to
convey the air of spiritual adhesion to the earth, of her *guilt-
lessly* occupying the volume of space needed for her blood
and innards, her musculature and fur.

Galvanized, obedient to the dictates my wife had planted
in me like tiny electrodes, I ran inside and got Charlie
Pienta's gun and, my heart drumming, cocked it open and
slipped in a green-jacketed cartridge of buckshot and cracked
it shut. I went outside. I hadn't walked around with a gun
since I toted that borrowed (from my best friend, Billy
Beckett, whose father worked in a sawmill) .22, squeezing
off shots at tin cans and perching birds. One bird, at what it
thought was a safe distance, dropped like a stone from its
branchlet and when I went up to it I had taken off its head,
clean, leaving a fluffy ball with wings and a chickadee's dapper black and white markings.

I have no declared appetite for killing, but sensing the
deer somewhere in the blue-tinted dusk, conscious of me as
I was conscious of her, was more exciting than anything I
had done lately, including making love to Gloria. She is still
handsome, with her crown of ash-blond hair, and dresses
with a beautiful trim sternness, but there is no faking that
tight lean knit of a young woman's body. Her instructions,
which I was following as blindly as Assyrians in the time of
Hammurabi followed Ishtar's, had been to scare the deer
with a blast.

I had the mail under one arm—bills and catalogues and a

few early Christmas cards—and the gun under the other
when there she was, suddenly, standing sideways in the driveway, closer to me than the chickadee had been fifty years
ago. I slowly set the mail down on a bare spot (the snow
melts first on the black asphalt) and then straightened and
aimed the shotgun ten feet above the frozen silhouette's
back (it was a good direction, there are no neighbors that
way for a quarter of a mile) and squeezed the trigger.

Nothing. The trigger felt welded fast. The safety catch
was on. Trembling but not panicked, I examined the unfa-
miliar gun and found no catch, just the flip lever to uncock
it, and at last realized I must set the hammer with my
thumb. Though there was no noise, my haste and frustration must have generated a scent that communicated itself
to the deer, for with a burst of astonishing easy vigor she
bounded over the wall there—low on the driveway side,
with an eight-foot drop on the other—and on into the deer-
colored woods. I fired, blindly, into the mist of the dusky
trees where she had vanished. The noise was enormous—
flat, absolute—and the kick against my shoulder rude and
unexpected. For what seemed a full minute there was a faint
pattering in the woods, like sleet, as the buckshot settled
and dry leaves detached by the blast (the oaks and beeches
hang on forever) drifted to the cold, hushed earth, the forest
floor whose trackable paths and branchings were sinking beneath the rising tide of darkness. My mail glimmered on the
driveway like white scat.

Gloria, coming home, was thrilled to hear that I at least
had fired Charlie Pienta's gun. She kissed me with a killer's
ardor. After dinner, thus rewarded and stimulated, I checked
the yard just in case, and, sure enough, against the snow I
saw the deer's hungry silhouette nibbling at the round privet
bush by the birdbath. I lifted the loaded, cocked gun and

fired, high, but not so high that I didn't think that a few pellets would sting her flank. To my amazement the deer didn't
move. She just kept nuzzling the bush, chewing its outmost
leaves, like a wife ignoring your most vehement arguments,
having heard them before. It was only when, at last sharing
my real wife's indignation, I moved toward the deer as if to
throttle her with my hands or beat her with the gun butt
that the creature, with a shadowy surge of her extended
head, loped off, as if awoken from a trance.

As my reward for coming over to her side against the deer,
my wife offered to make love to me in any position I chose.
I like it when she lies on top, doing the thrusting, and also it
is bliss to fuck her from behind, with no thought of her own
orgasm. But by the time we went to bed, after dinner and
the network news and a glance at Channel Two, and did a
little reading—*Scientific American* for me and for her the
competition's Christmas gift catalogues—we were both too
sleepy to act upon our new rapport. Outside, in the dark, a
wobbly patch of life upon the blue snow, the deer perhaps
browsed, her soft blob of a nose rapturously sunk in the
chilly winter greenery, her modest brain-stem steeped in
some dream of a Cockaigne for herbivores.

"Perhaps": the word is like the little fork in reality when a
quantum measurement is made. Each time that we measure
either the position or momentum of an elementary particle, the other specific becomes, by Heisenberg's indeter-
minacy principle, unknowable. The "wave function" of the
particle collapses. Our universe is the one containing our
observation. But, some cosmic theorists aver, the system—
containing the particle, the measuring apparatus, and the
observer—continues to exist in its other possible states, in
parallel universes that have branched from this moment of
measurement. The theory is called that of "many worlds." It

is intellectually repulsive, which does not mean it is not true. Truth can be intellectually repulsive. From the same verifiable quantum formulations arises the possibility that our universe, born from nothing, was instantly boosted, by the gravity-reversing properties of a "false" vacuum, into an expansion so monstrous that the universe's real limits lie many times beyond the matter of which we can gather evidence with our farthest-seeing telescopes.

———————

My wife's two sons, Roger and Henry, and her daughter, Carolyn, with Roger's wife, Marcia, and Carolyn's husband, Felix, have come for Christmas. It is nice to have the big old house trembling with other footsteps and the murmur of multiple domestic discussions. The rooms, even to the third floor, are permeated by the scent of woodsmoke from the fire the boys keep going in the living-room fireplace, which my wife and I rarely use. We just want, after dinner and the news, to get upstairs to bed. Often we are in our pajamas and nightie by eight o'clock; we have made a joke of it—"Damn it, you won again!"—as if it is a sporting event, the race to bed. But in fact we are in a more serious race, to the death. Which of us will die first? We look each other over every day, appraising the odds. I have given her five years' handicap, but two of my grandparents lived to ninety—hill folk from up near Cheshire, tough as beef jerky. When my mother died, and her meagre heirlooms descended to me, I gave the squinting, thin-lipped photographic portraits of her parents to the Pittsfield Historical Society. But I have never been back to see if they are hanging on the wall.

By Christmas all but one of Charlie Pienta's shotgun shells were used up in scaring off the deer, but still she kept coming back, nibbling, at dawn or dusk, when the snow was blue. Snow that falls this early is slow to go away; it sinks in upon itself and hardens. Despairing of my effectuality, my wife through her network of Garden Club colleagues reached a young man from Maine who had grown up hunting and who loved venison. Slim and politely spoken, he came and stood in the driveway, listening to Gloria's tale of cervine persecution. Even though hunting season had passed, he promised to come back the day after Christmas and see what he could do. He drove a tomato-red pickup truck, a Toyota. She confided to me that he seemed too much of a boy to do the job; she wanted her hunter to be big and grizzled—a twin of me, with a less oppositional character.

We had to attend a Boxing Day celebration provided annually by an English immigrant we knew. We asked my stepchildren and their mates to stay in the house, lest they be shot. We made nervous jokes about not wearing deerskin and pulling in their horns. Throughout the Boxing Day lunch—lamb, creamed broccoli, pear tart—we envisioned carnage, which robbed the food of taste. But when we came back, around four-fifteen in the semi-dark, all was quiet. There were the tracks of truck-tire treads in the driveway but no pickup and no trace of blood in the snow. Our five guests were gathered safely around the fire in the living room reading their Christmas books. Marcia—who is so like Carolyn, with the same shiny brushed brown hair, straight nose, aristocratic brow, and confident candor of expression, that I keep forgetting who is Gloria's daughter and who her daughter-in-law—looked up and, with a trace of her Philadelphia drawl, twanged, "We never heard a shot. There was a lot of walking around looking very solemn, but no shots. Sorry, you two."

Again, it seemed to me we were on a certain branch of

possibility, and there was another in which something had been killed, and then, ramifying, many things were killed, everything—a universe packed black with death. This universe, I saw as the log fire settled with a flurry of sparks, was one that we were all certain to enter. We must have sinned greatly, at some juncture long buried in our protozoic past, to deserve such a universe. I devoutly wished that there was not this cruel war between the deer and my wife.

"Isn't that the pits!" Gloria said. "That deer is *always* here at this time of day. I bet he scared it away with his show-offy dumb truck. I *thought* he looked too young."

"There were *two* men, Mom," Carolyn said. "The older one was the more committed. He walked all around the yard, into the woods, looking for deer clues." Yet another word nicer than "shit."

"Did he say he'd be back?"

It turned out that nobody had gone out to talk to him. We had told them to stay indoors—we had planted those electrodes in their heads—and they had obeyed.

Yet they are ambitious and intelligent. All except Henry have Ph.D.'s. Roger and Marcia teach at the University of Pennsylvania, where they met before the war. Carolyn and Felix are racier, living in Washington Square, amid the pieces of New York University. Carolyn paints. Darker and an inch taller than Gloria, she reminds me of her father, a Boston University economics professor who made the mistake of moving with his family to the same North Shore town where I was lurking. All four young people have his erect dignity, his habit of pausing before an utterance, and a deference to your opinion that leads you to suspect, in midsentence, that you have it all somewhat wrong. Henry is less academic, and lives nearby, in Salem, picking up a living at computer, VCR, and cell-phone repair. None of her children quite have Gloria's pale fire, though of course Marcia and Carolyn stir me a bit. They seem, for all their impenetrable grooming and manners, not quite content. Carolyn's paintings border on the pornographic, and Marcia has a childish streak that comes out in a startling baby voice, which I take to express, toward me, deflected aggression. When I give her the glancing kiss to which my stepfather-in-law status entitles me, she just perceptibly twists her face away, her chin tucked into her clavicle so that I have to plant my mouth on her hair-swathed ear or else go burrowing, like a ferret after a snake, to bring my lips into contact with the skin of her cheek; her shoulders hunch up and sock me in the chin. She pokes fun of the course she helps teach—"Systemic Decompensation in Patriarchies, with Special Emphasis upon Slave Narratives"—and wistfully talks of going into fashion design. Her sketches are of Hollywoodish ball gowns, slinky lounge pajamas, see-through blouses, high-necked dresses with slits up to mid-thigh. She gets headaches, and puts on wraparound sunglasses to ease the pain. I wonder if "headaches" is a code for menstruation pains. It disturbs my retired calm, having a menstruating female in the house again.

Among the anti-deer methods that my wife has tried is scattering human hair over the hedges and bushes. I was humiliated to ask at my barber shop for some hair clippings, but they jollily gave me a whole transparent garbage bag full of the stuff, a single day's sweepings. Young glossy hair, glinting reddish hair, hair with gray in it, straight and curly hair clipped in the hirsute fullness of life—the giant bagful, eerily light to hoist, savored of atrocity, of those orderly death camps in the middle of the last century which ended forever Europe's concept of itself as civilized and of the Western world as proceeding under a benign special Providence.

The Deer

The deer are supposed to scent humans in the hair and flee in repugnance and terror. Another stratagem her Garden Club fellow-members urged upon Gloria was to have me urinate at critical spots on the lawn. It had to be male urine, a human buck's scent. I obliged a little, by the euonymus hedge and near the birdbath, but the project was too undignified to be carried out systematically, in the winter cold. And the deer seemed unimpressed, or else after an initial repugnance she accustomed herself to the hostile tang in the air.

The young fill a house with the smell of heavy late-morning sleep, and of nightsweats of fear as they confront life in all its branching possibility and need for decision. Menstrual fluid, epidermal oils, semen—all such effluvia in overflowing supply.

If my wife were to die, I used to think that I would look up women from my past, residues of passionate affairs thirty years ago, but lately I have begun to think I would seek out only young whores, with tight lower bodies and long, exercise-hardened limbs, and put the problem of my erratic erections to them like a tricky tax matter laid before a well-paid accountant on a clean, bed-sized desk.

Two days after Christmas, having been out looking for an excuse to fire Charlie's last shell, I came into the living room still holding the gun. Roger and Marcia and Carolyn and Felix, who had been reading and burning my laboriously split logs, all pretended to scramble for cover behind the furniture, shouting, "We're leaving, Pop! We'll go!" They call me "Pop," saving the more affectionate "Dad" for my former rival.

When they did actually head south, two days before New Year's Day, Roger offered me his thoughtful opinion that the week of constant woodsmoke from the chimney was what had kept the deer away. They would be back, he thought. He is the closest, academically, to their father, who has remarried and moved to Mexico, where the economy is sounder than in our fragmented, warhead-pocked States. Roger teaches cycles and is accustomed to making predictions.

I woke in the middle of one of the first nights of the New Year—2020, a jeering staring number that once denoted perfect eyesight—stricken by dread: my professional usefulness over, my wife more of a disciplinarian than a comfort, my body a swamp in whose simmering depths a fatal infirmity must be brewing.

And worse and somehow larger than any of these major concerns loomed my bad playing of a three-no-trump hand in a friendly game of bridge that evening with Grace and Stanley Wren. I allowed Grace to pull my stopper king of clubs from the board, and when I yielded the lead on a low heart trick she ran the clubs and set me; all I would have had to do, I saw clearly now, to hold on to the high club was to draw out the ace of diamonds, avoiding the unfortunate hearts. Bridge always churns me up with the recognition of my intellectual limits: for this reason I generally avoid playing, just as, years ago at U. Mass., repeatedly outplayed by nimble-headed computer nerds from Boston's western suburbs, I gave up chess, which I had loved as a child back in Hammond Falls, playing opponents even more childish on a board set up on the oval rug braided of rags beside the cast-iron wood stove that heated the back end of the house. I liked all those areas—chess, science fiction, movies, comic strips— where my father in his grimy workclothes was a stranger.

And always this nagging elderly need to urinate, besieging my groin as I lie trying to coax myself back into the sickly-sweet therapy of dreams. Dreams: there sex still revolves with surprising force, turning a phantom woman into a hairy moist center of desire hot as a star, and there excrement overflows the bowl like a fetid volcano, or I find myself, naked, obliged to defecate at a dinner party, in close proximity to the bejewelled hostess as I strive to maintain a polite conversation and she to ignore my rumbling, spurting bowels. Humiliated and self-disgusted, I awake, and from the bathroom window see that something has triggered the burglar floodlight to come on on the side of the house toward the sea—the back side, as I think of it.

The light's alarmist burning, spreading into the bedroom, had given me the false impression of approaching dawn. It really was still in the middle of the night. It had snowed some inches, and the fresh powder, I observed, was marked by several uneven lines of medium-size tracks—deer tracks.

The creature's habit is to set one foot behind the other to make almost a straight line of indentations, so that I am reminded of that little sharp-toothed wheel from my grandmother's sewing box, with which she would trace a chain of perforations onto paper dress patterns. What wistful, twisting canker of hunger had driven the deer back to us? She had bestirred herself from the tent-shaped shelter of some great hemlock in a remote woods. Fresh snow seemed to drive the animal to risk proximity to the gun, the shouts, the golf balls. The tracks led to the front of the house, where there was nothing green save straggling rhododendrons, their long leaves rolled by the cold into dry cigar shapes, and pachysandra buried beneath a foot of icy white, and those leucothoë plantings that have never, I tell my wife, looked like anything but jungle weeds.

God, how suddenly savage and ruthless Grace Wren seemed, running those clubs on me, cashing in even the five and the two for tricks! As if no friendship existed between us at all, as if we had never danced and flirted together, my lust coating us both in sweat. She had had a good pert figure before her bosom expanded and sank. She has stopped dyeing her hair, and the wiry, salt-and-pepper look is not unattractive. How stupid and vulnerable I was, without my stopper king! Perhaps this was my dream's day-remnant—my humiliation as we sat elbow to elbow at the card table turned into a helpless outpour of foul-smelling excrement. I had played shittily. Oh, horrible! I tossed and turned beside my oblivious wife, feeling those deer tracks outside as a love letter I could not answer and replaying the bridge hand until, trying to remember if the queen of spades was in my hand or the dummy, I slipped from the great magician's agitated sleeve into the false-bottomed box of sleep.

A week ago, Henry, the younger of my wife's sons, and his local girlfriend—an amazingly skinny, pale, supple redhead whose father runs a TV-and-VCR repair shop in Swampscott—and I ran down to pick up milk and orange juice and a bag of so-called Smart Food, popcorn flavored with cheddar cheese. Coming back up the hill, the Subaru, bought new last April, gripped the slick and sluggish road surface admirably, and I felt youthful, reliving teenage moments propelling the boatlike old family Plymouth through a Berkshire blizzard, back from a date that had steamed the car windows. My wife's son, in a flourish of automotive showing-off, likes to back a car into our narrow two-car port, fashioned by the son of the previous owner from the wooden shell of an old greenhouse. For some reason, maybe to impress the skinny redhead, I thought I should do the same. Henry jumped out, in the exuberance and cockiness of youth, to help guide me. Distracted by his gesticulations, and driving in a bulky coat and clumsy boots, with the windows obscured by vapor, I rubbed the back of the Subaru against a white wooden inner wall of the old greenhouse. It was a subtle sensation but I knew disaster when I felt it.

That side of the car was in shadow, and my stepson kept reassuring me, "It's nothing, Pop, I don't think it will even show," but in the morning, with the sky pure blue and its light reflecting from the drifts of fresh snow as in a hall of mirrors, the damage was clear and extensive. Gloria was furious—as furious at me as she had been at the deer. Again, a helpless possession of hers, an ornament to her existence, had been chewed by a predator. "It'll cost a fortune," she told me, with diamond-hard satisfaction. "A thousand welders minimum."

She had won a point in our battle to the death. I was incompetent, senile. I couldn't argue. And yet I had been somehow jostled into this abysmal mishap by the frisky young people who had accompanied me, whereas I could only blame myself for that badly played bridge hand.

My wife and I know dozens of women and a number of men who seem content to devote hours of each day to the practice and perfection of their bridge. What is wrong with me, who resents the energy spent in development of a skill whose end product is a scribbled bridge pad, a set of scores fading into the void? What doesn't fade into the void? The rest of their lives these bridge players devote to the cultivation of their roses, the trimming of their hedges, the feeding of their faces, the tidying of their homes, the maintenance of contact with their children and grandchildren and socioeconomically identical acquaintances, the travelling to Florida and to Maine in the suitable seasons—all activities that leave no trace. What is wrong with me, that I want to leave a trace, by scribbling these disjunct and jumpy notes concerning my idle existence? Spoiling paper—no worse and no better than scribbling on a bridge pad.

There is, among the indeterminacies, a universe in which, undeflected by my stepson's overstimulating presence, I opted to drive the Subaru straight into the carport without a scratch or a dent. What would that universe be like? It would be one in which Gloria would have one less weapon, one less I-told-you-so, to wield against me. It would be like the one I am in, only with some other vexation crowding to the forefront of my brain—the tiny, conscious part, which floats on a primeval sea of hunger, sex, and semi-automatic bodily functions.

I read last night about Neandert(h)al man. He has a history of sorts, it turns out. He was an evolutionary offshoot of slender *Homo erectus,* who migrated from Africa into Europe a million years ago or less. Though glaciers advanced and retreated, Europe was generally cold. Neanderthal (let's keep the old-fashioned, pleasantly incorrect "h") men developed the short, thick, conservative bodies of Arctic dwellers today. They were so strong that their muscles, knitted to our bones, would snap them. Their own bones are often found broken, perhaps in battle with giant elk, bison, and those long-horned extinct oxen called auroch (plural). Though the Neanderthals' relics show some progress in flint-working, they evidently never got the idea of projectiles—no slings and arrows for them. They had to grapple with their prey close up, and the patterns of their broken bones correspond most closely to, of all contemporary professional groups, rodeo riders.

Pre-Neanderthal men toppled hundreds of animals and thirty human colleagues into a cave in Spain three hundred thousand years ago; the first true Neanderthals date from seventy thousand years later. Fifty thousand years later still, glaciers so heavily descended upon Europe that the conti-

nent, for the next fifty thousand years, was empty, as far as
the fossil record shows, of human beings. Think of it! Ten
times the span of recorded human history pass, and men are
squeezed from the European record of stones and bones.
But evolution was not sleeping. When the glaciers retreated, the Neanderthal skeletons were more massive, and
the hundred-thousand-year heyday of their subspecies began. They made fires. They buried their dead with flowers.
They fabricated flint knives and dug postholes for wooden
dwellings, but left no tools for stitching; they must have
worn their animal hides untailored. They had big noses and
receding chins and foreheads. Their skulls include the hyoid
bone that indicates a voice box; coöperative hunting and the
passing on of even crude practical skills demand some level
of communication. The Neanderthal people left no art, unless one counts a polished tooth from a baby mammoth,
possibly used as a shaman's amulet. Shattered bones and
skulls suggest that they practiced cannibalism.

They co-existed for ten thousand years with Cro-Magnon
men, men anatomically like us, who forty thousand years
ago came into Europe from the Middle East with projectiles, sewing needles, improved hearths and shelters, and art.
Neanderthal man slowly vanished; his last remains are
found in southern Spain, a few jawbones and femurs and
tools going back to about thirty thousand years before
Christ. It never occurred to these harried, dwindling primi-
tives to cross the Strait of Gibraltar into warmer Africa.
They were a conservative, dull-witted, rather hapless crew,
never very numerous—a few thousand at a time, roaming
around in packs of about thirty. There is a slight slenderness
to the later fossils that some paleoanthropologists take as
evidence of interbreeding with *Homo sapiens*. Fat chance,
say other paleoanthropologists; it was ever nothing but war,

mutual abhorrence, and murder between the races. Most Neanderthal men died before they were half my present age. Some day I will be as forgotten, as dissolved back into the compacted silt, as your typical grunting, lusting, hungry, broken-boned Neanderthal man. I simply cannot believe it! And that is certainly stupid of me.

I took the train to Boston yesterday, to conduct a little business at the old stand. The Lynn marshes were vast and virginal from the train windows—a brilliant arctic vista. In Boston the snow had already been translated to a dun-colored mush and an inhospitable shortage of parking space, even in the lots. My former partners at Sibbes, Dudley, and Wise were cordial, but harried—competition is everywhere, stiffer than it used to be, and young blood is bubbling up through the firm, stressing the sclerotic arteries. The relaxed, discreet air that Boston money used to affect—in pointed contrast with noisy, obnoxious New York money— no longer obtains. Post-war, the numbers are down and the heat is up. I got out none too soon. I made my pile when it was a relatively easy effort.

A number of secretaries have been hired since I left; my presence kindled no spark of deference or potential engagement in their moist, clear, searching eyes. I was out of their food chain. I played the cordial antique fool, the only role open to me. My business—a sizable municipal-bond redemption for my faithful old client Mrs. Fessenden, and some finicking mutual-fund readjustments for my own portfolio—was too quickly done. After respectfully observing how my old office has been cut into four "workstations" by frosted-glass partitions (Ned Partridge, a meddlesome tech-

nology groupie whom I was always itching to get fired as office manager, could scarcely contain his triumph), I had little to do but walk up the hill to the Athenaeum, graze on the
English newspapers, and then make my way across the hill
to Cambridge Street and through Charles River Park—
every sidewalk and street awkwardly narrowed by heaped
snow—to North Station and rather ignominiously catch the
four o'clock train home. Boston had little use for me now.

Two images from my expedition stuck in my craw:

In North Station, a young woman, bundled against the
weather in a long parka and a checked muffler, accidentally
turned her face toward mine as she blew a bubble of bubble
gum. The primitive man within me prickled at this casual
uncalled-for protrusion of insolent mock-nakedness, a round-
ness out of her mouth pinker and more blatant than an exposed breast or penis, there in the chilly damp gloom of the
station, which is a much drearier, barer place since the renovations that substituted Fleet Center for Boston Garden.
At the same time, twenty-five years ago, they raised the platform to be level with the floors of the cheesy new plastic-
seated cars, a handicapped-sensitive improvement which
denies normal passengers the old jaunty sensation of swinging *down* into Boston. And they enlarged and enclosed the
waiting area where we all used to stand in the fresh air,
which was bracing after a day of inhaling recycled gases
within our sealed office buildings. To discourage permanent
perching by the homeless, they took out many of the friendly
wooden benches in the station itself, which has been robbed
of all its old shops save a diminished version of the fruit
stand. There is no place where you can buy a candy bar. A
sickening smell of hot cheese wafts everywhere from a
pizzeria that has been installed at the end where the cretins
who attend sporting events in Fleet Center might be

tempted to coat their guts with fat and gluten. In this place, for decades a daily station of my pilgrimage, the young woman unthinkingly showed me her pink bubble, and then wolfed it back, seething with bacteria, into her oral cavity.

And, secondly, on the ride home, gliding past the marshes which were dark now, making the window into a mirror, I saw my own gazing eye, in three-quarters view, unexpectedly close in the black glass, watery and round, like the watchful dark orb of a deer. A deer eye, fearful and alert—hostile or neutral, I couldn't quite tell. We cannot think or feel with the brain of another creature but we can see its eyes, those sensitive organs which the brain protrudes. My reflected face loomed inches from mine, the skin a dirty metallic color, skimming along in mid-air, transparent to the industrial shapes and receding lit windows, like the visage of a spy from outer space, an evilly staring alter ego. It gave me a start, and forestalled the nap I had scheduled for myself, the fifteen minutes of sleep that mark the end of a commuter's day and fortify him or her for an evening at home.

———————

Another foot of snow has fallen on top of the two feet already on the ground. I waded out across the front lawn to take down the Christmas lights that we run up on the flagpole as our part of the annual pretense that God descended to Earth in a baby's body. The neighbors expect it. I've been told that even ships at sea—the lonely-looking oil tankers that, like long cardboard silhouettes on a slow string, edge into Salem Harbor—appreciate it. But my wife, who has strict ideas on many topics, says that nobody with any taste keeps lights up after Twelfth Night. Her father never did. Twelfth Night came and went, and there was no thaw in sight, so I seized this even mildly sunny day, the sun a white blur in a high thin cloud cover.

Walking through snow up to my crotch turned out to be an ordeal almost comical in its severity—worse even than those childhood memories we distrust in hindsight, of eye-high drifts and tunnels from the front porch. My yard, where I amble back and forth in the summer practicing chip shots and setting up croquet wickets in anticipation of a visit from my grandchildren, had become huge, an antarctic continent. Every step sucked at my entire leg with the force of gravity on another, much larger, planet. My boots quickly filled with snow—a chilly, sticky sensation that came back to me from sixty years ago. Extracting my leg from each socket was like pulling a giant tooth. I wondered if the deer was watching and could hear my grunts, my laughter at my physical plight. Her velvety white-rimmed ears would prick, her eyes would show no more emotion than my own bulging eyes in the flickering black window of the commuter train. Suppose my heart decided to flip shut—to knock off for an eternity-long coffee break—at this moment. Would the deer come and sniff curiously, would the smell of my hair still frighten her, would the universe branch and carry me intact into another portion of endless space? Are the funnel vortices of black holes the passageways whereby we enter the afterlife?

But I was already on another planet. Each step a comical struggle, I fought my way to the pole on its little flagstoned platform—a conceit of the previous owner, a nautical man who loved to stand and take in his view of Massachusetts Bay. I dug down to where the ends of the Christmas light cords had been pegged or tied to a handy bush. The experience was archaeological, really, and made me feel, as my numb fingers grappled at the knots, the cold connection between the buried and the present.

So much snow wraps the world in cosmic feeling. The euonymus hedge, no longer defenseless, is rounded in its thick
white armor like a futuristic motor vehicle. A transcendent
sparkle rides the surface; microscopic icy prisms send rain-
bows to my retinas. I am immersed in the white blind brute
reality of nature, heartless and beautiful. I am in the rushing
waterfall, the thunderhead cradle of blue new stars in a
proximate galaxy. Beneath the dazzling skin of snow, a
whole lost world waited to be born again, its details—blades
of grass, pegs holding knotted ropes—faithfully tucked into
the realm of the potential. I coiled the strings of Christmas
lights, stiff and lumpy with ice, into their cardboard box and
carried the box to the third floor. From the third-floor windows I looked for deer tracks, but of course there were none.
She must be huddled in the tent-shaped shelter beneath a
hemlock, the wet dark orb of her eye watchful. To stick a pin
into that bulging eye—that would be a wicked thrill, a tunnel into another world.

Instead of deer tracks I saw curious paths between the
trees, the oaks around the driveway, from one trunk to another, and then vanishing, bat-shaped dents in the snow.
It took me surprisingly long to deduce that these were the
body-prints of squirrels, only half hibernating, quickly
floundering from one tree to another. But what makes them
think one tree might be an improvement over another?
A bed of grass in one, a cache of acorns in another. Like
rich Manhattanites, they scuttle from Park Avenue to Wall
Street and back, minimizing their moments on the ground.
On this scorched planet we human beings are not yet quite
alone; there is still other life. Squirrels, rats, deer, the last
rhinos and cheetahs. Insects, of course, in their undis-
mayable selfless multitudes.

And then the next day, or the next, awaking too early, un-

settled by the hyperactive, menacing weather—Gloria is
falling in love with the different channels' weathermen, and
can tell them all apart—I was walking in the pre-dawn semi-
dark down to the mailbox, where the delivery man throws
the newspaper, sparing himself the trouble of our driveway.
Above me a two-thirds moon hung in a sky already blue. I
looked up at this apparition and tried to see it as it is, a ball
in space, illuminated by a single light-source. The direction
of the source was clearly indicated by the way the light lay;
it was somewhere over my shoulder. The sun was in the
southeast but not yet risen. I tried to make myself realize
that the moon was hoisted into the same light that had not
yet touched me; there is no other light; it soaks the inner solar system, in whose interplanetary spaces there is no night
and day; and this light would *not* soon be lifting over the
horizon behind my left shoulder, beyond the cluster of
quaintly named local islands, but in fact the surface I am
standing on and all surface continuous with it to the horizon
of the sea and beyond was plunging *toward* the sun, like
the floor of a vast airplane crashing, a vast curved floor
monumentally, imperceptibly spinning in the direction *dead
against* that in which the sun like a knob in a slotted groove
would arc across the sky to make another day in my minuscule, clinging, transitory, insectlike life. Inside my curved
skull I approached this spatial visualization as if approaching the edge of a windswept cliff or steep slippery-tiled
roof; then my mind darted back, dizzy, into the safety of
pre-scientific stupidity. I could not at all visualize how the
moon—its waxing and waning; its presenting always the
same face to the Earth; its monthly revolution; its tug on
the tides—fit into this gigantic toy of gravity with all its
balls of matter. Everything went flat for me; the snow-packed
driveway beneath my feet stopped moving.

How curious it is, given the scientific view of the universe as ultimately causeless and accidental, that the moon and the sun are the exact same size in the sky, as we see in a solar eclipse, where the fit is so exact that Bailey's beads of sunlight shoot out rays through the valleys of the moon. No wonder men for millennia took these two heavenly bodies, so disparate in astronomical fact, to be twin gods—competing brothers, or a brother and sister safeguarding different aspects of the human soul. The kinship did not have to be. In another easily imagined system there might be two moons, or five, or none. There might be two suns, a large and a small, locked in a gravitational embrace, setting and rising at opposite ends of the horizon. Somewhere beyond Jupiter our space-exploring vehicles show the sun as another star, no brighter than Venus from our planet's vantage. One of the scientific sages I admired as a boy, a kindly prune-faced dwarf who appeared on public television, educating the masses, said that, if all our cosmological wisdom had to be passed on to a benighted future in a single sentence, the sentence should be *The sun is a star.*

The sun is a star. Christianity said, God is a man. Humanism said, Man is a god. Today the sages say, via such Jainist cosmogonies as string theory and the inflationary hypothesis, that everything is nothing. The cosmos is a free lunch, a quantum fluctuation.

The deer awakens, starving, in her tent of hemlock boughs and comes up to the house, placing and lifting each foot in an almost straight line. My wife is away, eating up the world with her errands, consumer and merchant both. The deer nibbles at our euonymus hedge, its edges exposed by the recent thaw, at first warily, then voraciously. She becomes as she eats a young lean-bodied whore, whom I invite into the house. We take care to brush from the front-hall Oriental, a little red, blue-bordered Qum, the pieces of melting snow that fall from her narrow naked feet. We go up to the third floor, where among the cobwebs and bat droppings there are discarded beds and down quilts, held in reserve for my stepchildren. Her thin body slowly sheds its chill, its shivering (all the little downy hairs of her body erect), and she serves me with a cold, slick expertise, her mind elsewhere to preserve her dignity. What I love most about the encounter is watching her walk back and forth to the bathroom, her flanks stately, her step silent, all but the crease between her buttocks tan. The bathroom fixtures up here have not been changed since the house was built in 1905; they are porcelain antiques, moon-white. My groin pleasantly aches from its unaccustomed friction. My semen, still coming in the sluggish way of an old man's body, leaks onto my thigh, and thence makes a telltale stain on the sheet. The sheets are changed only once or twice a year, when a child comes to visit. I will have to call the local taxi, to get the girl away, off my property. The driver hangs out, over a scummy cup of cooling coffee, at the drugstore in the village. I am leaving clues, I realize. My body fluids are leaking out into the community. When I become frightened, for my prestige and safety and domestic peace, I tell myself she is a fantasy, a branching not existent in the palpable universe.

Walking down to the mailbox this morning, I observed in the mounds that the plow heaped on either side of the driveway, and in the ice and packed snow receding on the asphalt, the patterns of melting—the ornate undercutting, the fragile lace left behind by liquefaction and evaporation, the striations of successive snowfalls, some damper and icier than others. The snow rots at its own indolent pace, its innards crawling with bubbles of meltwater like wood lice.

In the southeast there are low thin clouds, violet rimmed with a sickly tangerine color; crumbling flakes of this metallic Day-Glo color float free and oddly mirror in the heavens the two islands, Baker's and Misery, that float in the view from our hill. Overhead, in a sky already the powdery blue of mid-day, there are two moons—a half-moon drinking the sky's blue through the seepage along its thin edge, and a smaller, even paler, more papery moon. If the first occupies, like the sun, approximately a half-degree of the celestial hemisphere's 180 degrees, this second is no wider than a sixth of a degree. It has a honeycomb appearance, with a pair of scarcely visible appendages, stubby dragonfly wings.

This moon was man-made—a space station set in orbit three thousand miles above the Earth, one-hundredth of the first moon's distance, by men before the Sino-American Conflict dissolved the governments able to maintain the shuttle ships. Earth abandoned its satellite, and the colonists marooned there survived for a time amid their tons of provisions and their solar-powered greenhouses. Then, as the world watched in horror the television broadcasts that were maintained with the generator's last volts of energy, the space-dwellers one by one died. This episode, become mythic, has inspired any number of bathetic retellings in the popular media, even if all of us who dwell on Earth are in a position exactly the same, if on a larger scale. Indeed, it is not impossible that the colony, in its giant honeycomb of hollow struts and exquisitely stretched sheets of insulating foil, still holds a few live crewpersons, surviving on protein tablets and hydroponic lettuce. The scattered surviving populations of the Earth lack the technical resources to send a rescue mission aloft, even if there were a will. This second moon, with its own phases and periods of eclipse, hangs in the sky as an embarrassment, a bad conscience. Once my species had been strong enough to put it up there, and now it is out of our reach. Like its larger natural brother, it was a half-moon today, struck at the same angle of solar radiation, half dissolved in the blue, translucent like a mirage. The moon's two power-gathering wings seemed, as I squinted up, an optical aberration, like the feathers of iridescence that spin off from the sun when you squint at it, or when you emerge from the sea with drenched lashes and corneas stinging from the salt.

The mailbox stands beneath several hemlocks. Their shadows make the snow slow to melt on this slope of driveway, an icy tunnel in wintertime. But, as I turned, *Boston Globe* in hand, to climb the hill, the hairy red sun, just lifted above the gray treetops of the woods, struck the bare asphalt at a low angle that brought into relief the parallel scratches left by the lawn service's plow. I had never noticed them before. They seemed ominously ancient, Egyptian, these man-induced grooves, as if slaves had dragged one huge stone across another in the construction of a pyramid so gigantic that death itself would be defeated.

———

Our late-January thaw continues. Looking down upon my lawn from a third-floor window, I marvel at how the bushes and hedges are completely freed and how much green grass has been exposed. Where I struggled heroically, braving a heart attack, out to the flagpole to remove the Christmas lights, a ragged green path exists, on which, if I wished, I could stroll out to run up the American flag. But I spare the flag the winter winds; already it is so frayed the stripes are coming apart at their ends, each becoming a thin pennant.

On Cape Cod, the snow has receded to the point where some golf courses are open. Yesterday a friend, Red Ruggles, invited me to drive down, with another friend of his, a retired airline pilot named Ken Dixon, and to play a round at a course of which a friend of Red's is a member. The member, who is our age, was suddenly too sick with something—gout, arthritis, the flu—to join us, but he phoned us in as guests. Red is not exactly retired, although his two sons have taken over the daily routines of the fish business he founded in Gloucester. While driving his Dodge Caravan down Route 1 and through Boston to Route 3 to the Sagamore Bridge and Route 6, Red kept picking up his cellular phone and talking to the distant places—Vladivostok, Punta Arenas, Dar es Salaam—where "product" (fish) can still be found and bought. He gives the greeting in the local language—"*Dobrii dyen!*" "*¡Buenos días!*" "*Jambo!*"—and then speaks in a loud English. He calls everybody "friend." He makes all these calls, I think, in part to impress his helpless passengers and in part to maintain sentimental contact with the shreds of what had been his fish empire. The fact seems to be that the world contains fewer and fewer fish. The oceans are as exhausted and mined-out as the land. Much of Red's cellular-phone time is spent reminiscing, with the person on the other end, about great hauls of yesteryear—multi-vessel shipments of frozen product that steamed across the Pacific like convoys in wartime and around Cape Horn to the bustling, venerable wharves of Gloucester, catch after catch. The planks of the wharves, in his telling, were slick and rank with cod liver oil.

It took a tedious two-hour drive to transpose rocky, oaky

Cape Ann into Cape Cod's sand dunes and pitch pines and salt-bleached shingles. But there *was* golf, on a course that was all rounded hills, grassed-over links—an opulent succession of freshly exposed breasts and thighs, little hill upon hill, with comforting swales and clefts and bulges between them. There were no flat lies, but no bare ones either. The grass under all that early snow had not had time to brown and harden. The greens held frost beneath a thawed quarter-inch that ripped open when a ball hit. I felt masterly and tender, repairing these wounds with a two-pronged plastic U and tamping the scar smooth with my shoe. It was lovely to be out and swinging. Among all these green bulges the flight of the ball felt especially penetrating. A good drive tended to catch a downslope that added yards. Ken hit one that, on a 420-yard par-four, wound up at the 150-marker. Two hundred seventy yards! And this from a silver-haired former pilot who is very deliberate and a bit cautious in all his preliminary moves, as if just before takeoff.

A few surviving white drifts in the sand traps and along the shaded edges of the fairway heightened our sense of adventure. The air was cold but not still—I put on my winter gloves only toward the end of the round. We had the course to ourselves: Ken, Red, and Ben, which made a euphonious scorecard. I was low medalist, by a stroke or two, but lost money at the game of skins we played. On one hole with four skins riding on it, I had a stroke advantage but then three-putted, with hateful senile nerves. Short on my lag, I pulled my four-footer. God, how I hated myself, while Ken and Red crowed.

Driving back through the rush hour was worse than after a ski trip down from North Conway. A hamstring in Red's left leg began to seize up, but there was nowhere to stop on the Southeast Expressway, full of cars pouring, with red taillights and white headlights, into and out of the ghost of Boston. This approach from the south used to be thrilling, the glass skyscrapers looming closer and closer and then burning rectangular and golden all around you as the expressway climbed upward out of the Chinatown tunnel. But with the completion of the so-called Big Dig in 2002, it became one long tunnel up to Causeway Street and the giant looping connectors to Charlestown and the Mystic River Bridge. Neglect has taken the futuristic shine off of the long subterranean stretch; the dead lights and the fallen tiles go unreplaced. Flickering in and out of shadow, the blue-tinted buried highway is spooky, the spookier for our knowing that above its dim roof rests a blasted swathe—formerly the old elevated highway with its constant traffic jams—of weed-ridden parks, stilled carousels, pot-holed jogging paths, straggling shops and restaurants doing a bankrupt imitation of the Faneuil Hall Marketplace, and other such rotting wisps of a vision of civic renewal. Few of the Chinese missiles made it this far, but there were pro-Chinese riots, and the collapse of the national economy has taken a cumulative physical toll. Looking back at the city's profile from the dizzying cloverleaf above the Charles, we saw the blue-glass, post-modern downtown buildings darkened in their post-war desolation, and rusty stumps of projected construction that had been abruptly abandoned, as too expensive for our dwindled, senile world.

One advantage of the collapse of civilization is that the quality of young women who are becoming whores has gone way up. No more raddled psychotics or puffy, dazed coke addicts for the discriminating consumer: twenty-year-olds who would once have become beauticians or editorial assistants, nurses or paralegals, have brought efficiency and comeliness to the trade. The prostitution rings advertise under such names as Velvet Sensations, Unadorned Fantasies, and the like, not just in the *Herald* and *Phoenix* but in the *Globe* and *Christian Science Monitor.* Anything for a welder in our new world. The commonwealth scrip is sepia, the tint of the former governor's red hair; it was hastily issued when the dollar hyperinflated, so the frozen wheels of commerce could begin again to turn; the engraver was a Republican.

Deirdre—Deirdre Lee, she confided to me on her last visit, her third, a last name being a treasure evidently as worth withholding as a whore's kiss on the lips—now moves about on our third-floor love nest with the briskness of a wife, remaking the bed, bundling our used towels for the washer and dryer. I can't rid myself, as I entertain her, of the uneasy feeling that Gloria will come back, slamming all the doors downstairs, clattering up the steps, exploding with icy-eyed fury at the homemaking prerogatives that Deirdre has usurped. It is not clear to me that Gloria is dead; I have a memory of wheeling and shooting her with Charlie Pienta's shotgun through the living-room window, but when I went back inside there was no body. It was a moment of measurement. I felt the universe crackle and branch.

Deirdre also steals material things—two silver-plated candlesticks, and an exquisite little French clock with a gilded face and a case veneered in mother-of-pearl—that Gloria had brought to the marriage. I brought nothing from the Berkshires but my maternal grandfather's china mustache cup and some bone-handled dull cutlery that I can still see my father's workmanly hands, callused and ingrained with machine grease, plying upon a tough Thanksgiving turkey. My mother's anxious face is framed between his cocked elbows as she waits to augment each set of slices with mashed potatoes, gravy, peas, and cranberry sauce, on one of those terrible holidays of childhood, those dry-mouthed group penances we owed the calendar's faded gods.

When I dared reproach Deirdre with her thefts today, she looked me up and down with her expressionless brown eyes—tarry coffee into which some pale flecks of nutmeg had fallen—and said mulishly, "I do plenty for you."

"But, darling, I *pay* you. Even more than you asked, the last time."

Our lovemaking had some of the excitement of an auction, as she volunteered, in a breathless whisper, to perform or submit to a variety of acts beyond the basic missionary in-and-out. She even, as I tried to move my tongue from one lovely smallish uptilted breast to the other—tan but for the little triangles of a thong-bikini bra—specified, "Twenty-five welders extra if you suck both."

"You bitch," I panted, liking this and knowing she liked it too, this damp tangle of commerce and hostility amid the friction of our naked epiderms. "Fifteen. Not a penny more. Your tits should be part of the package. I mean, I'm paying you for your *time*, not for each itty-bitty bit of you."

"Thirty-five if you suck so hard it hurts me," she countered.

It had not occurred to me until this moment to hurt her. Now it seemed an inviting idea. The universe had branched.

"*Ow*," she said, within a second, looking down maternally from within the massive Sphinx-mane of her bushy black hair, the side nearest the window glinting on the crests of its dishevelled curls. Her broad young face, simply but impressively carved but for its blunt and visibly pored nose, loomed a muddy brown, a sandstone tint, insofar as my eyes could pull color from the murk of the ambient dim windowlight.

She was somehow Egyptian in this light, pharaonically opaque.

"You're lying," I protested. "That didn't hurt."

"I'm very sensitive there. Especially when I'm ovulating."

"If you're so fucking sensitive you shouldn't be a whore," I told her, slobbering on, so the small glossy slope of her profiled breast shone by virtue of what must have been, beyond our sheltered grapple on this lonely planet, the moon, the barren uninhabitable moon hanging above the yard's retreating snow.

She was maddening me into an inflamed condition such as I had not experienced since the sweaty backseat tussles of my teens, with their excruciatingly grudging advances, piece by piece, into the forbidden, sacred terrain of a female body. "Let's do it with you on your knees this time," I suggested hoarsely.

"That's fifty more welders." Her hard little voice, with its Massachusetts accent, which erased the "r" in "welders," sounded a touch hoarse also. "Doggie is normally seventy-five more."

"How about up—"

"I don't do that," she quickly said, then added, "for less than three hundred."

She had put herself in doggie position, presenting me with the glazed semi-rounds of her tight young buttocks, and, visible in the moonlight between them, the lovable little flesh-knot of her anus, suggestive of a healed scar. Here, too, the sun had failed to penetrate, deep between the tan buttocks, making a slim white crescent. I wondered if it was Revere Beach where she sunbathed so diligently, her swart skin fearless of the keratoses that cancerously dotted my horny old hide. The Columbus-haters are right: we Northern Europeans should never have veered south across the roiling Atlantic into this dazzling New World. It was a pit-falled Eden; it was forbidden fruit; we drank too much and lost our faith. We began to speckle and rot.

I slapped her solid glazed butternut ass, with its infantile puckered aperture, so decisively that she tumbled onto her back, her eyes stung into life by the blow. I noticed those wounded, tear-moistened eyes nevertheless flick with professional satisfaction toward my triumphantly swollen member, its undischarged juices swirling their intoxicants through my veins. My prostate ached with the forthcoming discharge. I told her calmly, "You can take that hypothetical three hundred and—"

On her back, where I had tumbled her, she laughed at my nicety. "Stuff it," she finished for me. "Go ahead," she teased. "Do it, you old fart." Pronounced "faaht." She spread her legs a bit; her thighs were paler inside than out. "But not up my ass for less than three hundred. Those membranes are delicate. That's how people used to get AIDS."

"Shut up about your ass all the time. Your cunt will do fine. I'm not one of your sicko pervert customers."

She was heavily furred, her forearms swirling with dark down. Her pubic hair was so oily it would have been irides-cent in a stronger light. So she could wear a thong bathing suit, she had shaved all but a central strip, which stood straight up like an old-fashioned typewriter brush. I imag-ined I saw a gleam of responsive moisture between the elephant-gray lips of her vulva. Her cool fingers seemed to be guiding me in but in fact held me off, even as I crouched to thrust home. Deirdre murmured into my ear, "Hey, wouldn't you like me to sit on your face? I could do that and blow you at the same time. For only a hundred extra—I'll give you a deal."

"You bitch, will you shut up about money?" But I hesitated. Her offer was tempting. She knew her man.

"But not so much that I come," I bargained. "I want my seed inside you. You money-grubbing cunt, I want to prong you up to your eyeballs."

She shuddered under me involuntarily. Her face like the face of a girl being mussed in the backseat of a family Chevrolet was built all of shadows, a ruin of little slabs. "Jesus, I hate men," she said, conversationally, as if I had become a disinterested anthropologist. "You're all so fucking proud of nothing—just *nothing*."

"Oh yeah?" I said, pronging her. "That nothing?"

"Nothing," she said, stiffening like a scared child beneath me.

"How about *that?*" She was young and slender and unexcited, with a virgin womb and a never-distended cervix. I knew I could hurt her, and gave a pelvic thrust that pinched my old prostate gland; it, too, wanted to retire, after pushing toxic effluents through its knotty core for fifty-plus years.

Her dark eyes widened and went watery in the shadow my head was casting. Her face sank a bit deeper into the black nest of her widespread hair. "Ow," she did admit, sweetly.

After Deirdre left, bounding down through the woods with her lifted tail showing more white than anyone could expect, I noticed that Gloria's silver quail were gone from the dining-room table. One bent down pecking; the other lifted its beak. I had given them to her on a bygone Christmas, on a lower limb of the thick gray tree of the branching past. Heavy silver—one had to be careful setting them on the table, lest their feet scratch the finish—they would melt down to a lump worth a few lousy welders, a bargain quickly struck with some cheating fence. The nether world preys on its own. I felt deeply ashamed, as though cancer had invaded my body. I would beat the thieving slut black and blue next time, tying her wrists and ankles together with pieces of the waxed cord that I had once bought to replace the rotting sash cords of the old house, and which I thought was still in the cellar. I would screw her until she squealed for mercy, and toss her out naked into the snow, and not pay her a red cent. If she beat sobbing on the door, I would pelt her with golf balls.

With Gloria gone from my side, the bed seems huge and cold at night, and the house reveals vast creaking depths as the unsated February winds whistle and roar outside. I have been taking Sominex to get me through the empty hours of the night, but then, fearful of becoming an addict, I abstained last evening. Sleep came with a satisfyingly dull and solid book on former President Gore—I never read fiction; after all its little hurly-burly what does it amount to but more proof that we are of all animals the most miserable?— but then I awoke in the whining, spitting dark. Furtive footsteps were detectable below and beyond me, faint as thumbprints on black glass.

In the breakdown of order, the criminal element has proved to be the only one with the resources and ruthlessness to rule. I pay protection to a pair of spivs, Spin and Phil, who come out of the local underbrush, and am allowed to reside on my little hill for somewhat less than I formerly paid in combined state and federal taxes. Of course, Spin and Phil aren't trying to make the world safe for democracy, or to administer a sensible but humane welfare program. It is not likely that I will be allowed my domain, defenseless as I am, forever, but for now, in the improvisatory confusion of the new world taking rough shape, I am allowed a space; I am overlooked. The new powers do not provide all the services the old did, but water continues to move through the town pipes into my own, and electricity flows. It amused me that in order to make their last collection the ambassadors from the underworld had to plow my driveway for me; thanks to them I could shop, and the local taxi could bring Deirdre to me. The footsteps that I seemed to hear I reasoned to be imaginary, because the world is so empty now; there are hundreds of empty houses where the starving and the disease-ridden can take shelter. The population pressure, for at least a time, is off.

I rose to urinate. Not wishing to agitate my neurons by turning on the bedside light, I groped toward the narrow pale slit behind which the bathroom night light feebly gleams. It was the two-slit experiment, it occurred to me, that embodied the paradox of quantum reality—a single photon, passing though both slits simultaneously, was able to project a striped pattern of interference with itself. I perhaps would have fallen back to sleep but for a snag, a nagging realization that I had not taken Sominex. After an indeterminate motionless time, I gave up trying to trick my body into thinking it was asleep; I rose again and turned on the light, not my own bedside lamp but Gloria's, reaching across the stretch of bed as cool and as smooth as a marble tombstone, to switch on the lamp. By some law that had evolved early in our marriage, the alarm clock, a Braun quartz travelling clock, lived on her side of the bed.

But she, like me a light and anxious sleeper, always kept its face turned so that its luminescent hands would not greet her eyes in a wakeful moment. I had to stretch, cursing, to press the switch and turn the little black box that contained time in its two endless spools. Two-fifteen! Not three hours of sleep! It seemed incredible to me that at that hour I would not fall asleep again, but in the long featureless blur of shifting positions and churning brain (like a cement mixer full of dry rocks, the same rocks over and over, never consolidating into pourable wet concrete) this did seem to be the case. I was tense, waiting for the first signs of dawn, a change of tune, a distant car—some *event* to trigger a relaxing realization that there existed a world other than my howling brain. As the wind outside died, my brain got noisier, senselessly tumbling alphabet games and previews of tomorrow (in which nothing in particular was scheduled to happen, just a dental checkup and a teatime visit to one of my grandchildren, and in the evening a television show on the cosmological implications of the new deep-space evidences gathered by the venerable Hubble Space Telescope, a show I would be too exhausted to enjoy unless I could now fall asleep) and comparisons between Gloria and Deirdre (whose body was not as comforting as Gloria's, which although softer was also warmer, infiltrating calories into the bed covers, whereas Deirdre's hard lithe form was cool even in the heat of coitus; after she would leave, by that disreputable taxi whose glowing rooflight I watched from the upstairs window circle my driveway and then pull away like a momentarily captured planet, shivers would overtake me and I would rush to put on a sweater) and all sorts of clattering useless mental debris including a rock-hard fury at my stupid self, my foolishly, helplessly rotating brain.

I could not shake free of myself. Whenever my thoughts loosened enough to permit a glowing, nonsensical mirage to peep through, my hungry consciousness leaped upon the glimmer with the triumphant thought *I'm falling asleep* and thereby snuffed it, closing the peephole into blissful rest. In the disorderly blizzard of waking thoughts I now and then prayed to the vibrating shadows, silently running the mutinously non-stop inner speaker through the paces of the Lord's Prayer or a simple beseechment, *Dear Lord, for Christ's sake, let me fall asleep.* But no remission in my torment was granted. God was a vibrating patch indistinguishable from the featureless others in the fuzzy Rothko that insomnia painted on the ceiling. The sheet beneath me was a bed of bent nails, of dead coals.

Then, before dawn, the surface of silence was lightly ruffled by the purr of a car coming up the driveway, the soft squeal of its brakes, and the thump of Gloria's *New York Times* arriving on the porch. Then the car's purr, shaped like a vortex in the sink, retreated down the driveway. The *Times* came to the door; the *Globe* just to the mailbox. I reminded myself I must cancel the subscription. This daily bulletin from another exhausted, blasted city, doubling the burden of paper to be set out fortnightly in the orange recycling bin, had always struck me as a snobbish excess. But I did not yet quite believe that she was gone. She existed in my brain and in my dreams. Sometimes in my dreams I find her bloodied and even headless corpse on the living-room carpet—an ethereal rose-and-sky-blue Tabriz that set us back twenty-four thousand dollars when dollars still counted. So the *Times*es keep coming, with their news of crack crackdowns and motor-mouthed mayors and uncollected garbage and public schools run like prisons and subways that are warrens of mayhem and disease.

Finally, the radiator close to my ear began to tick, at a signal from the thermostat, and my tense frame slackened. Soon the old pipes would companionably chug, chitter, and bang. I was not utterly alone in the universe. The house, well built at the other end of the last century, in slightly slumping over the years has reversed the pitch of some of the pipes, which therefore collect moisture that explodes when the rising steam encounters it. I pictured the little plastic wheel in the thermostat, marked with the numbers of the hour, and the little tripping protrusion I had myself poked into a small hole at the numeral 6, and the leverage this minuscule plastic protrusion (they came in two colors, red for day and blue for nighttime) would exert on the adjoining small wheel that would tip a bead of mercury in its inch-long vial, completing an electric circuit that would activate the furnace. That little bead of mercury, balanced on a temperature-sensitive spring of two annealed metals with a different expansion rate—brass and steel, at a guess—was more of a friend to me in the endless night than almighty eternal God.

But, believers will respond, God gave Mankind the wit to construct thermostats, and this manifests His benevolent existence. I was suddenly too relaxed to argue. The radiators had been resurrected and were shouldering the task of watching over the house. My vigil could cease. But by now, near seven, sunlight, arriving earlier each day, shone in a heartless white stripe below the window shade, and it was time to get up, groggy, disconsolate, and doomed to oblivion though I was. The day was a hostile dare I must take, with a commensurate hostility.

———

The chores of living: the brushing of the teeth, the shaving of the cheeks and chin, taking extra care around the lips, which invariably wear a pursed, haughty expression, the expression of a stranger. My mouth over the years has sunk into a downturned, faintly sneering expression, like the mouth of a death mask, slightly lower on one side than the other. Luckily, I was always rugged-looking rather than handsome, so the wreck of the flesh—the eyelids so sagging their folds snag one on another and need to be rubbed back into place upon awaking, the double cords of throat wattle, taut only when I lift my chin to shave beneath it—dismays me relatively little. The meaningless geography of an old face: the odd dark spot on the edge of one upper lip, the inexplicably sensitive patch along the left jaw, the actinic bumps that have returned after their enraging treatment with Efudex. It resembles the moon's geography, which once afforded room for hypothetical canals and seaports and which has proved, now that we have walked upon it and photographed its pores, obdurately meaningless, a study in enlarged non-significance. A pimple of a hillock here, a blue-gray *mare* there, a rumpled dark side. But not an anatomy: bleak evidence, rather, of heavenly happenstance.

Though I gave it up over thirty years ago, when pitiable tobacco-addicts were being banished from restaurants and offices and being made to stand outside on the sidewalk in all weathers, I still miss smoking, if only because it deadened my sense of smell. A clammy pungence arises to my nostrils from pockets of my body when I, lifting first one leg and then the other, remove my pajamas. No amount of soaping in the shower long suppresses scents which I do not, myself, find disagreeable but remember Gloria complaining about. Yet she herself, in the sodden relaxation of sleep, emitted odors I would never chastise her with. Alone in the house with my unnarcotized nose, I scent what I fear may be a fire in some plastered wall or combustible corner of the cellar but what I deduce is only the Kellys burning wood in their fireplace a wedge shot away. A few carbon atoms in the air; how do our nasal receptors find them, out of so much mere bland oxygen and nitrogen, and digitize them into signals that activate the brain? The brain protrudes the eyes, but molecules seek out the smell centers within it, at the back of the cave. There, matter meets mind.

I undress my body, shower it, dress it again, in slightly different clothes. No need any more for the crisp business suit and shirt; the same beige corduroys and pilled blue sweater will do, with clean underwear and a maroon turtleneck of fresh-smelling cotton. My papery bare feet with their purple etching of veins beg for their socks and ever more shapeless moccasins. We are the herders of our bodies, which are beasts as dumb and bald and repugnant as cattle. Death will release us from this responsibility, which grows, morning by morning, ever heavier. This morning, having completed the last tightened lace of my dressing and preparing to make my constitutional down the driveway for the *Globe*, I looked from the window and saw on the seaside lawn one of the deer that, now that Gloria is gone, browse untroubled on our shrubbery. This one, munching a crescent into the euonymus hedge, seemed less than full size, and gazed up at my face calmly. His (I felt it was a half-grown buck) muzzle was surprisingly coarse, seen head-on, as lumpy and stupid, around the dark-grained and convolute nostrils, as a cow's. I was beginning to see deer as stupid ruminants rather than heraldic apparitions. Gloria had not been wildly wrong to hate them. The animal slowly scented danger in my watching—my white face as much a signal as his white tail—and stalked off, with an affronted dignity, across the flagpole platform and then down toward the driveway.

An inch of wet snow had fallen while I had been wrestling with insomnia. From another upstairs window I saw that the black tire tracks of the man still bringing Gloria her *Times* had stopped—stopped as if his chariot had become Elijah's or Phaëthon's and taken flight—at the base of the steep curved section. Dark footprints, however, brought the story down from the realm of the supernatural: the poor fellow, not wishing to risk slipping off the curve, had, like the FedEx man two months ago, after the first snowfall of this snowy winter, got out of his vehicle and walked.

The *Globe* delivery man always prudently stops at the mailbox. As I, having squeezed my feet into my L.L. Bean Maine Hunting Shoes, walked down to retrieve the morning paper, I observed in addition to my own tracks (which imitate chains laid closely parallel) others: the clustered four paws of the hopping rabbit; the stately punctures, almost in a line, of the deer; the dainty marks, shaped like pansies, of the Kellys' cat, who comes over here to stalk the Y-footed birds that feed on our purple pokeberries; and a troubling set of prints, as widely spaced as the deer's but larger and multiply padded. In trying to picture the animal I could only imagine a lion. A smallish lion. One reads that, as the woods of the Northeast encroach more and more upon cleared fields, bears and coyotes and mountain lions are spreading south. As our species, having given itself a hard hit, staggers, the others, all but counted out, move in. Think of those days when the hominids were just a two-footed furry footnote lost amid the thundering herds of horned perissodactyls. Why does the thought make us happy?

Deirdre is becoming a little too familiar. Instead of submitting to my sexual whims, she prefers to give me the benefit of her feminist rage. "Why are men so cruel?" she asks soulfully, with a little-girl rustle of her head on my shoulder.

"Natural selection," I tell her. "The killers survive, the killed drop out of the genetic pool. Same reason," I go on, "women are masochistic. The submissive ones get fucked and make the babies and the scrappers don't. The meek inherit the earth."

I'm not sure she has been listening. "Jesus, I hate men," she says, off in her own world of memories and strictly localized intellectual reference.

I permit myself to get angry. "You keep telling me that. Where would you be without them? A lazy ignorant cokehead like you, what are you fit for except turning tricks? And you're damn lucky to have found an old sweetheart like me, instead of some crazy young buck who'd beat the crap out of you."

"You're not so uncrazy, Ben. You're crazy about being Frenched, I notice." Toying with my white chest hair, curling it around one index finger, while her headful of wiry oily wool tickles my shoulder and the side of my neck.

It is true, the sight of her plump lips obediently distended around my swollen member, her eyelids lowered demurely, afflicts me with a religious peace.

"And horsing around with my asshole."

Yes, that, too. Her vagina, Deirdre's unspoken accusation ran, was less favored by me than these two orifices designed for other purposes, for ingestion and excretion, and to this extent I was a pervert. My own sense of it is that, at age sixty-six, I am still working up to the vagina—that Medusa whose sight turned ancient men to stone, that sacred several-lipped gateway to the terrifying procreative darkness. I was not yet, at three score and six, quite mature enough to face its blood-empurpled folds, its musty exudations. I was still a boy shutting his eyes when the vaccination needle went in. My working-class doxy sensed this and disliked me for it, even as she wearily roused herself from my side and prepared to nurse me into arousal.

"You rich leech," she told me. "You've never had to get down into it, have you?"

"What do you mean, 'into it'?"

"Into the dirt where the rest of us grub. You called me a money-grubbing cunt last week. Thanks a lot. Just because I didn't get born a fat cat and can clip coupons all my life—"

"Nobody clips them any more. It's all in computers. Anyway, I was born poor. Out in the west of the state. We lived in a town north of Pittsfield called Hammond Falls. There was a river downtown and a bunch of brick mills, mostly empty by the time I came along. Our house, which had belonged to my mother's parents, was up the hill, out on the outskirts, an old farmhouse. Except it was narrow and dark, like a city rowhouse, close to the road, surrounded by these sloping fields going back to cedar and scrub maple. I went to U. Mass., when it cost almost nothing, and met my first wife, and we came to Boston, where I went to the B.U. Business School on student loans, and became a stockbroker. I changed my accent, to blend in. I suggest you change yours too, darling, if you expect to get anywhere in this very class-conscious commonwealth."

This nearly made her spit, naked as she was, crouched on the bed. "Commonwealth, well, la-ti-da darling, yourself. What a liar! We should both wash our mouths out, me from sucking your stubby dick and you from being a liar. I can see all around this house, it's full of inherited stuff."

"It's Gloria's. My late wife's."

"Who says she's late?"

"She's not here, is she?"

"No, but she wouldn't be, would she? With me here. Unless she was a real AC-DC."

In a rage of annoyance—she was re*sis*ting me, in every re-

sentful fibre—I seized her brown arm, which was propping
her up over my belly like the leg of a beast poised to drink.
"Who says it's stubby? *You're* the liar. If it's so stubby why do
you gag when it's only halfway in?"

She sullenly pulled her arm away, revealing four white
finger-marks. "Ow. O.K., not stubby. Stinky, though."

"You should talk. You're like low tide down there—low
tide next to a sewer outlet."

Deirdre brushed a mass of her curls back from one ear,
contemplating thoughtfully the erect refutation of stubbiness which my surge of violence had pushed through my
blood. "You guys hate us, don't you?" she said musingly.
"Cocks hate cunts."

"But they love mouths," I crooned to her, and fell into a
state of beatitude as her lips absent-mindedly enclosed me,
and her brown hand, narrow as a hoof, worked the skin at the
base up and down, into a moist tingle mounting heavenwards.

"We hate you, too," she told me afterwards, when I was
too languid to hurt her. "You own us, but we hate your
guts." She had come back from the bathroom, after a tumult
of flushed toilet and expectorated mouthwash, in a clear-
headed, combative mood.

"Who's this 'you'?"

"You rich creeps. I never got into one of your houses before. Usually the tricks are guys with no background, Irish
or eyetie, you know, who have a little money they can't hang
on to. They don't want to hang on to it. They're too
Catholic. Down deep they think it's holy to be poor. Only
the Jews and you Wasps aren't ashamed to hang on to
money, to sit in heaps of it and roll in it and smear it all over
yourselves—disgusting! You think you're so great God *likes*
your being stinking rich."

"Darling, I agree. I must learn to spend. That thing you just did was worth every welder."

"Two hundred."

"It's usually a hundred fifty."

"You had a lot of come today. I nearly choked."

"I love it when you nearly choke."

"I know you do, you prick. That's what my father began by having me do, blow him." Her eyes narrowed as she looked into the past, preparing to match my confession with her own.

"Hey," I said, "do I need to hear this? I'm no therapist. I'll start charging *you* by the hour."

"I was eight. My head came up to just the right height on him. He said to do it, I didn't know, I thought it might be normal. He was my father, he said it was all right, who else could I trust?"

"You could have gone to your mother."

"*Tchaa!*"—a catlike snarl. "She was worthless. She would have slapped me and called me a liar. She didn't *want* to know. He was all she had, too."

"I'm sorry, dear, for calling you a liar."

"O.K. I appreciate your saying that. I'm a hooker and I steal, but I don't generally lie. It's too confusing, it makes another world. So I stick with the truth, generally. Except when I said you were stubby. You have a nice prick."

"Don't break my heart."

"You can't take a compliment, can you? You hate me too much. You hate needing me. Guys do. It must feel funny, having that business hanging down outside you have to keep feeding."

"I feed *you*," I said, and felt compelled to embrace her, her pliant slim waist, the long brown supple abdominal stretch between the wispy ghosts of her bathing suit, and I felt her harden, in fright at my confessed need and in calculation of how best to employ it to her advantage. I was her slave, my slave's slave. I whispered into her ear how I wanted before I died to pump a ton of jism into her, into her mouth, into her little puckered asshole, into her huge warm cosmic cunt, pump it all as some kind of glutinous silvery bridge to the next world, and she was saying, "Uh-huh, uh-huh," automatically, calculating how to put my craziness into a profitable harness.

Our mothers wipe our bottoms and praise our first babbled words, our nurses at the finale tidy up and maternally murmur amid the mess of our dying, but the women who out of whatever motive swallow our seed through one of their holes deliver the acceptance that matters. They drink our groins' milky tears. Through the bodies of women men conduct what tortured dealings they can with the universe, producing serial murder and morganatic marriages and a Morgan Library's worth of love letters, novels, and death threats. Women don't ask for this, true. But what *do* women ask for? as a maligned sage at the far end of the last century infamously inquired in all innocence.

———————

Between bouts of lovemaking Deirdre and I have taken to exploring the house together, naked. I turn the thermostat way up for the adventure. Gloria kept a thrifty cold house, and when I wasn't looking would sneak our bedroom window open an inch or two even in the bitterest January weather. She would even raise the storm window, which she ordinarily said she couldn't do because the little spring catches would break her fingernails; but, in the attempt to freeze my old gray head fast to the pillow, she would take this risk. When I began wearing a knit watch-cap to bed, she mocked me, and would pluck it off in my sleep, to ensure that I awoke with sniffles and a fatal dry cough.

My slim young companion and I explore seldom-visited chambers of the far-flung old house. It was built by one of that legendary race of Boston rich who came to this shore for the summer cool, before air conditioning, their untaxed dollars engaging armies of Italian masons and Scots-Irish carpenters. Seven fireplaces, no two alike, in Ionic, Doric, and even (in the living room) Corinthian modes. Palladian windows, columned verandas. A fully finished third floor, and a basement with a plastered ceiling. Over the course of more than a century, the plaster has lost its grip, and chunks of it litter the remoter regions, including a mysterious room whose floor is the jagged ledge the house was built upon. This rough chamber, which knits the structure to primal matter, has always rather frightened me. It lies beyond the laundry room and the servants' bathroom, where the thick old porcelain toilet goes months unflushed, its oval eye of water scummed with plaster dust. A steam pipe arrives at its safety valve in the farthest, rock-bottomed chamber, and the hissing, as from a captive serpent, startles us. Deirdre exclaims in disgust at the dry filth, the decades of unswept plaster fragments and whitewash flakes and flecks of crumbling brick and mouse droppings and bits of mouse poison, all accumulating on her sticky bare soles. I tell her, in the ardor of this strangeness, that I will lick them clean, even though I die of it. My genitals dangle in the cloistered cellar air; I love how her body beside mine displaces dead space. Faint musty and oily whiffs spring from her flesh and hair and dart deep into my nasal passages. I keep touching her, lightly, guiltily, the way we touch a smooth statue or a rough-textured canvas when the museum guard is not looking.

We go up the cellar stairs. Naked we move through the main floor, past Gloria's Chippendale dining chairs and mahogany table of many leaves and teak-veneered breakfront laden with Meissen and Limoges china and filigreed Victorian wineglasses with ruby-red stems, our dirty feet tracking cellar crumbs over the blue Tabriz. I inspect the rug for bloodstains but can see none, in the bald winter light. I exultantly, fearfully feel our joint intrusion as systematic desecration. Our filthy bare feet, our Edenic nudity. If the white FedEx truck were to flash around the driveway, the driver would see us through the Palladian windows. I am getting an erection, mounting the carpeted stairs with this body lithe as a boy's beside me. When I glance down at her, she has sullen, swollen lips and a blunt blob of a nose—an obtuse muzzle. We survey the second floor, the rooms the boys lived in before they went off and got married. Some rock posters and car posters are still up. My mistress is younger, I realize with a start of shame, than even the younger of my stepsons. Our relationship abruptly seems exploitive. I take her cool sharp elbow and lead her up the back stairs, to the third-floor "safe" room, with its special alarm that must be deactivated with a switch in a closet, where Gloria keeps or kept her special family treasures—jewels inherited, in unwearably ornate settings, from great-great-grandmothers; silver platters and teapots too heavy to use at less than a state banquet; vast punchbowls of cut glass; boxes of turn-of-the-century first editions that her maternal grandfather paid to have shipped from England, along with his Savile Row shoes and dinner clothes, and that he slit, as he read, with a little ivory paper knife tilted in his signet-ringed right hand. Even men, men of means, attended to books then as if to carven caskets in which a crucial secret, a key to living, might be locked.

Another capped steam pipe hisses in here, overheating the slant-ceilinged small chamber. Its single window, a dormer, overlooks the lethal sea, with its ragged islands and pewter glare of shrouded sunlight. Deirdre, amid all this treasure, is frightened by something within herself—perhaps a chemical need, for a quick pipe of crack, or a surge of covetousness. I have shown her too much. I make a mental note to change the padlock, lest she and that pimp of a taxi driver return with criminal intent. Gloria's splendid ancestors, so confident in their luxurious appropriations, hiss crushingly in our ears. As if ashamed of her meagre assets—her momentarily young and healthy body, her willingness to play the whore—Deirdre folds her thin arms tight across her small breasts. Her wine-dark nipples are taut, as if from a chill. Fear like an odor leaps from her skin and clings to me, softening my erection.

What do we know about the Egyptian grave robbers? We know, by inference, that they were brave, risking the anathemas of the gods and execution by torture. They were clever, breaking into even the center of the great pyramid of Cheops and emptying it before the archaeologists arrived a millennium later. They were persistent, gutting of treasure, by the year 1000 B.C., every known rock tomb save that of the golden-faced boy-king Tutankhamen, which had been haphazardly concealed by a pile of stone rubbish from the excavation of another tomb. Tomb-robbing was a profession, a craft, a guild, practiced by whole villages such as that of Gourna, located above the Valley of the Kings, and connected, possibly, with the honeycomb of royal tombs by deep-dug wells. The thieves' tunnels rival in extent if not finish the sanctioned passageways of the pharaohs' engineers. The divinely inspired technological achievements of the tomb-builders—false stairways, monolithic booby traps, passageways hundreds of feet in extent—were matched by those of the sacrilegious thieves, who conquered even the labyrinths of Amenemhat, constructed by the shores of Lake Moeris. Thieves were angry, vandalizing everything they could not steal: levering open giant sarcophagi, ripping apart mummies like jackals at a leopard's corpse, hurling precious vessels and statues with such force against the walls that dents and smudges of pure gold remain in evidence. Their fury was a way, perhaps, of combatting the gods, whose vengeance they could not help fearing. Yet their crimes were beneficent, performing the useful service, modern economists inform us, of restoring gold to circulation— bringing it back from unsound investment underground, counteracting the severe trade imbalance that this world kept incurring with the next. Tutankhamen's golden coffin alone weighed two hundred fifty pounds.

What did the robbers, breathing the adhesive dust of damnation, scraping through crevices of a predatory narrowness, do for light? The builders chiselled by the light of the sun, which was bounced around corners by circular reflectors of bronze and, quivering like water, illumined the deepest recesses of laboriously hollowed limestone. But an outside member of a looting team risked apprehension by the hooded priests' police and death by slow disembowelment, flaying, or impalement. No torture was too extreme for the enemies of immortality; we robbed our victims not merely of life's passing illusion but of an eternity. We crept along holding before us lamps of translucent calcite, so the glow permeated downward as well as leaped up, a notch holding the twisted, serpentine wick in place and our fingers warmed through the alabaster. The smell of sesame oil was strong, enlarging the smell of our sweating bodies much as the flickering flame enlarged our shadows, which surged and lunged around us as we inched forward in the silence of the dead. Each piece of floor had to be tested for a pitfall— a precipice or a delicately balanced slab that would tumble our broken bodies onto the bones of previous trespassers. The light was ruddy on the painted walls; our flames were orange, with a blue base like the change of tint in the heart of a flower, at the base of each fragile petal. There were two of us: if one wick guttered out, it could be relit from the other. If both blew out at once, in a sudden draft from an intersecting passageway, we must perish in these subterranean tunnels and turnings unless I could strike fresh fire from the flints and dry grass I carried in my leathern waist-pouch. This method, though, was chancy, and the outraged gods would have breath enough to extinguish the fire again.

"The air grows worse," my accomplice muttered.

I ventured to say, though my larynx was clogged by fear as by a cloth stopper, "Mayhap we are approaching the House of Gold, where the mummy reigns, with his rotting nose and urn of foul innards. A pox on Horus! May Anubis dine on his own excrement in the life everlasting!" Insulting the dead and their gods braced our courage. We had come through the First Divine Passage, whose triple doorway had forced upon us two months' worth of gnawing circumvention, done in the secret stretches of the night, while the priests' guards slept, content with their bribes and stupid on fermented barley. We had negotiated the Hall of Hindering; its tangle of decoy corridors and stairs had been long ago decoded by a trail of henna powder, left by a thief himself now as dead as the Ruler of All in his onyx sarcophagus. Along the walls of a long sloping corridor, bright colors leaped forward into the lights of our lamps—scenes, crowded yet tranquil, of seasonal pleasures along the Nile, of seed being sown and grain being harvested, of fish being plucked from the transparent river waves painted as zigzags of a blue weaving, of cattle being herded and a hippopotamus being hunted, of workmen assembling a temple and dancing girls with heads of abundant knitted hair applying kohl to the rims of their softly staring eyes. Feathered ibises and ducks, solemn oryxes and monkeys accompanied the brown broad-shouldered human figures undergoing the rites of daily life, a life the dead king in his House of Gold was still enjoying amid his jewelled furniture and dolls of faïence—the faithful *ushabtiu*—in the chamber we had not yet reached.

Now the walls on both sides showed a procession bearing treasures toward this chamber, and hieroglyphic lists of the prayers that must be said to Thoth and Ra on the boat journey to the land of the dead. The masses of the stone around and above us pressed on our spirits, making it still harder to breathe. Centuries of stillness had thickened the air's taste. Carefully picking our way through an area of collapsed rubble, we came to the Hall of Truth, where murals showed the monarch's heart being weighed by Osiris, with Ammut squatting near at hand waiting to devour the heart if it was found unworthy. By the flutter of our lamps, the paintings were hasty, sketchy. The king must have died before the tomb was quite completed, because the murals ceased. The walls grew rough—the chisel marks slashing frantically in the wavering light of our naked flames—and the ceiling grew lower. Of the narrowing passageway that loomed to our lamps it was difficult to say whether it was fortuitously

unfinished or an intended trap. The slanting ceiling compelled us to lower our heads and bend our knees. When
crouching became impossible, we crawled in the pale dust
like crippled animals, hobbled by the necessity of carefully
moving the lamps ahead of us. A spidering of our double
shadows filled the dwindling space. The walls squeezed in-
ward so that we could no longer crawl side by side. A faint
breath, damp as if from a ghost of the Nile, brushed our
faces and made our delicate flames stagger. When they had
regained steadiness I made out in the dim dust a lintel leaning at an angle above a spill of rubble. The irregular aperture might have admitted, with not an inch to spare, the
head and shoulders of a slithering man.

My young companion had pressed up beside me, in a
space scarcely wide enough for one body, and joined his
lamp to mine to cast light into the space beyond. We saw at
the very edge of our lamps' merged glow what appeared to
be a giant gold face. Gold: the skin of deity. Black irises
glared from within whites pieced together of alabaster
flakes. Shadows flickered across the immutable great features in a counterfeit of agitation. The inert weight of the
stone all about us seemed to be meditating an action. We
talked in whispers, so as not to blow out our lamps with our
words.

"You go first," I said.

"No," came the sighed response, causing my flame to
shrink to its blue root on the fibrous wick before regaining,
orange and erect, its strength. "*You*, master," his light voice
urged huskily in my ear. He was in a sweat of fear; I could
smell it even through the dust.

"You are younger and more slender," I explained.

"But you are stronger and more courageous. You have
lived more life."

"There is nothing in there," I stated, fighting panic as his slippery, fragrant body pressed upon mine in our corset of mute stone.

"There is something."

"Our fortune, it may be," I insisted, attempting to wriggle backward, to let him slide forward. "Loot for a lifetime's worth of feasting. Go *in*, I tell you. There is *nothing*."

"Nothing is not nothing," he moaned. His gritty naked knees flexed convulsively into my chest; in the suffocating closeness I smelled his uncircumcised sex. As if by an impatient breath, both our lamps were blown out. Absolute darkness encased us.

ii. *The Dollhouse*

WHITE LIGHT knifes beneath the window shade a minute or two earlier each morning, in strict accordance with the planetary clockworks. The light is bald, assaultive, a supernal revolution removed from the lulling, sifting dawns of December and January, dawns which bid us roll over and drink another half-hour of delicious grainy gray sleep. On the bare roads strewn with salt and sand, on the scruffy lawns and fields whose grass lies matted in brown swirls like a species of carpet, on the metallic branches and twigs of winter's stripped trees, on the pebbles gouged up from beside the driveway by the snowplows and scattered across the asphalt, this light presses with a blank urgency, beckoning everything into a painful precision. The earth is like a nude woman flashbulbed in her bathroom at an awkward transitional moment of her toilette. Despite her wrinkled ugliness, we lust for her.

Other signs of earliest spring: On a wet day the lilac buds are visibly yellow, *pointilles* daily growing plumper and wetter in the gray atmosphere. Little mossy patches appear in the lawn, even before green snowdrop noses break the crust in the border beds. The birds are noisier in the woods; the crows gather in shuffling, ominous clumps in our oaks, and the mourning doves double and redouble their throaty cooing as they cluster in the thicket of mountain ash, sumac, and sassafras to the right of the driveway, below the little straightaway. Cumulus clouds appear, spaced in a sky of a guileless, powdery blue, and there is a twinkly carefree quality about the way the sea now wears its whitecaps. Even though a perishable March snowfall restores us for a few days to picture-book winter, these vernal signs persist and expand—cracks in the comforting encasement of hibernal sterility. Farther afield, willows yellow down by the pond on the Willowbank golf course, and along Route 128, where there used to be miles of overhanging trees, the surviving maples show a distilled red vapor in their massed ranks.

I was a student at U. Mass. in Amherst when I first rode Route 128. I was nineteen, soon to be twenty. In the spring, when the white light hit and the air warmed the trees into a chartreuse froth, a thirst would arise in our throats, there in that desolate inland campus at Amherst, that drab Satanic diploma mill, for the sight of the sea, and the sensation of sand beneath our bare feet, and the aristocratic scent of salt air. Josh Greenstein, my roommate, owned a white '69 Pontiac Trans Am convertible that looked like a bumpy long bathtub; we would giggle getting into it, as if it were brimful. Josh and his steady, Hester Rosenthal, who went against racial type by being blonde and blue-eyed, sat up front while we in back got the full benefit of the wind, which battered our eardrums and dried our faces tight as drumheads. We would drive north to Route 2 and then east through Concord to 128. The road, flecked with the beginnings of the glassy high-tech boom, passed through Burlington, Wakefield, Lynnfield, Peabody, Danvers, Beverly, and Manchester on the way to Wingershaek Beach in West Gloucester. Or we turned north on Route 1 to Crane Beach, in Ipswich, or farther north to Plum Island, off Newburyport. The terrain held clapboard houses few and far between, perched on the edge of greening lawns and fresh-plowed fields, amid steel-blue ponds and spatterings of forest in bud. Forsythia, dogwood, magnolia, cherry, and apple overlapped in a quilt of blossoms. In Topsfield, Route 1 dipped down to cross the gush of a swollen brown river. This antique superhighway went straight as a ruler from Boston to Newburyport, taking the hills as if with seven-league boots. When we crossed over to 1A, along the coast, winter-blanched salt marshes reached to where sky and sea joined. There were wooded islands in the marshes, and long straight ditches. Salt hay (can it be?) had been picturesquely gathered into stacks on wooden staddles. The air battering our faces had salt in it, and Josh and Hester sang along with the radio: "Delta Dawn," "Rocky Mountain High," "Killing Me Softly with His Song." Arrival at the beach parking lot had something heroic about it—we had had the vision and now, after many miles and many songs and not too many stops to pee and eat a hot dog, had attained it.

And who is this sitting beside me, wearing a wind-whipped red bandana and a squint that makes the planes of her face look romantic and detached, like a lean Indian squaw's? It is *my* steady, my girl and first wife, the fair Perdita. She was a lanky, taciturn, frequently tan art major who was to bear me five children and remain, loyal if unenraptured, my spouse to nearly the end of the twentieth century. Our children, though slower to marry and breed than we were, have now produced ten grandchildren—nine boys, and a final, adorable female infant. Born so close together, our children were fed and bathed and taken for outings as a close group, and to this day exhibit toward each other a symbiotic deference and regard. They married, for instance, strictly in the order in which they were born, and bore their children—two each—with the same sense of priority. Their generational mode is to have stable small families, in contrast to the large and messy and eventually doomed households in which they were raised. In further evidence of their conservatism, all reside within this state, strung out within an hour's drive along Route 128, so that the ancient highway bears familial as well as romantic associations for me. Its hinterland, out of sight beyond the thinned trees and hazardously sharp turnoffs, is rich for me with small backyards and electronically overequipped living rooms and soccer fields and elementary-school auditoriums where I have attempted, however ill-rehearsed, to play the role of grandfather.

The catastrophic dip in world population has not, oddly, brought back the stretches of forest through Peabody and Danvers that I recall. Perhaps there can be no replacing the landscape of youth. The towering, freshly leafing branches scudded past Perdita's profile; she squinted with stoic calm while an edge of the red bandana beat at her temple like a frantic pulse, her hazel eyes mere slits, her pursed lips cracked and dry. We smoked, and our cigarettes kept flinging sparks and hot ash on our faces and clothes. We whisperingly would confer, the destination at last reached, about asking Josh to put the top up on our return drive. A chem. major, on the gastroenterologist track, he wore thick glasses, had a bad complexion, and could be prickly about what he fancied his prerogatives. Hester, that flaxen-haired JAP, was oblivious to the discomfort of those in the backseat. In the tumult of the wind and scudding scenery my eyes fastened on Perdita's exposed knee, already tanned by sessions of semi-undress on the grassy slopes encircling squarish Campus Pond. When we at last arrived at the beach, and clamorously went forward to dip our toes over the edge of the continent, she would hoist up her winter skirt and expose her lean legs to mid-thigh. Holding her skirt with one hand, she would bend over the shallow, sliding shore waves like some kind of gatherer, a timeless figure from Millet, posing thus until the tumbling water's frigid grip hurt her ankles and she scampered back, laughing with the pain. When we all lay together behind a hot dune the grains of sand would fall from her drying bare feet one by one, like the sands in an hourglass that silently steal away even the most tranquil and disaster-spared life. I vowed I would live in sight of the sea, and I have.

Her feet were exquisite, now that I think about them—the pads of the soles thick and rounded, the little toes lifted off the ground and clearly vestigial. She was the most placid, the most adrift in nature's currents, of the women I have known, or perhaps that is the way I prefer to remember her, memory being no less self-serving than our other faculties. Her genes now float up toward me from the faces of my grandchildren, diluted by a quarter. My daughters startle me at times by their resemblance to Perdita, her way of absentmindedly posing, with a certain graceful solidity, as if letting some invisible current flow through them. The middle of my daughters has married an African, from Togo, and it has changed the temper of the entire family, for the better. Split, or extended, by divorce, we did not quite know how to be a family until the Africans showed us. Adrien has many brothers and sisters, in many countries, getting advanced degrees. Though very slender, he speaks in a deep voice, slowly, in an accent in which French and English elements are charmingly mingled. His great-great-grandfather, a clerk and translator for the occupiers, spoke German; Togoland was a German territory until 1914, when Allied colonial armies from the Gold Coast and Dahomey invaded. Would that the trench war in Europe had been resolved as quickly!—the entire maimed and vindictive century now past would have been different. Adrien presides over my children in a way I never did. My status, shadowy at best since my defection from their mother, a matter of sneak college visitations and shamefaced appearances at weddings and baptisms, took on a sudden refulgence with his arrival among us. My sins were brushed aside. His own father had lived in Tanzania, across the great continent, an implementor of Nyerere's *ujamaa*, and with an array of informal wives had bestowed upon Adrien a number of half-siblings. This was patriarchal behavior. I was given a Togolese robe of many colors, and took my place in the outdooring ceremonies whereby my two brown grandsons were presented to the sky god. I was given cards in which the appropriate blessings in Kwa were phonetically spelled; pronouncing in a loud voice, I tipped the glass of gin, a substitute for palm wine, three times (inwards, toward my breast, not outwards) to offer libation to the ancestors within the earth. Being an African grandfather was made realer to me than being an American father. My adult children, thanks to Adrien's African magic, suddenly had permission to love me again.

Adrien and Irene and little Olympe and Étienne live in one of Boston's endless western suburbs, a slice of land wedged, with its lone factory, strip mall, and playing field, a thrifty distance beyond fashionable Concord and Lincoln. I drive along 128, and then miles of 62. Their house stands in a tract of development on a hillside, with a view of muddy yards and abandoned plastic tricycles. Adrien and Irene go out, after a few grave and girlish, respectively, remarks to me, to dinner and a local movie house, while the boys and I watch some unintelligible (to me) cartoon video that has been thoughtfully provided, and then I try to put them to bed before their parents come back. This is the game, and they know we are playing it, and they tumble and frisk upstairs and down not quite defiantly, just making everything, from getting into their pajamas to brushing their teeth, maddeningly difficult. The house is full of masks and knotted, braided, beaded pagan symbolizations from Togo; a studio portrait of me, taken at the request of the firm at some stage of my advancement through the ranks of Sibbes, Dudley, and Wise, occupies a place of honor in the exiguous living room. Yet this fetish does not ensure discipline. The boys, dodging my bedtime attentions, have lovely pearly smiles, like mischievous Irene's when she was their age, but with lavender gums. Their eyes are of an astonishing inky solemnity—not a fleck of even nutmeg in the blackness of the irises. Their hair is pure Adrien: helmets of kinky frizz, pleasingly springy to touch. I can't stop petting their heads. Where else can I touch an African coiffure? It was something my life hadn't promised me. I wonder what barber, in this nearly all-white town, knows how to give them a haircut. They are seven and five. They like, amazingly, being read to, which I would have thought was too tame an entertainment for children raised among VCRs and PCs and CD players; Adrien teaches computer science at a local prep school and the baseboards of his house crawl with wires, plugs, adaptors, and winking power-surge preventers. So, lying between my grandsons on the bottom bunk of their bunk beds, I drone through one battered, shiny tale after another of fire engines and milk trucks, of elephants wearing trousers and party gowns, of bewildered kings and gentle giants and witches in shingled huts in forests where medieval Germany merges, in terms of housing, with the round huts of Togoland. After a while the springy soft heads nestling against my cheeks become less restive, and I make my first attempt at abandoning them to their dreams, an attempt which usually collapses in a flurry of scampering footsteps and brotherly blows and cries of recrimination. With a weary imitation of indignation and surprise I mount the stairs again and resettle them in their beds, only to find, on my next return up the creaking stairs, them together in the lower bunk, Olympe asleep but a glitter of wakeful black still caught in Étienne's long curved eyelashes. He fidgets against sleep's tightening grip. His bottom lightly touches that of his older brother, through their flannel pajamas; their round heads are side by side on one pillow. I never had a brother. Any moment, Adrien and Irene will be coming back, with a loud crack of the front door that often wakes the boys into a scamper of gleeful welcome. I notice, as Étienne in the dusk of the lower bunk settles into self-forgetfulness, that his bare foot, dilutedly brown, bears a cashew-shaped little toe as vestigially uplifted as Perdita's.

This is set down, I suppose, in the search for meaning. As one supernatural connection after another fails, the chain of ancestors and descendants—the transcendent entity of family—offers to solace us. But the dissolution of ego, which family demands, is just what we fight. Immortal DNA offers as cold a comfort as the transmigration of souls. If we can't take our memories with us, why go?

Spring for me has always been the season to fear death. I wake heavily, with something undigestible gnawing my stomach, in the intensifying white light. My idiot subconscious, meanwhile, responds to the time of year with dreams of sex. Last night, as Deirdre's lean body rested light on the mattress beside me—her long tanned bony back is heartbreakingly boyish—I dreamed I was making love to, of all people, Grace Wren. My woken self could not believe the passion with which I lay my body on top of hers (trumping it) and I ground my pelvis against the auburn-haired ace of hearts at the juncture of her legs. Her breathless face, her ample (but more youthfully, jauntily so; this was the Grace of twenty years ago) breasts, and that hairy crotch holding its responsive buds and folds were all under me with such passionate reality that my poor hard-on ached like a bursting bladder. In my dream the focus of my pain had recourse to her warm mouth, she was blowing me, she was giving me pure head, for she had no body, there was just her severed head with its closed eyes sucking. Horrors! I awoke with the monstrousness of it, the Dahmeresque atrociousness. It was as bad as something in Greek mythology or Aztec religion. The sexual parts are fiends, sacrificing everything to that aching point of contact. Society and simple decency keep trying to remind us of everything else—the rest of the body, the whole person, with its soul and intellect and estimable socioeconomic constituents—but in the truth of the night our dismembering needs arise and chop up the figments of our acquaintance like a Mogul swordsman gone berserk, and revolt us with our revealed nature.

During this same March night, while I was sleeping, a warm rain turned to freezing rain and then snow, depositing a candied crust on the reviving greenery, a white caramelization that sparkled on the skin of the driveway and in the buckgrass and wild blueberry that grow along the edge. The winter still had a kick of cold in it. Halfway down, I regretted not bothering to put on gloves and my little rubber hunting shoes, with their soles patterned in chains, for my morning walk to retrieve the newspaper. I slipped and slid. In the headlines, President Smith, that anonymous, derided man, was offering free farmland to citizens willing to go and work an assigned acreage of the depopulated Midwest. The Homestead Act anew. Little fragmentary sheaths of ice showered upon me as a chill breeze stirred the beech twigs overhead. This should be the terminal mood of my life, I thought: everything mundane candy-coated.

Deirdre got me to go to the Peabody mall yesterday; she had a whole list of depleted household necessities, including bathroom washcloths. With her cervine sense of smell she claimed that all of our washcloths inexpungeably stank. "What have you been wiping with them?" she asked me.

I blushed, answering, "Only myself. That's the smell of old age."

She alertly saw, out of those globular shining eyes of hers, that she had hurt my feelings, to a degree that might cause a rift. Hastily she told me, "You don't smell like that. You smell sweet, like a freshly powdered baby. The back of your neck, especially."

I wondered what she knew of babies. She was not as young, perhaps, as she seemed to me—old enough, certainly, to be a mother, of some child crawling or toddling down there in the murky valleys beneath my little hill.

The mysterious people who dwell in these valleys were out in force at the mall, in their windbreakers and blue jeans, their high-domed, billed bubba hats and their barbarically ornate running shoes. Retirees—who all seemed ancient to me, but some were perhaps younger than I—lounged in a daze of early Alzheimer's on the benches the mall provides, waiting for their shapeless wives to come claim them and lead them to the car. If they had a thought as we passed, it must have been that Deirdre was my daughter, or a hard-faced young escort from the nursing home. We entered the mall through Filene's; to swim in such an abundance of scarves and underwear and pointed vinyl shoes, in so pungent and deep a lake of artificial perfumes dizzied and dazed me. Spring, though not quite yet in the air, was in the fashions, and in the stir of consumers, propelled by the lengthening light out of their warrens into the wide clearing of consumerism. Young couples, tattooed and punctured visibly and invisibly, with studiously brutal haircuts, strolled hand in hand as if in a garish park of the purely unnatural, so deeply at home here it would not have surprised me if, with a clash of nostril studs and a spattering of hair dye, boy and girl had turned and begun to copulate. Malls have become a public habitat soaked in slovenly intimacy; its customers step naturally from huddling around television in their living rooms to cruising these boulevards of superfluity, where fluorescent-lit shops press forward temptations ranging from yogurt-coated peanuts to electric-powered treadmills. Elderly women had dressed themselves like kewpie dolls, in pastel running suits that suggested an infant's pajamas. I was the only person in sight wearing leather shoes and a necktie. Deirdre parked me outside Banana Republic and at the end of my ordeal took me into Brooks Brothers and bought me a striped shirt that answered some gangsterish beau ideal of her own. She has, it almost made me weep to think, a splinter of feeling for me somewhere in her polished brown machine of a body. Easy weeping is another sign of dotage, along with stinking washcloths.

My grandchildren, spread along Route 128 in the residential gristle between its ossified centers of commerce, tend to have—Étienne and Olympe aside—tony, English-tinted names: Kevin, Rodney, Torrance, Tyler, Duncan, Quentin, and Keith. The girl, perhaps inevitably, is called Jennifer. Where do my kids and their spouses get these monickers? Off of birthday-card racks, it must be, or the Winnie-the-Pooh page on the Internet. They all have their problems. Torrance was born a month premature and is delicate, querulous, and elfin; Tyler, his younger brother, was born two weeks late and has club feet and a prematurely sealed fontanel. Quentin suffers from chronic constipation, and Duncan is hyperactive: he will grab and shake a ficus tree or a floor lamp until the leaves drop or the bulb shatters. Rodney has reading problems, Kevin broke his wrist on the school jungle gym, and Keith is having a hard time adjusting to the arrival of his little sister, about whom so much sexist fuss is being made. And yet they all are dear, and half have learned to spell GRANDPA and send me, at their parents' prompting, birthday and Christmas cards. It quickens my senile tears to think of them all marching—toddling, creeping—into the future, lugging my genes into the maelstrom of a future world I will never know. Such brave soldiers, in what kind of battle, for what noble cause? The doughboys who swarmed out of the trenches into clouds of mustard gas had geniuses for generals by comparison.

If love between my children and me has achieved, thanks to African wisdom, a certain settled, ironical, negotiable shape, that between my grandchildren and the apparition that I form at the back of their tadpole eyeballs is pure chaos. I often try to imagine what they will feel when I die. A faint apprehensive pang, tinged with the comic, as with those boys who sneak off to the baseball game on the excuse of a grandparent's funeral. In their up-to-date eyes, I have lived in hopelessly old-fashioned, deprived times, so what can it matter, even to me, that I die?

Building the dollhouse for my daughter in the cellar—at the memory, my pen becomes impossibly heavy in my hand.

———————

Walking back up the driveway with the newspaper this morning, I was suddenly conscious of the noise, through the sparse intervening woods, of the sea; it had a new, louder voice. There was a warm, snow-eating drizzle in the air, and a wet wind during the night had activated our outdoor burglar lights, I noticed when I awoke to urinate. The air carried the thrashing of the waves on the beach with the urgency of fresh news, the yowl of a creature new-born. The infant spring has its own acoustics, I noticed. Walking a bit around the property a few days ago, I had taken note of the heavy-headed little snowdrops, and the first pale edges of daylily leaves in the drab soil, but these signs bore no glad message for me. This breezy moist sea-roaring possibly did. Such marine thunder, slowly grinding up the continents, must have sounded thus in our planet's earliest days, when the lifeless seas beat upon rocky shores now lost beyond all geological conjecture. This prezoic sea's invasion of my ear somehow cheered me. I liked the fuss, the stirring up. I walk carefully these days, trying to avoid any thought that will tip me into depression.

Deirdre in her renovations, as she bravely tries to oust Gloria's décor from a few corners of the house, sends me down to the barn with rugs and items of furniture she wants out of sight. Already, in this barn originally built to accommodate carriages and their horses, with troughs and stalls and a drain in the middle of a sloped floor for an Augean hosing, there is an accumulation of old bicycles and skis and collegiate lamps and chairs and hide-a-beds and cardboard boxes of textbooks that will never be consulted again. It is easier to keep these condemned objects here in a kind of life imprisonment than to steel oneself for execution out on the curb on trash-collection day. Such repositories, in garages and basements and closets and attics, pledge our faith in eternal return, in a future that holds infinite temporal opportunities for eventual reuse and rereading. Alas, time's arrow points one way, toward an entropy when all seas will have broken down all rocks and there is not a whisper, a subatomic stir, of surge. So to fumble and stumble around looking for a cranny of space in which to lay an old Oriental four-by-six whose American domestic career began in Gloria's father's grandmother's Danbury, Connecticut, foyer is a wallow in one's own death, in funerary spaces as futile as Egypt's treasure-crammed tombs.

I recognized a black English bicycle that Perdita and the children had given me one Christmas when I, wheezy and overweight, had complained of never getting any exercise. Its bell was rusty and its tires were flat and I had never ridden it much. A bushel basket splinted and stapled together by some artisan from the other end of Massachusetts over sixty years ago held a smattering of my childhood toys, which I had come upon in my mother's attic when she at last died. The toys seemed older than I—some bas-relief Mickey Mouse blocks, a cap pistol with fake-ivory handle, a tin Pluto who when wound up would whirr himself to the edges of a table and then, his weight shifting to a sideways wheel near his nose, magically turn back from danger. Could these toys have belonged not to me but to my father, that least playful of worried, work-degraded men? He had been a child in the Depression, when toys were still sturdily fashioned of tin and wood. In the barn I noticed pieces of rusted drainpipe I had saved when we had the house painted too many years ago, and a crude wooden table, covered with dribbled shellac, that little Henry had proudly built, with my grudging help, when there had been three of us living here. All these uselessly preserved pieces of the past were jammed suffocatingly in. In a kind of panic I roughly, angrily rearranged a few things so I could fit in the old carpet, a tarnished brass ship's lamp, a faded needlepoint footstool, and a pallid, washy watercolor portrait of Gloria's mother that Deirdre had replaced with a soft-focus tinted photograph of herself in her low-necked high-school prom dress. This duty done, I fled, gulping the air outside the barn like a man who had nearly drowned.

Once I did nearly drown in the dismal detritus of time. Perdita and I, in our earliest thirties, lived in a pre-Revolutionary house in the middle of a drowsy coastal town called Coverdale. We had a small but, what with our children and their neighborhood friends, well-used backyard, in a corner of which I would plant each year two rows of lettuce, four feet of parsley, eight tomato plants, and some mounds of zucchini seeds—salad ingredients, all, within a few strides of the kitchen door. Spring that year had thickened around me paralyzingly. In Boston, in the sealed-in fluorescent environment of Sibbes, Dudley, and Wise, I was able to function, but at home on weekends, as the trees budded and our plethora of children—four, and Roberta huddled, head down, in Perdita's tummy—trooped through the house with muddy knees and noisy grievances, a paralysis of depression hit me. I saw everything as if through several thick panes of smeared glass. No air circulated between me and the world. I went out in the late afternoon to dig up my garden plot and a single earthworm, wriggling blindly to return to its darkness of earth, seemed, from my towering height, an image of myself. Except that I was miserable and terrified and the worm was not.

Our eldest, Mildred, had an eighth birthday coming in May, and I wanted to build her a dollhouse. It wasn't to be a very elaborate one, just four rooms, two over two, beneath a peaked roof and a triangular attic, with perhaps a flight of corrugated-cardboard stairs connecting the two floors. I had the wood, the half-inch plywood, the six-penny nails, and the cans of white and gray (for the roof) and red (for the door and window frames and two-dimensional shutters) paint, but whenever I went down to the cellar to work on the dollhouse—it had to be when Mildred was off playing—a clammy sense of futility would ooze out from the rough old eighteenth-century foundation stones and try to drown me. Had my workbench been less rudimentary; had there been objects down there more companiable than an asbestos-plastered furnace, a filthy oblong oil tank, a stack of tattered wooden screens to repair and insert when I could find the time and strength, a tumble of cast-iron furnace guts—ash-coated coal grates and shaking levers—never taken away after the conversion from coal to oil, and a rickety set of bicycles covered with cobwebs; and had the dollhouse been a less makeshift and more intricate artifact by a more skillful carpenter than I, I might have cheered up.

As it was, a dreadful fatigue dragged at my mind and numbed my hands on the tools. The whole real house, with its dependents and its mortgage and its pregnant mistress, seemed to be pressing upon me down there. I had taken pride, at first, in Perdita's pregnancies, but by now the process felt stale, a stunt stained with Nature's fatality. Yet another new life coming underlined the passing nature of all our mortal arrangements. The house had seen many arrangements pass through it since 1750. I would die, but also the little girl I was making this for would die, would die an old lady in whose mind I had become a dim patriarchal myth, and her dolls would die out of the innocent fervent make-believe that gave them momentary life, and the spiders had died in their webs around me, waiting for prey that had never come, and it all seemed futile. The spider corpses were like little white gyroscopes, I remember, and the streaked foundation stones behind the piece of pegboard that I had crudely nailed up over the narrow workbench sweated, at that time of year, with moisture thawing out of the soil. There was no God, each detail of the rusting, moldering cellar made clear, just Nature, which would consume my life as carelessly and relentlessly as it would a dung-beetle corpse in a compost pile. Dust to dust: each hammer stroke seemed dulled by cosmic desolation, each measurement for my rust-dulled crosscut saw seemed part of the grid of merciless laws that would soon extinguish me. I couldn't breathe, and had to keep coming up into the relative brightness of the kitchen, and into Perdita's full-bodied presence, though her puzzled, wifely concern was part of the oppression. She had joined me in natural process; we had bred children, and together we would reap the varicose veins and decaying teeth of middle age. I blamed her; even at those times when, sensing my despair, she tried to lift my spirits with lovemaking, I kept blaming her, and was rapacious but sullen in response. She was the universe that refused to release me from its bonds. Spring and its seminal imperatives hung heavy above me; relief came, amid summer's unclothed flirtations, in her last months of pregnancy, as the beginning of an affair, my first. Its colorful weave of carnal revelation and intoxicating risk and craven guilt eclipsed the devouring gray sensation of time. My marriage, I knew, was doomed by this transgression, or by those that followed, but I was again alive, in that moment of constant present emergency in which animals healthily live.

But first, unable to face the suffocating cellar, I bought Mildred a dollhouse at the Boston F. A. O. Schwarz, with a hinged roof and tiny doorways and movable window sashes. I am sure she preferred it to the crude one I would have made. It stood in her room for many years, though the phase of life in which she could entertain domestic fantasies within its miniature walls and enthusiastically play with it soon passed. This period of my children's childhoods seems as I look back upon it one great loss and waste, through my distraction. I gave them shelter and went through the motions but I remember mostly sorrow—broken bones, dead gerbils and dogs, little round faces wet with tears, a sickening river of junk food, and their sad attempt, all five of them before they passed into the secrecy of adolescence, to call me out of myself into the sunshine of their love.

A line of geese overhead, honking. Not a V—for some reason, in their haste to return to the warming North, they all fly off the same wingtip, and form a single long diagonal line pointing toward the Willowbank Country Club. Green goose excrement makes the short sixth fairway, by the pond, free-drop territory, there is such an abundance of it.

And the sky has a cloudy wet-wash tousled look you never see in winter, when the sky knows its mind for certain. Spatterings of big drops abruptly turn to sunshine, making puddles flash like shields.

Driving back from a quick run to the former supermarket—mostly empty aisles now but word went out that they were expecting shipments of orange juice and chicken breasts in, and the lines would be only an hour long—I heard on the radio this man with a mellow voice from Minnesota reading an old poem about spring, and as soon as I got back I tried to write down some lines. *When March is scarcely here a color stands abroad on solitary fields that science cannot overtake but human nature feels.* This color *waits upon the lawn* (maybe I heard it wrong) and *shows the furthest tree* and almost speaks to the poet but *then, as horizons step or noons report away* (probably misheard), *it passes, and we stay.* It was like being a psychotic and hearing the sick neurons, the degenerate voices of the gods, broadcasting inside your head. I had never heard the sadness of spring expressed before: *A quality of loss afflicting our content*, and then something about *encroached* (it sounded like) *upon a sacrament.* Eerie, magical stuff. I never heard the poet's name.

Spin and Phil, the collectors for the local crime overlords, came up to the house for their monthly installment. Nine hundred twenty-five welders for straight protection, one thousand for the deluxe. The money must be in cash, in bills no bigger than twenties. I've been paying deluxe, on their recommendation, but today I asked, "What do I get extra for the deluxe that the straight doesn't deliver?" I think having Deirdre in the house now emboldened me. Though she is just a woman, she is one of them—valley people, people from beyond this hill.

Spin is natty, with a red-and-gray bushy mustache, a toothpick he rolls around in his mouth, and a nice tidy way of expressing himself, like an old-style movie actor. "Mr. Turnbull, what you get is active consideration, not just passive. With the deluxe, anybody gives you trouble, *anybody*, we come after them. With the straight, you get no hassle from us, but if anybody else gets on your case, you're on your own. Can you follow that?"

"Just barely," I say. "Suppose I paid you nothing, how would that differ from the straight?"

Phil is heavier-set, and still wears brown suits, which don't ever look pressed. "It'd be ugly, Ben," he told me, with a quick hitch in his shoulders that made his suit jacket hang worse than ever. "I don't want to have to think about it. I don't want *you* to have to think about it. Hey, this is a beautiful place you got here. Wood, though. Hundred-year-old wood, at least. Get to burning up on this hill, there'd be no stopping it. They don't make fire hoses long enough."

I intended to pay, but, as with insurance salesmen in the old days, or company representatives touting a public stock offering, I liked to tease them a little, to make them work for what we both knew was a societally condoned rip-off. "I don't *need* so much house," I told them. "With all the expense, I'm thinking of moving. It's not as if I'm not still paying taxes on top of everything else."

"Some taxes," Spin coolly sneered. "Local and commonwealth. I can remember, so can you, when there were federal taxes, and the structure in place to enforce the collection. It was called the IRS."

I said, "There's a lot of talk on the radio about starting it up again. A lot of people miss the federal government."

"Fat chance," Phil said, "after that dumbhead dust-up with the Chinks. They blew it."

Deirdre heard the male voices on the lawn, in the front circle, and came out with her hair in curlers and green cream on her face. "You creeps ever think of getting lost?" she asked.

"Watch your mouth, Dee," Phil said.

"You know Deirdre?" I asked.

Phil didn't answer.

"We went to high school together," she admitted. "He was a loser then, and he's a loser now. What are they asking money for?"

"Protection," I told her. "They see that no harm comes to me, despite the breakdown of law and order."

"Ha!" she said. "These two jerks saying they're the new law and order? Go inside and call the police, Ben. This is intimidation and threatened assault and arson and I don't what all else."

"Are there still police?" I wondered aloud.

"Sure," Deirdre said.

"You don't see them standing guard at road repairs any more," I pointed out, adding helpfully, "Maybe because there are no road repairs."

"They're too busy," Deirdre said, "locking up crooked morons like this and throwing away the key."

Spin contemplated her with a smile, shifting the toothpick from one corner of it to the other. "The police," he said, "are our colleagues. We all have a stake in returning order to the community."

Phil tried to reinforce the other man's smile by also leering. "Back in high school, Dee," he said, "they used to say you were a pretty easy lay."

The universe branched; I would come home and find her raped and her throat slit and a leering note pinned to the blood-soaked body.

"I don't give a fuck what they said," she said. "They used to say you were a simple-minded asshole, too. Get the fuck off this property and stop intimidating my—my husband."

I had to protest. "They're not intimidating me, darling. We have an arrangement, from long before you showed up, if you don't mind my pointing that out."

Boys versus girls: how often that's what it comes down to. Still, in this day and age.

Deirdre is like Gloria in that she gets excited—panics, really—when she feels her territory is being invaded. Her eyes, weirdly comic in their rings of green face cream, swivelled from one to another of us and then clamped shut; her mouth stretched sideways into a slit and the veins in her throat swelled as a terrible noise came out of her mouth, high like a siren but breathy, panting in little bursts. We all laughed, I the least heartily. "Darling," I told her, "this is the way things are now, since the war. We're all having to make new arrangements."

Deirdre in her blind fury lowered her head and tried to butt at Spin's and Phil's bellies; Phil grabbed a fistful of curlers and black hair and held her like that, her arms swinging, while Spin looked at me, the toothpick dangling from the middle of his lip, and said, "This isn't reasonable, Mr. Turnbull. We're just doing the collecting. We don't make the rules."

"I know you don't. I'll get the money. Gloria, you calm down. I mean Deirdre."

"You're *with* these creeps!" she cried, her voice muffled as Phil bent her head to her chest. "Against *me!*"

I raced upstairs, to where the bundles of Massachusetts tender were tucked beneath my folded undershirts. The old governor, with sepia hair and sleepy eyes, gazed out from the crude engraving. When the dollar exploded into worthlessness, not just states but corporations and hotel chains had to issue scrip. Ours has been holding its value pretty well lately, thanks to the revival of clamming and lobstering. With the plains a radioactive dust bowl, decimated Midwestern cities have been living on truckloads of New England mussels and apples from New York State.

The three interlopers had spaced themselves out on the driveway circle. Deirdre, putting her curlers back in place, was standing over by the euonymus bush, its brown chewed patches waist-high. Phil was sizing her up, wondering when to attempt a rapprochement. Spin was all business, standing just off the granite porch step; I handed him the money. The sepia bills looked worthless, with their rather supercilious engraved visage. Spin glanced at the welders but did not count them; he tucked the lot into his side coat pocket, taking care to smooth the pocket flap. He was jumping the season with a light checked sports jacket and dove-gray pegged slacks. He debonairly sniffed the air. "Next time we see you," he promised, "the grass will be green."

Phil pleaded with the back of Deirdre's head, "You get good value, honest. Without us you're totally vulnerable up here."

She refused to turn or say a word. I glanced at the two strong-arm men and shrugged apologetically.

"Want a receipt, Mr. Turnbull?" Spin asked me.

"I trust you," I said. "Take care."

"Explain to your little lady," Phil told me, "that the world's changed. It ain't what it used to be."

"She knows it," I said, feeling hostile now myself. It's one thing to be held up, another to be forced to give your approval. It's true, if they were not "protecting" me, somebody else would be. I actually have a pretty good life, compared with most of the people on this planet, in these sunset years of mine.

The sea earlier this March morning wore a look you never see in winter—a lakelike calm, a powdery blue so pale it was scarcely blue, with stripes of a darker, stirred-up color that might have marked the passage of a lobster boat an hour before. The daylilies, in a rock-rimmed bed on the right side of the driveway as I walk down it, are up an inch or two, and the bulb plants on the sunny side of the white garage show thrusting shoots as close together as comb teeth. An occasional boat—motor, not sail—appears on the water, and in the woods there is a stir of trespassers—teenagers on dirt bikes, sub-teens sneaking smokes.

Last night, stepping out into the misty chill darkness in a failed attempt to see a comet that has lately been much in the *Globe*, I was hit by a true scent of spring—the caustic and repellent yet not totally unpleasant stink of a skunk. One never sees them, except as a mangled mess of black and white fur on the road. But the odor of their existences suddenly reaches us, even through the steel walls of a speeding car, alerting us to the hidden strata of animal existence, whose creatures move through coded masses of scent, through invisible clouds of information.

A curious dream last night, whose details fall from me even as I write. Gloria and I were leaving Boston after some event, some little concert or worthy talk, probably at the Tavern Club or her club, called, in honor of Caesar's wife, the Calpurnia. The city, torn up by the Big Dig, could be exited only at "the top"—a narrow place of high traffic like the Mystic River Bridge. We were on foot, she leading. The mouth of a downward tunnel—an oneiric echo of the one under the old Charlestown circle, or the one named after a legendary baseball player—loomed confusingly, like the ambiguous exits off of Memorial Drive that suddenly shoot a car over the river or into Kendall Square. She led me to the right, along a concrete walk that stayed level—one of those ill-marked gritty passageways that skirt great new constructions. Except that it seemed to proceed along the edge of buildings that fell away beside me, on the right, dizzyingly. Gloria moved along, with that brisk impatience and obliviousness of the comfortably born, and I timorously followed along the obscure path, which bent now and then as if tracing the ramparts of ancient city buildings: the analog perhaps is with those medieval pedestrian ways around Court Square, in the shadow of the ancient gray City Hall, now a Chinese-war memorial.

Gloria did not acknowledge the screaming depths of vertical façade and jutting cornice beneath us, nor did I speak of them: I wrestled with my terror in silence. Then we came, among the building-tops, to a place where there was a gap— a dream image, perhaps, of the Mystic River—and I froze, too panicked to step across. But then somehow she doubled back and deftly traversed the perilous gulf with me and we were together on the opposite side. It was like a flickering at the climax of a silent movie, this transposition to the safe, the northern, side of Boston.

I awoke and it was not Gloria beside me but Deirdre, her lithe and lightly sweating body emitting a faintly harsh, metallic scent, her face tucked into the crooks of her slender brown arms, which were folded around her head with a silken relaxation as she slept the heedless, unshatterable sleep of the young. Perdita, the first woman I slept with on a contractual basis, used to awake, no matter how late we had come to bed, around dawn. To the sounds of her stirring about in the bedroom and then in the kitchen below, I would fall asleep again, as if to the sounds of my mother's morning housework back in Hammond Falls. Like the sun and moon, I as a young husband realized, men and women set and rise on independent schedules.

In the many years of my commuting, from 1977 on, there

were two memorable tragedies on the Mystic River Bridge. Just before dawn one morning an overloaded truck swerved out of control and hit a bridge support with such force that the upper deck collapsed, crushing the driver and stymieing the early commuter traffic, which had to halt at a precipice not unlike that in my dream; the bridge was closed for at least a year. Then, years later, a husband who had almost persuaded the public and the police that an unknown black man had shot to death his pregnant wife when their automobile strayed into Roxbury parked in the middle of the bridge and leaped to his death as the truth began to emerge: he had done the deed, long premeditated in a brain overheated by an infatuation with a younger, non-pregnant woman. To deflect attention from himself he had fired a bullet into his own abdomen, perhaps more painfully than he had intended. His suicide note admitted nothing and was full of self-pity. The incident made us New Englanders all wonder, *Inside every husband is there a wife-killer?*

Deirdre keeps a very messy house. The laundry accumulates in the hamper, the dishes in the sink. She even leaves banana peels and eggshells and crusts of toast rotting within the Disposall, when it is but a few seconds' satisfying occupation to switch it on, under running water, and listen to it grind such garbage away. Before she moved in with me, I had her enlist in NarcAnon, and she was initially enthusiastic and resolute, but I sense backsliding lately. Unaccountable fits of euphoria, with manically sexy and animated behavior, are followed by spells of withdrawn hostility. She is like a kite whose string is still held in my hands but whose distant paper shape I can see fluttering and dipping out of control.

The other night she wet the bed. I was astonished: I awoke at the sting of the warm liquid seeping through my

pajamas, and when I wakened her—she was sleeping naked—
and roused her to what she had done, she didn't seem to
comprehend. She fumbled with me at tearing off the wet
bedding, laying a dry towel over the damp place on the mattress, and remaking the bed with a fresh sheet, but seemed
still asleep, locked into some drugged continuing dream of
her own. In the morning I couldn't get her to talk about it,
and indeed I didn't press her too hard: it was embarrassing
to me, too.

Some kids—I presume they were kids—smashed a window and broke into the barn. I'm not sure of everything they
stole: Two bicycles, at least, that had belonged to Henry and
Roger. An inflatable raft, not much of a success, for use in
the pond, when Henry was still a little boy, and lonely on
our hill, his brother and sister already away at prep school; I
remember how he tried to make pets of the pair of ducks
that nested near the pond every spring. They produced a
chain of fuzzy ducklings that, one per day, would be pulled
under by the snapping turtle that lived in the bottom ooze.
Also missing were a number of the Mickey Mouse blocks—
they have some collectible value now—from my old toy basket, that weathered brittle bushel basket from the apple
country of the Berkshires. And a porcelain-base lamp and a
folded linen tablecloth that I seemed to remember from my
previous, depressing visit to this storage area, which had
claustrophobically reminded me of the cellar of the house I
once shared with Perdita, several worlds ago. Perhaps I had
not fled her but that basement, where I couldn't bear to
hammer together a dollhouse for a girl who would soon out-
grow it and add it to the world's wasteland of discarded toys.

I think the thieves were the kids I hear whooping and
crashing in the woods, now that the weather is warming.
Deirdre is certain it was Spin and Phil, "as a warning."

"What would they warn us about? I'm a model member of their club, paid up until the end of March."

"Ben, you're such an innocent. People always want more, more. They keep going until there's nothing left, until they've sucked you dry."

The image recalled to me too vividly her past as a cock-sucking prostitute. She seemed to know Spin and Phil too well. I wanted to slap her, to knock that stubborn out-of-reach druggy daze out of her. Her lips looked swollen and moved stiffly, like those of a person in the cold, though the day was sunny, if cool—one of the first basking days, when an atavistic streak in the blood begs you to crawl up on a rock, old turtle, and let the sun soak through your shell.

———————

Ken and Red asked me to go skiing with them. I said yes, though a little loath to leave Deirdre alone in the house all day—she has been acting so *dangerous* lately, with that reckless female self-disregard that presumably serves Nature's need to throw DNA around but frays the hell out of male nerves. I dragged my skis and boots up from the cellar, where they rest in the little damp laundry room next to the chamber where the jagged ledge sits like an uninvited guest, a chthonic ghost. The cellar of this house is a century-and-a-half newer and several orders of magnitude more cheerful than that of the pre-Revolutionary house that I once occupied with Perdita and my five dependent children. My present basement savors of upper-class self-regard in the early 1900s. The same ample scale of construction that obtained in the householders' summer living quarters was transposed, in a minor key, to a netherworld, for servants. There are foundations of pointed rust-tinged granite, partitions of white-painted brick, steam and waste pipes of cast-iron solidity, cobwebbed rooms devoted to the hobbies (wood-working, photography) of the sons of the previous owners. In the darkest and dampest of these—the old darkroom, its windows sealed with taped wallboard—I keep my skis. Since February a year ago, the last time I skied, the edges had rusted, I discovered. The windowless, subterranean damp had penetrated the weave of their canvas carrier, and atoms of oxygen had bonded with atoms of iron. Natural processes continue without our witnessing them: what stronger proof of our inconsequence? Bertrand Russell (I believe) spoke of human consciousness as an "epiphenomenon"—superficially there, a bubble thrown up by confluences in the blind tumble of mindless matter, like the vacuous brown curds whipped up by a fast-running brook.

We drove two hours north in Ken's gray Audi. Red had to forgo the global conversations with which he regales his passengers in his hyperequipped Caravan. Ken wore his old pilot's cap as we sailed up Route 93, through stretches of second- and third-growth woods and blank-sided industrial buildings—Reading, Wilmington, Andover—into New Hampshire. Above Concord, a lot of the condo developments wedged into the hillsides were charred shells. Abandoned when the flow of back-to-nature second-home buyers out of metropolitan Boston had been dried up by the disasters of the last decade, these standardized wooden villages had been sacked and set ablaze by the starving locals in their own back-to-nature movement. But Nature was slow to digest these mock-bucolic intrusions; the blue-brown hills with their precipitous rock outcroppings bore wide black scars festooned with tangled pipes and wiring. Electronic equipment had been one of the objects of the looting, but its value depended upon an electronic infrastructure that had been one of the first casualties of urban catastrophe and global underpopulation.

Loon Mountain was one of the few ski resorts still open for customers. The gondola had been closed for lack of Swiss replacement parts and the lift operators on duty had a bearded, furtive look. They seemed evil trolls, in their polychrome parkas and lumberjack shirts, mining the mountain with clanking, creaking ore-carts that went up full and came down empty. The overweight, pockmarked woman behind the ticket window asked to see my driver's license in verification of my claim to the senior rate. "Sixty-six," she said, having done the arithmetic with a frown. "O.K., sonny. What's your secret? Cheeks like a baby's. A mop of hair." Her coarse attempt at flirtation made me wonder if she had scented Deirdre's youthful body oils clinging to me, giving me an ungeriatric aura of sexual success. Ken and Red crowed at my blushes, and got their own senior tickets without challenge.

The conditions were lovely. The winter's many snows, first falling in November, had created an eight-foot base, and snow-making had kept it replenished. The surface was scratchy with yet plenty of loose corn to turn on, and there were no lift lines. The crowds were eerily sparse. A few brats with snowboards gouged their rude arcs into the shining slopes and hurtled up and over the jumps that had been constructed for them, and a few of us fun-seeking retirees made our careful, controlled way down the trails. Actually, only Ken could be called careful; his stiff linked turns are executed with studied knee-dips and pole-plants. Red, who has never taken a lesson, sets his skis a foot apart and just heads with a whoop downhill, turning only when his gathering speed bounces his skis into the air. His scarlet ski-hat dwindles rapidly down through the granite-walled chutes and undulating mogul fields. His employees in Gloucester gave him as a joke Christmas present a silver windbreaker lettered EAT FISH ALL WEEK FOR GOD'S SAKE in big capitals and today he wore that over a turtleneck and a Shetland sweater of undyed wool.

I have a staid but furtively daredevil style. I try to think of my feet, the weight on first one and then the other, and of the inner edges, where all my weight and intricate, unseemly innards balance as if on a single ice-skate blade. But my skis, their rust sharpened away by a hunchbacked troll at the ski shop, tended to run out from under me and nearly snagged me into a fall or two, until I remembered that skiing *is* falling, a surrender to the unthinkable and the fearful. Then I began to fly, to feel my loosened weight gracefully check my speed as I turned, left and right and then left again, into the fall line. We rise as we age; the older we get, the longer and more treacherous the distance to the earth becomes. To a toddler, the ground is a playmate, a painless bottom-bump away.

My legs—the knees, the quadriceps—began after four or five runs to ache so much I kept braking and gasping, while Red's hat vanished down below and Ken steadily, stiffly traversed his way out of sight. I was calling upon muscles that had been resting for a year. The years move into us; their cyclical motion is not their only motion. Pausing, gasping, I admired the sky, a bottomless gentian blue in which the two moons hung, their top hemispheres by some multi-cogged permutation of the celestial mechanism sunlit, so they looked like porous cookies being dunked in a translucent celestial brew. The valley with its twisting roads and stacked condos spread itself far below me, and at a bit more than eye level Mount Washington's white crest gleamed above the intervening darker crests. Everything here in New Hampshire was dun and brown and blue; the clear air arrived at my senses with the sharpness of a dog's bark, sounding somewhere unseen in the valley.

On the drive back, we were all three silent, stunned by so much unaccustomed fresh air and exercise. Our elderly proximity to death seemed a not unpleasant thing, shared in such companionable silence. The Audi's cruise control pulled us steadily southward. Snow thinned into dirty crusts along Route 93. On the right, at Concord, the elongated gold dome of the state capitol caught the day's declining light. Below Concord, at this hour, there used to be streams of headlights as the commuters returned to this low-tax haven from their daily raid on the coffers of "Taxachusetts." Now that golden stream was reduced to a trickle, on a highway engineered for six times the traffic. The mountains around us shrank and lessened. The radio, tuned to a Boston station that advertised Music for Easy Listening, became less staticky and more languorous. Ken's head, back in the pilot's cap, snapped out of a nod; Red had grunted "Jesus!" and grabbed the wheel from him as the car drifted out of its lane. Ken was sheepish, but we too had been at fault, for falling into our private reveries and not keeping up a stimulating conversation. Ken pulled to the side to switch places with Red and, settling into the co-pilot's seat, told us how through all the years he was flying he could never fall asleep as a passenger, no matter how jet-lagged. He knew too much, and kept listening knowledgeably to the engines for signs of trouble. Only when seated upright in the captain's scientifically cushioned black chair, with stretches of cloud or dark ocean or settlement-spangled land miles beneath him, and the automatic pilot securely locked into the controls, would he irresistibly sink into dreamland.

———————

I got back before seven and though the house was silent something had changed. An infinitesimal measurement had been made, and Deirdre and I were in another universe. There was an alteration in the air of the rooms. There was the scent of another man. She came downstairs languidly, already in a bathrobe. "I felt grubby after housework all day and took a shower," she explained. "How was skiing?"

"Beautiful," I said. "But Ken fell asleep at the wheel on the way back and nearly got us killed. Also, I can hardly move my knees, they're not used to it. Anything happen while I was away?"

"No, nothing."

"Nothing? Nobody call?"

"Some old lady. She was worried about the forty-point drop in the market today. I told her you were out having fun with some guys. She sounded sore about it. I said to her, 'Lady, he's retired. You can't expect him to sit home all day watching your pot for you.'"

"Mrs. Fessenden, it must have been. I should call her and make reassuring noises. I'll remind her she's a long-term investor and shouldn't worry about the ups and down day to day. These old people don't have enough to do, so they worry." I realized that from Deirdre's point of view I was also old. I had forgotten my age, in the afterglow of the ski trip. "What's for dinner, darling?"

"Oh," Deirdre said, with a shifty lowering of her long-lashed eyes, "I'm not hungry. I've been kind of nibbling.

There's some cold ravioli in the fridge from last night you could zap in the microwave."

"Thanks. Zapped ravioli, my favorite gourmet meal. Let me get out of these ski clothes."

There was a bareness to the house, somehow. On the way upstairs I glanced into the living room and the dining room to see if anything conspicuous was missing. In Gloria's time these rooms had been resplendent, showcases for the family antiques, but since her departure—disappearance? death?— the rooms had invisibly begun to slip into shabbiness. Even the rug, the great blue Tabriz, looked faded, up at the end with the French doors and the little oval-backed sofa whose ecru silk the sun was rotting as it traced its daily arc above the sea's horizon. There seemed fewer trifles—candlesticks and silver picture-frames and Limoges figurines. In our bedroom, I thought I had left a few of my bureau drawers out a few inches; they were all snugly closed, and the bed seemed too tightly made. Such tidiness was unlike Deirdre, even on a day that she said she spent doing housework. I sniffed. Was the ashy trace in the air a cigarette, or a ghost in the fireplace? The previous owners used to build fires up- stairs—one could tell by the charred bricks. They had used the house fully, confidently, as something theirs by right. The information on my olfactory cells decoded, suddenly, as a man in a baggy brown suit. His naked, plump, hairy re- flection was embedded in the mercury backing of the oval mirror, if I had the technology to recover it. The technology of the future will be able to reconstruct the exact location of every atom in the past from its position in the present, just as technicians at the factory can recover every key-tap fed into the computer's hard memory, even those obliterated by the command DELETE. One strange scientist, I read years ago in *Scientific American*, maintained that at the end of the time, which he called the Omega Point, the kind souls of a fantastically advanced civilization spread across the entropic or imploding terminal universe would painstakingly reconstruct and resurrect us all, every human being who had ever lived, me and a medieval stableboy and a Neandert(h)al auroch-hunter along with all of Gloria's ancestors and the millions of Chinese civilians killed in the recent lamentable Sino-American Conflict. It seemed an unlikely thesis, though one partially anticipated by St. Paul, and no doubt rigorous in its physics.

The intruder would have left traces, also, on Deirdre's nervous system, while I was clumsily courting ecstasy on the ski slopes. Going downstairs, I saw the carpeted steps as neatly aligned moguls, and imagined myself dancing, knees pressed together, from one side to the other, swerving around the newel posts on the landing. As I dutifully consumed my zapped ravioli, along with some tired broccoli whose browner florets I had cut away before tucking the stalks into the microwave dish, she hovered over me uncharacteristically. She was making an effort to be agreeable, though her conversational responses were sluggish, like those of a computer whose memory is loaded to capacity. No doubt about it, hers was getting more input than mine. "God," I said, rummaging in the chaotic fridge for something else half rotten to warm up, "it feels good to have had some exercise for a change! We should do more physical stuff, now that spring's in the air. How's your sex life?"

This startled her. "You should know," she said at last. "The same as yours."

"Is it? When did we last make love?" I asked.

She had the answer, dopey as she seemed. "Eight days

ago. Last Tuesday, after you got turned on by the new talking head on Channel Seven."

A crisp blonde woman with a glassy square cleft chin she tips up toward the camera as she reads the TelePrompTer through the lens. She has thin, darkly painted long lips that she rarely smiles with, except at the end, when she releases a wide satisfied smile that says it all. She is so cool and refined that she never banters with the weatherman or the oaf who does sports. "What a terrific talking cunt she is," I agreed. "What's on your schedule tonight?"

"Nothing." But she dragged the word out, teasing.

"Want to go to bed early? I mean, right after the news, before the skiing catches up to me and I start snoring."

"Su-ure," Deirdre said, "if you want to. I was going to wash my hair."

"Wash it afterwards. Let me mess it up first."

"Mess it up how?" Thinking perhaps of some perverse trick she had once turned. She was taut, like the bed she had made for a second time today.

"Oh," I said, reluctant to give her any satisfaction, "I don't know how. I don't want to feel inhibited, though, like your hair is offbounds. Wasn't there some frozen yogurt? Peach was the flavor—I can *see* the carton, right here, next to the frozen lemon cake. Where is it? Who ate it?"

"Who ate what?"

"The peach yogurt, you dope." She was reminding me annoyingly of herself the night she peed in the bed and refused to become aware of it. "It's gone. Let's unfreeze the lemon cake for tomorrow night. Let's get into bed first and think of a way we can mess up your hair."

"I don't like your tone," Deirdre said.

"I don't like yours, either."

"You seem hyper."

"You seem like you've snorted or swallowed or mainlined something and have something to hide."

"I'll be fucked if I'll fuck you in this nasty mood you're in, just because you say to."

"Some mysterious body has eaten all my peach frozen yogurt. Who the hell are you not to fuck me when I'm begging like this, when I pay all the damn bills?"

"I'm your wife, I guess you could say."

"I liked you better when you were a whore, frankly."

"Of course you did. Men do. Like whores better than wives."

"You were purer then."

"A man would think so."

"You used to auction yourself off, piece by piece."

"O.K., you bastard. A million welders, to come all over my hair."

"I don't have a million welders."

"Yes you do. I've seen the statements."

"Only a fraction of those assets are liquid, Miss Nosy. Let's say two million, if you tell me what you were really doing all day."

"I was doing housework and feeling fond of you, if you must know. I was thinking how much I wanted to go to bed with you when you got back from skiing with those jerks. I swept and cleaned the whole upstairs, and picked up winter sticks and stuff outside on the lawn." Tears, confounding me, had appeared like rheum on her lower lids, shellacking brighter the brown of her eyes. We are each a slimy apparatus of interacting liquids. Our olfactory cells are open nerve ends embedded in a thin mucus that dissolves the volatile molecules we scent. "There were these little puddles," she went on, her voice trembling, "of little turds everywhere."

"Deer scat," I said, abandoning my hopes of peach frozen

yogurt and giving Deirdre a timid, paternal hug. "Let's not go to bed," I said. "We're both in lousy moods. Let's see what's on TV."

"Yeah, that blonde bitch you have the hots for." She added, perversely aroused now, "Ben, I'll be a whore if that's what you want. Let's think of some fun way to get you off."

"Maybe while we're watching," I deferentially suggested, "that bitch on TV."

———————

Canada geese honking overhead are so common I don't even look up. Two visited the pond down by the mailbox, now that the ice is off some of its surface. It melts from the edges in. The geese, with their haughty black faces and pearly gray bodies, are intruding upon a pair of mallards who have been in the pond since black water opened at the reedy edges and where the flow in and out is swiftest. I stood by the mailbox watching the ducks one day; my watching alarmed them, and the little brown female tried to paddle away and ran into slush. The drake with his sumptuous green head followed, and so she found herself performing as an ice-breaker, paddling her way through the slush, beating her wings to give herself extra thrust as the ice thickened. Her struggles carved a sinuous trail—the handsome drake serenely floating in her wake—before cutting back to some open water farther from the threat that my silent presence posed.

Odd, how perfectly both duck and drake seemed to agree that the task was hers. The female of the species takes on the serious business, while the male wears the plumage.

I visited little Keith and Jennifer yesterday, in the mint-green Lynnfield ranch house occupied by my youngest child, Roberta, and her contractor husband, Tony O'Brien. Jenny is six months old, her big silky cubical head adorned now by a coating of fine fuzz that stands up with a comical erectitude, as if suffused with static electricity. As I spooned in pureed carrots, her splay-fingered, transparently nailed hands, agitated by the strangeness of this craggy old man feeding her, would wander into her mouth with the food and thus make along with the silver feeding spoon a confusion of substances and purposes. Her tiny blue fist captured and squeezed an orange blob, and then sleepily rubbed it across a gossamer eyebrow. *"Stop that,"* I said sharply, and my daughter—whose own infancy is still coiled somewhere in the gray neuronic tangle of my atrophying memory—explained patiently to me that babies learn first how to grip things and only much later how to coördinate the niceties of letting go.

From my own infancy on, I have ascribed to things—toys, tools—a hostile intent, bent on opposing and frustrating me. An only child, I selfishly think of the universe as a big antagonistic sibling. Despite my gaffe of speaking to Jennifer as if she were a typically obstructive adult, I was allowed to give her the bottle, warmed in the microwave exactly one minute; Perdita and I had had to heat bottles in water simmering on the stove and then test them on the inside of our wrists, with a little kiss of blood-warm milk my veins have not forgotten. A cosmic calm descended, of food and appetite colliding. This was as close as I would ever come to having breasts. When I experimentally tugged at the bottle, I was astonished by the force with which Jennifer's little mouth held it fast—again, serious business.

A defect in me, I fear, if not all male animals, is an inability to take serious business quite seriously. Feeding, fornicating, sleeping, dying—surely all a touch undignified and absurd. I used to marvel at the intensity with which Gloria would protest when I, at the wheel of one of our cars, would seem to her to be too close to another car, to be in the wrong lane, to be risking a slip on a patch of ice, or—and here I may have been guilty of teasing—to be insensitive to the dangers of the railroad tracks at the bottom of our hill. I liked to bounce over them without stopping and looking and, when the red lights were furiously dinging, to nose forward and see if the train was far enough down the line to take a chance and scoot across. What a squawking fuss Gloria would make, over her little life! Females carry the burden of the world, I think, but men the magic—the universal magic, the glittering super-dense sperm that spurted out of nothing to make the Big Bang. Male homosexuals, in my construction of it, disdain all the rosy, spongy allurements that nature has created to lead them fruitfully astray and go straight for this magic at which females also hurl themselves, defying destruction. Girls fall in love with serial murderers and with rock stars who like reptiles flicker their tongues between choruses. It hurt my feelings, it diminished me, when Gloria so furiously resisted the opportunity to die with me beneath the wheels of a commuter train. Once, as I slyly glided forward, she pulled out the car keys; another time, she opened the door on her side and would have jumped out had I not braked. Flirtation with death had no erotic charm for her. I was insulted. If not magical, men are not much.

A curious symptom, possibly fatal: when I stand holding an infant in my arms, my knees go weak, so watery-weak I fear I will fall down with my precious burden. An effort of will holds me upright until the fit passes, or else I ease my weight onto a chair. I first noticed this with my seventh grandson, Duncan. I nearly crumpled, there in the cream-colored maternity ward of the hospital. The boneless bundle in my arms, with a round face still blue from its passage through the vaginal channel, added seven nearly unbearable pounds to my own weight.

When I confided to Gloria my mystical symptom, she diagnosed simply a drop in blood pressure and prescribed water for me. She herself tried to drink eight eight-ounce glasses of water a day. "Drink and tink" was a beauty tip from one of her bawdy Calpurnia Club friends. It kept the skin hydrated from within, moist as a baby's, went the theory. I must say, baby Jennifer's skin is so delicious that I cannot restrain myself from pushing my cracked old lips against her semi-liquid cheeks, her solemn great smooth brow, her fuzzy pate fragrant of shapeless, powdery thoughts. It is enough to make one laugh and even scream with delight, these infantile textures and aromas. I feel dizzyingly swept along by the whirl of life. I think that when my own children were infants I was too distracted by the world's business—by the unstoppable, fortune-forming bull market that persisted through my thirties—to inhale. Not until the Crash of 2000, when the addled computers deleted billions and billions from the world economy, did I look up at my children, who were teenagers by then.

Jennifer is a charmer; we all tell her so. Her brother and eight male cousins, all of whom she has met, reinforce her power. She is a sacred larva being stuffed with royal jelly. It is she who will take the male magic into herself and carry the Turnbull DNA, diluted by half with some O'Brien stuff, toward eternity. Solemn in the authority of her slate-blue stare, the electric fuzz of her hair as yet colorless, she is a unitary person, with the full regalia of human interaction at her command. When she closes her mouth on the liquefied carrots and untidily smiles, I am pleased; I was hurt and of-

fended when, at the beginning of the visit, she hid her face
in her mother's shoulder at the strange sight of me. We vie
for her approval; I have an unworthy urge to tear her from
her father's thick arms and murmur in the velvety folds of
her ear how his contracting business teeters on the edge of
debt, how his creditors would have torn the shelter from
over her head but for my discreet financial interventions. I
am jealous of the young married life Tony leads, here in the
pastel tract houses of Lynnfield, with my dear daughter as
his chattel. Roberta stands in their little kitchen over the
electric stove, and from the graceful, drifting way she turns,
plastic spoon in hand, to attend to a gruff and complaining
remark of Tony's ("This kid smells like she needs a diaper
change"), it could be Perdita of thirty-five years ago in the
corner of my eye. Her elliptical physical style lives on in her
daughters, who choose husbands, I am repeatedly assured,
who resemble me. The resemblance eludes me.

Little sulky Keith and I are alike in this household: we
are insider-outsiders, inside but not altogether in, excluded
from the holy triangle of father-mother-infant. Keith and I
are outer layers being shed, helpless neglected witnesses as
Jennifer powerfully wields her spell, rewarding or dismiss-
ing those who court her favor. Roberta tells me that in the
early mornings, or during the baby's afternoon nap, Keith
would make his silent way into her room and heap his toys—
teddy bears, wooden trains, plastic telephones, metal dump
trucks—into the baby's crib, piling them on experimentally
until her entire body, including her head, was covered. Tony
has installed a lock on the door too high for Keith to reach.

They feed me well on these visits, and invite me to carve
the roast chicken or pot roast as tribute to my seniority, my
chiefdom; but I am always relieved to be off, out the door
into my car with its heater and radio, as if escaping a dis-

creditable past or removing my variable from an equation intricate enough without me.

———————

Crocuses are up in the driveway circle, at a spot in the bed where sunlight reflected from the granite outcropping warms the earth. Their colors, purple and white, seem a bit vulgar and trite—determinedly Easterish—compared with the pristine and demure ivory of the drooping snowdrop heads, an especially large cluster of which still glows in the otherwise lifeless woods. The earth in Gloria's beds looks friable, developing fissures as frost works out of the soil; a giant is heaving from underneath. The daylilies in the bed that I pass along the driveway are enough out of the earth to show a trifoliate, heraldic silhouette—pale-green fleurs-de-lys. The forsythia wands are lined with symmetrical buds, like saw teeth, but in this slow gray spring have not yet unsheathed their signal yellow flowers. Yesterday I spotted my first robin, strutting along the driveway's gravel shoulder in his familiar dusty uniform, gawkily startled into flight by my approach: a stuffy bird, faintly pompous in its portly movements, spoiled by the too many songs and poems unaccountably devoted to him. I was more interested, returning up the driveway with my *Globe*, in two small tan birds, one with a faintly rosy head, whose names I didn't know. They revolved in the net of the maple-leaf viburnum's pale and brittle branches, performing a kind of leapfrog, one perching on a twig lower than the other and then the other flicking to take a place above the first: some kind of courtship dance, carried on with a diagrammatic rigor.

Nature's background noise picks up: making the bed after tumbling a half-willing Deirdre in its sheets, and opening the window and its storm window a crack to let out our body smells, I heard a muffled thrumming that sounded too mechanical to be even a woodpecker's bill attacking rotten wood. Purely inorganic creatures exist on this planet, as yet a mere underbrush to the flesh-and-blood, oxygen-breathing fauna but indisputably existent and evolving, biding their time as did our own mammalian ancestors during the long age of the dinosaurs. The microscopic first forms, it is conjectured, arose in city dumps, or more likely dumps attached to the perimeter of vast army bases or nuclear-fuel plants wherein a soup of spilled chemical and petroleum by-products was energized by low-level leaks of radioactivity. Metal particles smaller than iron filings fused, propelled into a self-sustaining reaction perhaps by the chemical activity of oxidation accidentally placed adjacent to a fortuitous mix of chemical influences. These tiny resultant creatures, with an anatomy much simpler than their organic equivalents, still possessed complexity enough for reproduction, in the soup of industrial waste. A ghost of intentionality, as it were, within their already refined and processed constituents enabled the metallobioforms to experiment with varieties of anatomy much more prolifically than the essentially conservative, ateleological DNA-dominated organisms. Within two centuries of their first lowly, unwitnessed emergence—which could scarcely have taken place before the Industrial Revolution and the invention of combustion-powered engines—there were metal species the size and weight of tree shrews and field mice, and two distinct phyla.

One phylum, the "oil-eaters," "lives" off the traces of petroleum to be found on roadways, in asphalt and in natural upwellings of tar, and on beaches, both rocky and sandy, heavily affected by oil spills. The other, the "spark-eaters," takes energy from electricity itself, as found in still-functioning electric fences and cables, whether overhead or underground; like arachnid ticks, they penetrate the insulation and cling until sated. These metallic pests never need to sleep or mate; they are free to devote all their days to consumption, which includes the search for oils, natural and artificial, whereby their parts can be protected from corrosion, rust, and friction. The spread of their population seems limited only by the amount of material which mankind has used and discarded. Where a territory needs to be cleared for their access to some chemical resource, they quite mercilessly exterminate the local organic wildlife, leaving the shredded bodies to rot and attract organic predators, who are then themselves slain, from the feet up. The heads of some trilobite-sized species—resembling giant wood lice—are miniature chain saws.

Television commentators go through spells of alarm over the threat of these "pseudozoans," since science predicts the evolution of ever larger and more voracious forms; this development seems remote, however, among the many more urgent issues of survival on our blasted, depopulated planet. The pseudozoans, or metallobioforms, or in popular parlance "trinkets," seldom venture out of hiding in daylight. They keep to the dumps that fostered them and the oily, electricity-rich underground realms of cities, but lately have been spotted farther afield, in wilder areas. So perhaps it was a pseudozoan whose mechanical thrumming I heard, mistaking it for a sign of spring.

Now that April is here, Deirdre and I took Gloria's mulch— buckwheat hulls and oak leaves, held down by boughs I hacked from a hemlock—off the rose bed, on the sea side, on a breezy Good Friday. Looking down the hill, toward the left of Mrs. Lubbetts' house, we could see the spume of breaking waves on the beach, silently flashing up and drifting away. A seagull was suspended in mid-air, level with our eyes, its flight into the wind holding it motionless. Inside, our cheeks ruddy, we had rum in tea and felt more companionable than for days.

On Easter, she surprised me by wanting to go to church. She said it would be bad luck not to go. Thus Christianity, once an encompassing cathedral built on swords and crowns, holding philosophy in one transept and music in the other and all the humanity of Europe and the Americas in its nave, has died back to its roots of mindless superstition. We went to the nine o'clock service in the church of her childhood, a shabby United Something (Presbyterian and Methodist? Congregational and Reformed?) with windows that were half lozenges of clear glass and half sickly Biblical scenes from that furtive first-century world of violet and saffron robes and wistful, genteel Aryan faces wedded to the gesticulating poses of Jewish rabble-rousers. The high, airless space, with its creaking pews, smelled of camphor and beeswax and the gaseous excessive heat of a furnace stoked up once a week.

We had come to the children's service, which was the one Deirdre remembered. Ten years ago she had been a girl of thirteen. Whereas I ten years ago was much as I am now, only with a thicker, browner head of hair and a five-days-a-week commuting habit. The children in the congregation rustled and prattled and squalled so that the voice of the young clergyperson, a woman with glossy Joan of Arc bangs and straight short sides, could hardly be heard. She read from Colossians 3 ("Set your affection on things above, not on things on the earth. For ye are dead, and your life is hid with Christ in God") and prettily embroidered the Resurrection story in John 20 into a woman's story—the adventures in feeling and relatedness of Mary Magdalene.

It was she who, before dark, found the stone taken away from the sepulchre on that first Easter, and the sepulchre empty. "Then she runneth," the Gospel tells us, and met Simon Peter and "the other disciple, whom Jesus loved. . . ." These two competitively raced to the sepulchre and concurred in its emptiness, but for the neatly folded burial linens, and raced away again. Men! Always rushing on to the next thing! Mary stayed, and wept. While weeping, she stooped and looked into the sepulchre and saw two angels, one standing at the head and the other at the feet of the empty place where the body of Jesus had lain. They asked her, "Woman, why weepest thou?"

Why indeed do women weep? They weep, it seemed to my wandering mind, for the world itself, in its beauty and waste, its mingled cruelties and kindnesses. I once saw Perdita break into tears within, I believe, the Church of San Miniato al Monte in Florence. It was a lesser sight, on the far side of the Arno, with a barrel-vaulted interior of black and white stripes, receding mistily, as I remember it, up several levels toward the altar and choir. Shocked by her tears, I touched her and asked her why, thinking I was somehow to blame. "Because it's so beautiful," she got out. Gloria, a reluctant weeper, nevertheless was hard to console after the death of Lily Bart in *The House of Mirth*—Lily, the barren heroine of a barren authoress, imagining a child nestled asleep beside her as she dies. And there were tears in Gloria's eyes when she came into the house a spring ago announcing that the deer had eaten all her tulips. My mother, mired in poverty and boxed in by my father's limitations, cried often in my childish witnessing, over some domestic frustration or new manifestation of bodily decay. Her teeth gave her a lot of grief, first in their twinges—so keen they started tears—and then in the disfigurements of their piecemeal loss, pathetically patched by additions to a little pink partial upper plate she kept in a water glass in the bathroom. She had been, by the evidence of old photographs, a pert, fair, small-boned and freckled country beauty, the baby of the Kimball family from Cheshire. At the kitchen table during a quarrel—my parents' quarrels were always about the same thing, it seemed to me, about there not being *enough*—she would fold her arms and hide her grief-reddened face in them, terrifying me, for her face was the face of life to me, and I could not bear to have it hid. I witnessed so many tears of anger and frustration and pain on my mother's face, there in our bleak house on the shadowy northern side of the hill on the road out of Hammond Falls, that I wonder if my heart was not permanently hardened, to save me from a lifelong paralysis of grief. Stuck it seemed forever in latency and then the helpless middle teens, I would burrow away from the family sorrows into the warm corner of the kitchen behind the wood stove, or go upstairs in summertime and lie across my narrow bed, and read science fiction—*Amazing, Astounding,* those cheerful pulp monthlies costing only fifty cents in the Sixties—or popularized cosmology, by Asimov or Gamow, in plastic-wrapped volumes borrowed from the Pittsfield Library. Implausibly remote, radiant, exploding facts relieved the pressure of the immediate bare facts around me—the kitchen linoleum with its black-edged worn spots, the pine thresholds so often scuffed they dipped in the middle like tired mattresses, the thin painted doors with their black latches, the beer-blurred gleam of defeat, almost crazy, in my father's eyes when he came home later than usual from work. Giant realities—God's facts—lifted me a bit out of it all and out of my poor skinny claustrophobic self.

The clerical collar gleamed white on the slender girlish throat of our sermonizer. It seemed a provocation, like the forms of mutilation, nipple and tongue rings and livid tattoos, with which the young scorn their own flesh and announce their scorn for us, the unpunctured and tattoo-free. Above the rustle and whining of the children I heard her preach, "Mary answered the angels that she wept because they had taken away her Lord and she did not know where they had laid him."

One can see Mary Magdalene, over the gap of a decade less than two full millennia, giving way to a fresh gust of tears with this confession of confusion. They were young, all these disciples and camp followers of the youthful Messiah—younger than many a contemporary rock group.

Then the question was repeated, by a new figure, a man standing behind her. "Woman, why weepest thou?"

Supposing this new presence to be the gardener, in this garden near the place of crucifixion, Mary said—steadying herself now into a certain dignity, drying her streaked cheeks with the backs of her hands, not really looking at this man—"Sir, if thou have borne him hence, tell me where thou has laid him, and I will take him away."

This carnal passion of hers for the body, though a dead body, our female exegete glides over, her little hands gracefully flitting from the sleeves of her robe.

"The strange man, whom she has mistaken for the gardener in this disorienting place, says her name: 'Mary.' She turns and says, '*Rabboni*,' which is to say, 'Master.' At this point, she must have reached out in the joy of recognition, for He says, 'Touch me not.' *Noli me tangere.* Jesus spurns her instinctive attempt at contact. Why?"

In her expectant silence we could hear the children squirming in the creaking pews and one infant whimpering against the pressure of his mother to keep him quiet.

Superposition, I thought. Before Christ ascended, He was in what quantum theory calls superposition—neither here nor there, up nor down. He was Schrödinger's cat.

"A little later in the same chapter," our inquisitor preached, "Jesus invites His disciple Thomas to touch Him, to ease Thomas's doubts. Thomas has said he will not believe in the risen Jesus unless he sees in His hands the print of the nails, and puts his own hand in the wound of sword-thrust in Jesus's side. Jesus obliges. He lets Himself be intimately touched to ease the other man's doubt. It is a guy thing. For Mary Magdalene, seeing must be believing. Jesus tells her not to touch Him because He is not yet ascended to the Father. He is in a fragile in-between condition. Still, He has some orders for Mary: she should go tell the disciples that He is risen. Mary obeys. Like so many women in the Bible, she accepts her subservient role and obeys. But because she needed to weep, to stay at the tomb and come to terms with her feelings, it was she and not Peter or the other disciple, whom Jesus loved, usually identified as John, son of Zebedee—it was not these but *Mary* who first sees the risen Christ and who hears her name pronounced by Him: 'Mary.' For the people of Biblical times, spoken language was as good as a touch, each word lived in their ears. They didn't have TV, they didn't have MTV or animated holograms, for them the spoken word was the hottest entertainment around. 'Mary.' '*Rabboni.*' 'Touch me not.'"

The child in the pew ahead of me, a toddling male with a

runny nose and hair much the same translucent lemon color as his snot, had become fascinated by me, and distracted me from the minister's concluding peroration, her parallel between Mary's confusing Easter experience and the way in which Christ sneaks up on all of us, in the morning mists, in the semblance of a gardener. Amen.

As we bowed our heads in the post-sermon prayer I was intensely conscious of the body beside mine, familiar and yet not, Deirdre's meekly bent back sheathed in a stiff purple dress I had never seen before. I moved my elbow on the pew-back to touch hers and she pointedly moved hers away. *Noli me tangere.* I pictured her tan skin and supple half-shaven underparts beneath the vulgar shine of her crocus-colored dress with its starchy white collar. Her submission to this service, to the giant male ghost it bespoke, roused me. Like many of the younger women here, she wore no hat, no Easter bonnet: her "big" hair, its oiled curls inflated by a hairdresser's patient teasing, was her headdress. Somewhere, Saint Paul devotes many verses to the vexed matter of how women should shave or cover their overexciting hair.

The clergyperson was stationed at the door, though the day was cold, alternating spells of pale sunlight with unseasonable spittings of snow. She greeted Deirdre by name, but after a hesitation that showed a long gap of attendance. When introduced to me, she darted her sensitive bright eyes back and forth between our ill-matched faces before granting me a firm little handshake and an abrupt smile I must call boyish. Her teeth were as straight and neat as her bangs.

I like these contemporary females, stripped of so much of the devious nonsense the rise of capitalism imposed upon women.

I liked, too, my drug-raddled consort's dragging me to church, this homely brown church out of Protestantism's

fading, working-class middle range. There was a nakedness
in that, a bared need. Gloria had been an old-style Episco-
palian, resenting any tampering with Cranmer's prayer-
book language and any evangelical or feel-good pollutions
of the service, such as a homily at morning prayer or the
passing of the peace at any service. Perdita had drifted from
Unitarianism into Buddhism and settlement-house good
works. Both women were religious aristocrats, for whom
God was a vulgar poor relation with the additional social
disadvantage of not existing. For primitive Deirdre, something existed, hot, in the knots of her nature, that she was
unashamed to bow to. Though I *was* ashamed, I was also
somewhat primitive, and had willingly attended as an extension of my worship of her body.

We walked arm in arm out of a swirl of snow into a
pollen-colored cloud of sunshine on the way to the parked
car. I felt better for having done this—put Easter behind me.
Perhaps Easter is my problem with spring—the unreasonable expectation of it. That distant spring when I was too
paralyzed by dread to build little Mildred's dollhouse, I
went, gigantic in my numbness, out on a warm day and marvelled to find little swarms of tiny winged ephemerids already active in the air, jiggling together in some obligatory
procedure, offering themselves as a humble rung in the food
chain, though it seemed too wintry still for spiders to be stirring and for swallows to have migrated north. Snowdrops—
an early small amaryllis, *Galanthus nivalis*—have always
worried me: if flowers exist to attract insects, where in this
just-unfrozen world do the insects come from? Well, here
insects were, in my muddy backyard, and if these gnats were
not oppressed by death, why should I be? A vast camaraderie
of living cells, all doomed to disintegrate back into insensate

dust, cheered me for a moment. I shouldered my life—my house, my four and a half children, my two cars, my half-acre—and moved on, toward this present moment in time.

———————

Tax time. Though no one takes it seriously—the District of Columbia is entirely given over to deserted monuments and warring gangs of African-American teenagers, who have looted every office of its last stapler and photocopier refill cartridge—a ghost of federal government exists in Maryland and Virginia, too weak to do anything but send out forms, which I sentimentally file in the drawer along with my pre-war returns. Deirdre is very upset that I have allowed Phil and Spin to raise the protection money again—from an even grand to thirteen-hundred fifty. Spin explained that their own expenses have gone up, what with the teenage competition coming out from Lynn, moving up the coast. "They don't go by any rules, Mr. Turnbull," he explained to me. "To them killing is nothing—it's not a last resort, or taking care of business, it's for sheer entertainment value. You don't want those babies to get into your pocket—they'll take it all, and then hang your hide out to dry."

Macho, rumpled Phil was offended by his partner's betrayal of fear. "They're kids," he said, "for Chrissake. Fifteen, sixteen. Some even, Jesus, like ten, eleven. Kids can't stand up to experience. We're professionals, right? We provide a service, we keep our bargains. Our clients trust us, right, Mr. Turnbull?"

"Right, Phil."

"Any of those Lynn kids show up on your hill, you know how to reach us. You have the phone numbers."

"I do."

Phil's eyes slid over to Deirdre, who always comes out-of-doors when she hears men's voices on the driveway. "How's she treatin' you?" he asked me, as if she couldn't talk for herself. "She keepin' in line?"

"She's my little lady," I told him, not liking his tone.

"I could tell you some stories," he said, "from the old days. Huh, Dee?"

"Tell all you want. It still leaves you as a A-1 asshole."

His eyes did a dance from her face to mine to Spin's, and he held his tongue, with an effort that pushed his head forward like a bison's. They didn't want to offend me, they wanted to keep the scrip flowing.

But Deirdre was roused. She asked me, "Whaddeya give these guys anything for? They couldn't do anything if you really needed protection. Look at 'em—they're scared shitless of these little kids from Lynn. Wait'll the Russian gangs from Mattapan get here. These are two-bit punks, Ben, and you're their only patsy."

"They've taken good care of me so far," I told her.

Spin seemed startled by my support; his toothpick bobbled under his mustache as he said to Deirdre, "Hear that, smart cunt? And this is one smart former financier talking. Outsmarted his way up the ladder from utter nowhere out in the western part of the state."

"How'd you know that?" I asked, startled in turn.

Phil smirked, checking if Deirdre took this in. "We know everything about our clients," he said, "we need to know."

"Fuck you two," she said. "When those kids from Lynn get here you're both going to wake up plugged some day. Or with a smile cut into your throats that'll make your mouths look like assholes."

Phil took this in and winked at me. "You watch her, Mr.

Turnbull. Back in high school everybody said she could suck dick all right, but that's not the same as dependable."

Spin was pocketing the April money. To end the conference, he said, "Trust us," but the words had a shaky ring even in my ears.

Back in the house, as their rusty old Camaro wheeled down the driveway, I explained to Deirdre that what they charged was so much less than what the government used to extract that it was a bargain, regardless of how real their alleged protection was.

"Yeah, but when there was government, there were things like the FBI and the Federal Reserve Board to keep things stable. There was structure," she told me. "Structure is worth paying quite a lot for. Without it, you get just survival of the brutes."

"Where did you hear all this?" I asked. "It doesn't sound like you."

"A program on television the other night, when I couldn't sleep. I get jittery; it's too quiet here at night. You were dead to the world. It talked about the Roman Empire. You know how, before it broke up, it made the spread of Christianity possible? All those roads and soldiers—Christianity would never have gotten out of Jerusalem without those roads. And it needed to get out of Jerusalem. It would have been squelched by the Jewish establishment. The Jews hated it, though it *was* Jews at first."

I was amused; this young person under my roof was trying to grow, to learn, to orient herself in the world as it now was. She wanted to live a life. My amusement was cruel, of course. I said, "I have to tell you, Deirdre, that I don't much care what happens in the world. I've had my years in it, by and large. You've arrived as a late kicker, one last joy, and I'm grateful. But time is running out for me. What Spin and

Phil and the kids from Lynn do with the world is up to them. I just want to buy a little peace, day by day."

"You *can't* just cop out," she said, getting wild. "What about *me?*"

"What about you, my dear? You're comfortable, aren't you? You're fed and housed up here. You're a lot better off than when you were turning tricks three or four a night and getting ripped off by the escort agency and terrified of being slashed or strangled by some sicko who could never come to terms with his own libidinous impulses."

"Yeah," she said. "But there's not enough here for me to *do*. Everything I want to do to change the place you resist, because Gloria wouldn't have done it that way. Gloria, Gloria. Ben, it's *boring* for me here. Even banging you, you seem to want it less."

"I'll want it more," I promised, "when it stops being spring. I just get down in the spring, I don't know what it is. We'll be fine, eventually." Some of that ancient dollhouse panic began to rise in my throat, thickening it. "Stick with me, darling. There's nothing out there but—" But what? Paganism. Imported Oriental gods, fraudulent magi and seers. The decline of Rome.

The lilac buds are two-pronged, showing the first unsheathing of leaves. Each sharp forsythia bud reveals a gleam of yellow. The daylilies are now well up—clusters of scimitar shapes. The peonies are a red inch out of the ground. A lone daffodil blows its golden one-note above the sagging crocuses in the driveway circle. The dead lawn shows a green blush. It is all up with winter and its low-ceilinged safety.

Rounding the pond back from a nocturnal trip to

Christy's convenience store for nibbles, milk, and orange juice, I heard the peepers—I rolled down my window to hear them better. The noise was like armor, metallic, composed of overlapping shining scales, ovals of sound beaten thin, a brainless urgent pealing chorus that filled the air solid, whether rising from the mud or descending from the trees was hard to tell in the dark. The sound hung in mid-air, nowhere yet everywhere, like last month's skunk smell.

The next day, a steady spring downpour drummed in the gutters and whipped against the windows with an insulting sting. Deirdre in a morose sulk did aerobics to an antique Jane Fonda tape of Gloria's while I rummaged in the encyclopedia and the seldom-consulted family Bible, nagged ever since Easter by thoughts of St. Paul. Without him, there might have been a Christ, but there would have been no Christology, and no crisis theology. From the standpoint of two thousand years later, his travels seem wormholes in petrified wood, the already rotten eastern end of the Empire, dotted lines traced from one set of ruins to another, or to empty Turkish spaces where even the names Paul knew—Lystra, Derbe—have been wiped away by time's wind. Antioch of Pisidia, where Paul founded the first Galatian church, deteriorated over the centuries into a rubble of marble blocks and broken aqueduct arches; the site was not rediscovered until the explorations of the English clergyman Arundell in 1833. Iconium, rivalling the second Antioch as a center of Christianity in inner Asia Minor, consisted of, after Paul's visitations, a patriarchate with many lesser churches on the slopes of the surrounding mountains. A city located in a flowering oasis surrounded by desert at an altitude of three thousand feet, Iconium had been founded by the Emperor Claudius as a colony of army veterans; these, together with Hellenized Galatians and Jews and ethnic Phrygians, made up the population. Poppaea, Nero's wife, appeared on the settlement's coins as a goddess. In later days Iconium became the residence of the Seljuk sultans of Rum and the headquarters for the Mevlevi dancing dervishes of Turkey; the Armenians of the region remained loyal to Christianity but were savagely slaughtered during World War I.

It was in Iconium that Paul encountered Thecla, a pagan girl who, falling under the spell of his preachments on virginity, became a saint and, in the terms of the adoring Eastern church, "protomartyr among women and equal with the apostles." The apocryphal *Acts of Paul and Thecla*, composed by an imaginative priest in the second century, contains the only known physical description of Paul, as "a man of small stature, with his eyebrows meeting and a rather large nose, somewhat bald-headed, bandylegged, strongly built, of gracious presence, for sometimes he looked like a man and sometimes he had the face of an angel."

The ages have not found it easy to love Paul, for all his feats of marketing Christianity to the world. Marketing it, nay—inventing it, and Protestantism as well, which after fifteen centuries at last took up in earnest his desperate, antisocial principle that a man is justified by faith and not the works of the law. What an impossible item, after all, he was selling: Christ crucified, unto the Jews a stumbling block, and unto the Greeks foolishness. To the Gentiles Paul appeared too Jewish—a Pharisee, a temple spieler—and to the Jews too much infatuated with the Gentiles. There was too much hair in his nostrils, too much moisture on his rapid lips; the hunched-over little tentmaker, bald and gnarled, had been twisted into something superhuman by his fit on the road to Damascus—a bragged-of burst of light that had left him hyperactive, insufferable with a selfish selflessness that laid him repeatedly open to scourgings and filthy abuse. Greek poured from him in an ungrammatical, excited tumble, and I, called John Mark, cousin of Barnabas, resented the way in which my pious and prudent older cousin on his own island, among the friends and relatives that had welcomed us on this our first mission from Syrian Antioch, was insidiously displaced as the leader of our expedition.

The turning point came in New Paphos, at the far end of the Roman road from Salamis, where we—Barnabas and Paul and I—had landed to preach among the synagogues; the governor, Sergius Paulus, like so many of his patrician class of colonial officials a foppish dabbler in poetry and philosophy, summoned us to his court, to dispute with the crowd of learned fools he had collected about him. Prominent among them was Barjesus, one of those Jewish magicians called Elymas, which infiltrated everywhere in those sick times of sorcery and febrile Asian cults; this snake-tongued man heckled and contradicted Paul's account as the self-designated apostle strove to set before the governor the intricately bold claims of our faith. At last Paul turned with fury in his eyes and—as ragefully as, within the memories of believers, he had led the persecution of Stephen, hurling rocks and curses alike upon the fainting martyr—Paul called Barjesus a child of the devil and an enemy of righteousness and a perverter of the ways of the Lord. His lips frothing and his eyes rolling upward as they did before one of his fits, Paul told Barjesus, "The hand of the Lord is upon you; you will not see the sun for a season." What happened then was incredible: the mist of darkness enveloped the man and he fell silent, but for begging to be led from the hall. Naturally, Sergius Paulus was impressed, as the Romans were always impressed by a show of cruelty. The governor asked for private sessions of enlightenment as to this Messiah crucified and risen, and the new dispensation that He had brought into the world.

It disgusted me to see Paul preen upon his conquest among our occupiers, and yet I was too young to protect my good-natured cousin from the tentmaker's grandiose impulses. Paul was on fire now with the desire to spread our word westward, into the vastness of Asia Minor, with their mongrel, uncircumcised populations. He wished to sail to Ephesus, because he believed that the word of Jesus, like a Heavensent plague, would spread best from the teeming ports. He had to settle for a ship to Attalia, on the same swampy coast as his native Tarsus, only to the west.

The mountains called Taurus, snow-capped, slowly rose beyond the prow. It was Paul's mad dream to climb into those mountains and evangelize the high cities that had provided goat's hair to the making of his father's tents. He remembered from his childhood many amiable shepherds and traders who wandered down into Tarsus with their woolly fragrance. He assured us that the Galatians were not such barbarians as we Judaeans thought; they were inclined to religion, an appetite being fed at present by fraudulent wonder-workers such as Apollonius of Tyana and Peregrinus Proteus and Alexander of Abonoteichos. The names tumbled from Paul's mouth like cheerful imprecations; he loved language as it spilled through his lips, and often in his darting eyes was a glint I can only call merry, a gleam of sheer mischief kindled by the hyperactivity of his Godstruck brain. He was beset by fits wherein demons bent him double backwards, and suffered periods of disabling feebleness; he carried in his bent form more pain than he wanted us to see.

Peter had not been like this. He often visited the house of my mother, Mary of Jerusalem. His hand would rest on my head; he would joke in his soft Galilean accent; he would praise my schoolboy Greek and mock his unmannerly own and promise me that some day we would travel together, with me his translator, as far as Rome itself. He was a tall broad man, erect, a rock, his beard turned alabaster-white even in the fullness of his manhood. He had known Jesus all day long, for three years, and had been loved by Him. Paul had never known Jesus, had only heard His voice in a cloud of thunder and sheet of light, never in the quiet human company of a roadway, a field, a fishing boat, an up-stairs room at suppertime. He had never touched Him, or joked with Him, or caught wind of His bodily functions, or seen Him flirtatiously treat with the women who followed with the disciples. Paul had an unreal sense of women and of Jesus, that made his ideas of both, and his professed love of both, extravagant. Our Lord's miracles had been daylight matters for Simon Peter; he and his brothers James and John alone witnessed the raising of Jairus's daughter. He and those others who had known Jesus well were men of the Law, seeking to understand among themselves in exactly what manner the Law had been fulfilled by the Lord's preaching and healing and resurrection and His subsequent appearances to the faithful. But when I was enough grown to travel and to spread our glad news among the synagogues, the invitation came not from kindly Peter but from Barna-bas, my mother's nephew, chosen by the church at Antioch, in company with Paul upon their return from Jerusalem, to journey abroad.

We walked up from the unholy seethe of malarial Attalia, along the Kestros River, past groves of lemon and orange trees, to the magnificent city of Perga. Here began the road into the mountains. We rested the night. The roguish innkeeper told us of the Isaurian robbers who beset travellers and disposed of their bodies in the icy mountain lakes. Also of wolves, mountain lions, and the bears for whom the mountains were named. Paul scoffed, saying he had God's direct mandate to preach to the Gentiles; God would protect us.

We set out in a chill morning mist. The path was bordered by wild cactus and prickly pears taller than ourselves; as we ascended there were pines, firs, and giant broomcorn; and when we lifted our eyes to the heights we saw great cedars swaying in the wind. And these were but the lower ridges. The path narrowed, becoming stonier and doubling back upon itself; the river, which had accompanied us for a while, fell away beneath our feet in a final cascade of rushing water.

Without the river's prattling voice, we could hear the wind above us, bending the cedars and sharpening the edges of the rocks. A narrow pass, between a face of red rock sweating ice-melt and on the other side a plunging precipice, brought us not to a crest but to yet more steeply upward vistas. Paul scrambled ahead, Barnabas plodded after, dragged by the other man's zeal, and I paused, stunned by the sheer extent of mountain walls before us, ridge after ridge, the farthest crowned by snow though April was well advanced.

We all have our revelations, on the road to Damascus or elsewhere. I called out my refusal to go any farther.

Paul skidded back down, pebbles scrambling and spilling from beneath his sandals, which were as dusty and cracked as the horny gray skin of his feet. "What's this, my son?"

"Rabbi, this is madness. There is nothing above us but barren mountains, with all their perils, and then highland cities that are merely rumors to us. Where are the synagogues, the ghettos, that will give us shelter and audience?"

A brief laugh showed Paul's ragged brown teeth in his black beard. "The Jews are there, my boy, if not in such numbers as you have been accustomed to in Judaea, Syria, and Cyprus. Wherever the emperor has established order, our brethren will already have ventured, pursuing the trades that demand patience and close vision, observing the close-woven old laws of the Torah, every jot and tittle."

There was this teasing scorn with which he spoke of the Jews, though he was a Jew. I asked, anger rising in me, "Is it to bring Christ to these sparse colonies of the circumcised that you ask us to risk our lives in a freezing wasteland?"

"To the circumcised and the uncircumcised," he said. "In Christ neither circumcision nor uncircumcision avails anything; nothing avails but faith which works through love. In Christ there is neither Jew nor Greek, slave nor free, male nor female. If you are Christ's, then you are the seed of Abraham, and heirs according to the promise. You have heard me speak thus many times, John Mark; why do you now seem to dispute?"

I was a young man and had no wish to dispute with Paul at the height of his power and evangelical urgency. Yet I had taken in the tales and sayings of our Lord before I could walk, for my mother's house was the first in Jerusalem where the followers of the Way gathered. The Last Supper was held in her upper room; the apostles met in the same place after Jesus ascended, tongue-tied in their amazement. At times I felt His presence with those that were gathered there, and I knew in my heart when His message was being perverted. "Our Lord said," I told Paul and Barnabas where they had paused on the steep path, resting their packs at the base of the wall of sweating red rock, "that he came not to abolish the Law and the Prophets but to fulfill them."

Paul said quickly, in his hurried tumbling voice, no longer

smiling, "If righteousness comes though the Law, then Christ died in vain. Christ died that all nations might be saved. *All* the nations, not just the nation of Abraham. Until the coming of Christ, the Law was our tutor, but since the revelation of faith we are no longer under a tutor. We are free, in Christ's love."

"But Christ came from Abraham," I said, "and his disciples came from the synagogue. If the Gentiles need not be circumcised to be converted, and may continue to eat meat that is unclean by the laws of Leviticus, then Christ need not have been a Jew."

"He chose to be a Jew," Paul said, "as the Jews were themselves chosen. But now that He is come there are Jews no more. We who are Jews by birth know that we are justified by faith in Christ and not by doing what is in the Law. If the Law could create new life, then righteousness would indeed reside in the Law. But Christ ransomed us from the curse of the Law by becoming the thing accursed, since it is written, Accursed is everyone who hangs upon the tree. Christ and Christ alone is the new life, given for all nations, even for those savage tribes beyond the boundaries of Rome, and not for just the children of the Law."

I held my ground there on the tilted path and said, in the face of Paul's increasing agitation, "Surely the Law was not given to Moses and our priests to be a curse, but to keep us clean among the unclean, to keep us distinct in our covenant. If Christ annulled the Law as thoroughly as you say, then virtue is what each man says it is, and righteousness becomes mere self-proclamation. The Gentiles will come to Christ as if walking from one room into another, without humility or ritual, without discipline or pain."

Paul's eyes surrendered all their craft to a blaze of passion: he held out his arms as if he stood before us crucified. "I have been stoned and flogged," he said, "for proclaiming Christ's victory in love. I have forsaken in this life all shelter and safety. Yet, my doubtful young friend, I rejoice in my suffering. Those who belong to Jesus crucify their flesh. They die to this world, that they may live in the Spirit. What matters circumcision then? What matters cleanness, and the manner of meat, which, as our Lord has said, all goes out through the bowels! I say to you as I said to Peter when in Antioch he flinched from eating with the Gentiles: You hypocrite! Jew and Gentile are one in Christ! I say to you that no man who puts his hand to the plow yet turns back is fit for the kingdom of God!"

Barnabas tried to intervene, wounded to see such hard words used on his young cousin. But I felt freed from deference by Paul's fury and intemperance, and justified in my suspicion that he was twisting the Master's Word in his passion to convert the world, to make everyone and no one a Jew. Participating in Stephen's death, and hearing that martyr curse the stiff-necked people who had ever persecuted their prophets, Saul had taken into himself hatred of the Jews, though he himself was the disputatious and hot-blooded quintessence of one. When our tempers had somewhat cooled, and we had partaken together of a handful of olives and some hard bread softened in a nearby freshet, there in that shadowed pass an hour's climb north of Perga, Barnabas arranged with me to descend to Attalia and take passage back to Caesarea and Jerusalem. He loved me, yet believed that he had been commissioned by the church at Antioch to accompany Paul and must do it even though it lead to death.

Also, I think, he scented glory in Paul's path.

Others have written of what befell them in the cities of southern Galatia. They passed safely through unseen bandit gangs and late blizzards in the wild region around the Cilician Gate, through the canyon worn by the Kestros. They made their way along the heights to the east of the vast blue lake and the great mountain, Sultan Dagh, beyond. In Antioch, where some of the citizens were given to the worship of the Persian god Mithras and others to the lewd goddess Cybele, Paul fell prey to blinding headaches and spells of feverish debility, but made many converts among the pagans; then the priests, waxing jealous, drove him and Barnabas from the city with a scourging. In Iconium, Paul met Thecla, and his heated words seduced her to tread the path to martyrdom. Again, after much fruitful preaching to the Gentiles, he was driven from the city by the Jews, who represented to the Roman authorities that Paul urged not only heresy but subversion, claiming that a certain King Jesus was the true ruler of the eastern Empire.

In Lystra, Paul healed a cripple, and the ignorant people hailed him and Barnabas as Mercurius and Jupiter and would have even worshipped them as gods had not Paul rebuked their superstition. There were few Jews in Lystra, but elders came from Antioch and Iconium and persuaded the people to stone Paul; he who had helped stone Stephen was left for dead outside the city, but by a miracle survived. He and Barnabas went on to the village of Derbe, where they founded the last of the Galatian churches, and returned to Attalia and thence to Antioch by the same way they had come, westward through Lystra and Iconium and the Pisidian Antioch, visiting the Christian congregations they had engendered there despite the enmity and persecutions of the Jews, who could not but think their initial hospitality had been betrayed and their ancient covenant cheaply assigned to a multitude of the uncircumcised—to Roman soldiers and Greek tanners, to women and slaves, to Asians and

Cappadocians, Phoenicians and Scythians, to legions of barbarians hitherto mired in superstition and the pleasures of the flesh.

Though Paul's missions took him ever farther afield, to Thessalonica and Berera in Macedonia, to Athens and Corinth in Achaia, to Ephesus until driven thence by an uproar among the silversmiths whose trade in idolatrous images of Diana was threatened by his preaching, and some say even to Spain and, by my own certain witness, to Rome—in spite of all these travels the Galatian churches remained the dearest of his children, being the firstborn, and the object of the first of his epistles which have been circulated and preserved.

Myself, John Mark, known in manhood by my Latin appellation, in time I reconciled with Paul. Nearly twenty years after we parted angrily above Perga, I was with him and Peter in Rome. Our congregation there, beseiged and small, had long been promised a visit by him; he sent ahead of him a long and eloquent letter, as a spiritual gift, speaking many things of Christ. In Rome Paul was a prisoner for two years, writing and receiving all who came to him for instruction and inspiration. Cities are unholy places, but their mobs were needed for the spread of the Word. In country air Christ's message melted into birdsong. Rome was Antichrist's capital, and its capture essential to our campaign. I had been in Rome some years previous, as Peter's interpreter and secretary, before Paul was brought there. It was then that I began, in my rough Greek, to set down those things I had heard of the life of Jesus.

Paul and Peter together met martyr's deaths under Nero Claudius Caesar, who, goaded into ever greater infamies and follies by his evil wife, Poppaea, blamed the Christians for the conflagration which many whispered had been set by his own hand. Peter was crucified upside down, in mockery; Paul as a Roman citizen was cleanly beheaded, three miles outside the city wall, in the Salvian Marsh.

I was spared by God from Nero's slaughters in order that I might write an account of our Savior's life, set down simply, in the plain words I heard from Peter and others of the men and women who knew Jesus when He was alive among men, casting out demons and feeding multitudes, healing with the spit of His tongue and delivering His Word in parables, not speaking from a cloud like an Oriental magus nor conjuring away all difference, decreed from the days of Abraham, between Jew and Gentile. Challenged by the Pharisees, He answered text for text, and conferred on the mountain with Moses and Elijah, as witnessed by Peter, James, and John. This I, John Mark, set down on parchment, where it cannot be changed and will endure forever.

In the woods today I surprised a butterfly, or, rather, he surprised me, the first of the spring—a Mourning Cloak, with dark wings rimmed in pale bands. There is a tint in the woods that exactly mimics the smoke of spring fires. The elongated red beech buds float in constellations within that gray-barked tree's laterally spreading branches. Forsythia's cutting yellow has broken through at last. Downtown, the Bradford pear trees put forth a show of cool, fluorescent white. The maple trees, Norway and sugar and swamp, produce a chartreuse froth of what seem leaves but closer inspection reveals to be up-springing greenish flowers. The view into the woods is nubbled and dimmed where in a week or two will stand a curtain of opaque verdure. There is now, in late April, a heavy sweet blurring of things, a vapor of oxygen-rich exhalation as green life begins in earnest to churn the elements in its billions of photosynthetic cells. The pond where the peepers cry at night has morning mist on its face. The dead lawn suddenly is revived and a few days short of needing its first mowing, and the daylilies hide tufts of flourishing grass in their little jungle. I saw my first dandelion at the edge of the drive. The house's rain-streaked windows reveal a runny golden-green saturation; a ruthless steeping invades nature, rotting everything it does not feed in its surge toward soggy plenitude, toward the flood of brainless, jubilant growth. People as well as plants feel it, a reckless excess of stimulants in the air; there are suddenly children wild on the streets, clogging the doorway to the convenience store, raucously scraping their skateboards and roller blades along the sidewalks, flaunting their pasty winter skin in shorts and baggy untucked T-shirts. Where have they been all winter, these children? They are spontaneously, repulsively hatched, like the flies that now buzz and bump on the inside of the kitchen windows, stupid in the warmth. Driving out to Route 128 along Merchants Road, I see a weeping cherry tree, no less spectacular for being familiar, making its annual splash of purple-pink against the chilly white of a star magnolia in the next-door neighbor's front yard. Violet-tinted magnolias plume everywhere, fat and pale as harem women, and even along the driveway my poor little spindly pear trees have devised a few blossoms, at one of which I saw a sleepy bee bumbling, my first bee. On Route 128, for no practical reason, there was a thickening of traffic—another spring phenomenon, garaged cars released and the itch to travel awakened.

I returned from a visit to two of my grandchildren, Torrance and Tyler, sons of my older son, Matthew, and his lovely, utterly blonde, slant-eyed wife, Eeva, a Finn from Rockport, an elfin child of its granite quarries and artists' colonies. They live in Gloucester, among drug addicts and out-of-work Portuguese fishermen, in a sprawling do-it-yourself house one block back from the sparkling, under-utilized harbor. Torrance is delicate, dark, and fey, with enormous girlish eyelashes, and club-footed Tyler sturdy and phlegmatic, with a Lapp streak in him somewhere. Both boys are heartbreaking if I focus on them, which is not easy to do; their fraternal tussles and sporadic forays into Grand-father's attention span compete with Eeva's explanation of the particular herbal tea she has opted to serve her aging father-in-law. And my true focus is upon my own child, Matthew. Of all my children, I feel guiltiest with him, though he is unfailingly cheerful and inscrutably benign. But in just the alacrity with which he comforts a squalling son I read my own conspicuous absence in his young life, off in Boston not only working the requisite ten-hour day but undergoing the post-hours male bonding, at the Federal Club and Brandy Pete's and the Parker House bar, that a se-curities business needs, to cement contacts. In his patently monogamous affection for Eeva I read another rebuke, a de-termined reaction against the suburban polygamy that even-tually produced my divorce from his mother. Like Perdita, Eeva has an artistic side, manifesting itself in carved lumps of linden wood and rather wonderful shapes of melted and half-blown glass. Her female beauty, in its full-figured prime at age thirty-four, sweeps over me with the fragrance of steeped chamomile flowers, orange peel, rose hips, lemon grass, hibiscus flowers, chicory, stevia leaves, allspice, and honey—the well-mulled combination of them excellent, she assures me, for blood pressure, regularity, and skin tone.

Her arctic eyes narrow and she becomes a Finnish witch during this incantation. She left out the beneficial effect of sexual potency, I guiltily imagine, to spare my son's fastidious feelings. He is pleasantly vague when I ask how his freelance architectural career is going, and when I stand, full of no-fat, no-sugar cookies, I feel that weakness in my knees which I associate with the extra weight of a child in my arms, though both boys are too big and wriggly to hold.

In the car, swerving around the circle that leads from Gloucester onto Route 128, I realize with a start why Torrance had so many new toys to show me and why both he and his mother glanced with a certain inquisitive alertness toward me as I sat, the perfect guest and eager consumer of health food, in the center of their oatmeal-colored sofa. It had been the boy's birthday. If not this very day, somewhere toward the end of April. I had totally forgotten it. How old would he be? I tried to remember the hospital circumstances of his birth. He had crouched in a transparent plastic basket like a little skinned rabbit, fighting to live after being born prematurely. We all felt through the plastic how hard he was trying to live. Eeva had wept, because she could not nurse him, could not help him. Now he was eight. A critical birthday, marking his entry upon the third and final quadrennium of childhood, before the onslaught, at thirteen, of puberty's stormy weather. It had slipped my poor old empty mind. I would call Matthew and lamely apologize—one more wound inflicted on this, my most innocent child, my uncomplaining son—and rush back onto 128 and to the penitential Peabody mall for some garish and superfluous present as soon as I got home.

When I got home, my mood of guilt and self-loathing took some of the sting and surprise out of finding the house dishevelled, the great rose and blue Tabriz rug stripped from the living-room floor amid other depredations, and an ill-written ballpoint note from Deirdre on the hall table:

Dear Ben—

I'm sorry I just can't take it any more, life here is too boring, tho' I know you try. We are just too different. I try to please you but I know I don't a lot of the time. Also to be honest I miss dope too much. It takes me to another place which is the one way I feel good about myself. We took some nice things but left you plenty, Phil said you owed me something, it's part of women's rights.

Be well always my darling,
D.

Then the rusty draw-gate of my heart lifted to admit torrents of regret. As I went around the house checking on what had been stolen, I mentally inventoried instead her tight buttocks, like two perfect bronze hemispheres but for the arcs of white her thong bikini cut into them; the taut terrain of her spine and scapulae and attendant back muscles as she relaxed into sleep beside me; her tough-talking mouth forming its dulcet and docile O around my stirred-up member, down—down with a determined gulp like a child's swallowing a dose of noxious medicine—to its tickly-haired root. She had wanted to be more than my lewd toy, my sex object, but I had ignored this silent plea. I had failed to take seriously her instinctive attempt, this last month, at spring cleaning, so inflexibly had I consigned her and our life together to the category of squalor. But the hormones of nest-building were in her as in every woman. I had given her attempts at homemaking no help; I had wanted only like some horn-brained buck to fuck her and between bouts of my erratic potency to ignore her. A shaky sense of irredeemable guilt rotated in my stomach as I mentally reconstructed her face, her shining round brown eyes as vulnerable as bubbles of jelly a stray needle might prick, her Sphinxy mass of ringlets, her blunt moist muzzle of a nose. I tormented myself with remembering the silken rivers of dark body hair that loving inspection discovered everywhere on her limbs, and the girlish secrets between her legs, the semi-liquid pink split pod with its magical pea and the drier other aperture like a tight-lidded reptilian wink. Her excitable quick way of moving through the house, the fits of sluggishness that buried her all afternoon in the bed, only a cushion of dark hair and a single shut eye visible in the tumble of covers. Lost, gone, all lost, and I had no appetite for another whore, even if I could find the thread to one in the anarchic tangle that stretched below my hill.

The house had been ransacked as if by a pair or trio of morons—some items of little value taken, some precious pieces left. Perhaps there was some bizarre code of fencibility operating, leaving Gloria's grandmother's finest Staffordshire china untouched in its mahogany cabinet and taking a plastic-and-aluminum coffee-maker that I never used, having sacrificed coffee decades ago to the obscure deities who control blood pressure. The living-room rug—what a weight for them to wrestle with!—was the greatest loss, but its absence exposed a maple parquet whose beauty had been long obscured. Each piece of surviving furniture was now doubled by a dim mirror-image in the floor's waxy surface. Deirdre's thefts seemed as random as a lover's heart, which chooses to cherish this or that inconsequential detail of the beloved, and ignores features that could be universally agreed to be worthier. I always liked, for example, the way Perdita could never give up smoking or drinking, and went around all summer in bare feet so dirty the soles became black, and disliked the way she was always trying to help less fortunate others—sending money to Ethiopian charities, putting in a day a week at a Dorchester settlement house. I want women to be dirty, and focused solely on me.

Deirdre and I had together proved helpless before the gathering needs of the grounds and garden. The plants and weeds were coming along in a rush. The daylily leaves in the bed beside the driveway were as high as my knees; a few tulips had popped open in the far garden. The peonies needed to be propped: even I could see that. Gloria had always done everything, and supervised what she could not do. She had ever been on the telephone to lawn services, tree services, sprinkler-system maintainers, greenhouses, nurseries, and spent muddy-kneed hours out in the garden beds, digging, planting, transplanting, mixing manure and peat moss, mulch and loam, wearing a big battered straw hat we had once bought in St. Croix on holiday. I had liked the dirty way she looked, with earth smeared on her cheek where she had rubbed a mosquito bite with a muddy glove, and the way she, dog-tired at dusk, would leave all her caked and sweaty clothes in the laundry room, including her underpants, and walk upstairs nude, past her staring ancestral antiques, to soak her aching body in the tub, leaving me to put a quiche or a defrozen meat loaf in the oven for dinner. Men like being useful. I had liked serving my naked queen of tilth.

iii. *The Deal*

O N MAY DAY, when I went into the open shed that serves as a garage, a shadow swiftly dipped down from a rafter in the corner of my eye, and I knew that the barn swallows had returned, to build their nest. How they find us in the continental ocean of green I have never understood, nor if they are the same birds, or a pair containing one of the old offspring. Their mysterious arrival used to mark the true beginning of summer for Gloria and me. A few days later, she herself showed up. I had not shot her, or if I had it was in another, slightly different, universe.

"Where have you *been?*" I asked, a bit timidly. I was unclear as to how long she had been gone; as I age, holes in my memory develop, and because they are holes it is difficult to gauge their size.

"You *never* listen when I tell you where I'm going," she said. And she proceeded to tell me where she had been. It was true, as her red lips vivaciously moved, with that rather annoying little self-satisfying roll of her jaw during a theatrical pause, my mind became a blank in which isolated words like "conference" and "the gift shop" and "Singapore" nonsensically bobbed. Could they be having conferences of gift-shop owners in Singapore? She was going on, "And at the Calpurnia Club, we had a *won*derful lecturer on English herbaceous borders. I asked her about deer and she said in the United Kingdom they were only a problem in Scotland. But another member, a *dar*ling woman called Polly Martingale from Dedham—she said she's an aunt of a protégé of yours at Sibbes, Dudley, and Wise, Ned Partridge—"

"That slimy son of a bitch is no protégé of mine."

"—she told me about a product you can get called AgRepel. It's made up of the ground-up shoulders and whatnot of cows. It smells like death. She gave me the phone number of a man in Boxford who carries it and I want to call him right now. Don't argue, Ben. For once in your life don't be oppositional."

It was a plea of sorts. I had wanted to blurt out some explanation for the missing Tabriz carpet and coffeepot and the other fencible goods but no explanation came; my mouth hung open foolishly. I wondered how many of Deirdre's curly black hairs were visible on the bed linen, along with how many of our telltale love-juice stains. Gloria gave me a quick probing look out of her frosty blue eyes. Five years younger than I, she is as alert as a bird on the lookout for worms in scanning me for signs of the inevitable decline that will leave her with a widow's well-heeled freedom. So many of her friends are widows, sole proprietresses of bank accounts no longer joint; blithely, at last, they command to be done all the home projects—the airy wing added to the house's gloomy core; the indoor lap-pool; the resurfaced driveway; the elaborate garden fence, its crisscrossed slats doubling as a trellis for roses and clematis; the screened-in gazebo beyond the garden, for reading and romantically solitary reverie—that the wretched husband, alive, would have forbidden. She envies these women the liberty their weeds betoken. To blunt her death-wish for me it has become my habit to deny Gloria nothing, even though some of her home projects, such as lining our bathroom with mirrors and ripping out the old bent-nosed nickel faucets for brass, Swiss, inhumanly streamlined fixtures, seem bizarre to me. Why all these mirrors in which to count our multiplying wrinkles? Confronting myself in the shaving mirror has become the major hurdle to each day. With the mirrored cabinet door ajar, I can see myself from a dizzying variety of angles, my profile when I bend close receding into that slightly curving infinity a pair of mirrors can conjure out of nothing. The first time I saw my own head in profile, with its slack, opisthognathous jaw and rather flattened back to my skull, I was nine years old, being fitted for my first grown-up jacket at the England Brothers department store on North Street in Pittsfield; I was horrified, discovering this ugly brother inside my own skin. He was a stranger, not any kind of twin. He looked Neandert(h)al. Now I see that ugly brother with his hair thinned and whitened and his dead-looking earlobes elongated as if by African magic, and his eyes shrunk as if by a New Guinea headhunter, and his skin blotched with pink sun-damage and shattered capillaries, not one but dozens of him parabolically receding in the astronomical complexity of Gloria's multiple mirrors. Still, to live with a woman a man must learn to accommodate her instinct to improve the nest. We are condemned, men and women, to symbiosis.

"I am *not* oppositional," I told her.

The AgRepel, which came in large plastic buckets from Polly Martingale's man in Boxford, looked like lumpy, dirty white clay and indeed did smell of death. But subtly: we had to get our noses down close to inhale the slaughterhouse redolence, and we wondered, as we lined the rose beds with it and scattered lumps beneath the euonymus and yew bushes, if the deer would lower their heads enough to be repelled.

"Wherever there's deer shit, put it," Gloria directed.

"'Scat,'" I said, "or 'spoor' or 'pellets' or 'turds,' if you must. But don't keep calling it 'shit.'" I felt she did it, by now, to offend me.

"It's shit," she said. "Because of you and your laziness I have to get down on my knees in my own garden and kneel in tick-lousy deer shit."

She sounded in my ears not unlike Deirdre; I wondered if one of them had absorbed the other. I protested unconvincingly, "Their excrement doesn't have the ticks in it. The ticks go from their hides onto field mice, somehow, and *then* they bite people. But only when they need to."

The tick and the disease they carried were rather unreal to me, but very real to Gloria. Her face in the shade of its Caribbean sunhat went white with fury at the thought of the deer invading *her* property and the spirochete invading *her* bloodstream, bringing chills and fever and aches and possible heart damage and arthritis. People even died of it, she assured me. This omniscient Mrs. Martingale knew somebody who knew somebody from New London who had gone into the hospital and just *died*.

I marvelled at how thoroughly Gloria was involved in this world, and not, like me, drifting away from it on a limp tether. When I stopped having to take the train into Sibbes, Dudley, and Wise each weekday, I split—so it feels—into a number of disinterested parties. My wave function had collapsed.

The Deal

Against much inner resistance, knowing full well that a child's innocent heart was being used to blackmail me into sitting still for a fund-raising lecture, I drove an hour along 128, at the height of the morning rush, to participate in Grandparents' Day at Kevin's private school, Dimmesdale Academy: all boys, fourth through ninth grades. The grounds spread on the edge of the birthplace of the Revolution, Lexington, a bucolic layout at the end of a winding street of posh colonial-style homes, at their halcyon best in the spring froth of blossom and new leaf. Kevin has recovered from his broken wrist and at the age of eleven is a limber and athletic blond with childhood's shambling manners and inaudible voice even though his head comes up to my shoulder. His paternal grandparents have retired to Hawaii but Perdita was there, her carelessly bundled hair liberally interwoven with gray; she had always scorned hairdressers, nail polish, and all lipstick but the shade, a milky pink, fashionable when she was in college. I was late, and had trouble finding the registration desk amidst the welter of little clapboard buildings built one at a time since the institution's one-room-schoolhouse beginnings in 1846. The label identifying me, by my own name and Kevin's, kept peeling off the lapel of my excessively tweedy coat. Though some grandparents looked ten years younger than I, and some as many or more years older, I was basically among members of my own generation. We had experienced birth in the conformist Fifties, adolescence in the crazed and colorful Sixties, and youth in the anticlimactic drug-riddled, sex-raddled Seventies. We had by and large dodged our proud nation's wars, the Cold War skirmishes and then the hideous but brief Sino-American holocaust. AIDS, before the development of its astonishingly simple and effective vaccine, had afflicted marginal portions of society, homosexuals and drug-takers and the children of the poor, but not us. Those of us here still held winning tickets in the cancer lottery, and had not fallen to any of the accidents, automotive and industrial and cardiovascular, that thin the ranks of active Americans. It was amazing to me how many we were: white-haired and arthritic, we were like the specialized plants that spring up a week after a forest fire has apparently swept all life into ashes. And our multitudinous grandsons were there to carry mankind deeper into the twenty-first century, to the brink of the unimaginable twenty-second.

I was indignant to have driven an hour and sacrificed a morning of my dwindling life, but there were grandparents present from Arizona and Florida, shaming me once again with my relative lack of family feeling. My passion to survive had only been partially placated by childbearing. Perdita had come out from Boston, where she lives in the semi-slum of the South End with a man considerably younger, called Geoff—diffidently artistic, as is she, and gay in part but perhaps not in the part turned toward her. Lankier even than when I first saw her in the Sixties (on the steps of the Du Bois Library, wearing tight jeans colorfully patched on both buttocks and a belly-exposing tie-dyed halter, puffing what, from the miserly way she pinched it in her fingers, was clearly a joint), she has let the years evolve a hundred florets of intersecting wrinkles on her face, and wears her grizzled hair constrained by a few hairpins, probably rusty. This gaunt old witch contains a beauty that I am one of the last on earth to still descry. To me she will always be that maiden on the shore, whose wet bare feet shed drying sand grain by grain in the cupped warmth of a back dune.

Linked now only by our progeny, we followed Kevin as he conducted us on a tour of the school—the new gym with its gleam of raw steel and unscuffed hardwood, the strained computer facilities, waiting for a donor to expand them— and sat side by side as the headmaster outlined his vision of the future and a choir of unchanged male voices piped through some madrigals and simplified Broadway show tunes. Perdita possesses that strange faculty of first wives of being instantly intelligible. "Dandelion," she murmured, and I knew she meant the woman two rows before us, with a head of hair as purely white and as evenly coiffed on her skull as a dandelion poll.

"Muffin," I answered, and she knew I meant the head-master, a youngish man both rotund and orotund. The cat-egory had been hers, a piece of private college slang back on the U. Mass. campus, dividing all humanity into three types, of which another was "horse" and the third I had forgotten. Could it have been as simple as "bird"? If our universe needs only three dimensions (plus time) to exist, and if three kinds of quarks, with their antiquarks, make up all the hadrons, and three primary colors all the stripes of the rainbow, a triad of categories might be enough.

"Rodney—" she began.

"Still has reading problems," I finished. This was Kevin's younger brother, who lacked and would lack all his life the loose-jointed ease of his sibling.

"Less so, Mildred says."

"He must have inherited post-linearity from Carol." Carol Eliade was their father, and my oldest daughter's husband— a son of Romanian immigrants, and a wizard, before the war, at keeping one step ahead of the Japanese in the minia-turization of computer chips. The war (which was perhaps less between us and China than between China and our protégé Japan, over the control of Asia, including separatist Siberia) had left Japan too ruined to compete, although the resilience of a demolished nation is always greater than seems possible. Fresh shoots push through the hot ashes; weeds spring up in new mutations. Global disaster had left intact the faint chemistry between Perdita and me, like a cobweb uniting two rotten old branches. In the math class, which was doing exercises in decimals, I was stimulated by her presence to participate in the riddling drill, which involved a string of solutions that spelled out a trendy phrase, in this case LOVE IS COLOR BLIND. I was still searching for the "B" when Perdita softly pointed out that the little boy sitting next to Kevin had already finished. "He does this every day," I pointed out in turn, with a competitive snarl that made her laugh. She would always see me as an academically aggressive, socially insecure college student.

Our forty-seven-year-old cobweb broke as we kissed our grandson goodbye and left Kevin running on the newly green, still muddy school field, rapidly shifting a lacrosse stick from hand to hand. The sky always looks so big over flat school fields, with their population of children scurrying in chase of their distant futures, while ominous silver-black clouds unfurl overhead. Driving back to 128, I observed that spring was further along west of Boston than on the North Shore—the green maple flowers, now a chartreuse dusting on the roads, had yielded to half-unfolded leaflets, and tulips were already up in red and yellow rows, along the white picket fences.

"How was the precious Perdita?" Gloria asked on my return. "Still anorectic?"

"O.K.," I said. "Not unpleasant."

"Why would she be unpleasant?" she asked. "She's got

this lovely boy-lover in Boston, and still collecting alimony from you."

"I'm not sure he's an actual lover," I said. "My kids say he's gay. I've never met him."

"And did you pay any attention to Kevin?" she asked, having decided that Perdita was an unprofitable subject for her to pursue. Yet the subject nagged her. My renunciation of my former wife had never been quite complete enough to suit her. She was a systematic woman, Gloria, and there was a residue of Perdita in our life that struck her as an impurity—dirt in a corner, as it were. Yet for me to give her what she wanted would be to expunge Perdita to an unreal degree, leaving me with a clean-swept past. Kevin was a safer topic: "He was dear," I said. "Still very innocent, even though I swear he's grown two inches in a month. He was touchingly pleased I came; I guess I had somehow communicated my resistance to driving all that way on a weekday." Weekdays and weekends were still different to me, out of intractable habit.

"Well," she said, "you might explain to him that he's one of ten. You could spend all of your time being a grand-father."

"Instead of being a useless housebound retiree," I said, a touch—an almost subliminal touch—combatively.

But my attitude toward Gloria since her return is meek and grateful. She has taken on the lawn and the plantings and wrestles with them and the workmen who come and go—lopping branches, scattering fertilizer—daily. Beds are re-edged; mulch is laid down over Preen. Miraculously, as the greenery outside the window rises into its Maytime flood (the beech leaves unfold like batches of tender umbrellas being raised; the hosta's unravelling tubes have sprung up all along the driveway), the interior of the house also prospers. The quail reappeared one morning on the dining-room table; dimly remembered doodads cluster more thickly on the mantels and end tables in the living room; one day, I don't doubt, the great blue living-room rug will reappear, like a revived lawn. Under Gloria's impassioned care the violated house is healing. Soon there will not be a single telltale scar of my transgressions.

———————

I awake each night around four and after urinating in the bathroom have trouble sliding back into sleep. Some vague wedge of dread jams the process. Gloria, unlike Deirdre, snores, not loudly, usually, but with enough variety of pauses and syncopation to keep me listening. The bed seems a slant surface from which I might fall into an abyss. That acrophobic dream about leaving Boston had widened a crack in me. I used to get back into sleep by trying to remember the dreams I was having, but my dreams these days are repellent shambles of half-forgotten faces contorted by the stress of old predicaments—unwanted pregnancies, amorous alliances swelling out of control, professional reversals in the antiseptic offices on State Street, children's clinging illnesses, the wounds and rebuffs they would bring home from school in tears, houses in Coverdale whose rugs and wallpaper are soaked in the acid humidity of domestic boredom and discontent, all shot through with a numbed but breathing version of the terror I felt in the basement with Milly's unbuilt dollhouse. Dreaming, I am unhappy, and yet in morning light I resist waking, lying in bed, collapsing into another doze, long after Gloria's footsteps have begun to make the house's well-built endoskeleton of joists and studs and beams tremble with her energy.

Walking down to the mailbox to pick up the *Globe*, I observe how freshly green leaves displace the forsythia's confetti of yellow petals, and squint up at the new object that has appeared in our heavens. Like the halo of iridescence that sometimes appears among cirrus clouds, it needs noticing, its very vastness, out of all earthly scale, being a kind of concealment. It is at least twenty times wider than the moon that Newtonian mechanics has appointed to be Earth's companion, and thrice again that than the abandoned honeycomb men placed in orbit before the cataclysmic war. This new moon, visible at night as a faintly luminous lariat slowly moving across the paralyzed sprinkle of stars, by daytime is imprinted on oxygen's overarching blue like the trace of a cocktail glass, a sometimes silvery ring of pallor. It may have existed—theories run—in prehistory; it may have hovered over the dinosaur herds, the first amphibians, the dead continents before the seas evolved life-forms more complex than algae. It is a spaceship, that much is clear, from somewhere either in our galaxy or even from another galaxy, for its appearance in our sky indicates that, unless against long astronomical odds its origin is but a few light-years away, its makers and steerers have with an unthinkable technology cut through the physical knot of space-time—have found a way to travel from point to point by the power of the mind. That mind was an alien element in the material cosmos has long been intuitively recognized, but scientists only toward the end of the last millennium formulated its primal place among the forces of creation. The particles smaller than a quark, it was reluctantly proclaimed, are purely mathematical, that is to say, mental. Further, the cosmos is exquisitely constituted in all its chemical and atomic laws to provide enough duration and stability for the evolution of intelligent life. Until such intelligence exists, the universe in only the most preliminary sense exists, somewhat as a play or script exists in textual form as a precondition of its being acted, its sets knocked together, and its lighting projected in three dimensions.

It has been abundantly shown by computer simulation that a universe less than fifteen billion years old and less than fifteen billion light-years across, containing fewer than a billion billion (10^{18}) stars, would have been too small to produce carbon-based life. We—and algae and earthworms and angelfish—needed all those exploding supernovae to make the heavy elements; we needed all the dark matter to slow the pace of gravity so life could emerge. In a universe wherein the gravitational fine-structure constant would be 10^{-30} instead of, as it is, 10^{-40}, everything would be 10^5 times smaller and 10^{10} times denser; our sun would be two kilometers across and burn with a hot blue light for a life of a single year. A planet equivalent to Earth would orbit this star once every twenty days and would rotate once every second, giving it two million days a year. But in the crowded, stronger-gravitied universe, stars would be tearing dark matter away from one another, and the planetary life-forms that might evolve—no bigger than bacteria in any case—would quickly perish. Sufficiently benign conditions require an initial density parameter set with an accuracy of one part in 10^{60}. These are the odds against mind's being a blind side-product of material forces: one in 1,000,000,000, 000,000,000,000,000,000,000,000,000,000,000,000, 000,000,000,000.

And yet I am insufficiently reassured.

The Deal

The slender torus that floats beyond the clouds but lower than the moon shows that somewhere in the universe mind has triumphed over matter, instead of antagonistically co-existing with it as on our planet. But the minds, or giant mind, behind this perfectly circular intrusion into our skies do not, or does not, communicate. Inspection with telescopes, where such instruments have survived the war, discovers no surface features, except for areas of slightly higher smoothness that may be viewing ports. The pale ring hangs up there like a dead man's open eye. Are we being studied as if by an ideally non-interactive zoologist suspended in a scent-proof cage above whooping, head-scratching tribes of chimpanzees? Or is it that there can be no more language between above and below than between a man and an underground nest of ants? Yet myrmecologists *do* communicate, in a fashion, with ant colonies, as does a small cruel boy who pokes a stick into one. We gaze upward at the staring ring and wait for the stick in our nest, the thrust of the Word beyond our poor words. It does not come. Only psychotics and publicity-seeking liars ever get abducted, and no detectable rays, from radio to gamma, emanate from the hovering spacecraft. Perhaps its projection here from the vastness of elsewhere consumed all its energy; perhaps it has simply nothing to say, having passed beyond the word-generating friction of ego-resistant space-time.

So we go about our low business within our shattered civilization as if the enormous low-lustre torus were not there. Many maintain it is not there. Today it seemed to me fainter, more nearly melted into the blue, as if slowly giving up its inscrutable mission. Mass illusions are common throughout history, sometimes manifesting themselves in elaborate consensual detail. Yet my belief remains that the object—

seven hundred kilometers in diameter by the best esti-
mates—is real, though composed of a substance impalpable
on Earth.

———————

The dread underlying my dreams may be surfacing in reality. There have been more sounds and signs of activity in the
woods, now that half the trees are in fresh leaf, making a
spotty curtain of green. Yesterday I heard hoots and thrashing sounds in the direction of the railroad tracks, and then
a regular hammering too loud to be a metallobioform. I
walked through the old hemlock planting, past the thick
clump of snowdrops, its heavy-headed ground-breaking
flowers melted away like their namesakes, with only a tiny
hard green nub left as evidence. Everywhere on the forest
floor the carpet of dead leaves is pierced by an oval, shiny,
not quite symmetrical leaf—Massachusetts mayflower, I
think, also called "false lily-of-the-valley." And goutweed is
springing up, and the miniature red leaf of burgeoning poison ivy. Out of sight of the house, wilderness begins. Dead
branches are strewn underfoot; fallen dead trees lean at a
slant on the still-living. Some sunken brush piles date from
the reign of the previous owner, when he and his sons
were young. Others, less settled and covered with needles
and leaves, arose in my earlier, more vigorous days here.
Ragged, tufted, littered granite escarpments divide the woods
here into high and low land; trespassers seeking a way to
the beach have worn a wandering path roughly parallel to
the creek that creeps, trickling and twinkling, through the
marsh that bounds our land. The escarpments make a series
of bowls in which interlopers, usually youngsters, feel sheltered and hidden enough to suck on their cigarettes and six-

packs, purchased a few steps away, across the tracks where the commuter trains hurtle. The voices and clatter arose from a bowl guarded from above by the spiky trunk of a long-toppled pine, and out of the sight of the tracks. I spied them from above—three young men with dark hair and what seemed heavy torsos clad only in thin white T-shirts, though the May air is cool, and promises rain.

They looked up startled—the human face, a flashing signal in our eyes, even in the side of our vision, as vivid as a deer tail—when I descended, with an unavoidable snapping of dead wood. I felt naked without a gun, though I had no reason to suppose that they had guns.

"Can I help you?" I asked—the standard proprietorial opener. I could feel my heart pumping, my blood rising in counter-aggressive reflex.

The sarcasm escaped them. They looked at me mutely. They were not Americans of direct African descent but distinctly dusky. Portuguese and Spanish blood had in some nocturnal tropical byway swerved to add a Negro tinge to olive skin. Distrustful brown faces, with black eyes as lustrous and vulnerable and angry as Deirdre's or the gelatinous orb that gazed back at me from the gliding train window last winter.

I restated my question: "Are you aware that this is private property?" They had begun to build something, with no tools other than one rusty hammer, a coffee can full of nails, and a hacksaw pitifully ill-suited to cutting wood. It was hard to guess, from the few branches they had aligned and insecurely fastened together, what kind of structure was intended, here on a slightly raised knoll of land amid the creased granite boulders.

"Who say?" one—the tallest—asked in turn.

"I fear that I say," I said. "These eleven acres are mine. If you doubt me, let's go together and call the police." Our little local downtown, with a blue-sided public telephone beside the convenience store, was not many steps away, across the railroad tracks. Haskells Crossing, our village is called; every crossing, on the B & M line between Gloucester and Boston, was named in the old days, and some of the names stuck, though the old Haskell estate has long been broken up into two-acre house lots. These boys had followed the tracks north, to a better life.

Another of them snickered, but was enough uncertain of the decorum of the encounter to avert his face, so that he directed at the leafing forest floor his mumbly reply: "Yeah you do that. You go find them, mister. They just love to come runnin', those police do."

The older, bigger one felt sufficiently on firm ground to offer a proposal. He spoke carefully. "We just want to make a little place here in case it rains."

"A little *cozy* place," the other speaker said. He was trying, I gauged, to match my initial tone of sarcasm. He was the nimble-witted lawyer of the group.

I was feeling ownership of this spot sliding out from under me. I looked at the third boy, the darkest and most slender; he seemed not much older than Kevin, and not as tall. "There is nothing cozy about this place," I stated firmly to him. "From this time of year on, there are tons of insects. There is poison ivy and scratchy briars. At night there are bats." My sense of it was they were city boys, out of Salem or Lynn but not all the way from Boston. "A few years ago," I told them, "there were rabid raccoons; one bite would kill you." Saying all this to the youngest gave me the courage to face the biggest and say in a voice artificially level, "I suggest you get off my land now." My hand at my side did itch for a gun, even that borrowed .22 with which I had beheaded the chickadee fifty years ago.

He said, expressionlessly, a surprising thing in reply: "Phil say you pay him rent."

"Phil? You know Phil?" I was as relieved as if Phil were a dear friend, to have a connection established between these youths and the adult world.

The little lawyer, as if not wanting his client to speak for himself, interposed, "My older sister, she know Deirdre. She told her the land all empty."

"It is not empty," I said. "I own it." I shifted my ground, perhaps disastrously. "There's lots of empty land, since the war." I was conceding an abstract squatters' rights, to entice them to go elsewhere.

"Less lately," the leader told me, with his deadpan factic-ity. His lips seemed stung and numbed by the words he was forced to utter. "Less now than there used to be. People movin' around."

The youngest one, whom I had appealed to as an image of my touching, grateful grandson, with a sudden wide wave of one thin and limber arm gave a pronouncement almost po-etic: "All these trees and dead rocks, they're not doin' any-body any good."

"They're doing *me* good," I told him in a grandpaternal tone. "Me and my wife. They're part of our living space."

My tone, or this curious term, made the lawyer of the group snicker again, and then as if to cover up this lapse he pleaded, his widening eyes focused on my face and daring me to look away, "We was thinkin' just a little watchin' post for the summer. Cold weather come, nobody can use it, promise."

"Watching post? What would you watch?" This was my

instinctive reply, but a wrong one. I should have instantly rebuffed the seasonal inroad. I was rusty at haggling.

The older one smiled, or at least his blunt, numb appraisal of me and my potential as an obstacle softened. "A lot of stuff goin' on" was his answer.

"He means pedestrian traffic," the lawyer said. "You may not know it, man, but tons of people use this path as a way to the water. We'd be doin' you a favor. We'd be keepin' people from gettin' up to your house."

"All these favors for free?" I asked—another mistake, a sarcasm taken as a concession.

"You said it," the spokesman eagerly agreed, his eyes staying fixed on my face in a kind of shining impudence. "No charge, absolute protection. We'll be makin' the place more tidy, too. Cleanin' up all this crap."

It was an area which I visited, as my physical activities became more restricted, no more than once or twice a year. When we first moved here, Gloria and I walked to the beach every week and roamed the woods stacking brush and planning bonfires. No more: this site was mine only by law. A litter of beer cans and plastic soda bottles had built up.

The leader reached down and picked up the hammer. In his plump olive fist it became a weapon. He said to me stolidly, "You ask Deirdre and Phil."

"No," I said, sounding prim and excited even in my own ears. "I will speak to my wife about this. And the police."

"Uh-huh." "Sure." "You go do that, mister." All had spoken, to reinforce one another; the three boys drifted closer together to make a dense unit that, by some force of anti-gravity, propelled me, my face hot with anger and fear, back up the hill. As I climbed the slope, which was slippery with dead needles, my heart labored and raced. Around me in the fresh leaves raindrops began to tick. Rain would chase the interlopers away, was my cowardly consolation.

But I did not, yesterday, describe the incident to Gloria. I did not want her to know more about Deirdre than she had already guessed. The house was healing. Even the useless old coffee-maker that had been stolen had reappeared in a lower kitchen cabinet, tucked behind the extra soup bowls. I did ask her, though, if she would like to borrow the shotgun back from the Pientas. I told her I had seen deer scat in the woods.

———————

Now in the suburban streets where some kind of order is still maintained, and even in the yards of those houses which are abandoned and boarded up or else burned-out shells, the vibrant magenta of crabapple outshouts the milder pink of flowering cherry, the dusky tint of redbud, and the diffident, sideways-drifting clouds of floating dogwood petals. The stunted old apple to the right of the driveway, much topped to keep it from intruding on the view, puts forth a scattered show of thin-skinned white tinged with pink, like an English child's complexion. The lilac racemes, once tiny dry cones the color of dead grapeskins, are turning large and soft and pale. Nearer to the house, the fattening azalea buds are bright as candy hearts.

However luxuriantly the crabapples down in the village are blooming, there is one in our side yard, toward the Kellys', that is half dead. Gloria, in a dictatorial whirl restoring the order that I had let, in her absence, slide, asked me to cut it down. "Give it a chance," I pleaded.

"It's had its chance," she said. "Do it, or I'll call the tree service and they'll charge three hundred welders and another three hundred to feed it into the chipper. You're always complaining about money, here's your chance to save some."

"Suppose I cut my own hand off."

"You won't," she said, in a tone of stern dissatisfaction.

Reluctantly I descended into the dank and spidery basement, sharpened the chain saw link by link with a dull round file, and adjusted its tension with a wrench and screwdriver. It has taken me years to get the trick of this adjustment; the clamp on the blade is out of sight, so one must feel one's way, as with sex or (I imagine) a root-canal job.

Quick-moving spring clouds shuffled sunlight in and out of the cool breeze off the sea. Being half dead meant that the tree in its other half was alive, with a pathetic dutiful effort of sap and cell division pushing a scattering of buds toward the cloudy, gusty sky, even as the lower branches snapped off like a mummy's fingers. As the saw—voracious and smooth-cutting in its first minutes, its bite juicy with fresh bar-oil— sliced off the dry lower limbs, I came to higher, smaller branches still moist, with green cambium, and I called Gloria over before I proceeded. She looked where I showed her the round wounds oozing water, and sighed: "Ben, you never pay attention, but every year we go through this. Some boy with the yard service cuts out the dead wood and we decide to let the rest go and see if the tree will thrive. But it doesn't. It doesn't thrive. Some bug is at it. Or it just isn't happy in this spot; it's never been happy. Too much salty wind, or the ledge is too close under the soil, or something. Cut it down. Now is the time. We'll find something else that will be happier. Probably an evergreen—a Douglas fir or a blue spruce." Seeing me still hesitate, with an expression on my face that must have been pained, she said, with one of the few smiles she has granted me since her return,

"Sweetie, you're overidentifying. You can't be sentimental if you're going to maintain a property. Here's your choice: let everything go to wrack and ruin so the value of the place drops to next to nothing, or else put this *very* unhappy crabapple out of its misery."

There was a pleasure, actually, in slicing up the helpless tree, amputating inwards, as the severed limbs accumulated in a high tangle on the lawn, and then cutting up the trunk in fireplace lengths as it stood there, a tall stump. The saw resisted, binding in the wet wood. The poor tree was still sending up sap to phantom buds. I dragged the limbs to the burning pit and stacked the trunk lengths in the garage, to be split some winter day. I too was half dead, but my other half was still alive, and victorious. The tree had gone from being my brother to being my fallen enemy. I gloated over its dismembered corpse, and resheathed the dull chain-saw blade in its sheath of orange plastic spelling STIHL.

This was days ago, in the tentative buddings of another season. Today, summer arrived, though it is still May. In Boston, the television said, the temperature hit ninety, and was close to that along the North Shore: the air of a different planet has taken over. The refrigerator works up a sweat. The sea seems sunken, greasy, like the concave underside of a silver ingot. The lilacs explode into pale violet and go limp, so that the branches sag out toward the driveway, brushing the sides of the delivery trucks that grind their way up through a haze of exhaust and pollen. Gloria goes off to Boston in a slinky summer dress that clings to her hips. She leaves it to me to put up all the storm windows remaining and to pull down the screens, and to install the air conditioner in our bedroom. It waits all winter in the closet under the attic stairs, beside the old bureau—a relic of my marriage to Perdita and one of the few items of furniture in the house I can call my own. When I wrestle the air conditioner up into my arms it has put on ten more pounds of weight; lugging it through three doorways and settling it in the open window, where it precariously rests on the aluminum fins that seat the combination windows and screen, stretches the outer limit of my strength. But the year I cannot lift it will bring my death closer in a quantum leap, so I manage to succeed, grunting and cursing and even exclaiming orgasmically in my spurt of muscular effort.

Gloria is not here as an audience but she is here in my mind; I am trying to make her feel guilty *in absentia*—a hopeless game. After a certain age marriage is mostly, its bitter and tender moments both, a mental game of thrust and parry played on the edge of the grave. If she finds me dead of a heart attack with the air conditioner in my arms she will never forgive herself: good. Why does she insist on having the thing installed, when in a day or two the weather will turn cool again? There is a magic moment, as the ponderous box teeters on its fulcrum of aluminum fins and I struggle with one free hand to lower the wooden sash so it slips into place behind the air conditioner's frame, when if I lose my sweaty grip the whole intricate and cumbersome caboodle will fall two stories to the flagstones below and sickeningly smash. This, too, would be good, teaching Gloria a lesson.

But it has not thus far happened. And will not this year. The metal monster secure, I tug out the accordion pleats of plastic that, screwed into metal holes, fill the rest of the window spaces, and plug the pompous three-prong plug into the socket that waits all winter for this moment, and turn on the chilling hum (with a low rattle in it as if it needs to clear its throat), and leave the room. Gloria is the one who must have air conditioning; the Hottentot secreted deep within me, the African grandfather, likes the heat undiluted— humidity-laden, lazy-making, caressing my limbs like an oily loose robe.

Outside, the heat has pressed from nature a host of fresh smells, musty perfumes of renewed rot and expanding ten- dril. The trees now have a blowsy look. Even the oaks, the last to leaf, have augmented their drooping yellow catkins with red-tinged miniature leaves, jagged and many-lobed. Stimulated by my triumphant wrestle with the air condi- tioner, I ventured into the woods, where I heard, close at hand, tapping and laughter. The acoustics of this acreage are such that sometimes voices and radio music from the town, across the tracks, sound uncannily near; but these noises seemed to arise beneath my feet. I took the gun.

Hosts of insects have been awakened within the thickened leaves and shadows. A dead millipede, half crushed as if by an unknowing footstep, lay on the bathroom floor this morning. I puzzled over it, the terrible tangled intricacy left behind by its absconded vitality, and, too squeamish to use my fingers, swept it up into a pan with a brush and dumped it into the toilet, and flushed. Until the flush toilet, did men have any true concept of the end of the world? Dozens of tiny mayflies were attracted to my sweat. Born to live a day, they were crazy for me; I was the love of their tiny lives.

The trespassers heard my footsteps, though I had tried to be stealthy. The three dun faces, darker now that the shade had intensified, were joined by a fourth, paler but still dirty- looking in the light here below the escarpments, near the path worn parallel to the creek still farther below. The fourth face was female, a skinny young girl's. Their little hut was a pathetic affair nailed together of fallen limbs, the buckling walls reinforced by forked branches broken off by last winter's particularly heavy snow and still bearing last autumn's leaves. For a roof, they had found some large scraps of gypsum wallboard, probably dumped by a local remodelling project and dragged across the tracks. They wouldn't hold up long in a good rain, I wanted to point out. But, peeking in, I saw an essentially cozy space, striped with light and furnished with a few metal-mesh lawn chairs stolen from somewhere in the neighborhood—not, I thought at a glance, from me. Mine had a wider mesh, and were safe in the barn. Where did they bed the girl, if they did?

Her presence among them lent a new tension to our encounter. Stringy and besmirched, she yet was a prize, slim and upright, with bony hips hugged by tight tattered jeans and taut breasts perking up her cotton T-shirt. She had a square jaw and a pale-lashed squint. No one introduced her; I gave her a nod. Her presence imposed a certain courtliness upon us, while bringing out a scent of danger and competition. I was carrying Charlie Pienta's shotgun, as if inadvertently. "I see you've finished your fort," I said.

"That's no fort," the biggest boy, the leader, told me. "We just use it to watch the path."

"And what do you see?" As if I were his captain and he reporting to me.

"Not much yet," he said, after a pause in which he grappled with the something wrong, inverted, in his answering my question at all.

The second in command, the quick-mouthed lawyer-type, sensed an opportunity to enlist me in their troop. "Not much yet, but what with the warm weather bein' here and schools gettin' out, there'll be plenty more for sure. They won't be gettin' by us."

"What'll you do?" I asked, genuinely curious.

"Turn 'em back, man."

"Suppose they don't want to turn back?"

"We have ways," the biggest one said, when his lieutenant said nothing.

"Well, this is very nice," I said, smiling at the stringy blonde girl, as if she and I could share a joke at the expense of these dusky thugs. "That's more than the police ever did."

"Police," the youngest said, the one that reminded me of my eldest grandson. "You ever call the police like you said you would about us?"

I turned to him, surprised and hurt by his challenge. "I'm saving them. I thought I'd give you guys a chance to clear out first. You know," I went on, my eyes returning to the girl, who must have been about fourteen, and had moved closer to the big mute leader—she was his girl, the gesture said—"this little hut of yours could be knocked down in ten minutes. I wouldn't be surprised to find it gone some morning when you show up. How do you guys get up here to Haskells Crossing, anyway?"

"Train," the leader said, as if obliged to speak by the pale girl's respectful pressure at his side. "From Lynn."

The little lawyer hastened to repair any breach this admission had made in their security. "Somebody going to be sleepin' here nights now," he told me. "Anybody mess with this place, he'll know it quick."

I shifted the gun to the other arm, glancing down to see if the safety catch was still on. The last thing I wanted was an accidental blast; but the tension inside me seemed capable of tripping the trigger without my touching it. "I haven't gone to the police yet," I admitted. "But the next time I see Spin and Phil, I intend to complain. I pay them good money to keep people like you from bothering me. They should be around any day now." In fact, now that I mentioned it, they were some days overdue.

The lawyer smiled, a lovable smile that tugged his upper lip high off his teeth, exposing a breadth of violet gum. "We about to tell you," he said, "Phil and Spin won't be comin' round. They asked us to do the collectin' in their stead. We what you call their proxies."

"Phil and Spin," the youngest said, with an expansive upward wave, as if their spirits had come to roost in the treetops, "they're delegatin'!"

"They're contractin' out," the lawyer amplified. "They gettin' too high up to do the plain collectin'; that's why they ast us. They said you a real good customer who wouldn't give us no bad flak. Some of these customers, they need persuadin'."

I was back, I felt with a happy rush, at work, in my office at Sibbes, Dudley, and Wise, doing a negotiation—shaving percentage points, feeling for weak spots. There were protocols to observe, procedures to follow. "How do I know," I asked, "you're empowered to act for Phil and Spin? Show me a document."

"You go show us Phil and Spin," said this lawyer in embryo. "Where they be, if they the ones collectin'?"

"The fact that they're not here," I said, "doesn't prove that you are their agents. Show me a written power, a document that Spin has signed."

"We don't go so much by documents," I was told. "We go by the facts on the ground. The fact on the ground is, Phil and Spin are phasin' out."

"Phasing out," I said, acclimating myself to a freshened chill of menace. "And you are suggesting that you're taking over their territory? Kids like you? You're playing with grown-ups, boys." I shifted weight, like a golfer doing his waggle, and the shotgun barrel swung lightly across the line of their feet and knees. They held their breaths.

Then the biggest of the three said, "You got a barn up there, right?"

I was surprised enough to hesitate.

"We been up there," he prompted. "Nice old shingled barn with horse stalls inside."

"From the horse-and-buggy days," I explained. "At the beginning of the last century. You know, the twentieth." I suspected they were quite innocent of history, of time. "Before the motorcar took hold, people still had buggies pulled by horses. You've heard of horsepower?"

Why did I want to teach these boys anything? I had no such impulse with my own grandsons.

"Be a shame," the biggest said, "that barn burned down. Lot of nice stuff inside."

Not so nice, really—bachelor furniture Gloria's sons abandoned in their social rise, a few ancient bow-topped trunks and a dismantled maple bedstead from the attic of my parents' house, an ornately gold-framed photograph of my mustached grandfather that I had not given to the Pittsfield Historical Society, spare or non-functioning power gardening tools, boxes of books that had overflowed the shelves in the house. Junk, but each a page of my life and a grief to lose to flames and ashes.

"You're actually saying you'll burn my barn down," I stated at last, to keep the negotiations clarified.

"He not sayin' no such thing," the lawyer intervened. "He sayin' only be one cryin' shame that barn started to burn. Up there on that hill, not much water pressure even if the fire fuzz do manage to show. Public services spread mighty thin these days. They be sayin' Haskells Crossing too poor to buy gas for the fire engines, these big old expensive pumpers they have from the old days."

I was impressed by his store of civic information, but I addressed the biggest boy, whom I thought his associate perhaps underestimated and overprotected. "If I do pay you the protection money, how do I know Spin and Phil wouldn't also try to collect? I can't pay double. That wouldn't be *fair.*"

At least that much was left of the United States after the Chinese war—a belief in fairness, rudimentary rights guaranteed to everyone regardless of creed or color. The boys accepted my point, wide-eyed there in the dappled, cavelike, buggy woods. As the sun passed noon, the shade deepened and dampened the air, and mosquitoes had begun to bite. Each of us in our conference now and then needed to flick a hand in front of a face being buzzed, or to slap a bare arm being bitten. In a universe only slightly otherwise constructed in its subatomic parameters, I reflected, there would have been time only for mosquitoes and sea slugs to evolve before the sun gigantically expanded and then titanically collapsed. "I would want a receipt," I told them, "and a guarantee that I won't be solicited by anyone else."

The second in charge told me, "We not so much into guarantees and receipts—we not signin' anything the police could use."

"You told me there are no police," I reminded him.

This made the pale girl smile. "Enough around to hassle you," she said. "That's all they're good for."

Her speaking up seemed to put us all on the same side of an unspoken gender divide. I advised the boys firmly, "If you are going to go into business, you must learn business methods. You must create a structure of *trust*. People aren't going to give you something for nothing, I don't care what kind of a world it is." As if this elementary lecture relieved me for

the moment of further obligations, I turned to the skinny female and asked her as if at a party, "And what is *your* name?"

She had smoky wary eyes, greenish. Her nose was straight,
with sore-looking nostrils. Her lips were thin, without lipstick; they began to smile in the complicity of politeness,
then she checked herself with sideways glances at her companions.

In the murky shuffling light, infested with the stabs of
swirling bugs, the most talkative of the boys became more
childlike and aggressive as the girl's ability to talk another
language came into play. He cocked up his oval face at me
and puffed out his lips. "She don't need to tell anybody her
name," he said.

"Doreen," she said in a voice soft but distinct.

"Are you from around here?" I asked her. My cocktail-
party courtesies seemed to stun her protectors. I was asking
her, as she sensed, what she was doing with these dusky
hoodlums.

"Near here," she admitted.

"A girl guide," I ventured. Guiding the interlopers from
Lynn around the local terrain: a girl Judas.

My politeness, my grave mature manner, no longer tempted
her. "These are my friends," she told me sharply.

I pictured her naked with the biggest, most stolid boy,
in the loosely built hut, while the other two kept watch.
She would serve him, inexpertly, fumblingly, but serve him
nonetheless. I resented her, knowing that tonight, lying beside oblivious, Boston-exhausted Gloria, I would want her,
this wan slice of forest sunlight, as I rarely wanted anything
any more. I would shift from my left side to my right side
and back again, imagining Doreen and me embowered in
the slitted light of that buggy, slapped-up hut. I would resist
relieving myself by setting my hand on my genitals—lumps

of obsolete purpose in wrinkled sacks of the thinnest skin—
knowing that Gloria would spot the semen stain when she
made the bed. I would become again an inhibited pubescent
lying sleepless and scared of unseen powers in that narrow
house on the hill above Hammond Falls.

I doubted that Doreen sensed my lust, it would have
seemed so ridiculous to her. But I could have been wrong. I
have never decided how alive women are to male desire,
their own sex tucked enigmatically between their legs, and
how much simply adrift they are, waiting for an irruption
whose unpredictability is part of its appeal.

The negotiations could go no further now. "I need some
proof that you guys are collecting for Spin and Phil," I announced, and then was immediately unsure if I had said it
aloud or merely thought it. In either case my self-assertion
was absorbed in the moist caverns of thickening greenery as
I, holding the comforting shotgun, ascended the slippery
slope up to my house.

———

Lobster boats, bright white in the glazed blue morning, with
red bumper rails, have reappeared in the bay, sentinels of
their patient, barbaric harvest. Each evergreen branch wears
a fringe of fresh pale growth; the Austrian pines have
erected candles inches long, all it seems in a few warm days.
Along the driveway, Siberian iris carelessly dug into the
daylily bed have flowered; their complexly folded heads of
imperial purple lift on slender stems above the matted jum-
ble of long leaves whose emergence as individual fleurs-
de-lys I so eagerly noted not many weeks ago. In the circle
in the front (or the back, Gloria would say) of the house,
bridal-wreath blossoms bend their thin branches low, and

enkianthus hangs out its little red-tinged, berry-size bells, beloved of bees. One day the fat and turbanlike rhododendron buds are about to pop, and the next day they have already opened, with azaleas and lilacs still unwilted, heaping extravagance upon luxury. Can there be enough bees to process so much pollen, so much nectar? The heedless June rush of it—the moon full and the color of cheddar as it rises through the eastward woods, the watchful torus at seven in the morning as faint as a watermark in expensive blue stationery, the dry bit of honeycomb most vivid at noon, unattainable and abandoned in its orbit. It rained last evening; at dinner we could see through the kitchen windows the soft sheets of rain released by the evening drop in temperature; the late light was dimmed by the downpour, whose silver threads thickened and shimmered like strummed harp strings against the backdrop of now-solid green. This morning, a wreckage of shed azalea blossoms was strewn on the drying driveway's splotched asphalt.

Bringing back milk and orange juice from the so-called convenience store—their convenience more than ours, I think—I was startled as I exited (now that warm weather is here, one has to step over baby strollers parked just outside the door and dodge ungainly boys sucking on candy bars and soda cans while squatting wearily on skateboards) by a long-legged woman in shorts, her hair grayed in quietly dashing stripes, a smile springing into her face like an advertisement for faithful flossing. Did we know each other? I thought not, but we well might have. Her lean, purposefully conditioned body and crisp tan Bermuda shorts, her canary-yellow polo shirt and discreet pearl earrings bespoke the clean and breezy class I had aspired to. We might have met in hallways muffled by plush carpet, at a fast-moving get-together in a Boston apartment before Friday-night Symphony, or beside the striped straightaway at a girls' day-school track meet, she young enough to be my mistress but old enough to have discarded a couple of husbands, each of whom had left her more comfortably off than she had been before. Or perhaps she had proved true to her first cotillion partner, and together they sat out the world's recent melt-down like a fast dance they did not have the taste for. They settled for a sloping lawn, a heated swimming pool, twin Mercedes whose vanity plates say HIS and HERS or RAM and EWE. As we passed at an angle there on the soda-stained sidewalk perhaps she sensed, between her legs or at the lim-bic back of her brain, my adoration. She flinched, or stiff-ened, as if walking through an automatic door. I would more than have died for her—I would have lived for her.

Born poor, I suppose I am fascinated by the upper classes. Lazily they accept me among them, too confident them-selves to care that I am an inwardly sardonic alien. Golf sea-son has begun, and I am over at the club three or four times a week, mingling at lunch, blending into the Wednesday and Saturday foursomes. Some of these men have never held a job. Their life stages have been marked by a succession of games: the child, introduced by his nursemaids to croquet and badminton and then given tennis and sailing and eques-trian lessons; the boarding-school boy, hardened at soccer and ice hockey and lacrosse; the college man, persuaded to risk his bones in the football line and test his eyes and nerves on the baseball team, while skiing becomes second nature on beery weekend trips into the White Mountains and the underwater high of scuba-diving is assimilated during rummy winter vacations to the tropics; the suburban hus-band, partnered with his wife at paddle tennis and matched against his old college roommate at squash; the country squire, ten pounds heavier and rosier in the face, caught up in the physically lighter but financially heavier exertions of polo and yachting; the paunchy man of distinctly mature years, passionate for the pedestrian challenge of golf and the poky interplay of Sunday-morning mixed doubles; and the stoop-shouldered dotard, still amiably feisty, extracting competitive thrills from billiards, bridge, backgammon, and yes, croquet again, in a more formal, white-clad version.

When St. Peter still sat guard at the pearly gates, how would he have judged these lives so devoted to regulated frolic? Not to mention the time-consuming fussing at the fine details of personal comfort, appropriate costume, fashionable vacation site frequented by like-minded others, and three sufficiently ceremonial meals a day? *Nothing achieved*, St. Peter might have inscribed in his golden ledger, his ever-write quill of angel feather checking off one more admissee to the voluminous, red-lined columns of the damned. But no; his angelic pen hesitates above the lambent parchment, then, moving across the ledger's gutter to the opposite page, indites with smiling resolution, *No harm done*, adding a checkmark to the cerulean tabulation of the saved. The elect of New England expect no less, and it is hard to imagine how Heaven could be an improvement for them over their earthly days. The minds of these purely ornamental men are well fortified for the playful monotony of chorally praising God, where sinners, accustomed to variety in their fortunes, would be driven mad.

The summer cycle of, to amuse us old guys, weekend sweeps and senior tournaments has begun, and last week I found myself playing in the third-flight finals against my buddies Red Ruggles and Ken Dixon. My partner was Fred Hanover, a dear, dimly known fellow-member considerably older than I, itself endearing. He is a former club champion. Flashes of calm prowess flicker between spells of topping the ball and of obsession with the sound his pacemaker is making in his chest; he has trouble not listening to his own heartbeat as his life is mechanically ticked away. He and I had avoided simultaneous collapse and ding-donged well enough to beat two previous pairs of oppponents. But playing against Red and Ken was strange for me, on a Sunday morning when the grass was still soaked and a chill breeze cut through my ill-chosen golf shorts.

We teed off in a flurry of friendliness but by the second nine, with the holes even, I had no trouble hating our opponents. My having played so many rounds with them fanned my smoldering fury at Red's sloppy, muscular whacking—his forearms thickened by a youth of scale-scraping and oyster-shucking—and Ken's excessively deliberate, time-wasting style, as if running through a long mental checklist before taking off. While the retired pilot hung for what seemed minutes over the ball before unwinding into it with his maddening mechanical consistency, I could not stop staring at, and detesting, his shoes, white shoes which were oddly thick-soled, like the single shoe a cripple wears to even out his stride. But these were *two*, two shoes exaggeratedly shoelike, like the corny shoes in old-fashioned comic strips, though unimpeachably serious and white. Still, some unfair advantage, or sneaking presumption, seemed involved, and when my turn at last came to drive on the par-five tenth I could not control an impatient quickness in the backswing and on the downswing an overeager boost from the right hand, my right elbow flying. The ball was pulled to the left but, by the same bad mechanics, sliced so that it curved back into the center of the fairway. I settled into the fairway wood with a restricted backswing and moved the ball over the traps and mounds to within fifty yards of the green. Meanwhile, Fred, with a good drive, muffed his second, third, and fourth shots, looking up each time and producing an agonized yelp and an agitated gesture as if to pluck the ticking heart out of his chest. His fifth shot made the transverse bunker and he picked up; the hole was on me. Both Ken and Red had been scrambling and it looked as if a par would win it.

The pin was on the front left of the green, perhaps twelve feet in. I planned a little bump-and-run down through the medium rough that on the second bounce would dribble onto the green and ooze to within a tap-in of the hole. It was as vivid in my mind as a tinted, crosshatched illustration in a how-to-play-golf book. Fred slouched over to my side, with his kindly, sun-battered, games-wise face, his thatch of dry old bleached hair pointing this way and that in the breeze. He pleaded in a soft voice, "Go for the center of the green, Ben. Get safely on."

He had not in the two previous days ever ventured advice, however in need of it I might have been. He felt pressure, and was communicating it to me. My cunning little bump shot, which had tingled like a done thing in my hands as they lightly gripped the pitching wedge, went up in smoke. "Really?" I said.

The former club champion didn't back off. "Get it on the dance floor," he said, his jaw clenched as if these were his dying words.

With masterful self-control I did not chunk the chip but flipped it down the safe, close-cut part of the slope so that the ball skipped onto the green, winding up twenty-five feet from the hole. "Grrrreat," my partner gratefully growled. He had been so insouciant these two days, his anxiousness grabbed at me now. It was only a game, wasn't it? I felt almost dizzily tall, walking onto the green with my putter. Fred had picked up, Red had skulled his chip clear across the green, but Ken had methodically—after hesitating so long I thought his cogwheels had jammed—chipped to within six or seven feet. If he sank it, he would salvage a par, and that thought led me, just under the scum of consciousness, not to lag but to try to sink, for an unbeatable birdie.

I was too stirred up to take note of the slope of the green here, or the close mowing that had left the grass the color and texture of toast. I charged the putt and in utter horror, as Fred grunted in the side of my vision, watched the ball (an unlucky found Ultra) skim across the left edge of the hole and nightmarishly keep rolling until *I was outside of Ken.* An abysmal embarrassment and incompetence possessed me; I walked to the hateful Ultra as if hiking to the ends of a sere and radioactive earth, then, hunched over, went blind, while blood beat against my eardrums like a raging prisoner. Blindly, numbly I lined up my second putt and stabbed at it and of course missed it, out to the right, ignoring the obvious break.

"Sorry, Fred," I said aloud, wishing him and all witnesses to my wretched three-putt dead. Even Ken's missing his makable seven-footer did not assuage my shame; it had been my hole to win and I had blown it. I had blown it, I secretly believed, because my partner had inserted his own competitive passion into the Zen zone I was attaining; but there was no way of saying this, and no way of redeeming my jejune blunder but by winning some holes. The harder I tried, the worse I got, overswinging, lunging, "swishing" the clubhead at the last fractional second, letting my right elbow roam away from my side to gain imaginary leverage. In the face of my uselessness, Fred plucked up some ancient proficiency; we scrambled and scrabbled up the slopes of this Sunday-morning match and ended two down on the seventeenth hole. We could have won it, and all my fault we didn't.

The Deal

Three-putting from twenty-five feet. I couldn't stop replaying the hole in my head; I took a sleeping pill but woke up at three in the morning back on that tenth green, dizzyingly tall above the receding putter-head, whacking the ball over and over again miles and miles past the hole while Ken, in his unbearable shoes, looked on in smiling wonder, as if a stewardess had just told him she would spend their London stopover in his bedroom after all, and my partner just out of sight around the corner of my skull grunted as if I had punched him beneath his pacemaker. I writhed; I thought of shaking soundly snoring Gloria awake; my eyes cursed the blank ceiling while my teeth suppressed a scream; I wondered what the point of human life was at all, if such dreadful things could happen under the sky.

Next morning, Memorial Monday, while saluting rifles rang out in unison in the town cemetery and television commentators put on their solemnest faces to chat for a minute about the millions who had given their lives *pro patria* in the recent war, Gloria told me I was taking golf too seriously. She wondered why I didn't give it up, especially since she could use all the help I could give in the garden, now that warm weather was at last here.

Give up golf? I love those men. They alone forgive me for my warts and stiffnesses, my tainted breath and protruding nostril-hairs, my tremors and white-capped skin cancers. My golf companions too are descending into deterioration, and trying to put a good face on it—joking, under the striped tent the club has erected, with a cold Beck's in one hand and an oily clutch of salted peanuts in the cupped other, over their own losses and lapses, life being a mess and a scramble at the best, men put here on Earth with hungers they must satisfy or they will die, and then they die anyway, men, men and women too, because for this ceremony of distributing prizes (Ben and Fred, Bradford Flight runners-up, *clapclapclap*) women, the wives and girlfriends and daughters and granddaughters of the players, have come to the club and are helping fill the tent with human talk and laughter, the chink of glasses and chomp of finger-food, the women in their perky summer skirts and knit polo shirts, women trim and lean and sun-weathered like the woman I saw outside the convenience store, women with their bright soprano voices gilding the brave baritone babble while unseen beyond the tent top the sad moons of transcendent witnessing and hollow endeavor lose and refind their pale shapes among the leisurely, operatic scurry of the fat clouds. Even Gloria came, stealing time from her garden, out of loyalty, wearing that straw hat we had bought years ago on St. Croix. I was touched, and gave her cheek a kiss in the cool shade of the sunny old hat, souvenir of our chummier days.

Going down to the barn to retrieve our two Have-a-Heart traps—deer aren't our only marauding pests; Gloria claims the woodchucks are just waiting in their endless burrows for her flower garden to ripen—I discovered a human body propped against the barn doors, in a sitting position on the plank ramp. I don't come down to the barn every day, and the smell of decay was ripe, much stronger than AgRepel. There is *musty*, which is what the AgRepel seemed, and *fetid*, which is what I catch when I inadvertently bend down over a toilet bowl whose under-edge has long evaded the scrub brush, and *stinking*, which is what a skunk, not entirely unpleasantly, does. Then there are *putrid*, *nidorous*, and *mephitic*—blasts from the rotting heart of nature, where Satan with his foul breath writhes encased up to the waist in God's implacable ice. We turn our faces away, ashamed for Creation.

The body was Spin's, I could tell by the mustache, and the natty combination of blue pin-striped button-down shirt and yellow paisley necktie with matching pocket handkerchief. His putty-colored summer-weight suit had been weathered out of press by wet nights and the bloating of the body within. The face, round and unformed now as a child's, was a mottled set of cheesy colors. A toothpick had been thrust into one open eyeball, like a martini olive—a childish cruelty in that—and the bludgeon or rocks that had been used on the top and back of his head had also been forcefully applied to his mouth, perhaps to loosen teeth thought to be gold. The corpse had attracted a cloud of buzzy supplicants, and the hands, rigid and hammer-fingered because of the pooling of blood in the tips, were crawling with small brown ants.

Even as I gagged, choking down regurgitation's burning acid, something in me soared free above this slumped puddle of deactivated molecules, soupily breaking down en route to their next combination. On the golf course one often passed the litter of a dove or rabbit torn apart by a hawk or fox or owl: a discreet little splash of feathers or fur, as temporary as a dandelion head. Except for the plastic threads in his suit and the tips of his shoelaces, Spin would melt back into the woodsy mulch like a gutted mole. The gallantry of his attempt to dress and talk well, above his station as an enforcer, had fled and mingled with the atoms of the air, purifying their cobalt blue. We had usually ended our monthly conference by professing how much we trusted each other. In ungrateful, chaotic times, we had built up a relationship.

I raced back up to the house. Gloria was off somewhere, I

hadn't been paying attention when she told me where, to the hairdresser or the pedicurist or aerobics or a Calpurnia Club luncheon or lecture. I was alone in the house with my heaving chest and the noisome, clinging afterscent of Spin's physical remains. I called the number for the police listed at the front of the telephone book. It rang three times and then a sugary automated voice clicked in, telling me to press the number 1 if this was an emergency, to press 2 if I wished to report evidence concerning a crime, 3 if I was requesting information concerning traffic conditions or the payment of traffic fines, and 4 if I wished to speak to the police for any other reason. I punched 2; the same sweet and unhurried voice told me to press 1 if the crime was violent, 2 if it involved theft, 3 if a white-collar crime, and 4 if it was a matter of a neighbor creating or maintaining a public nuisance or any other violation of civic order. I was beginning to sweat; I felt walled into a steel box. I punched 1, and then 4, and the voice told me pleasantly, with spaces between all the words, "We're sorry. At present, all lines are occupied. But please stay on the line, and a representative will be with you shortly. We value your call, and apologize for this delay."

Then came some recorded easy-listening music, old standards in arrangements with strings and without vocals. From my childhood I recognized the Beatles' "Penny Lane" and from my teenage years their "Get Back." The absence of the original lyrics was a political statement; since the war, the nominal government in Washington did not want any particular voices and themes that might cohere into rebellion. From the years of my marriage with Perdita there came "Call Me," by Blondie, and "Like a Virgin," by Madonna, both ghostly and purely soothing when severed from the rasping of their provocative chanteuses. I hung up, tried the procedure again, varied the procedure, but never succeeded in producing a human voice. For a tantalizing second there was a gap in the switching of automated circuits, but then the voiceless music closed in again. The police were impregnable behind their computerized deflectors. I dialled 911 and it was busy. I tried the fire department and got, on musical hold, some baroque tintinnabulation, Bach or Vivaldi, I didn't wait to determine which.

I hurried back outdoors. The birds—grackles, and a pair of raucous mockingbirds, and the nesting barn swallows— were filling the air with an excited squeak and twitter not much less mechanical than the incidental noises of evolving metallobioforms. The June sunshine beat down like a flattening template, giving each leaf and grass blade its shape. I ran down to the barn—a little lane once used by carriages and roadsters—and, as I had feared would be the case, Spin's body was no longer there on the plank ramp, leaning against the barn door, whose last coat of paint clung in green flakes like so many iridescent insects. There was just a shadow of dampness where the body had rested, and a lingering stench.

The corpse had been a message, in lieu of a certificate, and the boys had taken it away once it was read. I was being watched, though my quick visual search of the woods revealed only receding depths of fresh leaves, lobed maple and triform hickory and serrated beech, leaves invading and nibbling at the carbon dioxide, forming ragged caves and tunnels of air worming their way down to the tracks and the creek. I was apparently alone on my vegetable planet. A few burnt matches had been left on the barn planks, beside the two-legged shadow of dampness, as a hint of further dire possibility.

Without considering an alternative action, I walked down on the slithery pine needles, gripping trees here and there to halt my sliding, to the boys' hut. Only the biggest one was there. For the first time, without the intercession of the would-be lawyer and the mollifying presence of the youngest boy and the skinny blonde girl, I felt his weight as a man, his lethal capacity. My face must have shown the shock of my discovery, for he permitted himself the smallest of smiles, under the broad brown nose and opaque black gaze. "So," I said, with a conspiratorial casualness, "you *are* qualified to make the collections."

"Thass right. Spin, like we said, he took early retire-ment."

"Phil and Deirdre?" Why did I care? My voice had trem-bled.

"They're still around, maybe."

"Is the monthly charge the same?"

"We were thinkin' maybe it should go up a little. What with us providin' on-the-spot service."

He had mastered the corporate "we," which diffuses and masks all manner of brutalities and denials. "How much is a little?"

"We were thinkin', how about two thousand a month? You owe us for May. That makes four."

"Two and two still make four. That's some increase, from thirteen fifty to two."

He shrugged. Though I thought of him as the big one, he was several inches shorter than I. Even weightwise, I was bigger than he, though my pounds could not be mobilized like the rubbery pounds of youth. The chinks in the hut, I noticed, had been stuffed with moss—defense against insects if not yet the cold—and the gypsum-board roof replaced with some plywood scavenged somewhere. They were learning. America is one big education. Two thousand was a lot of welders, for a retired man in a chaotic economy, but it was still far less than the old government had extracted from me, in dollars, for its wars and universal medical care, its mad schemes of spaceships in the sky and equal opportunity for everyone. It would be hard for a boy from Lynn to grasp how much a white financial adviser could stash away over the years. He was asking peanuts.

"I'll have it for you tomorrow. I need to go to the bank for so much scrip. But I want something for it."

He was silent, blank.

"I want you and your buddies to stay down here on this side of the—" I didn't think he'd know the word "escarpment." I gestured and said, "these big rocks. Stay away from the barn and the house. I haven't mentioned any of this to my wife but if she finds out you'll be in another ballgame. She's a lot tougher than I—nowhere near as reasonable. She has that female thing of territoriality."

He still stared silently. There was nothing in my assertions and threats that deserved an answer perhaps. All the concessions had been made; I felt a certain craven pleasure and relief.

"Deirdre say," my opponent said at last, graciously to end the conversation, "you scared shitless of your old lady."

The spring is so advanced into near-summer it has turned soggy and lost all shape. Azalea, dogwood, lilac, the blossoms of fruit trees are all withered and fallen into the detritus of moist earth. White is the color of the moment—lilies of the valley, bridal wreath, the maple-leaf viburnum that clings to the steep bank in drooping pulpy limbs that take root at their tips. This sinister plant, when on the way down to the mailbox I put my face close to one of its wide compound flowers, has an odor of decay, echoing the mephitic aura around Spin's body. I can't believe the boys are going to drag that body elsewhere, to prove themselves to another protection customer, but I would have heard, I think, the sound of a shovel digging a grave on my land; you can't go down three inches without striking a rock. They came up, all three of them, as far as the barn to collect the packets of sepia paper I had withdrawn from the bank, and Gloria had spotted them from a third-floor window.

I explained who they were—the successors to Spin and Phil.

"I think you're ri*dic*ulous," she told me, "to have anything to do with men like that. And now boys. I wonder if any of them would like to work for us a few hours each week, helping out on the grounds? I'm *dev*astated that Jeremy is thinking of giving up school and going to Mexico."

Mexico, which had remained neutral during the Sino-American Conflict, was attracting many of our young people as a land of opportunity. Those who were denied legal admission were sneaking across the border in droves, while the Mexican authorities doubled the border guard and erected more electrified chain-link fences. They were talking of a Chinese-style wall, along Aztec design lines.

"I don't think these boys want yard work. They're into criminal activity, and very dangerous. You let me deal with them."

Gloria had been thought when young to have promise as a dancer, and until her mid-teens had taken ballet lessons. Whenever she wishes to assert herself, she straightens her back and splays her feet, as she did now. "Ben, you really shouldn't be handing them money. It's pouring it down the drain and giving them a false sense of reality. Call the police. You say there aren't any, but I see them all the time—just yesterday morning, three of them, all young and in uniform, were directing traffic around the collapsed road on the way to Magnolia."

"They were moonlighting," I said. "Or else it was bandits in stolen uniforms. They rob the armored trucks and UPS vans."

"They were *very* courteous to me."

Jeremy had come to us from a local fundamentalist college. He had a handsome but small head no wider than his powerful, flexible neck, so that at moments he displays a serpentine grace. I had become dependent upon him; his appearance on a Saturday or Sunday morning would galvanize me into an attack on the outdoors I no longer could muster by myself, however earnestly Gloria nagged. Together, Jeremy and I would lop, haul, dig, Preen, trim, mow. He had long slipped away from fundamentalism and would confide, if he seemed sluggish, that he had been hitting the bars in Gloucester and had gone on to some girl's apartment. But his natural Christian mannerliness spared me any details that might have made me jealous—whether the girl had a roommate, if she got into the act, if the girls did anything to each other while he watched—details my thick skull craved, out in the laborious sunshine. Jeremy can start all the power tools—the leaf blower, the weed-whacker with its spinning nylon string—that gum up, for me, on their infuriatingly viscid and approximate mixtures of oil and gasoline. As we grub away side by side at some desolate patch of garden which Gloria wants to restore to the supposed state of glory it enjoyed in the fabled days of household staffs and freshly imported Italian gardeners, I reflect on how little it takes to breed a relationship: paternal and filial feelings flow between us like inklings of sexual attraction. One day when a black hornet stung me below the eye, his voice shook in worry and concern, which I tearfully shrugged off. He admires my limberness as we scramble about on the rocks with armfuls of clippings for the burning pile or the compost heap, or together shinny into the ornamental apple trees to clip off the upright suckers that are poking into Gloria's view of the sea. I encourage him to go to Mexico. I tell him he is lucky to be young in a world that is full of gaps and the opportunities underpopulation affords. My world when I was young, I tell him, was crammed with other so-called baby boomers, so that I advanced and made my little pile only by means of twelve-hour days and claustral conformity to the fully staffed pecking order. As he ducks into his old Nissan with a supple undulation of his sinuous bare-naped neck, I feel an erotic pang.

Sex seems everywhere, now that humid heat has become a daily thing. Warm weather creates sexual hallucinations. In the waiting room of my periodontist, the smiling hygienist summons a male patient (not me) upstairs to a "blow job," or so I hear her say. Near the beginning of my vast dental experience there was a Miss Edna Wade, assistant to Dr. Gottlieb, one of two Jews in Hammond Falls (the other ran the little local movie theatre, which closed in the Seventies). In cleaning my teeth, Miss Wade pressed her great round breast against my hot ear until its wax melted and I feared the zipper on my fly would rip.

With Gloria off to Boston on a cluster of her errands—shopping for slipcover material, having lunch at the Calpurnia Club and tea at the Ritz with a pre-war friend from the Winsor School, topped by a facial and a pedicure—and the outdoors a forbidding jungle, I went to my cache of pornography, which is tucked behind a uniform set of sturdy Bible commentaries once owned by Gloria's reverend great-uncle, and excited myself with the absurd combinational permutations of a paperback called *Rex and Flora: Virgin into Vixen*. When my erection, in response to Flora's expert administration of fellatio to a delivery boy, had attained full stretch, with my left hand cupped nurturingly about my balls, I admired it—the inverted lavender heart-shape of the glans, the majestic tensile column with its marblelike blue-green veins and triple-shafted underside. Stout and faithful fellow! My life's companion. I loved it, or him; erectile heat suffused my system with the warm blood of well-being; for these pumped-up instants I felt no need to justify my earthly existence; all came clear. I wished that my neck were as flexible as Jeremy's so that I could dip down enough to do an adoring Flora on myself, imbibing at least that first translucent drop of pre-cum (as the porn books spell it) if not the thicker, curdled cream my swollen old prostate gland sluggishly releases, minutes after my climax.

If I did not have so many friends, at the club and at the office, who have had prostate operations and suffer the indignity of incontinence and the desolation of impotence, my erection might have been less prideful. Often enough in my youth it had been a mere embarrassment, an inconvenience to be cleared away, dismissed with a hand or a handy vagina, so as to get on with life's real business. What was so real, I now try to remember, about that business? Showing up on the dot of 8:35 a.m. at Sibbes, Dudley, and Wise, playing honest Iago to the blind and innocent Othello of the filthy rich, trying from the safe distance of State Street to outguess Wall Street in its skittery, dragonish gyrations—chimerical and numerical ephemera, in the backward glance. Nothing as solid and real, I feel, while my grip on my best self slackens, as this stiff prick, a gleam of tasty pre-cum unlicked at its tip.

I am conscious as my days dwindle of how poorly I have observed the world. The plants in their pulpy, modest complexity; the styles of sky and sea which like the whorls of fingerprints never quite repeat; the precise tint and fit of the rust-stained chunks of granite the vanished Italian masons built so lovingly into walls and terraces all over this property and its miles of brothers along the North Shore. Sitting on the toilet yesterday, I suddenly saw as if for the first time the miraculous knit of the Jockey underpants stretched across my knees. Tiny needles, functioning in cunning clusters at inhuman speeds, had contrived to entangle tiny white threads with perfect regularity to form this comfortably pliable, lightweight, and slightly elastic fabric. Engineers had planned and refined generations of machines, giant looms deploying batteries of hooked needles scarcely thicker than a hair yet containing moving parts, minuscule springs and latches, to duplicate mechanically the intricate knitting action of patient human hands. On all sides I am surrounded by such wonders of fabrication, those of human creation most decipherable but no less deserving of praise than those of that blind weaver, Nature.

But in fact I am dull and disintegrating. Strange complaints send dispatches along the neural network. A sharp little come-and-go pain beneath my left ear—the first cry from a lymph node choking on cancer cells? A sensation, upon awaking, of a film upon my eyes, obscuring vision for a half-hour into the day. Sudden thrummings and twitching just beneath the skin of my face. Sudden urgent urinary requests from below my belt. Not to mention arthritic finger joints, nocturnal stomach aches, and the mysterious mur-

murings and twinges the heart emits as it labors away day and night in the mushy total darkness within my rib cage. Which of my many interior slaves will first rebel and bring down in a chain of revolution my tyrannical reign? How much thankless effort these visceral serfs exert to maintain idle, giddy, fitful consciousness upon its throne inside my skull!

This morning a radio voice between doses of Offenbach and Buxtehude promised temperatures in the eighties; the sea, I noticed, was smoky in its flat calm, somewhat the way it is on the coldest January day, when the sub-zero air pulls vapor up into its crystalline nothingness. The widespread mist this morning blurs the horizon and all but obliterates the little dark strip that is the South Shore—Hingham and Cohasset and all that—where useless old lecherous men are also rising and putting on exquisitely manufactured underpants.

Walking down to the mailbox for the *Globe*, I pause to study the pink laurel, just now, in mid-June, coming into bloom. Each apparent single bloom, as with my spent rhododendrons, is a cluster of small sticky-stemmed pink-white flowers, each a strict pentagon with a deep-green center, a decorative circle of blood-colored angles and arcs, and ten stamens whose dark-red anthers are socketed halfway up the pentagonal vessel's side, each white filament arched like a catapult spring, the pistils erect and ruddy-headed in the center, the whole formation as precise and hypnotically concentric as a Hollywood water ballet filmed from above. Amid such patterns infinitely multiplied we make our aimless way; nature's graph paper, scored in squares finer than a molecule's width, deserves tracing less coarse than our erratic swoops of consciousness. All this superfine scaffolding, for what? The erection for a few shaky decades of a desperately greedy ego that tramples through the microcosmic underbrush like a blinded, lamenting giant.

———————

The two pretty laurel florets I had on my desk to pose for my description yesterday are shrivelled today to the size of squashed insects. Their etched petals and pistils and anthers had been mostly water and are now returned to the vapor of the air.

And, walking down the driveway, I saw that though the Siberian iris are gone and the daylilies yet to bloom a few white iris have hoisted their flags—those floppy petals that each have, I discover in Peterson's *Field Guide to Wildflowers*, distinct names. The upright one is a standard, the lower one a fall, and the smaller ones are called, it seems, style arms.

Gloria's peonies are in full fluffy romp, and her roses a few days short of unfolding. A clump of great phallic lupine lords it over her small garden behind the former greenhouse, a garden fenced in by a balustrade salvaged by the previous owner when he tore down the seaside veranda. The lupine petals are miniature pouches, purple and white distributed up and down the stalk like school colors in a cheerleader's pom-pom.

And birds. It has been a wonderful spring for birds. The mother swallow pokes her tiny sharp head over the edge of the nest as she furtively sits hatching her clutch. A shiny brown bird hangs upside down in the farthest extension of the drooping hickory twigs outside my window, worrying at something invisible to me—a grub, an arboreal sweetmeat of some sort. Robins, it has come to me sixty years after my first-grade teacher, Miss Lunt, made so curiously much of

them, spend more time hopping along the lawn and driveway than they do in flight or on a branch; and their flight has
a frantic beating barrel-bodied quality, like that of pheas-
ants. Without knowing it, they are forsaking the air. In some
millions of years robins may be as wingless as dodos and
great auks but, instead of extinct, as common as rats, and as
little cherished. In noble contrast, the swallows dip and flip
through the ether as if they own the invisible element.

Beatrice was in the neighborhood with her two boys and
came by for tea. She and Allan live in Wellesley; of my two
sons he has more nearly taken my path through life, beginning, however, not in semi-rural poverty but in suburban
comfort. He works in Boston finance, not as I was, a hand-
holder of individual rich widows and booze-sodden scions,
but as the assistant manager of a mutual fund, that marvel-
lous device whereby even the slightly monied masses can
partake in a conglomerate portfolio. His is called Pop-Cap,
or Low-Yield, or Slo-Grow, or something. For a time he
was in Chi-Hi, specializing in issues trading on the Hong
Kong and Shanghai exchanges. The great war put a crimp in
that. Yet, since by the terms of the Sino-American treaty the
island was reassigned back to our faithful allies the British,
Allan sees wonderful opportunities ten or so years down the
road, when mainland China becomes less radioactive and
reacquires an infrastructure.

Beatrice is dark-haired and beginning to go stout. But just
beginning—her face is a pearly madonnaesque oval with
sumptuous long black eyebrows that thicken toward the
bridge of her nose, giving her an aristocratically vexed look.
Beneath her pinched white nose her rosebud lips are often
pursed and sulky. Her figure's growing opulence was em-
phasized in a crisp summer frock, coral in color, that exposed her upper arms and when she crossed her legs, as

we sat on the side veranda, gave me plenty of pale thigh
from which to avert my eyes. Having so ripe a young
woman—"young" changes its meaning; she is about thirty-
five—as my guest (Gloria being off to a Garden Club
conference in Framingham on the diseases and parasites
common to flowering shrubs) had a lyrical illicit side, an in-
cestuous shadow we tried to disperse by sitting out here in
the afternoon sunshine while Quentin and Duncan played
on the lawn. Played, that is, in spurts of about five minutes;
Quentin, though older, was sluggish and suspicious and kept
dragging himself to his mother's side, thumb in mouth
though he is almost six, while his three-year-old brother hy-
peractively scampered and skidded from rock to bush to the
croquet balls and mallets I had brought out of a spidery corner of the gardening shed for their visit. I had also found a
semi-deflated soccer ball, which in one minute flat had vanished into the nebulous, depressed area of prickly wild roses
just off the side lawn.

"Duncan hit me," Quentin said, removing his thumb for
the time it took for this utterance. "With one of those
sticks," he said, popping his thumb back in and rolling upward to his mother's face eyes the same seductive sherry-
brown as her own.

Beatrice still smokes, endearingly. Accepting the child's
heavy head on her bosom without burning him or spilling
her tea intensified the look of black-browed vexation that I
found attractive.

"Mallet," I said, pedantically grandpaternal. "Those colored sticks are called croquet mallets. You're supposed to hit
the ball through the little hoops with them. They're called
wickets. Shall Grandpa show you again?"

I had shown them once. Little hyper Duncan had listened
intently and then with a whoop of glee had whirled through

the layout I had set out, whacking each wicket until it went flying. Now the child, dressed in flowered bib sunshorts, had toddled to Gloria's rose bed and was rapidly tugging off buds, chanting in anticipation of our rebukes, "Naughty! Naughty!"

"Dunkie, you cut that out!" Beatrice called, but lazily, wearily, in a rote tone the child could ignore. She dragged on her cigarette and let her voluminous exhaling express depths of quiet desperation. The smoke made its way among Quentin's glossy curls, and the child solemnly blinked his pink eyelids. The languor of the child's frail, unambitious white limbs disturbingly suggested to me how my daughter-in-law would dispose herself in bed.

I raced off the porch to rescue Gloria's roses, which had been a bit tough-stemmed for Duncan to damage much. He had pricked himself on a thorn, and his little square stubborn face, yellowish with a child's unthinkingly acquired tan, creased and wrinkled as a wail of protest built up inside his chest. He squinted up at me dubiously and then, with one shaky suppressed sob, held up his pricked thumb to my face. It was sticky like an old penny candy against my lips; his face gave up on holding back tears. I lifted him into my arms and, though my knees threatened to buckle under the weight of his soul in that curious elderly reflex of mine, carried him into the shelter of the porch.

He showed his mother his wounded thumb. "Grandpa kiss," he said.

"Thank you, Ben," Beatrice said. "I can't keep up with him."

"Beatrice, who could?" Our first names leaked into the sunny air like rumors of an affair. Undressed, she must have as many white knobs as a thunderhead. "How's, uh, Number One's number-two problem?"

"Some days he seems to have the idea," she allowed, passing the teacup and saucer around Quentin's obtrusive curly head, "and then he loses it. When Al and I talk poo to him he looks at us as if we're incredibly crazy and in *very* poor taste. I guess it *is* sort of disgusting if you think about it. Like a lot of things. But don't normal children, if it feels good, forget about its being in bad taste?"

"I would think," I said, as if I personally didn't know. I shied my mind away from picturing my daughter-in-law settling her white bulk on the toilet seat and letting her ample fundament part to give nature its daily toll of fecal matter. Feels good, does it? Here on the veranda, as the westering sunlight advanced like a slow tide across the porch boards and lapped at our feet, the click of her cup and the sigh of her exhaled smoke seemed embarrassingly loud. The buggy heat held the muted smells of excrement, sex, death. The kousa dogwoods that Gloria had had the tree service plant, over toward the yew hedge that screened us from the Kellys, bloomed in their unsatisfactory way: white bracts strewn among the green leaves like pieces of paper sewn to the upper side of the boughs. I searched for a topic to fill our silence. "How's Allan liking his work?"

Beatrice responded pouncingly. "He *loves* it," she exclaimed with exasperation. "All that computerized buying and appraising. He can't stop talking about the wonderful Asians, the ones that are left, their enterprise and diligence and so on. I think he thinks Westerners are relatively decadent, and overweight. Like me. I feel I should be Japanese or something to please him. One of those little Thai beauties he comes home raving about after one of his trips to Bangkok."

Both boys had begun to wriggle in our arms at the mention of their father's name. Duncan became a bundle of wiry muscle; as he and Quentin returned to the mallets and balls on the sunstruck lawn, the older boy's movements were by comparison mincing, female, constipated. He had inherited, perhaps, my melancholia. I thought of it as coming upon me in old age, but in truth I had always moved on the edge of depression. The house in the Berkshires had step-worn floors and moldy wallpaper clinging to the plaster walls of the narrow stairwell. Oilcloth on the kitchen table, linoleum on the floor. Fields of sallow corn stubble outside, and the unheeding rush and swoosh of traffic along Route 8. Great headlong loads of cut logs, tree corpses, went by, from the pine plantations to the north, whose murky aisles of trunks showed a few splotches of sun and hid bear-shaped intimations of mortality. The doll's house in the neglected basement. The marauding deer in a ruined world. The blurred corpse of the millipede. The laurel florets shrivelled to nothing. As a child I loved life so much the thought of its ever ending cancelled most of the joy I should have taken in it.

"Gloria's not much here, is she?" Beatrice asked, showing me her profile as she gazed toward the boys, softening any malice in the question.

"Gloria," I said loyally, "is astonishingly busy. She works like a dog on this place, and then rushes over to the gift shop. Her two partners, she says, are utter featherheads. And then there are appointments with her hairdresser, her manicurist, her aerobics instructor—I can't keep track of how many people she has on her personal maintenance crew."

"Gloria is very beautiful," Beatrice said, but listlessly. "Maybe an aerobics class is what I need. That, or give up alcohol. They say you drop five to ten pounds right away. How do you find it, Ben, not drinking?"

"Like waking up in Kansas every morning. But at least you don't have a headache or a lot of fuzz in your mouth."

"I need the lift," she confessed. "Allan says it's all right, the Asians drink like fish. He says they never had their heads fucked over by the Judaeo-Christian God. The Japanese killed the missionaries, and the Chinese let them in here and there but never let them get an audience with the emperor. Just kept them waiting outside the palace for generations. *Duncan, stop that!*"

The smaller boy was tormenting the older, by gleefully pretending to pull down his pants. Young as Duncan was, he knew where his brother's weak spot was. Quentin wheeled frantically, trying to fend him off. The mockingbird had set up a sympathetic screeching from within the big yew bush the deer had nibbled. In mating season the bird had amused us by perching on the top of the flagpole, leaping up with a complicated call and turning in mid-air and then settling on the top of the flagpole again. The boys' agitated whirling was like that, only suffused with Quentin's embarrassment and little Duncan's ferocity. "Poo!" Duncan kept shouting with fierce glee. "Poo!"

Sunlight had crept up our ankles and bounced dazzlingly off the glass top of the wicker table and the china cups and saucers. When Beatrice bent forward to douse her cigarette in the remains of her tea, sunlight plunged down her coral-colored neckline into the socket of damp, warm space between her breasts. The kiss of the doused cigarette hung in the air. "They're at each other like that all day," she said. "I pray for first grade next year." Her eyes stayed fixed on her plump hand, where it hovered with opened fingers above the cup of cooled tea. Her eyebrows had knit up a vertical wrinkle between them. How nice it would be, I thought, to be beneath her and feel her breasts sway, heavy and liquid, across my face, my open mouth, my closed eyelids.

In his desperation Quentin had seized a croquet mallet and I feared would do his savage little brother an injury; I raced out onto the lawn and took the weapon from him, while snapping, "Stop it! Enough is *enough*." The boys, with their workaholic father, were so little used to masculine discipline that both made teary faces and ran to their mother, where she sat on the white wicker sofa in a kind of slumber, a non-intervening goddess. She took my intervention as a criticism, and bestirred herself to depart, replacing her cup on my tray, and attempting to stand. Quentin slouched against her so tuggingly that one strap of her frock slipped down a rounded brown shoulder and bared a milk-white strip of bulbous boob. The darker, areolar flesh around her nipple would be pimpled, I figured, with a delicious roughness. "That was darling, Ben," she said, readjusting her strap without hurry. "Good tea. You must bring Gloria to Wellesley one of these days; I need all kinds of advice with the garden. It's getting out of hand, just like the children. Allan works these beastly hours, but the fault is mostly mine. I've become such a slob; all I want to do is sleep all day and eat all night, and then throw up in the morning." She stood, and yawned.

"It sounds like—"

"It is. We've been keeping the news to ourselves, hoping it would go away. Seven and a half more months, I can't stand it! I'm too old to be making babies."

"Bea, that's *beau*tiful." I lurched toward her, barking a shin on the glass-topped wicker table.

"Or plain stupid," she said, closing her eyes and letting herself be kissed on the cheek much as Duncan had let me kiss his pricked thumb.

"How much of a secret is it?" I asked.

"You can tell Gloria, but not your children, if you don't mind. Allan's a little embarrassed, he doesn't want Matt especially to tease him. It wasn't planned, of course. We don't believe in more than two."

"That's very old-fashioned of you. The world must be re-populated," I told her.

"For another slaughter of some kind," she sighed. "Still, I wouldn't mind if it were a girl. Among the cousins, the tide seems to have turned that way."

"Give Jennifer a little competition," I said encouragingly.

"Competition," Beatrice said, closing her eyes once more and shuddering. Standing in the slant light, she was cut di-agonally in half, like the big-eyed queen of spades. She wears her glossy hair centrally parted and twisted up into a chignon, so the nape of her neck shows, with its symmetri-cal swirl of fine uncaught hairs. To put one's lips into that down: like an armpit, but softer.

"Makes the world go round," I finished for her. "That's thrilling," I said, trying to strike the right briskly enthusias-tic fatherly-in-law note, "about the baby." But the prospect of an eleventh grandchild made my life feel even more su-perfluous and ridiculous, lost in a sea of breeding. The three Wellesley Turnbulls buckled themselves back into their claret-red Mazda with a smoothing show of familial affection and sticky kisses, but the visit left me depressed. My exchange with Beatrice had been all irritable foreplay, ending in biological jealousy of my son; through the inter-play of his two boys I had looked down once again into the dismal basement of life, where in ill-lit corners spiders brainlessly entrap segmented insects, consume them bit by bit, leave a fuzzy egg sac, and die. All those leggy spider corpses, like collapsed gyroscopes, that we see dangling from cobwebs—did they perish of starvation, having spun a web in vain, or of old age, in the natural course of things, after years of drawing upon Medicare and Social Security?

Lonely, frightened, I walked into the woods and down the slope, grabbing branches to prevent a skid that might break old bones, to see if my friends from Lynn were at their post. I could hear voices, including a female voice, halt as my steps crackled on the sticks underfoot. An extension had been made to the hut, a wing roofed in the corrugated opaque plastic sold in lumber-supply depots and framed in crisp two-by-fours—no more dead branches as supporting timbers. There was a raised plywood floor and a wall of mosquito netting. Two shadows lurked behind the netting, and the face of the blonde girl appeared in a parting. "Oh it's you," she said, in a voice flat but not especially hostile.

"Am I interrupting anything?"

"Just sittin' and socializin'," the other shadow called out. It was the loose light voice of the youngest of the three boys. "Wasn't you just havin' company?"

"My daughter-in-law and two grandsons."

"That's some red Mazda she drives. Drives it fast, too."

I didn't like the sensation of being spied on; Gloria and I had bought this place because of its privacy. "Where're your two associates?" I asked.

"Out hustlin'," the boy said.

"Doing stuff," the girl amplified, distrustfully.

But I had paid up my tribute until the first of July and was determined not to be rebuffed. "I see you've added a screened porch."

"The bugs were gettin' bad."

"You said it." I slapped loudly at three, one real and two imaginary. "What's it like in there? Must be nice."

They were reluctant to respond, but were too young to be coldly discourteous. "Have a look," the boy called, and the girl lifted a piece of the netting so I could stoop and step in.

It was heavenly inside the tiny shelter. The stolen wire lawn furniture made the perfect minimalist fit, and there was a spare chair for me. Sunlight filtered through the corrugated plastic roof as an underwater tint of speckled green; the trees in my woods took on a vaporous, gesturing presence outside the walls of mosquito netting, which had been fixed to the floor with a tidy row of rocks.

"Just thought," I said, seating myself, "I'd come down and see how you're all doing."

"Not complainin'," the boy said. Until, the implication was, my visit gave him cause for complaint.

The girl was, a shade, more forthcoming. "José and Ray are off on business," she volunteered.

"Good, good," I said, stretching out my legs expansively. "That used to be me, off on the train to Beantown every day, working eight, nine hours at the least, eyeball to eyeball with the other sharks. The trick was to get control of some rich widow's millions and then churn the money for the benefit of your broker friends. Or administer a nice juicy trust for point eight percent per annum. Pension funds and retirement plans—they were another boondoggle; the poor fat cats couldn't make head or tail of the quarterly statements. People who have money, by and large, have a subconscious wish to lose it. A kind of financial death-wish—the species' way of balancing things out. You've heard the phrase 'Rags to riches to rags in three generations.' Or am I talking too much? I love the netting; it makes this into a really enchanted interior. Another couple of rooms and you might turn this into a little seafood restaurant." I noticed, through the opening into the first room, walled with branches and roofed in plywood, a bedless mattress striped with slivers of sunlight, like a nest of golden straws. "It must be tough at the end of the day for you guys to go home to your slummy triple-deckers, or wherever you live."

"Not too tough. Night is really spooky," the girl said. "There's *things* out there. Ticking things."

"I squash 'em with *rocks* when I see 'em," the boy announced, his spindly arms showing how, in vigorous arcs.

"My name's Ben," I told the girl. "I believe yours is Doreen. Nice to meet you. How old are you, may I ask? Fourteen?"

"Just about," she agreed.

"And you"—to the boy—"must be about the age of my grandson Kevin. He's eleven."

The child wordlessly nodded, vaguely feeling that much more conversation with me would be a betrayal of his peers. He saw that I was a smooth talker when I wanted to be.

"I'm sixty-six," I told him. "Imagine that. When I was your age, if anybody had told me I'd be sixty-six some day I'd have laughed in his face. When I was young they used to say, 'Don't trust anybody over thirty,' and now look at me."

He looked, with his eyes like globules of oil. I asked him, "Shall I call you Kevin Number Two?"

His eyes went to Doreen and outside to the spectral trees and back to me. He knew giving up your name was a possibly fatal concession. "Manolete," he murmured, just on the edge of my hearing.

"A great bullfighter, once upon a time," I told him. "A fine and famous name. Carry it proudly, Manolete, as you perform in the arena of life. May your *pases* always be pure and the crowd ever award you both ears and the tail." Lest he think I was mocking him, I explained to him, "It's time that does it. It turns you from eleven to sixty-six in what feels to you a twinkling. Once gone, time leaves no trace. It's out there in space, out of reach. The arrow of time. Some scientists think its direction is reversible in quantum situations, and others think it would be reversible if the universe were as smooth at the end of time as it was in the beginning. I can't quite picture it myself." I turned back to Doreen: "How are Ray and José doing, at business?"

"O.K., I guess." She didn't sound convinced.

Manolete, named, was liberated into one of his sudden large gestures, sweeping a hand toward the ceiling, whose tint seemed to hold us at the bottom of a dirty swimming pool. "A lot of old clients from Spin and Phil, they say, 'Fuck off.' They say, 'Show me.'"

"Well, you showed *me*," I pointed out.

Doreen, not to be excluded from our male conversation, volunteered, "They've been killing the people's pet dogs and cats and leaving them at the front door, but a lot of these rich people say all the same they don't want to pay anything."

"People are selfish," I told them. "What you need to do in an operation like yours," I went on, "is to establish *trust*. Phil and Spin, people trusted them. They didn't necessarily *like* them, but they could re*late* to them. You all have the disadvantage, may I say, of seeming a little young."

Manolete's arm darted toward me like a sword. "Young, we show them *young*. We got the guns, and we don't give no fucking damn no how!"

"Well said," I said. "But what you need, to convince people like me, is something written. I know people your age hardly even bother to learn how to read, but that's how the people you want to convince deal with one another. With something in writing. Suppose I were to give you an endorsement. It would go something like, 'I, Benjamin Turnbull, of this address et cetera, hereby declare that these young entrepreneurs and enforcers of order have supplied their services to me in a thoroughly satisfactory manner. What they promise, they deliver, so help me God. These fine young men can be trusted.' How does that sound?"

"It sounds like real old-time bullshit," Manolete said, but with a smile, here underwater.

Doreen asked, "Why would you do that for us?"

Her torn jeans and loose T-shirt and rough short haircut did not conceal that at thirteen going on fourteen she had the beginnings of a figure. Slender pliant waist, budding breasts. At one end of the fertile continuum Beatrice was at the other of. "I like you," I said. "You've brought some fresh faces into my lonely life. And you're repelling trespassers for me, right?"

"'Pay or go away,' we tell the ones on the way to the beach," Manolete said, with one of his pent-up gestures.

"Exactly," I said. "Also, it seems to me, if I gave you such a written endorsement to establish your credibility in the neighborhood I might be entitled to a discount."

"Discount?" Doreen asked. "How much?"

"Oh . . . what would be fair? Let's say ten—no, fifteen—percent. Fifteen percent off the monthly charge. Don't answer me now. Take it up with the other two. But point out to Ray and José that it's the only way to get their racket on a respectable footing. I would write the endorsement in blue ink on my engraved stationery, that would show everybody it was authentic."

Mosquitoes, as the long June afternoon slipped into damp shadow here on the eastern side of the hill, were finding their way through gaps in the netting. I slapped several as they approached my ear. Odd, that I who cannot bear to kill a spider, and used to hate it when one would suicidally crawl into the wet paint of some home repair, am heartless about mosquitoes, though they are all prospective mothers seeking a drop of blood to nurture their progeny. That telltale whine of theirs—I wonder why evolution has failed to silence it, through the survival of the unsinging. But evolution has its curious perversities and warps and failures to deliver the obvious. "You need bug repellent," I said, standing but taking care not to hit my head on the translucent corrugated roof.

"We got it," Doreen said, less friendly as the light clammily ebbed from this fragile space of shelter. "But it doesn't work worth squat on those ticking things."

"I squash 'em," Manolete boasted again.

Gloria must be back from Boston or wherever she has been. I could hear through the trees the surging motors of cars, but whether on our driveway or elsewhere I couldn't tell. The acoustics of this hill have always been deceptive. Conversations at the gas station downtown sound as if they were just outside the kitchen window, whereas in my study upstairs—my journal-keeping room—I fail to hear the FedEx truck come up the driveway. By the time its roar strikes my ear the heedless truck is around the curve by the daylily bed and out of sight, having knocked one more low-hanging branch off the hemlock.

"And you have a cooler for drinks, I see," I said, spotting the white of Styrofoam glowing in a corner of the other room. "For a modest fee, I might let you string up electricity from a plug in my garage. It would take a lot of extension cords, but you could have a fan, and a lamp, and even a little refrigerator. Not free, of course."

"Hey, Big Guy," the boy said. "We like it the way it is. The way it is, it's our own thing."

That "Big Guy" had been worth the slippery trip into the woods to hear.

The longest day of the year 2020 A.D. happened to be rainy and misty, its early dawn and extended dusk hidden in a white wet mass of droplets. The day was a long pallid worm arching up out of darkness and back again. The paper as I write curls limply and rejects the abrasion of the graphite.

In Gloria's garden, the peonies are already rather blown and by, though a few buds, their tightly packed silks stained as if tie-dyed, still wait to unfold. The huge white ones have scattered edges and spots of vermillion like bloody clues. The two-toned lupines are by, but the towering foxgloves are at their peak, as are yellow columbines, delicate dancing minikins that seem to disavow any connection with their stems. Bouncing Bet has escaped from the borders to mingle with the weeds out by the old hotbeds, which have been reduced by time to a rubble of broken glass and dried putty.

She cut some roses from the rounded bed toward the sea and won a number of second-place ribbons at the June Garden Club competition. I think she would have won first if she had waited a few more hours to cut her entries, which had opened too wide by the time of the evening judging. The contest is not so much for growing as for cutting. Now the contestants sit about the kitchen in water glasses, as opulent as old actresses, and the ribbons dangle in the library, their strings pinched between the six volumes of Winston Churchill's history of the last great war but one.

I made an obligatory, multipurposed excursion to Boston.

There was a plethora of bare flesh in the train and in North Station and even the streets of the financial district, along its seam with the tourist traps and juvenilia of Quincy Market. Some tans were already ripe and hardened; young female buttocks, poking their hemispheres below the fringed hems of their radically abbreviated denim cut-offs, exposed here and there a pastel rim, shaped like a new moon, of bikini underpants. I thought of Deirdre.

And yet, by and large, how hideous people are! In Mass. General Ambulatory Care Center, where my dermatologist made his semi-annual harvest of my keratoses, sizzling them away with painful squirts of liquid nitrogen, none but the obese, the cankered, the demented, and the crippled crowded into the elevator with me. In the corner of my vision, faces scrambled, so that I had the distinct impression of a much-grafted and patched-together burn victim standing beside me, his face a chaos of ridges and blotches. But when I sneaked a glance in focus, his face was unscarred, and twenty years younger than my sun-damaged own. I practiced my new trick: by focusing mentally on a face in the side of my vision, I was able to generate an impression of swarming deformity on all sides of me, as if I were ascending in an elevator crammed with mutants or ghastly damaged survivors of the recent great war, their raw surfaces radioactive, their mutilation beyond plastic surgery.

In fact, except for the empty office blocks and the apathetic, sometimes deformed male beggars in olive-green fatigues, there is oddly little in contemporary America to recall the global holocaust of less than a decade ago. The national style has always been to move on. Business as usual is the pretense and the ideal, though the President and the legislators down in Washington have as little control over our lives as the Roman emperors in the fifth Christian century did over the populations of Iberia or Thrace. Even before the war, the bureaucracy had metastasized to the point of performing no function but its own growth. The postwar world dreads all centralized power. Our commonwealth scrip is printed not in Boston or centrally located Worcester but by six or seven independent small-town presses; the design varies widely. Still, electronic connections with other regions of the country are reviving, and commerce is imposing its need for an extended infrastructure. There is even talk of air service from New York to California, hit hardest by the Chinese bombers and further reduced—to near–Stone Age conditions, it was said—by earthquakes, brushfires, and mud slides. Reuniting the coasts is a dream demagogues make much of, on talk radio.

The first prize I ever won, awakening me to the possibility that there were prizes to be had, was a freckle contest at a church picnic; we belonged, half-heartedly, to the Cheshire United Congregational, with its skimpily equipped basement Sunday school and its tall plain-glass windows and its paint-poor pillared Greek-temple front. Puritanism lost its salt and savor as it moved west through Massachusetts; it seemed to me that the white light fell cruelly through the clear glass on our faces and Sunday duds, like the remorseless clarity under a microscope. What comfort did the watery Congregational creed bring, I wonder now, to my mother and father as they struggled with poverty, toothaches, chronic unemployment, and constant dissatisfaction? Never mind: as a child I used to win freckle contests, and, though the freckles have faded, the susceptible fair skin has remained, its squamous and basal cells seething with DNA damage. During the long wait in my dermatologist's office, I studied my fellow-patients with loathing. They all seemed much older than I, doddering and drooling onto the handles of their canes, when in fact they were probably my age. I still peer out of the windows of my eyes with the unforgiving spirit of a young man on the make. My heart spurned all alliance with these disgusting relics of the last, unmourned century; I sought, instead, collusive flirtation with the noticeably nubile nurse who at last ushered me into an examination cell and, handing me a folded robe of blue paper, indicated that I should strip. Why don't you strip with me, darling?

My dermatologist, himself a relic, gave me an abstracted going over and found nothing that needed the services of a surgeon. I rather enjoy excision, the decisiveness of it—one less set of diseased cells to lug around. He painfully squirted liquid nitrogen onto a few spots of actinic damage on my face and the back of my right hand. The doctor, whose own skin is soft as rose petals but a wilted brown, said that yet another vitamin-A derivative had been found to reverse, somewhat, the deterioration of dermal cells. I waved it away: "At my age—"

He tut-tutted. He was ten years older than I. "Don't underestimate skin," he told me. "It's the last thing to go. People die of a failed heart or a failed liver but never of a failed skin. In Irish bogs, you know, these corpses preserved by the chemicals in the clay, the skin holds up as well as the bones. We see five-thousand-year-old tattoos, clear and blue as the day they were stippled in." Yet, in his encroaching senility, he forgot to write me the presciption he promised, for the vitamin-A ointment.

Mrs. Fessenden, whose senility has advanced a notch, has developed the fixed fear that all her funds have disappeared in the electronic maze of computerized finance. It is a reasonable fear: data banks blank out, governments fade away, inflation makes a mockery of currency. But the genius of capitalism dictates that wealth, once established, endure, to lure others to labor for it. Wealth survives wars, idiocy, and high personal unworthiness. So from MGH I trudged through the acres of brick-and-concrete rubble (Government Center, they used to call it) where the John F. Kennedy Building and City Hall used to stand (both blown up by American sympathizers with the Chinese cause during the war, though all the inhabitants of Chinatown had been interned on the harbor islands) to State Street and my old offices at Sibbes, Dudley, and Wise. Here I had been happy; here I had been, in a small way, mighty. I often dream I am riding the elevator up, and finding everything beyond the receptionist's desk nightmarishly changed. It was necessary today to secure tangible proof for Mrs. Fessenden that she was still a wealthy woman, however the world wagged. Yet what could I get for her but more suspect computer printouts? They all looked alike and could mean anything, she said. With the grudging help of Ned Partridge, who now has a wispy assistant with the economical name of Gary Gray, I found in a back room of old-fashioned "hard" files some engraved Chicago Municipal Water Authority Board from the 1920s that had been left to her in her father's estate. They were beautifully ornamented with crosshatched fountains, overflowing urns, nude Nereids, and bearded heads of a jubilant Neptune. Along the bottom edge, above the lacily etched border, ran a tableau of a French fur trader, in company with two buckskinned Indians, surveying the horizon of Lake Michigan from the marshy mouth of the Chicago River. Another of Ned's assistants, a compactly built girl in a jade-green sheath that clung tightly to her honey-colored skin—Africa had recently bumped into Asia somewhere in her gene map—helped me take state-of-the-art color Xeroxes of these antiquated proofs of financial substance, and collusively agreed to FedEx them, at the expense of the firm, to Mrs. Fessenden in Chestnut Hill.

The air-conditioned offices in their shades of ecru fluorescence formed a kind of paradise and I was tempted to linger. Once I had been welcome here, and it was not the least unkind trick of time that I had become an alien body, a germ to be neutralized and expelled. The comely underlings understood this less well than the higher-ups. One of the disagreeable things about Ned Partridge's face, besides its papery indoor pallor, is the way in which his long lustreless nose somehow appears in profile even when he is looking at you head-on. In the Picassoesque scramble his fishy eyes seem to intersect, also. "The place isn't the same without you, Ben," he told me, with such evident insincerity that the mixed-blood beauty darted an eyelash-begemmed glance in his direction.

"You all seem to be managing," I said.

"Yeah, but there's no give-and-take any more. No fun."

"Was I fun?" I asked incredulously.

"There's no graciousness," he went on, avoiding my question. The Afro-Asian assistant demurely lowered her lids on the moist treasure, in its shining lashed vessels, of her gaze. As if I, a poor boy from outer Hammond Falls, had been the standard-bearer for fading gentility. "You still have Firman Frothingham," I pointed out. "He's fun."

"Yaah, he's still around, but between us"—his face jumped closer, out of focus—"Frothy's lost a lot of his fire, his *esprit*. It's all cut-throat now," Ned said, settling back into his chair with a shuffling of lips and nostrils. "Savages," he snorted. "Everybody carving out their little turf and pulling up the drawbridge. Bingo, and fuck you, Mac. Let Pat show you out, Ben—we have a new floor plan since you left."

Pat, indeed. Pat pat. As we threaded through the vanilla

lambency of the offices, I observed how her green sheath, with its split exposing a golden-brown sliver of thigh, fit her discreetly but undeniably steatopygous buttocks with enough snugness to declare their cleavage. Even her face, as it smiled goodbye forever, had its muscular bulges. She was a choice cut of meat and I hoped she held out for a fair price.

Then, expelled, I descended to the steamy squalid streets, with their throngs of ghastly hoi polloi. It was as if the world's population had never been halved. All the sickly marbled tints of Occidental skin spilled and milled about on Congress Street as I bucked through the tumbling flesh toward North Station. Within, the stench of the cheese and pulped tomatoes of Italian fast food nearly made me gag. Overweight girls in their random search for stimulation were staring right through me. The commuter train in summer becomes a cargo carrier to the North Shore beaches, and the vinyl seats take on an aroma of salt water and suntan lotion and of wet towels and sleepy sunburned young bodies dying to take a piss. As we age and appetite dwindles, I notice, we become fussier about our food—we smell unsavory ingredients that youth greedily gobbles up, and also resent the secretive fumes of breeding, from the sour fermented beverages that loosen our inhibitions to the post-coital puddles. Odorous rumors of all those necessary secretions and excessively clever gametes make us queasy.

I write this while doubting its truth. There is a rapacious splendor in the way our ugly, multi-digited species, with its absurd patches of hair and oversized skull, slaughter by slaughter covered the world in waves of anthropic fat, wiping out the mammoth and auroch and dodo and rhino and pressing the tiger and cheetah and *Sus scrofa* into unsanitary zoos, where they smell nothing on the night air but people—an ocean of human scent and excrement and semen. I am part of it, still; in the same shameful nook of me that craves perpetuation I am as carnal as ever.

I can remember that first, rapt taste, chalky and exalted like a primal malt ball, of childhood pornography. Grubby pages were passed around, from hand to hand, in that Dark Age of text duplication, in tattered mimeograph and even blurred carbon copy. There was an inspiriting prose tale of a sixth-grade boy whose teacher has him stay late at school; she mounts a ladder to affix a Christmas decoration and lets him look up her legs to see that she is wearing no underpants. Later in the saga she makes him taste her copious fluids and extracts from his fly his silver virgin rod. Amazing! We schoolboys wondered, Did such things truly happen? In some universe, perhaps, but certainly not this. I, a businessman in bud, asked myself who were the adults who showered such delicious fantasies upon us starving juveniles, and how such a business reaped its profit. Another item of sexual *samizdat* took the female point of view, in rhyme:

> I took out my tits, shyly proud of their size,
> And blushed as Ted's finger explored 'tween my thighs.
> I gulped when his member was thrust into view,
> But he bid me caress it, and lick at it, too.

How often I have wished I recalled more than this one stanza, and cursed myself for having an indifferent memory. But other boys were leaning on me, stabbing with smudged fingers at the fragile, often-folded hectographed copy, threatening to tear the revelatory text into fragments. One detail was unforgettable in its technical interest: as Ted prepared the heroine for her deflowering, he knowingly placed a pillow under her hips. Pillowy ass upon ass-kissing pillow: a sacred secret here, the vaginal canal lifted skyward at the proper tilt, like an ack-ack gun, to bring down ecstasy from on high. I hugged this rakish bit of sexual insiderism to my heart's foul underside but in the next fifty-five years have found less use for the tip than I would have thought. Education is so wasteful, so hit-or-miss.

In the first narrative, did the student then get up on the ladder, and the teacher, from below, rub her bare breasts against the boy's feet, in a sort of Biblical laving?

Or have I made all this quite up, in a suspect surge of recovered memory?

———————

Beside the driveway, the laurel bush, whose pentagonal blossoms seemed each a dainty marvel of biological design, has spread around itself a white-and-pink circle of such blossoms, shed, like a young woman who has slipped, while standing, out of her wide petticoats.

How much of summer is over before it begins! Its beginning marks its end, as our birth entails our death. *Urzeit gleich Endzeit*, somebody once said in the course of my hit-or-miss education. The lawn is dry and tan in spots; a minute or two is snipped from the ends of each successive day; the hard white sails against the bay's midsummer blue seem as unsubtle as the stencilled border of a pampered child's nursery. The leaves of the little English oak along the driveway show, I notice on my way to the mailbox, constellations of holes eaten by insects or their fuzzy-headed larvae. The grass and weeds have hastened to go to seed, knowing their time is short. The year is like a life—it is later than you think, the main business is over and done with before you fully begin. There is a kind of tidal retard in our perception of forward motion.

As I tried to explain to my protégés, an explanation for the puzzling fact—puzzling to physicists more than to ordinary men, who can imagine it no other way—that time's arrow moves in only one direction is that the initial singularity, the universe at the moment of the Big Bang, was utterly or almost utterly smooth, with the consistency of an orange popsicle, whereas the terminal singularity toward which all the billions of galaxies may raggedly collapse will be less smooth, or downright rough, like butter brickle ice cream.

It makes sense: all those blazing suns, red and swollen or white and shrunken or yellow like our moderate own, blue and new or black and collapsed, madly spinning neutron stars or else all-swallowing black holes denser yet, not to mention planets and cinderlike planetoids and picturesque clouds of glowing gas and dark matter hypothetical or real and titanic streaming soups of neutrinos, could scarcely be expected to converge exactly upon a singularity smaller, by many orders of magnitude, than a pinhead. The Weyl curvature, in other words, was very very *very* near zero at the Big Bang, but will be much larger at the Big Crunch. But, I ignorantly wonder, how does time's arrow know this, in our trifling immediate vicinity? What keeps it from spinning about like the arrow of a compass, jumping broken cups back on the table intact and restoring me, if not to a childhood self, to the suburban buck I was when still married to Perdita. On one busy summer day, as things worked out on everybody's schedule, it fell to me to fuck three women— Perdita in the morning, since I was going off on a business trip and we liked to leave each other "topped up"; another, a pretty but futureless interne bond analyst, at lunch hour, in the Parker House, after room service had delivered some club sandwiches and iced tea; and the third in my hotel room in Houston, an overweight gum-chewing whore I picked up in the saddle-brown bar over whiskey and frijoles.

Because she was a professional, I explained the situation frankly, and the sheer crassness of the explanation got me so excited that I wound up, to her drawled, grudgingly impressed compliments, coming twice. In all cases, my semen arrowed outward, into darkness, like the minutes of my manhood ticking away.

This morning I alarmed myself. While shaving, without thinking, I began to shave my chin and the area below my lower lip before I did my upper lip. It was as if I had forgotten for a second how to be me. My shaving procedure is invariable: soften whiskers with hot washcloth, lather bar in soap dish, shave right cheek and jaw first, then left, then upper lip, and lastly the tricky, knobby region of the chin, with its need to hold fast the lower lip with the upper teeth. I have cut myself more often in this region than any other, and save it for last. Suddenly I was tackling it out of sequence. My identity had been usurped by an alien who had not been briefed upon just this trifling detail; another hand than mine had taken over. It was as when a measurement is taken in the quantum realm of an electron's position or momentum, and the wave function collapses and another universe floridly sprouts on the spot.

All praise be to the holy Lord on this glorious day at the end of June. The sea is speckled with white crests—the manes of white stallions, the superstitious folk say, but for those of us sequestered in prayerful peacefulness on our island hill a divine sign of safety, as the scudding aftermath of a night blow strong enough to hold in their harbors the dragon-headed, square-sailed galley ships of the fair-faced demons from far Lothland. Rumors have arrived from across the

narrow water between our fastness and the Munster mainland concerning attacks ever nearer. The seafaring fiends
have no end of appetite and cruelty, to which Providence in
its miraculous patience lends scope so as to accumulate un-
gainsayable proofs toward the eternal damnation of their
souls. The saintly monks of Lindisfarne, the makers and in-
scribers of magically beautiful codices, were stripped and
tortured in June of the year 793 after our Lord's birth of a
meek virgin, and the raiders came again in 801 to set the
buildings afire, and in 806 to kill scores more of helpless
monks. St. Columcille's fair Iona has fallen with much massacre, and Inis Murray was quite destroyed, never to rise, in
the second year of this our terrible ninth century. Glen-
dalough, Clonfert, Clonmacnoise, and Kildare where none
less than St. Brigit rules as high abbess above a holy gathering of both sexes—none could withstand the evil from the
sea. The pirates with golden beards have penetrated even to
Pátraic's beloved Armagh and burned the blessed buildings
to the ground. The horrors that God in His mercy permits!
All to test the faithful, our learned abbot explains—to polish
up the devoted to be sparkling angels in the ranks depleted
by Satan and his defiant and banished legions.

And still, he says, to ease the fear from the unshaven faces
of the young among us, unlikely in the extreme it would be
for the Lothlanders to seek out our remote and rocky island,
poor as we are, thirty brothers and twice as many of sheep,
nine goats and a single dutiful ram, two pair of oxen to drag
the plow through our patch of low soil, and a pen of pigs for
the bacon to trade (we eat no meat) and for the squealing
when the rare strangers come up the lone flint path from the
shingle beach. A man like me, unable to read a sign save that
of the cross and the great dancing "X" which begins Christ's
name—Brother Guaire has shown me pages he has labored

on in the scriptorium, glowing designs that dizzied me endeavoring to follow them down to the end of the knot, all in inks the everlasting colors of jewels—a man like me, thrust by a hard-hearted whore of a mother, before I had the makings of a memory, upon the bosom of the church, and raised by it within the charity of God to serve my betters, gifted though I was with naught but an encouraging way with dumb beasts and the herbs of the garden, such a man, his chief joy the simple smile of creation and one meatless meal a day, bran soaked in goat's milk or sea bass with bread and uncooked beans, and the gratification of lying stretched cruciform on the dirt floor of his stone hut offering up his hunger and pain to the crucified God, such would not likely attract the fury of the marauding Antichrists from the lands to the north, where all is ice and bewhiskered sea-creatures with soulful eyes like those of men eternally condemned.

The highest pasture on our stony island consists of grass tufts nibbled by the goats; below the upmost ledges in the growing season sheep graze broad-sloped shoulders of green, the winter lambs near the size of their mothers now and all still as gray boulders in the golden morning sun, heads lowered to feed. The occasional bleat of a lamb imagining himself lost drifts down. A pair of hawks whistle one to the other as they hang watchful in the wind. The herbs and medicinal flowers in their frothy rows nod about my knees—the yellows of the cowslips and feverfew, the purples of hyssop and lavender, the dainty useful greens of mint and cabbage. Brother Vergil before he wasted away of flying venom and the weakness of age explained his arrangement by the humors: here thyme and hyssop, warm and drying herbs, to clear phlegm; there burdock and figwort, cool and dry, to cleanse the sanguine system of gout and diarrhea; here senna and hellebore to purge with their heat the clogging of black bile that induces constipation and melancholy; and there rhubarb and dandelion to counteract with their cool moisture the hot and dry tempers inflicted by an excess of yellow bile. Garlic and basil, coriander and goldenseal—the mute plants do hold in their roots and stems and calyxes and corollas a thousand responses to the multitudinous gaps and imbalances the body in its turmoil poses. God through His vast kindness knots into all the crevices of His flowering creation the essential juices of His peace and love, according to the code declared by the wondrously variegated patterns of the flowers and leaves. Dried aerial parts yield decoctions and poultices no malady can resist. For headache, lavender and feverfew; for boils, a poultice from feverfew; for sore throats, infusions of coneflower roots or loosestrife blooms, added to tincture of astringent, phlegm-reducing herbs like silverweed; for hemorrhoids, ointment of pilewort—there is nothing amiss in our workings without cure in God's garden. Even warrior's wounds slowly vanish under applications of self-heal and purple-flowered comfrey, called knitbone by the simple folk. Before the birth of Christ, so gracious is God, He was busy revealing these secrets to the pagan Greeks, the king of whose wisdom was named Aristotle. As I bend my back to the weeding of the aisles of my living church of silent adorers, I beg forgiveness for these many deaths by uprooting, for even weeds too humble to have a name no doubt contain properties that, knowingly extracted and combined, would join them to the chorus of cures. God created nothing to no purpose, though many purposes are yet hidden from us, to be revealed no doubt on the day when the living and the dead alike are summoned in their risen bodies to judgment, and all this finespun intricacy singing about us is revealed as but a filigreed shadow of the glorious true world prepared for His faithful. This day cannot be far off, the abbot says. Indeed, that eight centuries have been allowed to pass since our Lord gave Himself to torture and despair on the Cross would cause Paul and those other early saints to marvel at the fullness of time allowed obdurate Mankind for its own salvation. Those who study the mind of heaven agree that the world must surely end before the year 1000, since a year of more digits than the Trinity would be a certain blasphemy.

The pigs have started a sudden squealing in their pen of wattles and alder stakes. Looking toward the west, where our humped island like a sundial casts its shrinking morning shadow into the flickering silver of the endless western sea, a flock of sails in the fatal square shape has silently appeared. Slender, they sit on the bright sea with the symmetry of letters, the same dragonish upturn before the mast as after. Perhaps I have been the last to read them, rapt here among the rustle of the herbs, tending and gathering. Now my ears take in shouting from the direction of the abbot's house and the round tower. I run to the cliff's edge and see fair-bearded men with sun flashing from their close-fitting helmets wading in squat armor onto the shingle despite the roughness of the waves. Some have already arrived in our midst. Shouting and pitiful cries rise to disturb the sheep on their high shoulders of meadow. Their bleating and the slow heartbeat of surf on the beach below all but drown the overheard thuds of struggle. Monks in their sackcloth make no more resistance to broadswords and battle-axes than slugs to the gardener's knife. The careless growth at the cliff's edge clings with its cold dew and milkweed spittle as I hasten bare-legged away, casting aside my basket half full of fennel plucked for a meal that will now never be served. My stone hut's beehive shape came into my mind but this sanctum for sleep and for prayer would offer no exit with a roaring demon crouching

at the entrance. Beyond the lower walled edge, the cliff
breaks away into crevices and shallow trickling caves where
a man might outwait a storm. Gulls above circle and dip, curious over the stir but safely aloof. The chapel bell, costly
iron that nigh sank the raft that brought it a week's journey
around Dingle, begins to ring madly as if to shatter its own
Christian voice, jerked into clamor not by the pull of pious
hands but by the mocking strength of a Norseman inflamed
by mead and bloody plunder.

I catch my breath behind the shoulder of the stone milk-
ing house. Through the chinks of its sloping wall, which
release to my nostrils like a final scent of earth that of dung-
spattered fresh hay, I spy smoke curling from beyond the
oak chapel, the *dairthech* where so many times I saw the
gleaming chalice lifted up amid the intertwining chanting of
the brothers. I see that what is afire is the wide reed roof
of the *tech mór*, where we were accustomed to eat and talk,
not always without natural men's gaiety, and those who
could read would read at the tables, the leaves of parchment
turning stiff as wind-filled sails. Now from the chapel's entrance streams in gesticulating gobbets a parade of the long-
haired fiends in their furs and leather breastplates. One
holds aloft our precious chalice, its rim of silver filigree
picked out with enamels the bright colors of sheep's blood
and noontime sky: the pattern would swirl beneath my eyes
in the moment when Christ's blood, sweet and strong as
dark queen's honey, was tilted into my lips by the abbot's
white hands. My gullet would feel the thick warmth of God's
inmost being.

The Lothlander holding the chalice aloft now lowers it so
that his comrades in pagan brutishness can spit into the pristine vessel and, as with a maiden helpless in their midst, perform worse desecrations from the low parts of their bodies.

The Deal

The great altar candlesticks and fine holy cloths and the cedarwood reliquary inlaid with precious metals and containing the bones of the hand of St. Finnian all flow forth on the stream of booty. The illuminated Gospels stored in a locked chest beneath the chapel lectern have been torn apart for the jewels in the covers, and the bright pages are scattered and trampled. It is a devilish sight that makes my innards sicken for more than myself. Brother Guaire! His knots undone! The thatch of the *tech mór* shows flags of orange flame, and the smoke from this and other fires dyes the scene like the dipping close of a cloud livid with thunder. In the murky tangle of horrors I see the abbot's small head, pale and benign, being brandished on the end of a bearded fiend's pike. The bodies of my brothers, naked and dismembered, are tumbled into the sacred well whose miraculous fresh waters, drawn from beneath the salt sea, had sustained our settlement here. God has forsaken us, to test our faith. The animals as they are led away, roped and hauled or driven with staves, bellow as if on the way to slaughter, but it is not the animals being slaughtered. They will live for yet a while. In this universe turned upside down the chickens ascend in a sprawling of feathers as if to join the gulls indifferently soaring above the havoc.

And now a step sounds behind me. My enemy is come. He is young, though tall and shaggy in his armor. Fine-meshed iron mail covers a long-sleeved tunic of green wool heavy with salt spray. He seems newly minted in the foundry of battle; perhaps I will be the first man he has slain. I drive my eyes to seek his face. His helmet is a pointed brazen dome that extends to a flared nose guard. Golden hair flows to his red-caped shoulders from underneath his helmet. When he lifts his cinder-black battle-ax high in both arms, the curly fleece of his beard lifts to reveal the clasp of his cape—an iron face incised with round staring eyes, snake-like horns, and fangs: his god, the enemy and antithesis of my God. He utters some words in his musical heathen tongue. I crouch beneath him, lowering myself to make his ax travel a hand's breadth farther to reach me. I hurry my thought through one last prayer to Christ; like my doom now will He tower above my resurrected flesh in judgment, in the blinding light of the life to come. Though I sleep a thousand thousand years, I tell myself, it will be to me as an instant. But there are still things of this life to see. The infidel's dog-white teeth are bared. Terrors swarm out of his deep-socketed eyes like bees bringing home honey from the freckled pits of a tall blue foxglove. I see that the boy is as frightened as I. This instant of time toward which our lives have converged has two sides of terrible brightness. Killer and martyr participate equally in the sacrifice our Lord commands. Poison and medicine are the same extract. Darkness and light are one.

Summer asks that we co-exist with too many other living creatures. The vegetable efflorescence depletes one's morale. The sky loses color in the humid heat; the sea becomes a parking lot for sailboats. Orange daylilies lord it over the blowsy yards in the village; Queen Anne's lace and Bouncing Bet brighten the meadows; daisies and chicory dot the ragged roadsides. A dead eviscerated frog appeared on our driveway: dropped by a crow, clumsy or sated? The mysteries of overplenteous life. I ventured into the buggy woods and found the full delegation, minus Doreen, in the hut, smoking cigarettes. "It keeps the mosquitoes down," the biggest told me. He was José, I reminded myself.

"How's it going, gentlemen?" I asked the three.

"A lot of kids goin' to be tryin' to come through here to-morrow," the lawyer told me. He was Ray. Tomorrow was Independence Day. Haskells Crossing puts on a fireworks display that attracts masses from the village and beyond. Bare-chested Vikings, already drunk, lug coolers full of beer. No matter how repulsive and futureless these young males are, they always have girls with them, going along: it says something about our species. No man too bad not to attract a woman. If women were fastidious, the species would go extinct. Thug boyfriends pleasantly remind them of their thug fathers.

"And what are you going to do about it?" I asked.

The question was embarrassing. "Keep 'em in line," Ray finally offered.

"That's all? You should charge the people to get by," I told them.

"You want that?"

"What's the point of being here if you don't? Not so much they can't pay; keep it within reason. Say, three welders a head, five for a couple. Children in arms can get in free," I suggested.

Ray, the little lawyer, asked, "This with your permission?"

"Absolutely," I said. "For a cut, of course."

"A cut? How much cut?"

I hadn't thought it through but proposed, "Twenty percent. One welder out of five. That's not so much. How else are the people going to get to the fireworks?"

"Supposin' they say they won't pay?" José asked. In his plump, seamless face his opaque black irises had a buttoned-on look, an extra protuberance that may have been an illusion produced by their brightness, their luxurious lacquer.

I laughed. A laugh sounds sinister in the woods, dam-pered by the greenery. "You're asking me that? A big tough guy like you? Maybe I should find some new protection."

"You're sayin' kill 'em if they don't pay?"

"That seems extreme. And probably counterproductive. What you want is a happy line of paying customers. But, listen, this is your party. I didn't ask you to camp here, on my land. Let them pass if you want. You have bigger fish to fry, remember? How are you doing with my neighbors?"

Each waited for the other to speak.

"Not so good, huh?" I said at last.

"They comin' around," the lawyer lied.

Manolete gestured suddenly. "They be sorry when we burn their houses down. *Pfoom!*"

"We have a saying in business," I told them. "Don't kill the goose that lays the golden eggs."

Manolete, perhaps the brightest as well as the youngest, said in his abrupt, small-boy, explosive way, "Only eggs they layin' is tellin' us to get the hell off they fuckin' property."

"Mr. and Mrs. Kelly," Ray interposed, "were reasonable. We show them your letter. They say O.K., they'd contribute something, but only a part of what you paid, since they only have three acres to your eleven."

He was learning the language, I thought. "Tell them," I said, "that that may be so but there are six of them and only two Turnbulls. Maybe mention casually that you would hate to see any of their children kidnapped; ransom costs a lot more than protection."

They took this in, the three brown faces in the sun-slit gloom of their fragile little shelter. José volunteered, "Those Dunhams, they didn't come up with nothin'. They treated us like dirt. He has his *own* guns, the cocksucker said."

The Dunhams were a perfect couple, unless one considered childlessness a flaw. Their impeccable mock-colonial house, visible in winter, lay hidden in the leafy woods not two hundred yards from Gloria's back garden. Athletic into their fifties, they matched like salt and pepper shakers. Both lithe, both forever smiling though faintly formal even in jogging outfits, their skins glowing with the same shade of suntan, their hair tinged with exactly the same becoming amount of gray, they came from old New England families with about the same amount of money and cachet. The world's woes, and the woes that parenthood brings, had passed them by; there was a polished, impervious beauty about them that one itched to mar. Their only point of vulnerability was their animals. They had two prize Persian cats, a perfectly trimmed miniature poodle, and a piebald pony who grazed in summer in a little meadow carved from their section of the woods.

"You might think about killing one of their cats," I told the boys. "They let them out in the morning for exercise and to do their business in the shrubs. Just kill one, leave the body on the porch, and show up for collection the next day. You don't have to admit to anything, just don't deny it either. If they don't pay up then, do the dog, that damned yappy poodle. The horse—before you kill him, get some spray paint and paint his side. If he holds still for it, paint in numbers your monthly charge. Like an invoice on legs."

In our box of artificial twilight, with its smells of tobacco smoke and sweaty mattress and pine needles masked by plywood, the boys broke into laughter at my wealth of malice.

"Any ideas how we should handle Mrs. Lubbetts?" Ray asked.

I was enjoying this. I loved these willing boys, so superior, in their readiness and accessibility, to my own grandsons.

Pearl Lubbetts was a Jewish widow—Earl Lubbetts had made his pile in potato chips and packaged popcorn—who had taken on over the years the imperious, lockjawed, rough-and-ready manner of a Wasp matriarch. She was usually dressed in Wellingtons and muddy-kneed dungarees, directing teams of local workers on one or another project of excavation, forestry, resodding, or masonry. She had built a private sea-wall to protect her front lawn from the tides, and at a far corner of her property had constructed a modernist beach house which was, as it happened, the only structure in my seaward view, summer and winter. She had cleared the surrounding trees, so nothing impeded my sight line; with its bleached redwood siding and flat white Florida-style roof and its sundeck balustrade like a bone comb, it was an unignorable blot on my view. Metal and glass elements on the roof and walls—flashing, skylights, twirling vents, and complicated tin chimney guards—beamed irritating glints into my visual field, unanswerable emergency signals from the edge of the sea; no matter what the hour between sunrise and sunset, some reflective angle boldly bounced protons right through my windows into my retinas.

"You could burn down her little beach house," I suggested. "That should give her the idea that you are serious individuals. When you go to collect," it occurred to me to add, "you might want to wear suits, or at least a jacket and tie. It makes a world of difference, credibilitywise."

The boys consulted with one another in silent glances. Triangles of white flickered beside their shifting irises.

"Hey, how come you tellin' us all this stuff?" Ray asked me.

"I like you young fellas. I want you to succeed."

"What's in it for you?"

I let a beat of silence go by. "How about twenty percent?" I said.

"Ten plenty," José said.

Ray's eyes flicked sideways in surprise at being supplanted as negotiator.

"Ten on the protection, twenty on the admission fees tomorrow," I offered.

Ray took back the role of spokesman. "How you know we not be cheatin' you?" he asked.

"The sad way things are in the world now, we all have to work through trust. I trust you, it's that simple," I told them.

José, the biggest, was the one to rise, extend his broad but soft hand, and say, "It's a deal."

iv. *The Deaths*

INDEPENDENCE DAY: my American flag flapped noisily on the pole in an east wind off the sea. For a time it was tangled in its cord and twittered like an insect with one wing stuck on flypaper, until I loped across the lawn and lowered the striped and starred cloth and sent it back up the halyard free. Out there on the blue width of water, sailboats tilted in the morning breeze and sleek white stinkpots gathered on the evening calm to see the fireworks sent up from the public end of the beach. You could hear the sounds and music of beery parties already in progress. I wondered how my boys were doing collecting tolls along the path. Downtown, around the convenience store, white boys in droopy loose shirts and shorts and girls in tighter foxy duds watched the holiday seep away like spilled soda on hot concrete. The insouciance and innocence of our independence twinkled like a kind of sweat from their bare and freckled or honey-colored or mahogany limbs. Sometimes I think the thing I'll mind about death is not so much not being alive but no longer being an American. Even for the losers there is a liberation in the escape from divine order.

The Deaths

In Gloria's rose bed the blooms, so red and white and pink against the sea, are tired, their blown petals littering the smoothly mounded mulch of buckwheat hulls; but her back garden is profuse with odd-shaped flowers I cannot name. Yarrow? Artemisia? Snapdragons and nasturtiums in any case, nasturtiums with a curious flower-shaped blazon on their petals, the dirty tint of a tattoo. The clematis on the sunny side of the garden shed is amazing, clambering on its quick red stems up the lattice I had made and drenching the clapboards in a density of lush purple flowers banded like church vestments. Gloria cuts it down to a virtual stump every spring, and her faith is always rewarded.

Within the garage, the barn swallows, so slow to start their nest, have in a few weeks' time hatched their eggs. It happened today: the air was suddenly full of careening baby birds. They fly swervingly up and down, on the edge of control, like children first on a bicycle. There are three, and they rest from their adventure perched on the wooden gutter of the house as tightly together as if still packed in the nest, frightened by all the transparent space around them. Gloria and I had observed them, as we passed in and out of the garage, from the day they were hatchlings, blind mouths held preposterously wide open above the nest's edge, their tiny bald bodies wholly devoted to the strain and distension of sudden post-ovum appetite. Tirelessly the dapper mother and father dipped back and forth across the lawn and shrub planting, harvesting invisible insects. In a mere two weeks the helpless and hideous babies have been fed into feathers and wingpower enough to be launched, blue-backed and roseate-bellied, as darting, dipping predators in their own right.

The baby birds had swiftly become complete, down to their flickering white-flecked swallowtails. For a time they will stay on our property, learning from their parents (how?) the fine points of survival, but the mud cup of a nest, given fibrous strength with grass wands and pine needles, has been emptied. How do birds teach birds, elephants elephants, without language? Even imitation implies a simian brain. In less than a month our babies will fly to Peru, and the dry brown leaves of the crabapple will accumulate in the open garage, and the thin breath of autumn dull the verdure. The asphalt of the driveway takes on a different texture then, and scrapes differently under our shoes. Our shadows are drier, more dilute, and an expectancy of closure flavors the shortening days when the swallows are no longer here. But for now they are still with us, holding a family seminar in mosquito-catching, and the Fourth of July fireworks burst into sight a second ahead of their muffled bangs, as viewed from our front yard, on the sea side, in the moon-bleached sky above the trees' silent, merged, beseeching silhouettes.

Gloria went in almost immediately, saying the mosquitoes were biting her to death. I stood on the flagpole platform as our bedroom lights came on and the air conditioner started to hum. The town fathers, whoever they were, had managed to scrape from their depleted budget a handsome display. There were types quite new to me—hovering white flares that shot out from a two-leaved orange butterfly shape and encircled it for some lingering seconds; a giant silent chrysanthemum whose rays were blue at the tips and gold at the source; drifting constellations of cold white twinklers; and several fireworks that unfolded from within their packet of chemical reactions a sharply violent color I had never seen in the sky before, thus spilled on blackness in transient splinters. Combusted salts of strontium, barium, sodium, magnesium, and mercurous chloride etched their signatures on the dark firmament, an infernal rainbow owing nothing to the sun. Gloria's golden window clicked off just as the finale of overlapping bursts died away to a chorus of grateful toots from the assembled stinkpots. I felt chilled and bitten in the dark. Where was I to go? She hated it when I crept into bed and disturbed in her the fragile succession of steps whereby consciousness dissolves. As I turned away to tread the damp lawn, something rustled in the sunken area of wild roses beside the platform—where we had once thought to dig a swimming pool, a dream that lives only in our still calling it the "swimming-pool area"—and I sensed that another presence had been watching with me. The deer.

And a week or less after this, by daytime, the giant dim torus in the sky, the ghostly watermark on the atmosphere's depthless Crane's blue, grew larger, moving toward Earth. Vast and then vaster, it stealthily expanded until its lambent rim touched the sea's horizon and disappeared behind the treetops; it was encircling the visible platter of Earth; we were within it; our round planet was like a stake to its quoit. The torus's blue hole, for these many months no wider than ten suns across, had swelled to become the empyrean itself; the upper edge of its "matter"—for matter is just what it seemed not to be—sank, distending, and lost itself, a line of faint pallor, behind the lateral stretch of distant, mountainous summer clouds. All the while a creamy, weightless sense of irreversible reassurance was flooding me. It was near noon; I had stepped out onto the lawn in obedience to an impulse. The young swallows were still careening, a bit wildly, about, but the other birds were hushed, as during a solar eclipse, with its out-of-sync dusk. I remembered standing on a hillside in the Berkshires under a shouting clarity of stars and seeing a comet through binoculars handed me by my father's work-worn hand: a tailed ball of fuzz, not seeming to move at all.

I would not die, I realized; all would be well. All the fleeting impressions I had ever received were preserved somewhere and could be replayed. All shadows would be wiped away, when light was everywhere and not confined to loci—stars, hot points, pinpricks in nothingness. But just the concept of light, born of combustion and atomic collision, was too harsh for the peace that was promised within the torus. All the shards of my spiritual being united—Perdita with Gloria; the old Hammond Falls house, poor in possessions but rich in meanings, with my present mansion, poor in meanings; my children with my stepchildren and they with my grandchildren and all the world's uncomforted waifs. Time was a provision that would be rescinded; its tragedy was born of misperception, an upper limit of conceptual ability such as keeps the bee bumbling among the clover and the faithful dog trotting, loving but puzzled, at his master's heels. (I have lived with dogs, though have none now. In Hammond Falls we had a mongrel called Skeezix and then a female successor, Daisy, who was part cocker spaniel; then Perdita and I kept a succession of golden retrievers as nurse-maids for the children, and once bought, not cheaply, a bronze-colored Doberman who was run over by one of the last milk-delivery trucks operating in Massachusetts. Her back broken, Cleo writhed in the middle of the street for twenty minutes before a young town cop arrived to put a bullet in her skull; she writhed and yelped and kept begging us with her amber eyes to forgive her her misfortune, to still love her as she had loved us.)

That the joy of creation, flowing through the generations of birds and bacteria, human beings and arboreal titans as they rise and fall is not an illusion but an eternal basis, and that a heavenly economy to whose workings we are blind will redeem every one of our living moments and carry to

completion each inkling of beatitude: such blissful certainty
of universal reconciliation travelled like a great magnetic
field across the depleted planet as it was passed, as in a magician's trick, through the cosmic ring, which receded in the
midnight skies above Australia and vanished, a faintly glowing ringlet, in the vicinity of the constellation Octans. By
morning it had vanished from all but the most powerful
telescopes.

Everyone had seen it; everyone had felt it; yet news cov-
erage of the event was spotty and diffident. Different people, interviewed, gave different times and durations for their
mystical sensations. Exact words were hard to formulate.
Scientists and psychologists were quick to jump into print
with theories of mass hallucination powerful enough to affect even photographic plates. A growing school of opinion
holds that the torus had never existed at all—had not hung
in our heavens for years—or had been no more a three-
dimensional phenomenon than the ring arond the moon on
a foggy night. Doubt and mockery have become fashionable, on television talk shows and among schoolchildren.
T-shirts appeared on the young, displaying the torus encircling a question mark, or diagonally barred to form the
symbol for negation. Even among lovers, it was embarrassing to talk about the transcendent moment. Comparing
notes elicited disturbing discrepancies. It is true, the memory of bliss fades, like that of pain. I write my description not
ten days after the event in order to fix my own memory, but
even so, doubt has crept in. What really did I feel? People
are grotesquely suggestible, to facilitate sexual congress and
tribal solidarity. I feel depleted and irritable, immersed in
the poisonous and voracious growth of midsummer. Lately
I wake twice a night to urinate, and sometimes there is only
a dribble, and an icicle poke of pain in a nether recess of my-

self, a dark and inaccessible underside I have always preferred to pretend is not there.

Gloria brings flowers indoors—nasturtiums in shades of
orange and yellow overflow a fat stoneware bowl, and the
velvet purple of clematis burns for a day or two on the
mahogany table in the front hall, in a swirl-ribbed vase of a
blue as pale as her eyes. A burst of baby's breath hovers in a
water tumbler placed on the dining-room table, between
the silver quail.

While she was off at aerobics, I went out into our woods
to visit the boys from Lynn. Behind the barn I startled a
deer; with a thrash that set my heart to thrashing he or she—
a glimpse of russet flank, a flare of white tail swallowed by
the foliage—bounded into the impenetrable area, thick with
thorny greenbrier, this side of the Dunhams' paddock. As I
proceeded a bit farther, along a faint path my steps are wearing down the hill, I felt the heat of the creature's great pelted
body lingering in the air. Pieces of bright gray sky clam-
bered overhead between the treetops.

Only Doreen was in the hut, reading a textbook edi-
tion, shortened and simplified for junior high students, of that
twentieth-century master, John Grisham. She was a brainy
girl, it occurred to me, who had put herself only for the time
being on a low road. She was sizing life up, ready to experiment with it. Her stockinged feet were up on one wire chair
while she sat in another, its metal grid softened by a dirty
blanket folded into a pad. In the close heat of the cabin she
had taken off her T-shirt and was bare-armed and bare-
bellied in a white bra. My shadow, as I entered, dimmed the
glimmer of the startling undergarment; her face lifted and

also looked shady, smudged, a defensive sneer beclouding her lips. With an intentional gruffness I asked her, "Where are your buddies?"

"Out, doing deals. José and Ray got themselves suits like you said to."

"Does it make a difference?"

"Seems to. They say the people treat them more like they treated Spin and Phil. They cough up."

"Good. Didn't I say?"

"They look pretty silly."

"To you."

Our silence was not as uncomfortable as I would have predicted. With a sigh I sat on a third chair and looked out the square window, to take my eyes from the freckled breadth of her bony upper chest, the glossy rounds of her shoulders like inverted china cups, the single navel-dented crease across her lean belly. The square held an abstraction, a silent still gnashing of sharp-edged leaves and broken rock-faces and stabbing branches and scrabbly shapes of light-soaked sky. The boys had reinforced the stick walls with inch-thick plywood nailed to the vertical members so as to provide a crackless, relatively smooth inner surface for their shelter. This added privacy had imposed a cost: though bugs and prying eyes were better repelled, so was fresh air; when the door to the screened addition was closed, as it was now, an unstirring damp heat was sealed in. I liked it. I have always preferred the closed to the overexposed, the stuffy bed to the stinging shower.

I wondered if the boys had known I was coming. They watched me closer than I could ever watch them.

"So everything," I said, "is working out. I keep looking out my window to see if Mrs. Lubbetts' architecturally in-appropriate beach house is burnt down yet."

She took a breath, momentarily erasing the crease on her belly. "They said," she said, "you could touch me wherever you wanted, but no penetration."

I cleared my throat in the sticky air, anxious to avoid a mis-step. "That's very generous of them," I allowed. "Is this instead of giving me my cut of the take? And what do *you* want, Doreen? Not to be touched at all, I imagine."

"Maybe I wouldn't mind too much," she said, removing her feet from the wire chair and setting the Grisham in their place, marking her place by resting the bigger, unread half on the seat with the rest hanging down. "This book is awful macho and preachy." She stood up, taller and more womanly already, her blue jeans insolently tilted on her jutting hip bones and so low-slung they bared the hem of powder-blue underpants.

I was frightened, and set my fingers on the white skin of her long waist as if testing a stovetop or iron for heat. She was cool to the touch, surprisingly, and clean-smelling. As my warming hands timidly investigated the ins and outs, the givingness of her waist, the immature firmness of her buttocks, I had no intention of removing any of her clothes; but the skimpy elastic bra slipped off by itself with a shrug that was her idea. She helped it up over her neck and wiry ginger-colored hair mass. The shadows between her ribs flickered when she did this. Her breasts smelled powdery, like a baby's skull, and her nipples were spherical, like paler, smokier versions of honeysuckle berries. In whispers we debated if my tongue and mouth were included in the permission to touch. We decided they were. Her fingertips toyed with the whorls of my ears as she gazed down upon my poor old scalp, naked as a baby's beneath my transparently thinning white hair. It moved me, how much, in even so relatively undeveloped and flat-chested a sallow-skinned girl, her breasts were *there*, jutting, reaching, even; her sharp-chinned face loomed above mine like a mothering spaceship as I slurped and nuzzled and groaned. She graciously offered to touch me, where I jutted, to relieve my groans, but I said no, the boys had made a bargain with me, and I had preached trust to them.

"A hand-job wouldn't be penetration," Doreen said.

"It would penetrate my soul," I said. "I would become a love-crazed pest." As a reward to myself for this renunciation I slid down her jeans along with her underpants, cupped her taut, porcelain-smooth buttocks in my horny old thick-fingered hands, and planted a tongue-kiss in her shallow navel. How white her belly was! Her pubic hair was just a ginger fuzz, thickest in the center, but even so she had shaved the sides in conformity with bathing-suit fashions. I stroked the pimples where whiskers would grow back. What is this human need to mutilate the most precious and tender parts of ourselves? Nostrils, earlobes, nipples. Circumcision. Art, I suppose. Taking the knife of criticism to God's carefully considered work.

Abandoning Doreen with her jeans not yet tugged up, I hurriedly climbed the slippery hill, away from this low part of the woods. I was panting and tumescent. I had become anxious to reinsert myself back into the slowly turning works of my orderly world. The patch of heat where the invisible deer had stood and started was still there, on its spot in the path, inflaming my face. Gloria must be home by now. She mustn't see me like this, hot and bothered. One icy-eyed question would lead to another, and there was no re-sealing the pit of truth once it was open. The curve of her car, her teal-blue Infiniti, gleamed in the driveway. The island of repetitive safety I had carved from the world seemed abruptly precious. I spit the acid taste of honeysuckle from

my tongue, and emerged from beside the barn with my hus-
bandly smile already prepared.

———————

Over at the club, I had come in to change back into street
shoes after an irritating round in which Red and I were
beaten by Ken and a new sidekick of his, a younger man
named Glenn, Glenn Caniff, an airline freight supervisor.
There was no comparison between the way Glenn hit the
ball and we did—his best drives were sixty yards beyond
ours and took off on a different trajectory, low to the ground
and then rising along a parabolic curve induced by backspin.
His shoulder turn was exaggerated and his knee action too
loose, but when he brought the club flush into the ball there
was no stopping it. His chipping and putting weren't bad either. Usually with my intermittently picture-book swing
and Red's ham-handed forearm-power we don't lack for distance, but Glenn made us feel old and poky, and when we
tried for that little extra the wheels began to come off, into
the weeds. I topped two drives just up to the ladies' tee and
Red couldn't stop his right hand from wrapping the ball
around the left-field foul pole. The more frustrated we got,
the more smooth and affable Glenn loathsomely became,
and the more slowly and deliberately Ken played, giving us
that sleepy silver-haired boyish pilot's grin. Still, I sank a
long putt on the last hole, for a sandy and an extra welder
on our final press, so my concluding mood was not altogether disgruntled.

The other three, wearing soft spikes, had gone straight to
the members' porch for the drinks and peanuts and payoffs
and gleeful recapitulation of their best shots, but I was loyal
to real cleats (I love the menacing clatter they make on con-

crete and asphalt), which are forbidden on the wooden porch. Also I needed to urinate and to be alone a few minutes. There is something photophobic in me that can stand only so many hours of the unrelieved sunshine of boon companionship and seeks the shade of ill-tempered solitude.

The locker room, newly recarpeted last winter, when in one of the renovations urged by the younger members its friendly old green metal lockers were replaced with expensive, less capacious ones of varnished beechwood, appeared at first empty. But then with a start I saw a naked man emerge from the tiled shower room. He seemed terrifically hairy, and, with his broad chest and bow legs, he crouched, like an animal thinking of pouncing. Seeing me, he also started; he had been no doubt lost in the reverie that follows a shower—the steaminess, the forceful needling water, the face blindly held up to the primeval thrash—as the large rough towel reacquainted him with his tingling surfaces. It startled me to think that the club was now admitting such brutish-looking members: but then I reflected that young men all, even I in my prime, have a brutish aspect, unevolved since the age of tribal warfare and the naked group hunt for the sacred bear and hairy mammoth.

This menacing shadow in our renovated cave advanced toward me quizzically, blinking and dragging his towel in one hand. "Ben?" he asked in a light, civilized voice. "Aaron Chafetz."

Of course. My doctor. My new young doctor, unrecognizable in his shaggy skin, and nearsighted without his glasses. My doctor of many years, Ike Fidelman, four years older than I, had had a stroke. It hadn't much bothered me, since he had always talked out of the side of his mouth, with slurred, impatient diction. But he had abruptly retired and moved to the so-called Oregon Wilderness—Chinese missiles had devastated the cities, the bridges, the Boeing plant—to live with his daughter, who had become a Buddhist priestess.

"Ike," I had complained into the telephone, "how can you leave me in the lurch like this?"

"It's no lurch. A great boy is taking over the practice. He'll be up on all this new stuff."

"I don't want all the new stuff."

Ike had been homeopathic in his approach; Gloria called him the only Jewish Christian Scientist in the medical profession.

"You will when you need it," he told me. "They do magic with superlasers now, Ben. Thirty years ago I'd have a flipper for a left arm and a bubble in my brain. Good luck. Easy on the coffee, the booze, the fried food, and the young girls."

Had he forgotten how I had given up, at Gloria's urging, alcohol and caffeine altogether? In her guilt at secretly wishing me dead, she took an overactive interest in my health, from vitamin pills laid out beside my morning orange juice to a constant nagging about what I put into my mouth.

"Dr. Chafetz," I said, absurdly formal but unable to address him in any other way. A doctor is a doctor. We thought of shaking hands but thought better of it. Our costumes were disturbingly reversed: usually I was the undressed one. I had never seen his body before; its thickness and hairiness did not go with his thin ascetic face, his somewhat receding hair, his gold wire-frame spectacles. Without the spectacles he had had to come close, to identify me. I ignored the bestially bared body and concentrated on his face, pale and sensitive and shaven. He had a deferential, hushed manner, never more so than when he was testing my testicles for hernia and probing my prostate gland with a greased forefinger.

The last time he had done this it had rather scaldingly hurt, which I wasn't sure was normal. I had hoped he had not taken my tears for those of erotic gratitude. I can just barely make out, at the fuzzy far rim of my psychosomatic universe, how male homosexuals could get to depend emotionally on penetration of the narrow, fragile anal passageway, which makes the vagina look like a tough old catchall.

Another universe, thinner than a razor blade, sliced into the sinister locker room. Chafetz was a naked Jew, and I a uniformed good German recruited to guard an extermination camp, thus releasing a younger member of the master race to the Russian front, where the Slavs had shown themselves perversely reluctant to embrace the blessings of the Third Reich. The sky was low and smoky day after day. The sun was hiding its face. All color had ebbed from the world save the dull brown of dead underbrush and, nearer at hand, the occasional bright splash of blood. It was Poland in early 1944, winter. Iron ruled the bitter air—the iron of guns and of barbed-wire fences and of the rails upon which the steam engines dragged their crammed human cargo in iron boxcars. Thin snow on the hard earth was quickly flecked with particles of ash. The view from the watchtowers was of monotonous and swampy terrain that in the distance reluctantly lifted in low rows of blue hills that mirrored the low blue clouds, viscid and wavy, close above them. In between lay a bar of silver light, scored by slants of weak sun. Winter rooks circled above snow-dusted fields of stubble.

A sickness had settled in our bowels as the news from the Eastern front, however brazenly presented as strategic triumphs over helpless barbarians, ever more clearly spelled defeat. Allied airplanes, though downed in devastating numbers, kept bombing the homeland: droning flocks of them cruelly seeking to obliterate our wives and innocent children. The mongrel brutes of the Jew-polluted earth were pressing upon us with a sullen weight not all of the Führer's magic could dispel. A complicity of doom was coming to exist between us and the verminous prisoners. They stank of illness, of vomit and the yellow shit of dysentery, though we endeavored to keep them clean with frequent hosings in the open air, even on those mornings when the piss in the latrines was frozen solid. To this one as he stood nearest to me in the shivering line I said, camaraderie rising to my lips like the acid of nausea: "You will die, *sicherlich. Ohne Zweifel,* you are going to die. *Verstehst du?*"

What sick demon inside was making me talk such gibberish? There was no response from the young Jew. Perhaps he was not as young as he seemed at first glance. The young men generally died before the older, who were more gristly, less easily broken, their spirits longer welded to their bodies. This one stared past me, through me, with eyes like globules of black oil, the oil for which the Reich is starving. His white skin in the biting cold had a sallow waxen lustre repugnantly different from the clean pink purity of Aryan skin. His eyes were infuriating in their shining opacity. Even men totally at our mercy were capable, I saw, of insolence.

I continued, "*Schwein,* you must die, because you are evidence. Loathsome evidence. *Beweis abscheulich.*"

Even in the freezing air his waxen skin gave off a warm human aroma. I wondered how many treacheries and obscene acts in the bunkhouse had kept the fat on his bones. There was something horribly animal about the way his hunched neck thrust forward from his white shoulders, with their hideous Jewish epaulets of black hair.

"With all such evidence destroyed," I told him chummily,

"the world will never believe what we did to you people."
And I fought a nauseating impulse to throw my arm around
his shoulders, in a camaraderie of hopelessness, and to fiddle
with the hanging weight of his circumcised prick, shaped
like a turd leaving a warm ass but bluish-white, its skin thinner and finer than that of a woman's body anywhere. Instead
I lifted my sturdy Mauser rifle and smashed the butt into the
side of his expressionless, bestial, liquid-eyed face. He stag-
gered but somehow kept his feet. "Answer when I speak,
Jewish swine!" I shouted. The other captives, and the other
guards, and even the rooks drifting overhead, did not flinch,
as if they were from a still photograph and the two of us
from a scratchy, twitching movie. The movie was not black-
and-white, for the red smear on the prisoner's temple grew
brighter as I watched, and two rivulets trickled in parallel
down across his gaunt cheekbone.

I was beginning to panic in the search for something
friendly to say. A taste of iron had appeared in my mouth,
though no time at all, time as we understand it, had passed.
I brought out, "How was your game?" Having taken a
shower, he must have played a game—tennis, most likely.

"Good, Ben," he said in his thoughtful, preppy, deferential, and delicately hesitant way. "We got three sets in. And
yours?"

"Lousy as usual. It's like I have an enfeebling disease and
don't know it. I sank a putt on the last hole, though; that'll
bring me back." My auditor resumed rubbing himself with
the towel, discreetly keeping his genitals covered as he did
so. He was about to turn away; I blurted, "Seeing you here
reminds me, I must be due for a checkup."

Dr. Chafetz turned his back. Black fur covered his shoulder blades with symmetrical whorls like hurricane clouds

and formed a dark downy triangle at the base of his spine, above his buttocks with their more transparent gauze. "Sure thing," he said over his epauletted shoulder, with his accommodating, preppy ease. "Call my office for an appointment, Ben. We'll work you in."

———————

The midsummer refulgence takes to itself the dust of days. The trees' green is a duller tint, as if in a Barbizon painting whose varnish has darkened. Purple loosestrife, acres of it, blooms in the broad marsh we see from the fourth fairway, as its dogleg curves around a pond choked with lilies. Gloria's garden holds a fluffy, morning-wet profusion of cosmos and daisies, veronica and salvia, black-eyed Susans on their wavy stems and tall thistles with their little blue sea-urchins. This year, for the first time that I can remember, she has brought to vegetable health a single dahlia of an indecently vivid pearly pink, the lush electric flesh-blush of a maiden's labia.

In town, hydrangeas flourish by the porches, in color mostly that rinsed blue which suggests balls of laundry. Vacant roadside spaces play host to goldenrod and chicory. The goldenrod nods, bowing to its own allergen-rich weight, while the chicory aspires, its stems darting upward like lines connecting dots. On the walk down to the mailbox I admire the clusters of orange rowan berries on the two spindly trees that Jeremy and I spared last fall by the stone retaining wall, orange berries that, along with the tiny white berries, like beads of frost, on the cedars, suggest Christmas. From my bathroom window as I shave I notice a rusty tinge to the topmost leaves of the burning bush that has overgrown the path the previous owners had laid through their rock garden. Here and there in the woods, a sugar maple flashes the merest pinch of yellow while the other trees—the oak, the beech, the sassafras shaped like a Tiffany lampshade—hold on to their green monotone. On the little pears a few worm-warped bubbles of fruit are shaping up, and the blueberry bushes, I noticed the other day, are producing more cankers than berries, and their leaves have been chewed to lace by Japanese beetles.

In early August the dusks start shifting in, so there is an elegiac, dimmed, dry quality to the seven-thirty hour, which in July still abounds with blue sky, high clouds, and mental lemonade. The garage is silent—the swallows and their cheeping, dipping trio of hatchlings have departed for Peru, leaving the nest woven of mud still cupped against a rafter. The dew-whitened cobwebs of earthbound spiders are conspicuous on the morning lawn, as ominous as the streaks of cirrus where cumulus yesterday ruled. Monstrous fungoid growths have overnight appeared in the grass, some resembling the toadstools in children's books but others shaped, like cancers, by nothing but the random outward push of greedily growing cells. At a kick, the brown mass, tougher than it looks, scatters into meaty shreds.

Several days after my appointment, Dr. Chafetz called to say that the PSA test on my blood had come back with a reading of 11. He paused.

"Is that bad?" I asked.

"Not, not ex*treme*ly bad," he said, with his deferential hesitancy, a preppy near-stutter. "But it *is* high."

"What's considered normal?" I felt I was dragging information out of him. He was already deep in a medical crisis that hadn't yet pulled me in, and down. My mind was darting about within the meagre facts, looking for a way out.

"Anything under four," he said. "Even five asks for a second look."

I held stubbornly silent, annoyed at his embarrassment on my behalf. Whose PSA count was this, mine or his?

He offered, "Your prostate didn't feel unusually enlarged in my manual investigation. Or seem to have any rough spots."

Seem to have? What was he doing up there—gathering vague impressions? "Well, O.K. What's the next step?" I asked, so briskly his voice came out as not just deferential but boyishly scared. I was the Kapo, he the naked, shivering, doomed prisoner.

"A biopsy. In Boston. We have ties with an excellent man at MGH, a urologist. We'll set you up with an appointment."

Where did this "we" he was suddenly hiding behind come from? "What's his name?"

"Carver."

"It would be." I laughed, encouragingly. I had to bring the boy through this.

"Dr. Andrew," he, interrupted, went on.

"Handy Andy," said I, irrepressible, unkillable, immortal.

Hanging up, I wandered through the rooms of the house. It was as if each had been given a scrubbing; a film of the drearily familiar had been removed. The house appeared splendid, ample, priceless. It came to me as I passed through the rooms that I was and always had been a slightly different person in each one. In the dining room, with its torn and stained antique wallpaper of fantastical vistas through the ages—temples, grottoes, castles, cathedrals; Rome, Jerusalem, Athens, Nineveh; Alps and the Alhambra, snowy peaks and spiky cypresses—and its standing platoon of Gloria's shining mahogany antiques, I was courteous, hostly, with lurking eighteenth-century graces and a grave gray-haired timbre. In the kitchen, where I microwaved a cup of water hot enough to soften up a teabag and extracted a low-sodium pretzel from the breadbox, I was Everyman, a stomach on legs, a trousered relic of the paleotechnological era when refrigerators and electric stoves still had weight and thick skins. In the dark little library I became a crabbed squire, a cranky country hobbyist, a nineteenth-century-minded custodian of uniform sets of Balzac and Dickens, O. Henry and Winston Churchill (the statesman, not the American novelist). In the living room, which I moved through on my way to the veranda, I was momentarily a breezy, translucent person, a debonair proprietor of mirrored and velvet-hung spaces carpeted by a single great rose-and-blue Tabriz; I became a throwback to a romantic time of gin parties and yachting, a light-hearted butterfly emerged from the narrow and dour chrysalis of that asphalt-shingled farmhouse lonely in its tilted field of drab winter stubble, on the edge of a dying industrial town. From Hammond Falls to Haskells Crossing: not much of a pilgrimage, really, considering that I had had nearly sixty-seven years to nudge my way along.

The out-of-doors, too, as I settled on the wicker sofa (which creaked under my new weight of dread), loomed with a defining distinctness, a dazzling room of another sort, in which I was an insignificant insect rapturously enrolled, for these brief bright instants of my life, in a churning, shining, chirping, birthing, singing, dying cosmic excess. From the quasars to the rainbow shimmer on my dragonfly wings, everything was an extravagance engraved upon the obsidian surface of an infrangible, eternal darkness.

My pulse fluttered. I felt girlish with my secret. I told Doreen before I told Gloria. Doreen couldn't understand

that it was a big deal yet; she had no idea where the prostate
gland was and her whole face wrinkled with disgust when I
told her. Gloria statuesquely enlarged at the news into the
tragic grandeur of eventual widowhood. Long cast in the
role of wife, she had endured years of dull lines, but now at
last the part was proving worthy of her gifts. She foresaw her
new, elevated status and wished to do nothing henceforth
less than impeccably wifely and loving: I could see the de-
termination written on her otherwise smooth, broad forehead. She would see me through to the next world and then
take as her reward a singular dignity, no longer regent on
behalf of a senescent male but queen absolute. She would
pour forth the melody from the center of the stage.

The mornings have a nip to them now when I walk down for
the *Globe*. Certain tall yellow-headed weeds—hawkweed, I
think—have taken root in the cracks of the broken concrete
drying-yard and I bend down to pull a few on my way, and
throw them onto the burning pile as I pass. Since childhood
I have loved this month—the flat dry taste of it, the brown-
lawn look of it, bouncing the heat back up against your bare
legs, and the lack of any importunate holiday marring the
blank days on this side of Labor Day and the return to school.
   On Saturday Gloria directed Jeremy and me to dig up the
Siberian iris that has flourished on the stony slope behind
the two scrawny pear trees to the right of the driveway. We
attacked the clump first with shovels, which met too many
stones, and then with the mattock, which I swung with
powerful effect. Jeremy suddenly exclaimed and darted his
hand down to seize a garden snake liquidly wriggling away
through the grass. The little snake's undulant motion and

the sheen of its polychrome scales were so beautiful it shocked us both to see that its tail end was mangled and raw, oozing muddy reptile blood. A shovel or the mattock in my hands had caught it, a blow from heedless Heaven, as it coiled in concealed innocence. Jeremy put the snake gently back into the grass and it slithered off with unimpaired fluency, but I thought that a snake was not a ribbon that could be snipped anywhere: it had an anatomy, intestines and an anus, and no more than I could it live long with its nether portion crushed. I hate it when our human attempts to inflict order upon the land brings death and pain and mutilation to these innocents, whose ancestors enjoyed the earth for tens of millions of years before the naked ape appeared with his technology and enraging awareness of his own sin. I blamed Gloria, for having us remove this harmless, thriving clump of iris because it offended her frosty, simplifying eyes. Who are we to say what is a weed or a pest? Now the pretty snake, stricken in its perfection, must lie in some crevice feeling its slender body dam and slowly fail; a glaze of nothingness will close upon the little jewel of its unblaming brain.

Working alongside Jeremy made me try to remember working beside my own father. He could do things, up to a point: hammer and nail, handle elementary wiring and plumbing. He worked for a time for a roofing contractor, and though he said the heights didn't bother him he would come home complaining of how roofers cheated people, even the most trusting poor widow. He had a vegetable garden out back that he would stand in at the end of the day, and a workshed on one side of the garage full of aligned jars of screws and nails getting rusty. For a time he had a job on the floor of the GE factory in Pittsfield, but the monotony of assembly, he confessed one night at supper, made him physically sick. He went from job to job, with his poor skills, his indifferent attitude, his lack of a trade. We did complete a few projects together—a doghouse for Skeezix, a soapbox racer, with the number 9 in silver outlined in black—but generally he was too tired. He just wanted to sit in his brown armchair with the fake leather worn off the arms and watch television and have dinner brought to him. I vowed I would never get that tired in life.

Last night I was in the bathroom when the commuter train thundered, louder it seemed than usual, along the tracks on the far edge of the woods. In a few months, when the leaves are down, I can see the golden windows flickeringly flowing by. I clenched with love of the muffled racket, an ecstatic sensation dating from my earliest intimations of traffic, of large things hurtling past on the road into the valley. I love thunder, too—the cascading and smashing first in the distance, like a strawberry box yielding to pressure, and then wildly, dangerously overhead, thumping the roof so the window sashes tremble in their sills and the thin clear panes shiver against their putty, and then the semi-satisfied, still irritable receding mutter, as the sated gutters gurgle. *Things passing safely by:* this intensely pleased me. Now perhaps I am the thing that is passing, my body a skin I am shedding, with resistance at some points of attachment.

The biopsy was neither painless nor painful. Giving myself the Fleet enema the night before and then again in the morning, on the cold bathroom floor while studying the underside of the sink and waiting for my bowels to feel revulsion, numbed my spirit to the humiliation of the ultrasound rectal probe and then the actual harvest of the tiny plugs of tissue—preceded, each one, by Dr. Carver's murmured formula, "A little pinch." A little pinch, a little pinch, and I was back in my street clothes striding, a bit tenderly, with tin-

gling empty bowels, up Cambridge Street to State, where
the old gang at Sibbes, Dudley, and Wise seemed friendlier
than usual—perhaps my expectations of friendliness had
been lowered. I felt myself as a perambulating bushel of de-
fective innards, and they treated me with civility as an intelligence, a faded eminence.

The urologist had been a young man with a head of receding blond fuzz and a complexion that had taken a pink
humidity from the underparts that were his specialty. He
had a big-shouldered, stern Irish nurse who stayed with us
and, while the snipping was going on beneath the discreet
blue sheet, unexpectedly held my hand. It was one of the
many impersonal mercies that descend upon us, I saw, when
we weaken. Our host the world is extra polite, even effusive,
when with relief it sees that we are at last about to leave.

But I had not weakened. I was no snake with a mangled
tail. The tingling singed sensation at the upper tip of my
rectum merely goaded me to brisker efficiency, more aggressive know-how. I was there to do some shifting in my
and Mrs. Fessenden's portfolios, plus some few others still in
my care, away from cyclicals, which were in for a troubled
time now that the Asian low-wage platforms were giving
signs of revival amid the vast destruction, and into tech-
nicals—live-gene transplantation and atomic-scale minia-
turization, possibilities that at last were emerging from the
theoretical stage. The big windows looked down upon a
Boston of slightly curved streets traced between blocks of
brick-red rubble and commercial buildings abandoned—
some so precipitously the windows had not been boarded
up—after the dramatic population shrinkage. These empty
blocks seemed from on high a great bowl of opportunity.
We survivors were heirs to room for expansion, to a future
of unpredictable possibilities loosed by the relaxation of or-

der. Evolutionary change proceeds through small isolated populations; widespread species tend to stagnate in their own success. We had been horseshoe crabs and crocodiles; now we were nimble niche mammals, ruthlessly thinned, rapidly developing hooves, lemur-large eyes, and specialized gizzards. I would not see it all happen but it was in the air, a kind of planetary expectancy vibrant above the rubble.

Gary Gray was the one who dealt with me. He seemed less wispy—indeed, he had developed a little pot belly, rather preeningly displayed in the logoed T-shirt which has become standard business wear for his generation. I still feel naked without a suit, though my suits in retirement are going stiff and shabby on their cedarwood hangers. "Where's Ned, on vacation?" I asked.

"You could say that," he said, and his sidelong glance did not encourage me to ask more. My heart leaped up gleefully, to think that Ned had come a cropper. One's own rise offers a precarious happiness, shadowed as it is by the threat of reversal and others' greater triumphs; but the downfall of another provides permanent satisfaction.

"I could say that, but it wouldn't be the case?"

"Extended vacation would be the optimistic formulation." Gary grayly smiled. "He got in the way of the number crunchers. He had too verbal a way of expressing himself."

"And Pat? She was his assistant."

"*I* know who *Pat* was," he said, in an overemphatic, peevish manner that may have been a parodic declaration of his own sexual preferences. "She's made a sideways jump, to Sturbridge, Morrissey, and Blaine. They promised her some accounts, and a cubicle of her own, if she'd take night courses in financial management."

"She seemed very promising," I said. "A people person." I have never understood homosexuals: they make their

choice, or have it biologically made for them, and then become very caustic and indignant about the party they have
chosen not to attend—the party of breeders, of fertile male-
female friction.

"She was a *tramp*," Paul told me. "You can use this office.
But all the transaction codes have been changed; there's a
hard-copy printout in one of the drawers. The crunchers
don't like their numbers used by outsiders, even cherished
former insiders like yourself. She really made your heart
go pitty-*pat*, didn't she, Ben boy?"

He took his leer and his bellied-out logo (EXCREMENT
OCCURS, it read) away. As I fiddled and fumbled my transactions into the data bank, I felt suspended in space, with my
stinging tail, and a touch agoraphobic. I wanted to scuttle
out of this cubicled brightness into a friendly dark crevice.
More and more, off my own chronically paced property, I
feel frightened and disoriented. Boston for forty years was
my second home, but now it seemed hostile and featureless,
a void beneath my feet.

This was true even of a golf game in Brookline which Red
arranged with a member of the Country Club whom he
knows. When Red picked me up in his Dodge Caravan, and
began to talk on his cellular phone with Durban, South
Africa, and then Perth, Australia—what fish there are on the
planet are in the Southern Hemisphere, like sparkling
snowflakes settling in a glass globe—I felt vaguely kidnapped. Fear raced at the back of my mind like the trickle of
cold water that murmurs throughout the whole house when
the rubber stopper in a water closet is imperfectly seated.
Ken Dixon sat in the back seat, silent, whether from a wish
not to interfere with Red's loud, rambling discussion about
evanescent schools of "product," or because he, too, on my
transmission frequency, heard the murmur of fear, of a fatal

leak in things that was draining the world of substance. The course—its lunar outcroppings of black pudding-stone, its par-fives wandering past cliffs and up sand-bunkered slopes like metaphors of life's dreamy, anfractuous journey— seemed hollowed out, a shared illusion composed of electrons and protons spinning in a space that was ninety-nine percent vacuum.

Our host was named Les, for Lester Trout, one of Red's financial catches when he was trawling the Boston financial community for investors, before the war, in an enlarged freezing-and-packing plant. Les was a happy rich man, in shape and fine fettle. Golf had become his life; he attacked the course once a day in order to bring his handicap down from an eight to a seven, and next year a six. He uncoiled into the ball with a wonderful compact force; and after an especially successful shot would flash a predatory smile, inviting you to share his delight in his game.

On the par-three twelfth, I suffered a moment of delusion: I expected to see his nicely drawing nine-iron shot plunge through the elevated green as if through a drum of green paper or the scummy skin of a pond. But no, there was terra firma there, our ancient accretion of sedimented rock. The ball hopped, and stopped. I kept picturing how an orange forgotten at the back of the produce drawer in the refrigerator shrinks to a grayish-green orb that emits puffs of smoke like a pod of pollen.

My sense of unreality, as I moved through the veils of *maya*, helped me play a little better than usual; I felt indifferent to everything but returning myself to the matrix of my home surroundings—the curving driveway, the white house, the leafy woods, the kids in the woods, the deer, the wife, the flowers—and so swung easily, winning praise I could hardly hear through the murmur of terror leakily running at the back of my brain.

I exaggerate. The dynamics of the match did burn through to me. I was partnered with our host, who with his expensively developed superiority was giving so many strokes to the rest of us that when he faltered—and he was bound to falter often, with a putt that lipped out or a drive that sucked too far left—the burden fell on me. Whenever the pretensions of our low-handicapper were punctured, it became a match of Red and Ken versus Ben. In my betranced state I held up better than when paired with Fred Hanover against these same two buddies. The three of us, equally strangers to this pudding-stone paradise, had a certain furtive solidarity, though I was the evil host's ally. My distracted golf took on a quality I can only call coziness. The path the ball should follow was marked as if by broad troughs in the air; it was the reverse of that frequent agonizing feeling of a narrow correct path, a kind of razorback ridge which the ball keeps slipping down one side or the other of. Especially on the second side, beginning with pars on the short, blind tenth hole and the long eleventh with its sheer cliff and grassy transverse ditch, did I help my team; we wound up collecting two welders, which Les Trout tucked into his wallet as gleefully as if he had made another million.

I marvel, writing this down, at with what boyish games we waste our brief lives.

Time, I have read, was believed by Pythagoras to be the soul and procreative element of the universe. And it is true, rail against its ravages as we will, that we cannot imagine our human existence without it: nothing would happen—we would be glued flat against space like the schematic drawings with which mathematical gamesters illustrate the odd consequences if our three dimensions were reduced to two. Descartes claimed to believe that time is a series of ever-perishing instincts continually renewed by God in split-second acts of deliberate creation. This grotesque idea occurred to me as a child, and perhaps to most children as their brains awkwardly widen into metaphysics. Science begins with keeping track of time. The Mayans had calendars more accurate in arranging leap years than our own. Dwellers in the Andaman Islands keep a calendar based on the odors of seasonal plants as they bloom and die.

Each morning, I observe, the day displays a few more dead leaves on the driveway, a few more yellow patches in the stand of young maples reflected in the pond. Shaving in my bathroom mirror, I glance down and perceive a slightly more reddish tinge than yesterday's to the top of the burning bush, *Euonymus atropurpureus*, which grows in the terraced area visible from this window.

Gloria points out that I shave badly, for all the times I have done it. I skip bristles beneath my jaw and just under my nose; I don't go far enough down my neck, so unsightly long white hairs protrude above my shirt collar. She also claims, observing me through the rivulets in the steamed-up glass door, that I don't know how to shower—I don't use enough soap, and I don't pull back my foreskin and scrub. The wives of uncircumcised men get cancer of the cervix seven times more than women with circumcised husbands, she claims. So, go marry a Jew or be a nun, I think. It wasn't my decision; it was taken by old Dr. Hardwick and my mother, back at Pittsfield General on a September afternoon in 1953. Maybe they plotted to give my wives cervical cancer. There was some kind of collusion between dark-browed, young-old Doc Hardwick and my petite, sandy-haired mother; I could feel it in the way they paired up at my bedside when I had the chicken pox or mumps. I could hear it in their chatting over coffee downstairs, my father off at work and house calls already all but a thing of the past. In the more than three score years that I have had to ponder it, I think being uncircumcised perhaps the most valuable thing about me. My sheathed glans imparts a responsive sensitivity to the entire stumpy stalk that embarrassed me now and then in youth but served me well into advanced maturity; I am *Homo naturalis*, man unscathed, Adam before the covenant; and I am deeply hurt that Gloria levels these criticisms. Perdita never complained of my poor cumbersome body, though her silences, her increasing reserve, her way of grimacing and keeping her own sweet counsel in the end were more devastating than any utterance.

To Gloria I am a kind of garden, where she must weed, clip, tie, deadhead, and poison aphids. She can't believe that, after all these years, I sometimes set the fork on the right and the knife and spoon on the left; it would affront her no less if I came to the table without trousers on. At the weddings we now and then attend, to see time feed the younger generation into its procreative mill, when she and I dance she tells me to take big steps and to stop jiggling my shoulders. Slurping my soup, picking my nose even in the dark of the movie theatre, putting on a striped tie with a checked jacket—all these harmless self-indulgences excite her to flurries of admonition, and perhaps I am wrong to take offense. She merely wants to train me, like a rose up a trellis. As I age and weaken, I more and more succumb to her tireless instruction. She finds my driving doddery and dangerous, so it seems simplest to let her drive when the two of us are in the car. Docilely, before putting them on, I hand her my pajamas to verify that they are clean enough to wear for one more night; she sniffs the collar, makes a face, hands them back to me, and says, "The hamper."

Yet I do not fail every sniff test. Sometimes, usually just before dinner, when her biorhythm enters an amorous patch, she presses her nose into my neck and says, "You smell *right*. You smell *mine*. It's like a mother—she knows her baby by the smell. And the baby knows the mother." These elemental animal facts never lose their charm for her; she is so conversant with the language of scent that I fear she may catch on my face a whiff of Doreen's crotch, which I have won the right to nuzzle, down in the shack, and, her glossy thighs propped on my shoulders, to stir with my tongue—the scarcely musky, gingerly furred pink folds of it—as the closest approach to penetration that I will allow myself, or that my unstated compact with the boys from Lynn allows me. It is a rare event—they are branching out, taking their moll with them—and I scrub my face afterwards, with soap enough to mask a rotting mummy.

The other amorous peak of Gloria's biorhythm comes at night, between four and five, when she awakens in a nervous state. She hugs me, kisses my neck, murmurs invitations. Her aristocratic fingers timidly seek my penis; I slap at her hand, trying to preserve my dreaming state. Her nightie has ridden high on her body; she makes me curl my arm around her; her breasts glide into my hands as if leaping; her buttocks push at my slumbering manhood, which dully considers answering the call, weighing the pluses and minuses. "It's the middle of the night," I groan.

"I know, I know," she says pityingly, apologetically.

"Couldn't you save all this for daylight, darling?"

"I will, I will—good idea," Gloria says, breathily, meekly,

yet with a heartbreaking lilt of unquenched hope, as if I might pounce after all. We both know she will not feel this passion in daylight, there is too much to do, the world presses at too many points—gift shop, garden club, newspaper, telephone—and her passion is based in part upon my being asleep, babyishly defenseless and pre-sexual, exciting perverse desire. My brain fumbles at the cozy coverlet of the dream I was having (I was back in Hammond Falls playing pick-up baseball) while wondering if my duty as a man and an American was not to gouge myself awake and serve my needy wife. She whispers, "I'll go to the other room and read," and I fall gratefully back asleep. All my old playmates are there in the dream—Poxy Sonnen, Billy Beckett, Fats Weathersby—and the red-brick smokestacks downtown, by the river, are visible beyond left field as it slopes away.

It is not just me that Gloria finds exasperatingly imperfect. The lawn boys have no idea how to mow a lawn, the cleaning ladies leave cobwebs in all the high corners, and the dentist has placed in her mouth a grotesquely mismatching crown—too yellow, too big. Her smile is in fact her foremost charm, brilliant and broad, her teeth apparently perfect. My mother, who was still alive then, regretted my leaving Perdita and the children, but admitted, upon meeting Gloria, "Those teeth are worth investing in." Her own teeth had given her much trouble, and by her forties were mostly denture.

Since my encounter with Dr. Chafetz in the locker room and its medical follow-ups, my wife has tried to soften her criticisms. She looks me in the face after smelling my neck and abruptly her eyelids redden. I clasp her to me, knowing she is counting the days, the weeks, the years it may be; but the end of her captivity, her espousal to one unmannerly helping of male flesh, is in sight. I hold her, forgiving the unspoken. "You're so precious, so precious to me," she murmurs in her dear confusion.

Men are unreasonable in their contradictory demands on women. I blamed Perdita for not providing total care—for allowing me, in the indolent remissions of her own commitment, some freedom, which I misused. And I blame Gloria for smothering me with a care that nevertheless has not protected me from old age and its perils.

———————

As in the spring I had watched for the crocuses to open, and then the forsythia and lilac to yield each day a bit more of their color, so I watch from the bathroom window, as I shave, the leaves of the burning bush taking on, ever wider and more intensely, a reddish-purple tinge.

The biopsy came back positive: tiny sub-surface tumors in the middle left lobe, like rotten spots in a punky old chestnut.

I had a passionate desire to see Jennifer today and, after calling Roberta, drove over to Lynnfield. The baby was up from her nap and seemed pleased to see me—in her mother's arms, she held out her own little arms to me, wanting me to hold her. I felt desperately flattered. She is ten months old, on the gabbly, tottery edge of talking and walking. But the apparatus of challenge and response is still missing some neural cogwheels in her solemn, silky head. "What does the *sheep* say?" Roberta asked her, the refrain of a childhood book they read every night.

Jennifer pivoted her head to look at me as if I were the one being asked the question. "B-, b-," I prompted. She switched her head to look questioningly at her mother. She began to wriggle and get heavy in my arms. I put her down, on the kitchen floor, and for a second she almost stood, before cautiously flopping down onto her diapered bottom and then regaining an upright position by clinging to a kitchen chair. She looked up at the two of us with a guileless puzzlement, the broad bulge of her forehead like that of a pitcher waiting to be filled.

"*Baa,*" both Roberta and I told her, in a spontaneous father-daughter chorus. "*Baa.*"

The infant held on to the chair seat with one hand and put the middle two fingers of the other into her mouth, while staring unblinkingly upward, trying to imagine what we wanted of her. She removed the hand from her mouth and extended that arm as far as it would go and squeezed her spit-wet hand open and shut.

"That's *right*," Roberta's proud voice pronounced. "Bye-bye! Little Jenny say bye-bye!"

Jennifer smiled, pleased to have found our tune, and let the bye-bye gesture slowly die. Then another of her accomplishments surfaced through the mazy channels of her growing brain. She lifted both hands above her head—or, rather, above her ears, since her arms are so short all her gestures have a lovely stubbiness. Roberta instantly understood. "So *biiig,*" she eagerly crooned. "Jennifer is *sooo* big!"

The child, seeing herself understood, clapped her hands together, nearly missing.

"*Pat*ty cake," her mother obediently chimed. "*Pat*ty cake, *pat*ty cake, *bak*er's *man!*"

For these seconds, Jennifer, using both hands, had been standing on her own without realizing it; realizing it, she sat down in fright on the floor, and might have begun to cry had not Roberta swooped down and swept her up into a triumphant, overwhelming embrace. Thus women urge seed into seedling, seedling into fibrous plant. Girl babies excite our intensest tenderness because the pain of love and parturition awaits them, just as all their eggs are already stored in their tiny ovaries.

I had one cup of herbal tea and three low-fat ginger cookies and watched shy little Keith build and destroy two edifices of nesting plastic blocks; then Irene arrived with Olympe and Étienne, on their way back to west of Boston from visiting Eeva and Torrance and Tyler in Gloucester. My children and their spouses keep up a seethe of visitation and sibling interaction which no longer requires me or Perdita; we are emeritus parents, and perhaps always were somewhat absent. Our children raised themselves, with the help of the neighbors, television, and the international corporations that hoped to sell them something. My two soft-mannered half-African grandchildren endured with ironic smiles the clumsy bumptiousness of their little white cousins, whom they escorted and carried (Olympe lugging Jennifer like a sack, face outward, her stomach elongating so that her navel seemed about to emit a cry) into the yard while my two daughters, somewhat formally, settled to entertain their father. I did not share with them my recent diagnosis, nor they with me the depths of tribal gossip, presumably enriched by Irene's afternoon with the slant-eyed, bohemian Eeva. It makes me tired to try to recall what we did say—with what rusty banter I tried to revive my paternal role. In fact I was content to sip my second cup of herbal tea and watch the two girls, now women on the near and far side of forty, talk and gesture and demurely titter with the long-boned, self-careless grace of their mother when she was their age or younger. Perdita had been about their age when I had left her, amid scenes of such grievousness as would attend a dying. It was a dying, a killing, and we lacked the assurances which the last twenty years have brought, that other lives were coming, that we could live without one another.

We had married in 1978, toward the end of a decade of license, but we were an old-fashioned couple, really. We spent some weeks that first summer at her parents' place in remotest Vermont—stingy thin mountain land that reminded me of the Berkshires but which I was seeing from another social angle, as someone not obliged to wring a living from it. I was out of the B.U. B-School by then, and had been taken on by Sibbes, Dudley, and Wise. We would play gin rummy by kerosene light, and push an old reel mower across the bumpy lawn, and swim in an icy brook deep in the woods. Once I sneaked a little Instamatic into our gym bag and took a few photos of her naked, without her knowing, because I thought she was so beautiful. When she saw the prints she was horrified and hid them so that they did not surface until our divorce, when all our possessions were churned up. She had kept them in a linen drawer, under the paper liner. I asked her for them but she told me, blushing, no—they were hers. Her body, never to be so smooth and shapely again, but hers to bestow upon the next man. Like Russian dolls, I contain a freckled boyish ballplayer and Perdita *une jeune fille nue comme Diane se baignant.*

My daughters and I walked out of the little green tract house in Lynnfield to admire their children, all four filthily absorbed in making a racetrack in the bare dirt by the fence.

Along Route 128 as I drove east, tawny stripes of hay nodded in the lowering sun. Grass wants to die, to grow tall and set seed and die. Keeping it short and green in a lawn is a cruel and unnatural act, pro-Gramineae activists keep reminding us, as they are dragged off and pummelled by representatives of the powerful pro-lawn forces—the mower manufacturers, the great seed-and-fertilizer combines. When

I got out of the car in my driveway, an acorn pinged off the car roof and another struck me on the shoulder. The air was still summery and the sky the smooth blue of baked enamel, but the oak trees were letting go. *Let go:* natural philosophy in a nutshell.

Acorn shapes have been on my mind. My sinister locker-room encounter with Dr. Chafetz was but the lowest rung of a ladder of doctors I am climbing. Beyond the plump damp-handed urologist I have attained to a wiry radiologist, in his grizzled fifties but still exuberant over the wonders of technology, which accumulate even in times of social chaos. "Twenty, thirty years ago," he tells me, "you would have been a sure-as-shootin' candidate for prostatectomy—cut out the whole damn thing, and to hell with the surrounding tissue. Barbaric! They would saw away in there, in a sea of blood, and the patients would come out totally impotent and most likely peeing in their drawers for years, if they *ever* got sphincter control back. Now, with conformal radiotherapy, we shape the beam to the tumor exactly, and never even singe the colon or the bladder on either side. Precision! To the micron! They used to use only X-rays and some gamma rays to do the zapping—we're getting cleaner, faster results with beams of protons. We're not just killing these cells, Ben—we're inducing them to kill themselves, by a process called apoptosis—that's *a-p-o-p-tosis*—which the developing fetus uses to destroy embryonic gills, for instance. The body's discarding and weeding all the time, all the time. Plus there's all sorts of mop-up tricks you can do with radioactive implants and chemo. Prostate, for example"—the noun "cancer" had been dropped from the phrase—"by the nature of the beast is subject to a hormone therapy that produces an androgen blockade. Not quite a piece of cake, Ben, but close to it. A bagel, let's say."

Did I imagine it, or were more people calling me "Ben" since this crack in my health developed?

"Any questions, Ben? You've been following me?"

I hadn't, quite. When I was back in college, and had a big exam coming up, the closer it came the less I could concentrate on the necessary books: they developed an anti-magnetism which repelled my hand when I reached for them. Each of the finite moments until the test seemed infinitely divisible, with always the *next* particle of time the one in which I would face reality and at last concentrate.

Particles of time are not infinitesimal; they accumulate. I never used to be conscious of any scum on my teeth, any more than I was aware of any body odor or need to bathe. Perdita and I, I believe, always smelled perfectly bland, if not sweet, to one another. Now I want to brush my teeth all the time, even when I have not eaten since the last brushing. And my neck—why is my neck so sweaty when I awake? Pillow, pajamas, collars—an invisible pollutant has settled on them all, moment by moment.

On the walk down to the mailbox, I notice that the stunted pears are showing ruddiness on their warty little cheeks. But the wild blueberries, which I try to persuade Jeremy to skip over with his whirring weed-whacker, are oddly slow, this August, to turn blue. Or else the birds and those deer are eating them as they ripen. Some ferns are turning a reticent shade of brown. The fall is almost here.

I will miss you, sweet pages blank each new day. Here, have not one line but two:

———————

———————

Now—yes, there is still a "now"—the maples hold arcs and crests of orange like bouquets shyly thrust forward by a massive green suitor, and the horse-chestnut leaves are wilting from the edges in, and a faintly winy blush hazes some of the trees I see from Route 128, as Gloria drives me by en route to one of my now-incessant medical appointments.

She has decided to rip up all the cosmos in her garden. With a tentative tenderness she asks me if I want to come outside and—not help, of course—merely watch. Each step I take has an attendant difficulty and pain that makes the world—the green of the lawn, the transparency of space, the resilient solidity of the life-permeated earth—perversely delicious. Everything tastes the way it did in childhood, of newness and effort; each surface presents a puzzling, inviting depth of possibility, of future time without end. The year has made less progress than I had expected in the nearly four weeks that I was off in the hospital, with a view of brick walls and the rusty tops of city sycamores.

I have resolved to spare this journal dedicated to the year's passing any circumstantial account of the obscene operation that I have momentarily survived. It has left me incontinent for a while and impotent I fear forever. A soreness at the base of my bladder, a rasping burning lodged high in the seat of elimination (the devil's lair, in old religious lore) remind me of the violence done my unruly flesh. The operation was, as the wiry radiologist predicted, a twenty-first-century miracle of directed radiation—raw protons, aimed to a micron's tolerance by something called a delayed-focus laser—rather than the cheerful prostatectomic butchery of yore. Still, the negative effects and the factors of uncertainty are not as radically reduced as the celebrants of scientific advance would have you believe. Our bodies, which even in the year 2020 are the sole means by which "we"—we no-

bodies, so to speak—"live," retain a mulish atavistic recalci-
trance. To be human is still to be humbled by the flesh, to
suffer and to die. There are now three of us in the house—
Gloria, I, and my impending demise. Gloria's eyes are bright
with it; her utterances and gestures have an actressy crisp-
ness born of her awareness of this witnessing third party.
Herself as widowed, as mournfully, bravely free, fills her
mind much as the image of an idyllically happy married
woman gives direction to the fantasies of a pubescent girl.
She tries to be kinder, but in her enhanced vitality has more
edges, which cut into my heightened sensitivity. Just being
in her garish, painfully distinct and articulate presence has
become arduous.

Of my hospital stay I chiefly remember the white, syrupy
conspiracy of it all, like a ubiquitous, softly luminous ethereal lotion, and the eager complicity with which I entered
into the therapeutic rituals, the obligatory indignities, the
graciously shared disgrace. What an odd relief it is to shed
all the roles and suits and formal pretenses life has asked of
us and to become purely a body, whose most ignominious
and flagrant detail is openly, coöperatively examined and
discussed—cherished, even, as an infant's toes and burps and
turds are loved. Amid the pain and anxiety and helplessness,
self-love holds a little orgy for itself. Others, solemn, in
white, scurry in and out, vigorously participating in the in-
decencies, bestowing technical names upon the hitherto un-
speakable. Not even the most wanton whore, unhinged like
a puppet by her craving for cocaine, forgives you as much as
the night nurse who takes away the bedpan. Smilingly she,
in that phosphorescent hospital twilight wherein wink the
multi-colored lights of multiple sleepless monitors, gazes
down into your face and inserts into your mouth, like a tech-
nically improved nipple, the digital thermometer with its

grainy plastic skin. In these crevices of the nightmare, a deep neediness is put to rest.

I took an innocent pride, in short, in being a good patient—like being a good soldier, a morally dubious exercise in solidarity. I asked for no more pain medication than the authorities decreed, I made appropriate jokes in the intervals of my care, I admired the giant humming machines under whose poisonous focus I was periodically strapped, I was stoical about my hair loss and blistered anus; I minded only the infrequent sieges of nausea and the pathetic shrunken wreck the procedures made of my beloved genitals.

"What didn't you like about the cosmos?" I asked, with a sickly croak. In my frail sensitivity I imagined I could feel the damp of the lawn creeping up through my shoe soles— baroquely ornate running shoes, purchased to speed my convalescence.

"It didn't fit," Gloria stated firmly. "It wanted to take over the entire garden."

"It wasn't a good soldier," I amplified, in this new voice of mine that seems to have a permanent scratch in it.

"Exactly." Shards of earth and vegetation flew. Fistfuls of torn-up flowers stared skyward, lacking the nervous systems to realize that all those chemical transactions called life had been abruptly cancelled.

I felt—eerie, phantasmal sensation!—a trickle of urine warmly glide from my bladder into the plastic catheter, which conveyed it downward into the cumbersome leg bag strapped below my knee. The leg bag was flesh-colored, amusingly—as if I might enter a beauty contest wearing it, and it mustn't show. Sometimes it backed up, and urine already ejected once backed up as high as my flaccid penis, spilling down my thighs.

Big belling morning glories had climbed the green fence,
and the single dahlia in my absence had grown and prolifer-
ated into a small tree crowded with numerous blooms the
blushing color of a maiden's labia. There seemed something
rancid and evil about the garden—clumps of nameless livid
growths formed caves for slugs and havens for beady-bodied
daddy longlegs with ornately evolved venomous mandibles.
In fact moles, rats, and woodchucks did burrow and rum-
mage in the soft, much-mulched soil. Woodchucks nibble
off the tops of Gloria's flowers—they are especially partial to
poppies—so she heartlessly sets out so-called Have-a-Heart
traps for them, low rectangular cages whose doors fall diagonally and lock when the hapless animal treads on a central
trigger. In my absence she had caught a creature who had
calmly chewed an escape hatch through the 14-gauge galvanized wire. That must mean that she had caught a metallobioform, and that they were getting bigger. All the specimens
I had ever seen or read about could have slipped out through
the half-inch square mesh.

"Ben, as long as you're just standing there watching me
struggle, wouldn't you like to throw the cosmos into the
green cart and pull it down to the mulching pile?"

"Bending over is agony for me."

"The doctor said the more you exercised the better
you'd be."

"The doctor doesn't have a reamed prick and a bag of piss
strapped to his leg."

"You don't have to be rude about it." Another clump of
uprooted cosmos was flung and a spray of dirt speckled the
tops of my hitherto pristine running shoes. They were aqua,
turquoise, crimson, black, and white, with striped laces.
Gloria added, "The cart is in the garage."

The effort left me feeling I had dragged a load of broken concrete up the side of Mount Greylock. She told me, "While you were in the hospital, I was frightened. I kept hearing noises and voices in the woods."

A tension of guilt tugged at my wound, my seared and cleansed pockets of cancerous flesh. Though the delayed-focus laser in theory left the intervening tissue unaffected, in truth the flesh knew it had been violated, and why. Flesh knows everything, and forgets nothing.

"Oh?" I said. "I've been struck since I was home by how quiet everything is." I had been listening, in my captivity, for the Lynn boys, my adopted grandsons, to come to the door dutifully inquiring after my health, or for Doreen at night to come and hiss sexily beneath my window. I even scanned the driveway for her cigarette butts. My flesh remembered the scent of her cigarettes in the sweatshop closeness of the shack, and her malty smell, and the glazed hard place between her breasts, shallow taut cones tipped with honeysuckle-berry nipples. She liked—the only thing she admitted liking—my rapidly flicking them with my tongue. At night I would lie and listen for sounds of human life from the woods but there was only the contralto drone of the cicadas—a thousand brainless voices blended, like an inhuman radio signal from space.

"I know," Gloria said. Her cheeks as she lowered her eyes to weed bulged with a complacent smile. "I did something about it."

"What?" I braced for the answer. Any mental disturbance or anxiety tugs at the seat of my pain with its torque.

"Don't you bother yourself about it," she said. "But it worked."

And in my feebleness and maimed self-esteem I assented to her mastery of our arrangements, here on this hill, in our postwar, post–law-and-order twilight; I let it slide over me as one gravitational field, with only the slightest grinding of stardust, slides over another.

———————

Signs: the cicadas' monotone at night, and one bright-scarlet leaf on the slowly ruddying euonymus bush that I look down upon as I shakily shave, and white asters, early fall's signature bloom, everywhere—at the gravel edges of the driveway, and in the shadows beneath the hemlocks, and on into the woods, white asters with their woody stems and rather raggy-looking serrated leaves. How strange it must be, being an autumn flower, waiting while the others—the snowdrops and crocuses, the daisies and loosestrife, the Queen Anne's lace and goldenrod—all have their go at romancing the busy pollinators; and then, as the days shorten and the insect population grows sluggish and terminal, but for a few darting, reconnoitering dragonflies and aimlessly bobbing cabbage butterflies, to unfurl their modest, virginal, starlike attractions. What patience Nature possesses, I thought, as with grotesque caution, my rectum protesting every tensed muscle, I made my way down into the woods, terrified of slipping on a patch of pine needles or some loose dirt that would send me and my hypersensitive wound tumbling.

Gloria is watchfully home most of the days now. Her two associates—the other two-thirds of ownership—have taken up the slack at the gift shop. Her gossipy get-togethers at the Calpurnia Club, her shopping flings at the Chestnut Hill Mall, her Tuesday book group, her Thursday bridge afternoons over at the Willowbank have all been put on hold as she hovers about me like a cheerful, soigné vulture. She has found a new hairdresser, on Newbury Street, who has achieved a perfect tint, a pale platinum blond with a tinge of copper, which blends with the gray so subtly that her hair does not look dyed at all, just faintly unearthly: a halo, a crest for the emerging widow. Around the house, except when fresh from gardening, she dresses with an ominous formality—shoes rather than sneakers, dresses rather than slacks or jeans. Not quite church clothes, but clothes fit for the gracious reception of an unannounced, distinguished guest, whom I take to be the inanimate version of myself that I am hatching—the solid, peglike, ultimate Russian doll inside a succession of hollow ones.

But today she had to go off for an hour of dental hygiene in Swampscott, and I felt strong enough—barely—to make it out into the woods and down the rocks to the shack by the path. I keep fighting fantasies of falling and the catheter being rammed deep up into my bowels. As I gripped a beech sapling to halt my slithery descent, I saw over the shaggy shoulder of a granite outcropping that the kids' shack was gone. Not only was it gone, I observed as I drew near, but the ground for thirty feet all around it had been cleared as if by a lawnmower. A furious lawnmower: the old dry limbs and even the plywood and wire screening the boys had stolen for their little haven was shredded into bits, as if chewed and spit out. The ground was coated with fragments the size of my palm—tarpaper, aluminum mesh, laminated wood, corrugated plastic, cloth, rubber, and leather. It took me a minute to realize that these fragments were not from a rag heap but had been torn from bodies, bodies that were—where? There was in the air a smell not only of rotting mulch in an autumn woods, or of the boggy creek that seeped through cattails a stone's throw away, but of sweetly putrefying mammal. And, now that I knew what to look for, I had no trouble finding, in the evenly spread layer of debris, splinters of bone, withered shreds of skin barely distinguishable from the leaves that were starting to drift across the decaying layers of earlier years' leaf-fall, and blackened strips of what had been internal organs. I remembered the snake I had wounded. As best I could judge from the state of decomposition, a week or two had gone by; organic scavengers ranging from ants to foxes must have carried off much of the carrion.

How many bodies were here going back to nature (as if they had ever left) I could not estimate. My rectum was screaming, affronted by the effort of getting down the hill, and I still had to climb back up before Gloria returned with radiant, plaque-free teeth and invigorated gums. Not more than two, I guessed. José and Ray doing night duty. Little Manolete I could not bear to include in the slaughter, in my mind's eye. The metallobioforms had pulverized even the skulls; the tufts of shiny black hair scattered about like rabbit fur could have belonged to any of them but Doreen. I prayed—let's call it that—that she had not been present at the strike, but as I turned to leave my eye caught a bit of blue cotton with a white band such as might hem bikini panties. Beneath her tomboyish garb she did use to surprise me with dainty pastel underthings. Bleak as our relationship was, I think I was beginning to amuse her, and she would plan for our next tryst. The greenish glint of her eyes, which would deepen when my rough old tongue had worked on her for a while, had gone back to earth.

But such underpants could have been left in the shack in the natural careless course of events. Many of the cloth fragments were stiff with brown dried blood, and there was no blood on the scrap of blue, I saw as I held it, rubbing its fine knit texture between finger and thumb.

As I stood there in the circle of the massacre—as geometrical as if drawn with a giant compass—I realized that the metal vermin might be underfoot, about to bring me down. As nimbly as my catheter and leg bag permitted, I danced to the edge and beyond, where the undergrowth was still unchewed, still messy with fallen sticks and greenbrier and wild woodland asters. Hurting and hobbled as I was, I fairly flew up the hill.

Why had the metallobioforms decided to clear this space? Or did they, in the tangle of fine copper wire which did for their brains, "decide" to do anything? Dampness, the friend of organic forms, was their enemy, and this little knoll was the driest spot in the immediate vicinity. The trinkets were limited in their range by the parasitic nature of their energy; the "spark-eating" pseudozoans had to cluster near electric wires or, in the cities, mass-transit third rails, and the "oil-eaters" required an abundance of spilled petroleum they were likely to find, in a backwater like Haskells Crossing, around the Amoco station. After clearing such a circular patch, they must have had to scuttle or slither out across the railroad tracks (where they could snack on the drippings of diesel fuel and brake lubricant on the ties) into our little downtown, to replenish their exhausted energies. Many trinkets, like carrier aircraft whose missions took them just beyond the possibility of return, didn't make it; their junky, rusting bodies—most no bigger than ladybugs, which they resembled in shape, without the playful spots—littered the underbrush. But the species seemed to be extending its range nevertheless, and to be penetrating woodlands where before the war only organic wildlife had been observed.

Even back on my own lawn, I kept nervously checking my ankles and lifting my feet, imagining the remorseless, stinging bites gathering into a fiery buzz-saw force. Survivors describe, on television, an attack as like having one's feet and then legs plunged into a meat-grinder. Such must have been the experience of heavy, laconic José and voluble Ray and little inky-eyed Manolete with his droll propensity for jerky, ambitious gestures. They had been the last people on Earth who had hoped to learn something from me. Had I been here to counsel them, they might all still be alive.

A wild wet late September storm outside: trees tossing and tousling in the struggle with air gone mad. Leaves' pale undersides show in waves in the woods between my windows and the beach, and small fallen branches sodden with greenery litter the driveway at the front of the house, away from the sea, which Gloria calls the back. The oaks around the circle whistle and roar in their afflicted tops so that I expect to see one come crashing down or drop a giant torn limb. But this is no hurricane, just a friendly New England nor'easter; the wind relents just enough, like a disease that declines to kill us, playing with us to pass the time.

My catheter was removed a few days ago: a relief, in that the scaffolding of impedimenta in which I have been enclosed is thus reduced, but also an embarrassment, since it promoted me to diapers—Depends Adult Incontinence Pants. They get wet and heavy within an hour, and Gloria has tactfully set me up in the guest room with a rubber sheet over the mattress. I awake and change myself several times during the night; yet in the morning I am drowsily surprised by the transposition of our bedroom curtains and bookcase to the sparser, bleaker furnishings of the guest room. Its ceiling over in one corner is broken into a set of broad prismatic angles, to accommodate a short flight of steps on the third floor above, and I gaze, half awake, at this architectural disturbance as if it is a thing in itself, a crouching angular high shape sharing my space, malevolent but quiet, in lieu of a wife.

Gloria takes care of me but the house shakes with the irritable clicking and slamming of the partitions she has put up between us. She wants to keep dry. In my impotence I have ceased to be of any use. From her angle our relationship is all sufferance, and a noble non-complaining; she is earning stars in Heaven, as people used to say, and her virtue afflicts me with its hardness and glitter so that I cringe. What I loved about her in comparison with Perdita was this: lovemaking with Perdita mixed us up, the two of us, like a dark batter of flesh and desire, and rarely in the exactly correct proportions, so that one or the other of us felt cheated, and the other guilty, as if our sex should be a merger as precisely fair as the mixture of genes in our children; whereas with Gloria there was no confusion of responsibilities. I would use her, and she me, to achieve two distinct, unapologetic orgasms, sometimes simultaneous and sometimes not. This sexual clarity seemed worth laying down my life for—my respectability, my financial security, my children's happiness. As it turned out, the price was less than I had feared; life went on, the world continued turning, as it would in the wake of this fierce September blow, broken limbs and all.

I keep getting out of bed to paddle from window to window, seeing the world drenched, feeling my diaper sag toward another changing. In my days of young fatherhood with Perdita we had a diaper service, which would take away each Monday an ammonia-rich, water-laden sack, and give us square bundles of fresh, dry, folded diapers instead. No such service now exists. What I remove now I put in a green garbage bag that each Wednesday Gloria in the back of her station wagon carts down to the side of the road to take its place in some far-off landfill, for the delectation of future archaeologists. They will see us as faithful newspaper-readers and revellers in absorptive pads.

If I can no longer give her an orgasm with my stiff prick, my only use to Gloria is as a stiff corpse bequeathing to her liquid capital. In our feverish, catch-as-catch-can courtship, I more than once gave her an orgasm with my hand (in the movies) or foot (under a restaurant table) or with my mouth as she kneeled on a bed looking down like a mounded snow-woman with my head held firm between her melting thighs. But I fear that now she would find such resorts impossibly undignified for a woman of over sixty. I myself turned sixty-seven in the hospital, a quantum jump unobserved except by a touching shower of cartoony cards from my ten grandchildren, whose signatures ranged from Kevin's maturely subdued ballpoint italic to a crayon scribble from Jennifer, her little slobbery hand no doubt bunchily held within Roberta's.

I read a lot, in my ignominious, tender, doze-prone state, avoiding the emotional stresses of fiction—that clacking, crudely carpentered old roller coaster, every up and down mocked by the triviality, when all is said and done, of human experience, its Sisyphean repetitiveness—and sticking to the alternative lives, in time and space, of history and the *National Geographic*. This splendid magazine almost alone continued to print right through the Sino-American Conflict, bringing us beautiful photographic spreads, miles removed from the hateful clamor of propaganda, on the picturesque yak-herders in the yurt-dotted sandy backlands of the very empire we were striving to annihilate. Somewhere amid the nuclear blasts they found the ink, the clay-coated stock, and the innocent text to sustain that march of yellow spines continuous from the days of—explorer, writer, statesman—Teddy Roosevelt.

The overlooked corners of the maps and time charts fascinate me—the so-called Dark Ages, for instance, from the fall of Rome to the year 1000. Not only do these centuries contain the unconscious (to its citizens) permutation of Roman institutions into pre-medieval simulacra, and the incongruous sunburst of Irish monasticism while the Saracens and Vikings were squeezing Europe to a terrified sliver, but in humble anonymous farmsteads and workshops technological leaps never dared by the theorizing, slave-bound ancients were at last executed—the crank and the horseshoe, the horse collar and the stirrup all first appear in, of all apparently Godforsaken centuries, the ninth. By the year 1000 the wheeled Saxon plow, wind and water mills, and three-field crop rotation were extending a carpet of tillage the sages of Greece and tyrants of Rome had never imagined. Perhaps now, in the decadent and half-destroyed world that spreads below my hilltop, similar technological seeds are germinating. Decadence, like destruction, has this to be said for it: it frees men up. Men die, but mankind is as tough and resilient as the living wood that groans and sighs outside my window.

A big white truck roars in the driveway, splashing to a stop. Gloria, her clogs swiftly clacking, goes to the door and there is a surprisingly long, even an intimate, exchange. Stiffly pushing out of bed, whose wrinkled, odorous sheets have become my loathsome second skin, I move to the window and look down, in time to see the FedEx man—or woman; the hair is intermediate—turn away and get back into the driver's seat. He or she is tucking some sepia scrip into a leather billfold, and there is a thick leather triangle belted beneath the dark-blue shirt. I call for Gloria to come upstairs; she finally obliges. Her radiant, intelligent, mature face, framed by cleverly tinted ash-blond hair, is as painful to look at as the sun.

"Was that something for me?" I croak.

"No, dear. For *me*, believe it or not."

"What was it?"

"It was a transaction."

"Obviously. What sort of transaction?"

"Well, I didn't want to tell you, but FedEx collects a monthly fee now."

"For *what?*"

Her already bright face brightened further. "For *every-thing*. For the utilities, and road maintenance, and our protection. FedEx is taking over a lot of what the government used to do but can't. It's like the Pony Express, taming the West."

"Or Mussolini making the trains run on time." The allusion went by her; the last war had made World War II as dim as a post-office mural. I asked, "What about the nice people I used to pay protection to? Spin and Phil, and then the boys from Lynn."

"A bunch of pathetic thugs, darling. They've all gone out of business. FedEx is nationwide; they have a network that can put New England into touch with Chicago and California again. It's a Godsend, really."

"You sound like a commercial."

"When something is an improvement, I'm not afraid to say so, unlike some grumpy old cynics I know. You just concentrate on keeping your diapers changed, and do your exercises."

Kegel exercises—mental exercises designed to reactivate

the traumatized urethral sphincter. It was frustratingly difficult to locate with the mind those clusters of tiny muscles
(there are two, one around the rectum and the other around
the base of the penis) which we learn to manage not long after we learn to walk and talk, thus obtaining our ticket of admission to respectable human society. Well, I had fallen out
of the club. And I had never known that Gloria regarded me
as a cynic. In relation to what sunny philosophy of her own?
In a marriage, as our flesh matters less, our opinions matter
more. But I didn't want to argue, I didn't have the strength.
I said, "It looked from the window as though he was packing
a gun."

"She. A very nice, competent young woman was driving
the truck, Mr. Chauvinist. And yes, they do have to carry
guns, with their new responsibilities. They need to defend
themselves, and us, against anti-social elements. Those voices
I kept hearing in the woods—I told FedEx about them, and
sure enough they stopped."

"They were children's voices," I said, her revelation touching some other muscles in me I didn't know I had.

"They were trespassing voices," Gloria said, irresistible in
her clarity of purpose and conscience.

"Did it ever occur to you," I asked her, "that *I* might be an
anti-social element?"

"What you are is a very sick man who will get better if you
do your exercises."

"My trouble is," I confessed, "I don't even know if I'm doing them. I may be just tightening my stomach muscles."

"Think prick," she said. My fall has brought a new frank-
ness to our relationship, a tonic simplicity as in those far-
off days when we knew upon meeting that, if we had a
smidgeon of privacy and ten minutes of time, we would

fuck, cementing our bond, nailing down our hotly contested stake in each other. *Think prick:* nothing cynical about that.

The house is cold now in the mornings and evenings, but Gloria won't let me turn on the furnace. Her father, a rigid, pipe-puffing Connecticut squire, never touched the thermostat until All Saints' Day, she says. By the same calendar he switched from whiskey-and-soda to gin-and-tonic on Memorial Day, and back again on Labor Day. Seersucker suits and tweeds moved in and out of his closet as systematically as changing the guard at Buckingham Palace, and he never took his Mercedes out of the garage without checking the oil. He was a saint of proper procedures. On the coldest days before All Saints' Day, he would set a log fire in the Wilton living room, and they would all have tea, little Gloria's chamomile in a flowered cup, Mommy and Daddy's smoky Darjeeling poured from the blue-green pot with evil-looking long-tailed birds on it, and little cakes served on a tray by their faithful maid Mary, named after the mother of God. She had a pointed nose red at the tip, from the master's love of a cold house, perhaps. When Gloria touches me her hands feel icy. I wonder if I am running a permanent fever, my body furious at how it has been invaded.

Opening the kitchen cabinet to get down a mug for my morning tea (common Lipton's, in a tagged bag), I am blinded by sunlight and fear I might clumsily break something. The slant of sun is different, lower, now. We are past the solstice. The Earth is like a ship that has slightly changed course; we would not notice but that the sun warms the panelled wood of our cabin at a slightly different spot in the grain as we dress for dinner. Last night, getting up to change my diaper, I saw the half-moon tipped halfway onto its back, and I made myself realize, in my drowsy gut, that the moon's illumined half was turned toward the sun, which had plunged out of sight behind the Kellys' trees hours ago, but in the slant direction from which the moon was lit. Two balls in the sky, one bright, one reflective: it's that simple. We live among their orbits like dust mites in the works of a clock.

The storm gone northeast to Newfoundland, the weather is clear and calm. The sea has milky stripes of extra calm in it, and even the lobster boats on the far side of Cat Island look sharp and white and close. Twenty miles away, the shore of Hingham and Hull—where last July I could see fireworks go off, fuzzy and faint as comets—floats a sharp, detailed blue above a mirroring width of what seems sheer air.

Other optical illusions:

1. Shaving the other morning, I saw what seemed a giant bright-amber butterfly flapping frantically at my bathroom window, and only slowly realized that it was my stirred-up shaving water, into which I kept dipping my razor, reflecting electric light back into the window, semi-opaque at that newly shadowy 7:00 a.m. hour.

2. On the first day that I felt I had strength to walk down to the mailbox, I saw, as I shuffled ("One small step for a man . . .") through the turn in the driveway, a long dark silhouette of something perched crookedly on the mailbox lid. My first thought was that a great bird, a crane or buzzard or pterodactyl, had alighted there; my next, that a package too big to fit inside had been attached to the outside catch with rubber bands at a weird angle. Then, as I fearfully advanced, I saw the shadow to be a piece of low hemlock limb intervening in my field of out-of-practice vision. It was always there. I had not taken this walk for seven weeks.

The vines in the woods—poison ivy and Virginia creeper—
are beginning to redden, and the maples, each in its way.
The tall red maple, so called, gradually turns a sober burgundy, while the more impulsive, larger-leaved sugar maple
flashes into swathes of orange and a neon pink. The Norway
maples planted downtown in the village will yield a clear
yellow a bit duller than the hickories'. I saw from the car
window as Gloria drove me to the Lahey Clinic in Danvers
for some blood tests a splendid tall hickory whose outer
leaves, basking in the mellow September sunlight, were still
green, while the shaded inner leaves were already golden—
a core of gold, a flickering inner life sheathed in seemly
decorum; it gave the impression, as we sped by in the
Infiniti, of a captive girlish soul, a twirling dryad.

Roberta brought Keith and Jennifer to visit me—my children have become solicitous, fluttering bothersomely, al-
beit loyally, about the wreck of my progenitive apparatus,
whereby they came to be. In their adult, wrinkling faces I
still see the plump cheeks and candid trusting gaze of ten-
year-olds looking to me for protection and guidance and,
most difficult to provide, entertainment. How can I explain
that I must be left alone, without any pulling and hauling
from loving kin, if I am to heal? That I have had my use of
the world and my only salvation lies within, in tending the
altar of my wound and waiting for nature or the force beyond it to slide me subtly away from my own disaster, by an
invisible series of steps, into another world?

We fed Jennifer lunch. She kept taking the silver porringer, which cost a fistful of scrip at Firestone & Parson,
and dumping its contents on the high-chair tray and then
deliberately dropping the already much-dented porringer to

the floor. The fourth time she did it, with her challenging slate-blue stare directly on me, I exploded. *"Stop it,"* I said to Jennifer, and to Roberta, whiningly, "Why does she keep *doing* that?"

The baby, who had recently had her first birthday, was not used to being shouted at; her mouth formed a tiny circlet, with a bubble in it, before her lips downturned and she began to cry, to howl, and then to sob and sniffle.

Roberta comforted her. "Oh, Precious," she said, "Grampy didn't mean it; he's just forgotten what little girls are like." To me she explained, "Daddy, it's just her way of getting used to *space.*"

My daughter's remark, derived no doubt from some digitized handbook of child development, was helpful: I saw an affinity between the infant and myself, beyond our both being clad in diapers. With gestures and perceptions as fumbling as hers, I was getting used to *time.*

It is a curious entity. It doesn't exist, I have read, at the particle level: the basic laws of physics are time-symmetric, but for one tiny exception, the particle called the neutral kaon. Were it not for the neutral kaon, perhaps, buildings would self-assemble as frequently as they collapse, and old men would become young in more than their dreams.

In my dreams, I seem to roam a long harvest table heaped with the past eras of my life. One night, I am back in Hammond Falls High School, swinging down the locker-lined halls in my penny loafers and frayed blue jeans—frayed and torn up to the limit the school dress code allows, for beneath the anti-social pose I am a conscientious student, with a college career and lifelong escape from Hammond Falls my sneaking ambition. I chestily inhale effluvia of hair oil and cheap perfume and hormonal overproduction; I eye the knockout girls in their rounded sweaters and pleated skirts and anticipate a Saturday-night sally into Pittsfield with my pals—dinner at the Dalton Avenue McDonald's or Teo's and a movie at the Showplace or the Capitol on North Street, followed by apple pie at Rosa's or the Popcorn Wagon. City streets, illegal beers, lamplight reflected in black puddles, freedom and sin around the corner. The tender heat and latent violence of high school, its fast crass glamour, are all around me, along with the quaint orderliness of its hourly bells and scheduled migrations from room to room. Killers in our walks, we of the Class of '71 are yet as docile as concentration-camp inmates. Though the "system" is widely mocked and deplored, no better has materialized to rescue us from these locker-lined halls, with their hopeful, rebellious clatter.

Then I wake to my soaked diapers, the patter of squirrels on the roof, and the odd construction, like a crazy-angled coffin, buried in the far corner of the guest-room ceiling. With a deadly lurch in my stomach I realize I will never attend high school again, not unless time reverses. Another night, I am still married to Perdita, in our colonial house on East Main Street in Coverdale; we are vaguely surrounded by children in all sizes, but the real seethe is between us and our peers, the other young couples, all closeted in their homes yet dying to burst out, each marital partner helplessly seeking, as in a beaker of jiggled chemicals, to bond with another. A thrilling, tragic tangle of illicit alliances past and future is spread beneath us like a net beneath the flying bodies of trapeze artists; we are still lithe, though in our thirties. Our houses and gardens are neglected; our children signal for our attention in the corners of our eyes. The melting walls of domesticity, the too-many points of contact—with spouses, lovers, would-be lovers, still-living parents, children daily growing more complicated and knowing, cats and dogs whose sudden deaths underline the terror of it all—engulf my sleeping mind, steeped in its liquorous essence of Turnbull. Perdita, gorgeously and pitiably naked, is sobbing her eyes out in the pantry while a party we are giving is still going on; I am conscious of the social impropriety of her smooth, mythic costume, and awake, dawningly grateful that I need not any more unravel the reason for her grief.

What a prodigy of storage it is that all the stages of my life are coiled in my brain, with their stresses and stimulations. My present abject condition is another dish on the harvest table, a shipboard buffet heaped up backwards between the fluorescent soup of life at Sibbes, Dudley, and Wise and the plum pudding of the childhood Christmas when I got my first set of skis—wooden ones, and secondhand, I could see from the nicks of wear. Time in my brain has become a kind of space—areas of coiled cerebrum across which enlivening electricity idly sizzles in my sleep.

And yet the dominant atmosphere of my dreams is one of dread, of atrocity. Where does it come from? Mine has been a happy life, as these things go: war and plague have veered around me. New England was the most lightly bombed sector of the former United States. The Sino-American Conflict as a whole lasted four months, and was mostly a matter of highly trained young men and women in sealed chambers of safety reading 3-D computer graphics and pushing buttons, thus obliterating quantities of civilians who never knew what hit them. Millions more Chinese than Americans died. The poisonous fallout chiefly sickened the world's dark majority in their ghettos and unsanitary villages. And yet I terrifyingly dreamed, just last night, of a pond surrounded by boys with flexible sticks, like bamboo whips, who flayed the pale broad fish as they came to the surface for air. An earlier dream had been cobwebbed with a grimy wealth of mechanical struts and lattices, infernal machinery of some local or global conspiracy or witchcraft was closing in on me, thickening like digestive juices around a swallowed gnat; I escaped only by awaking. All this terror must be history—*der Weltgeist*. Nanobolts of cerebral electricity swarm across that part of my brain which stores racial memories, from Neanderthal butcheries on.

The post-solstice sunlight comes at me from unexpected angles, as if liberated. It lies, flecked with dirt from the windowpanes, on the page I am polluting with these scribbles, and blinds me as I rinse my cereal bowl at the kitchen sink, so that I nearly drop it, as if slapped. Squirrels frantic with the multitude of acorns needing to be buried scrabble heavily across the roof overhead. Geese in their endearingly imperfect V's honk very loudly. Everything outdoors is brilliant and ready to topple. The tilted sunlight glitters in the poplars and shines through the leaves; though they are still mainly green, they are thinning, losing substance. The dogwood in the circle reddens. Gloria has set Jeremy to pulling up brown hosta, while I in my infirmity cower indoors. Jeremy never did get to Mexico. We shed our dreams one by one.

A week has gone by. Time in my sense of it is fragmented and thrusts this way and that, like the ice jam around the North Pole. Some of it rushes by; the darkness of morning slips through a choppy, brilliant interval into the darkness of evening; sometimes an hour sticks straight up, unmoving. A number of trees have turned a blatant yellow. The tenderest maples, with small, scarcely indented leaves, approach the sensational salmon pink inside a whelk shell. The Bradford pears downtown, I saw through the car windows as Gloria took me on a ride to the bank and the post office, are as blandly green as in June. There is an odd variousness to it all; here in mid-October one beech is all golden jangle and glitter while its mate nearby hasn't turned a leaf. The burning bush that began to blush in August is still half green, while its smaller companion has quickly assumed a luminous magenta unreal to see. One of our dogwoods is a subdued brownish burgundy, while the leaves of the other are mottled, no two alike, each individually dipped in a saffron dye that skips dark curdled spots like freckles of rot on a pear's skin. A scrubby sumac, with flanged stems, that mingles with the wild roses shows an inky red, almost an eggplant color, while its leaves keep a pale mint green on their undersides. And, on their spindly, prickly trees, apples and pears—unbidden, uneaten, gnarled—and berries—white on the big cedar along the drive, black on the stalks of goosefoot maple—add to the visual harvest, along with Gloria's gallantly persisting roses and her thriving many-branched dahlia. Sunlight takes on a supernal value, reflected back from all this varicolored warmth of tinge; the broad sea blares a blue I would not have believed obtainable without a tinted filter.

I awake at night because of my wet diaper and, changed into a dry one, still cannot get back to sleep. The house creaks around me like a galleon shifting sails; from the third story come distinct bumping sounds, but the steady green lights of our alarm system indicate no corporeal trespasser. Wind whistles outside in the soon-to-be-naked trees. It is time to lower the storm windows. For reasons of thrift and coziness, I like to do it early; Gloria, who loves fresh air, puts it off as long as possible, to a day in November so bitter my frozen fingers smart as they manipulate the little corroded catches.

I return to the guest bed and wait for morning. The wind counterfeits the sound of the first train. I yearn for the first stir of traffic in the village. Though I will them to close, my ears open wide to drink the new day. The tense black surface of expectancy at last parts and the five-thirty train telescopes its onrush of metal wheels out from the amorphous sighing of the woods: the sound enlarges, arches into a volume that makes the house shudder on its rigid underlay of granite, and then swiftly sinks in pitch and volume as the train slows to a pause at the Haskells Crossing Station. Who can be getting on it? Who can be getting off? There is no going back into sleep; within a half-hour, the car that brings Gloria *The New York Times* will rush up the driveway and circle by the porch. I listen with every nerve for the sound of its approach, but it comes upon me with an unexpected closeness, suddenly next to the house, filling the silence with its automotive pomp—the wet slur of tires, the crackle of crushed twigs, the creak of the springs as the car swerves toward the porch, a groan of brakes lightly applied, the rapid ticking of the engine in the pause, and then, in one chord, the bump of the folded paper hitting the porch and the car's dismissive acceleration down the driveway. A cocky, synchronized performance, nicely perfected since the snowy winter mornings when the driver ignominiously parked short of the steep curve beyond the drying yard and walked the rest of the way up. To him, as he sails past, the house must look as oblivious as a white mausoleum in the half-light. Little does he know it has a consciousness: I am awake, a painfully alert ghost. All over the dark Northeast men and women are awake in that stir of mild misery we call life.

From these same windows—"front" I call them, though Gloria says the seaside faces front—I heard in mid-morning, as I lay there, shaved and fully dressed but recuperating

from my insomnia with a copy of *Scientific American*, a truck
roar up and Gloria's pure, bell-like voice, more familiar to
me than my own, mingle with a voice also, though less res-
onantly, familiar. I peeked down and over the edge of the
porch roof glimpsed my wife's bright head nodding in eager
conversation with a chunky man in the police-blue FedEx
uniform, with its tricolor stripe down the sleeves. Not a
package changed hands but a sheaf of scrip, from her hand
to his and thence into a worn leather satchel. The squirrels
are in a frenzy of gathering and hiding; one of them scampered along the roof above my head and when the FedEx
man looked up at the noise I saw his face; it was Phil. He had
not been rubbed out, then, when Spin was; like me, he lived
on. When the truck had roared down the driveway, I called
for Gloria to come upstairs. The tyranny of the sick is luxurious. She came. "Who was that?" I asked.

"The FedEx man, darling. Haven't you seen him before?"

"Why were you handing him money?"

"I *told* you, dear. They collect, in exchange for peace and
order. It was they who took care of those horrible children
who had built a hut in our woods and who were terrorizing
the neighbors; the rumor is it was *they* who burned down
Pearl Lubbetts's expensive beach house! It's quite wonderful, what they're doing. FedEx, I mean. The guards they use
to protect their shipments are being assigned to cities and
towns now. They want to bring back green money, that people could use in any state. There's even talk, the *Times* says,
of their moving the federal government, what there is left of
it, to Memphis, where FedEx has its headquarters and all its
airplanes. It's about time somebody took charge, before the
Mexicans invade."

The Mexican repossession of Texas, New Mexico, Arizona, and lower California had been an item lately in the

Globe, along with much else terrible—shootings in Dorchester, rapes in Mattapan—that had merely a literary relationship to me, sequestered in my own microcosmic geography and my seared, chastened body.

"It's a *net*work, so it can do *any*thing," Gloria was going on, with a flash of her beautiful teeth and a toss of her ash-blond hair much like those (the flash, the toss) with which, twenty years ago, she could cap one of her—our, might I say?—triumphant sexual performances. She would coax up an erection through a trouser pocket of my gray suit in the middle of Symphony or, unzipping my fly, while we were driving home from Boston at midnight through the neon carnival of pre-war Route 1. "People say President Smith has already resigned, but there's no way to tell."

At times I dream I have an erection, with a mauve head like a rabbit's heart, so hard and blood-stuffed a one it makes the veins in my throat sympathetically stiffen and swell; but when I awake and peek inside my soaked Depends, my poor prick is as red and flaccid as a rooster's comb. How could so superfluous an appendage ever have served as the hub of my universe? The *foolishness* of life hits me, stunningly, as the last plausible shreds of my dream dissolve and the suburban houris conjured by my desire—Grace Wren, sucking; Muriel Kelly, splayed—withdraw their wisps of white flesh, but there is nothing to laugh about.

Still, I burn to see Phil by myself, to ask what happened to Deirdre.

I live on a planet where the vegetation is golden, gold in all its shades from red-brown to platinum-white, but all refulgent, towering, superabundant. Red veins of contrast course through its infinite foliations; sheets of orange twirl and tuck themselves into quilted caverns of rustling shadow; a rain of cast-off leaves twirls and twitters down on the same diagonal as the westering light from our proximate star. Gold on this planet rusts; the atoms of its element are eager to combine with the blue of oxygen, the green of vaporized sulfur. Out of gold's volatile, ubiquitous substance are hewn and thrashed the beams of our homes, the thatch of our roofs, the bedding for our livestock. "Common as gold" is a phrase, and "gold poor." Yet we do not despise the element, but bask in its superabundance, which crowds every surface to the verge of the sea, itself golden, imbued as it is with aureate salts. Stalked heaps of gold froth compete with the clouds in their cumulus, and make a ragged join with the sulfurous sky, which the daily floods of local starlight dye a deep, heavenly chartreuse. Theologians make of this an argument for the existence of God: if the vast sky were any color less soothing than green, our lovingly fabricated eyes would be burned blind.

Today Phil was waiting for me at the mailbox, his white FedEx truck parked at the entry to our dirt lane through the woods. The pond was having a jolly time reflecting the blazing wall of maples and birches along its edge. A duo of ducks jostled the reflection with their widening rings every time they took off and relanded, or with comic deftness tipped up their tails to grab a bite underwater.

"How're ya doin', Mr. Turnbull?" Phil asked me. The somber blue-gray uniform fitted him better than his brown suits had. "That's some operation you've had, your wife's been tellin' me."

I shrugged. "They've got it down to a science now. A stream of pure protons, no bigger than a pencil lead, passes through the good cells and slices out the bad."

"Still, there are lousy aftereffects, she was saying. Your missus and I did a lot of chitchat when you were in the hospital. She's some swell lady, by the way. She knows her own mind and isn't afraid to express it: that's what I like in a dame."

I had never heard Phil talk so much; in the old days Spin had done most of the talking. "She likes you, too," I said. "She likes the way FedEx is going to take over and kill off all the anti-social elements and bring back the United States of America."

"We-ell," he said judiciously, with what I took to be official FedEx gravity; the corporations among their other roles have become the only teachers of deportment. "FedEx has got its competition." His eyes were small and close together, but on the other hand they were a light contemplative gray, the color of a machine's burnished underside, and were framed by unexpectedly long eyelashes. "But we're getting a handle at least on everything east of the Mississippi. The strategy is to absorb the little carriers first, and let UPS come to us when it's ready." He moved closer; a sour male essence wafted from his jowls and armpits. "Between us, they're working on a way to remote-control the trinkets, with radio signals; the little things' brains are just a few transistors, after all. Once the kinks are out it'll be the biggest thing in warfare since the taming of the horse."

"And the invention of horseshoes and the stirrup," I said. "Otherwise, warrior herdsmen couldn't have ridden their horses for invasive distances."

"You're losin' me." He frowned. "Hey"—his little eyes crinkled in anticipation of the jab to come—"how'd the old dingle-dangle like being knocked out of commish? You were some hot ass-man, to hear Deirdre tell it."

"Deirdre," I said. "Exactly. Tell me about Deirdre. What's happened to her? When Spin got killed, I was afraid—"

"Yeah, Spin," Phil said. "That was real ugly. The kids did it with rocks. Rocks were all the little suckers had—real crude. But you know," Phil went on, waxing philosophical, "Spin, great a guy as he was, led with his chin sometimes. Remember how he had to dress like some dandy all the time? That showed insecurity, knowing he was out there operating pretty much on his own. He didn't have what this outfit"—he touched the insignia on his breast pocket—"has. Esprit de corps. The world like it is, you can't go it alone. Impossible. They'll eat you up. That's what I told Deirdre. But the cunt, she don't listen."

The present tense was hopeful. "Where is she?" I asked.

He looked at me still humorously. "What you want with her now? Your dick's just a memory, the way your missus tells it."

"Gloria talks about it?"

"You know—in a very refined way. Like I say, she's a class act. What I really appreciate, she's got a head on her shoulders. She may not call a spade a spade, but she can dig a hole with the best of 'em, you know what I mean?"

People who have come up in the world become boring very quickly; everything they say is disguised bragging. He wanted to talk about his connection with Gloria, I wanted to talk about Deirdre. "You're not telling me about Deirdre," I said. "Did you and she, after she left me, live together?"

I tried to picture this oaf laying his sweaty sack of a body down beside hers with its slender bony back, its silken coating of fine flowing hair, and my anger was all at Deirdre, for allowing it, for giving away so cheaply what I had chosen to regard as precious. "For a while," he casually admitted. Not only were Phil's eyes small, but so were his ears—no bigger than teacup handles, and pressed tight into the spongy sides of the skull between the bulge of his shaven blue jowls and the bulge of his curly, springy hair. Between his hairline and his eyebrows there was little space for a forehead. "We palled around, she moved into my digs. But she's restless, Ben." When would everybody stop calling me Ben? I was not the world's friend. "She wants to be"—his gesture took in the flaming pond, the walls of woods, the vast presiding illusion of a blue sky—"out there. She's a whore, you know? She'll lay for you, great, but then she'll lay for the next guy. She doesn't give a fuck, literally. She's hooked on dope and this notion she has of freedom. I tried to beat the crap out of her a few times, but it didn't take. She didn't learn a thing. She's like some wild animal, you know?"

I didn't want to hear this, particularly, but I did like being able to talk about Deirdre openly—to drag with my tongue the sweet secret of her name out from the granular dark of my memory cells. The way she would pantingly negotiate the price for every new twist of lovemaking. Her tight butternut ass, with its white thong shadow, up in the air, the little flesh-knot between the glassy-smooth buttocks visible in moonlight that entered the third-story window at just the right celestial angle. The flat planes of her face harking back to the Egyptian Sphinx or some heavy Aztec head of solid sandstone, only transposed to a smaller, female scale, with modern nihilist nerves. The way her stiffish purple dress with its little white collar rustled beside me in church last Easter as the boyish clergywoman preached of how the risen Jesus said to Mary Magdalene, "Touch me not." Her searing wish—I felt it now, at last—to be sheltered.

I drew closer to Phil, as if to a squat radiator on a bleak winter day. There is a warmth in the proximity of a man who has fucked the same woman you have. It is as if she took off her clothes as a piece of electric news she wished him to bring to you. He has heard the same soft cries, smelled the same stirred-up scent, felt the same compliant slickness, seen the same moonlit swellings and crevices and tufts—it was all in Phil's circuitry, if I could but unload it. He was a healthy FedEx man, wearing the attractive uniform of power; he could afford to be casual about his conquests, but I no longer could. My sexual memories had become epics of a lost heroic age, when I was not impotent and could shoot semen into a woman's wincing face like bullets of milk. Deirdre's flanks in memory had acquired the golden immensity of temple walls rising to a cloudless sky and warmed by an Egyptian sun. Whore though he thought her, a nimbus of her holy heat clung to Phil—his oily black pubic curls had tangled with hers—and I moved another inch closer to him, as the two ducks on the pond suddenly tussled, with a quacking and thrashing that sent concentric ripples crashing into the reflected red image of the maples.

Phil mistook the reason for my intimacy. He thought working for the expanding FedEx conglomerate was the most important thing about him. He lowered his voice confidentially to tell me, "In a coupla months, we'll have the circuitry in place so we don't even have to collect in person; the monthly charge will be automatically deducted from your bank account. Neat, huh?"

"How do I know you won't deduct too much?"

"It's a matter of trust, like you always said. Trust us. You won't feel a thing."

"With you, did she come?"

"Huh?"

"Deirdre." I was shameless now, in my decrepitude. In a world of dwindling days, why wait to seek the truth? "Were you able to give her climaxes?"

"Hey, Ben, come on. What does this have to do with the

price of cheese?" He glimpsed my need and smilingly despised me for it.

"I want to know," I pleaded. "I miss her. Deirdre." Saying her name—did my penis stir? I felt *some*thing. "I wish her well."

"Like I said, she was a whore. Her coming wasn't the issue."

"I tried to make it an issue," I confessed. "I worked at it. But I could never be sure, she was so good at faking it. Her mind was always a little elsewhere, didn't you think?"

He saw that he mattered to me only as an emanation of our shared cunt, and he felt indignant. He cut me off. "On her next fix is where it was," he said. "They're all like that. They hate the tricks they turn, don't kid yourself, Ben. Hey, you don't look so good suddenly. Think you can make it back up that hill?"

"My doctors *want* me to exercise," I told him. "They *want* me to drop dead." As I shuffled my way up the curved asphalt, past the fruit trees with their rotting dropped fruit, the lilacs turning purple leaf by leaf, the sassafras shaped like an upside-down bowl, and the cedar with its frost of tiny berries, I decided that the stir of my penis at the mention of Deirdre's name had likely been just a leak of warm urine I had happened to notice. I resolved to work harder on my Kegel exercises.

Rain for three days, one of those fall nor'easters that knock the leaves from the trees and paste them to the wet earth. Still, the hickory outside my upstairs window has scarcely turned, but for patches of yellow. Agitated squirrels tousle it, clambering out on its downward-drooping twigs, and then scamper thunderously across the roof above my head.

The gutter at one end was plugged, and the overflow built up a puddle behind the pachysandra that was draining into a basement window. In a burst of vitality that alarmed Gloria, I put on my old foul-weather sailing gear and in the driving rain set up the extension ladder and climbed its slick rungs and, not daring to look down into the steep triangular space beneath my feet, cleared away a plug of twigs and leaves with my hands. There was primitive satisfaction in seeing a vortex appear and the level of water standing in the old wooden gutter go slowly down, obedient to the patient, omnipresent laws of physics. Childhood games: getting the elements back on track. Man as hydraulic traffic cop. Down on the ground I tried with the point of a pick to gouge a run-nel through the pachysandra to drain the puddle into the driveway, but gravity was against me. *If gravity be against us, what can be for us?* I liked being out in the rain, because it made my soaked paper diaper feel natural, a piece of saturated nature.

Inside the house, arranging everything in the laundry room to dry, I was aware of the heat from the radiators, as touched and grateful as if a faithful servant had thought to set out for me a tray of tea and warm scones. The house and its appurtenances of wiring and piping pursue an independent life, like a motherly, stationary megatrinket.

Gloria professed alarm at my exertions but in fact I felt invigorated, my face tingling. It was only in the evening, as I tried to read in bed a popular book about cosmology, that a terrific fatigue hit me—that degree of unforswearable weariness that brushes even the certainty of death aside in its haste to close our eyes.

Alive, I'm alive, I sometimes think now, listening to the

rain in the gutters, feeling the extension of my limbs beneath the soft sheets. What bliss life is, imagined from the standpoint of a stone or of a cubic yard of black water in the icy ocean depths. Even there, apparently, conglomerated molecules manage to light a tiny candle of consciousness. The universe hates death, can it be? *If God be for us, who can be against us? Nor height, nor depth, nor any other creature, shall be able to separate us from the* . . . Alive. A pitiable but delicious reprieve from timelessness. I think of all the sons of bitches like Gary Gray and Firman Frothingham who would just as soon see me dead and the pleasure of spiting my enemies warms my cooling heart.

The sky this dawn was a pink blotting paper, set above a sea whose blue presented the same misty, fibrous texture. In the foreground the golden trees looked sullen and darker now, curdled and rust-ridden, after the storm. As the leaves thin, the sky lowers again upon our awareness. Making my slow way down the damp asphalt, where flowing water has left drifts and eskers of pine needles, acorns, hickory nuts, dead twigs, and gravel from the edges, I seem to see, in broken arcs beyond the scudding, thinning rain clouds, the heavenly circle, the torus. Has it, in spite of the public indifference that attended its departure, returned, or is it a trick merely of refracted sunlight in a high mist of crystals—a white rainbow?

According to the book that proved such a soporific last night, the torus has a rhythm of appearance and disappearance over the aeons, like one of those comets whose elliptical orbits swing far out into interstellar space and by the old Newtonian laws predictably return to our sky. To generations its presence is evident and the source of omens, miracles, admonitions, and reassurances. People live by its wan light, sing its praises while they work, construe even their humblest bodily functions and pangs of pleasure and contrition as parts of a pattern the torus by its ideality establishes. Then it gradually dims, succumbing to mockery and disproof. The generations grow bored with repeating the pieties of their fathers; a cry for human freedom and self-expression rises against the skyey wedding ring, which has come to seem a shackle, or the lid of an oubliette. The chants, perhaps, drive it away. Since it never touches the planet with more than a sense, in certain transits, of global well-being, it can be ignored so thoroughly as to be practically non-existent.

The altars are slighted; the temples fall into mossy ruin. And yet an air of irresolution hangs in the emptiness. Public disorder increases. Telephone booths are vandalized; graffiti cover every stone surface consecrated to beauty and visual harmony. Children acquire guns and shoot each other as casually as images are flicked away on television; adults drown their disquiet and despair in alcohol. The world by itself is not enough; there must be another, to give this one meaning. And blood sacrifices are initiated by the tyrants who come to power in the resistless confusions and lassitude: giant drums and smoke pots call out to the red-streaked sky; drugged adolescents, chosen for their physical perfection, have their hearts cut out of their heaving chests by hooded priests wielding sea-green obsidian knives.

Eventually, in its own time, the torus reappears. Personal sanity and public decency are restored, but always with seeds, smaller and darker than mouse turds, of discontent and resentment sealed within the social order. The new cycle has begun. Those cycles occupy far more time than was at first thought: millions of years, rather than thousands. Time grinds the ruins of one epoch, its imperishable monu-

ments, into a fine sand that seems an utter desert to the fore-
bears of the next epoch as they emerge, hand in hand, their
nakedness clothed in leaves, out of Eden. And always overhead, silently clamorous, imperiously silver and pure, the
stars rotate and ever so minutely shift, forming new constellations, new arrangements in the sprawl of eventually dying
sparks on the velvet display-cloth of space. The sea through
the thinning trees wrinkles in red filaments that threadily
reflect the bloated, never-setting sun.

Walking back up the driveway, the *Globe* in hand, I glance
to my left at the sourwood tree that Gloria planted ten years
ago and am struck, hard, by its seasonal beauty—long oval
leaves, deeply creased like peach-tree leaves, overlaid one
upon the other in the lower branches to form a screen of
crisscrossing scarlets and browns and freckled yellows and
pinks and greens. Gloria has gone, yes, sour on this tree—it
grew too eagerly for her taste, between the pears and the
lilacs. It quickly towered over them, and heavy snows broke
off its overextended branches, which then sprouted an awkward spray of secondary shoots. She even talks of cutting it
down, after ten years of trial. The gardeners of the world are
unsentimental about correcting their mistakes. Perhaps I
have for it a certain fellow-feeling. Uncherished, rarely
glanced at, the sourwood is humming to itself a complex
chorale of autumn colors and at the same time extending
outwards, like so many long-boned feathery hands, its flowers, which are spent flowerets a third of an inch high orga-
nized into one-sided fanning racemes. It blooms even as it
sheds.

Then, around four this afternoon, when the sun was angled just right, I wandered into the seaward guest room—
not the one I sleep in, overlooking the driveway circle—and

was stunned by a window uniformly loaded, like a fabric pattern, with sunstruck butter-yellow hickory leaves. A window like an upright case of pure unfettered brightness.

I see now too late that I have not paid the world enough attention—not given it enough *credit*. The radio, between the weather and the stock report, releases a strain from Schubert's *Drei Klavierstücke*, a melody that keeps repeating, caressing itself in sheer serene joy, and I think of him and Mozart, dying young and yet each pouring out masterpieces to the last, rising higher and higher as their lives fall from them, blessing with their angelic ease the world that has reduced them to misery, to poverty, to the filth and fever and the final bed. My eyes cannot help watering, a sure sign of senility.

Gloria has found herself, through the agency of FedEx and its omnivorous networks, a deerslayer. He comes to the house in a dusty green truck, splotched camouflage-style, and parks in the driveway or else down at the entrance to the dirt road, beyond the mailbox. I shuffled downstairs to meet him. He stood just inside the front door, on the Qum rug. He is a man about my age, a bit smaller and more wiry, but with that same dry flattened gray thinning hair and those same horny splotchy backs to his hands. His hands tremble, from a history of drink or the beginning of Parkinson's. He has crowded-together, brownish lower teeth and a lovely gentle voice. There is something holy about him. He talked to me of "signs," meaning turds, in the woods, and of laying gossamer-thin blue threads across likely trails in the woods. He described to me how a deer, once struck by an arrow, will bed down immediately in a nest of brambles and let itself be

approached for the kill, since it does not associate the stun-
ning, unhinging thing that has happened to it with human
beings; it doesn't have the circuitry to make the connection.
This holy man is of the opinion that animals don't feel pain
at all as we do. They are of another, virtually pain-free order. He hunts them with a bow and arrow because of the
sport—he is, like me, retired; more happily, it would seem:
he once climbed poles and read electric meters for a living,
which may have encouraged habits of stealth and quick observation—and because he and his wife love venison. I had
never heard before of a woman liking venison, but, then, in
many ways I am still innocent, especially about women. The
two of them carve up the carcass and keep it in their freezer
for years, like a couple in a fairytale hut. The archery season
begins soon, in early November. He will set up a blind, in a
likely spot, and stand motionless in it for hours, beginning at
5:00 a.m. What monk in a cold stone cell could do more to
punish himself? He is another of Gloria's saints. Her father
was a saint of propriety; this man—named, like her father,
John—a nature saint, blending selflessly with the trees, and
brush, and rocks.

His existence crowds my universe, diminishes it and me,
yet I am curious to see what will forthcome.

Speaking of masculinity, Red and Ken came to visit me,
looking sheepish that they have not visited before. But the
golf season had been active until a week or so ago, and they
filled me in on the results of the Labor Day Weekend Four-
Ball, the Fall Mixed Gambol (you had to play with somebody else's wife, a source of endless titillation), the Senior
Men's Championship (over fifty-five), the Plimpton Super-
Seniors (over seventy, named after Ed Plimpton, a Mass.
Amateur Championship runner-up who had been a member
of the club), the Columbus Day Best-Ball, and a new tour-

nament scored by the Stableford system and named in honor of an assistant pro, Dale MacPhail, who had been killed in the war, obliterated in an Aleutian missile silo.

I sat uneasily in the library with my visitors. Gloria hates it when I leak urine onto the silk-damask-covered seat cushion of my favorite wing chair; she keeps telling me how much the reupholstering will cost. I tried to strike the correct, hostly, jocular note, but Ken, with his silver hair and bristling black eyebrows, kept looking like an airline logo, a kind of human eagle, and falling into a silent stare, just the way on the golf course he will exasperatingly freeze over a putt or short chip. Red had brought his flip phone in his pocket and it kept ringing, so he would withdraw into the hall and murmur about a fish haul in some remote corner of the world—the Seychelles, say. It was hard for me to believe that I had ever experienced ecstasy in the company of these men.

Yet, after they left, I was moved to walk through the kitchen to the back-hall closet, where I keep my golf clubs, and to open the door. The masculine pungence of sweat-impregnated grips and often-worn leather shoes swept out at me; hundreds of hours of my life had left their redolent film on this equipment. I could smell the rubber inside the balls and the tough compressed wood of the tees and the marshy rankness of the wet turf I had trod through, especially the turf of the sixth fairway, where the geese all deposit their tubular green shit and the black-shelled turtles bask on the rocks among which a sliced drive raises a supple splash. I longed to be back inside the body of the robust ogre who had left behind these smells.

"So, when do you think?" Ken had said to me at last.

"When what?"

"When will you be back on the links?"

"There's a lotta good golf left in November, Benny boy," Red contributed.

"December, even, if there's no snow," said Ken, his aquiline stare softening to a teddy bear's at the childish thought of snow.

"Come on, use your heads," I said. "I can just barely walk. Pee keeps bubbling out of me."

"You don't need to walk," said Ken. "We'll all rent carts. All you need to do is swing the club. You tended to swing too hard anyway. Too hard, and too quick. Swing slow, like I do."

"I always said," I said, "the day I can't walk the course is the day I give up the game."

Red snorted impatiently. "You can walk next year. Ride the rest of this. Get off your ass, for Chrissake. You look like a dead mackerel." His phone rang, or rattled, in his shirt pocket. He went out into the hall." "*¡Saludos, mi amigo muy caro!*" we could hear him shout.

It was hard for me to imagine my playing golf next summer. Another year, all those seasonal gears to turn, those heavy heavenly bodies to push into place. "Who've you been playing with?" I asked Ken.

He blinked and stared straight ahead, as if looking for a vision of those other players on the backs of my uniform Winston Churchill. "Oh, we've had some nice games with Fred, his pacemaker seems to be getting less loud, and we had Les out for the Columbus Day Best-Ball, he hit the ball real well, he has a new driver with a magnesium head and a glass shaft, would you believe? Also, some of the younger members—Glenn Caniff and his buddies, you should see Glenn powder that pellet these days, and little Mel Spiegelman, he doesn't look like he has a muscle in his body, but, wow, when he winds up . . ."

He trailed off, perhaps noticing the jealousy, the sadness his recital was inflicting upon me. I would be replaced, *was* being replaced, and would not even have a tournament named after me.

So when they had disappeared down the driveway in Red's Caravan I paid a memorial visit to my golf closet, and even took out the putter and thought of trying a few strokes on the big blue Tabriz in the living room. But it seemed too much trouble, and to refer to a self I had been quantum-jumped out of, into a new orbit.

When his green truck appears in the driveway—he is scouting the territory, drawing up mental maps—I try to go out and greet the deerslayer. He tells me things about nature I didn't know. One day he pointed out to me the ugly fungi that grow like monstrous tan brains on the lawn. He said, "Those are called hen-of-the-woods. They grow only in association with oak trees. Very delicious, cut and sliced and sautéed, or put into a spaghetti sauce. Soak it in salt water to get the dirt and insects out. Sometimes you find a salamander or two in there; they don't do any harm. Here." And with a black-handled pen-knife, the kind that men used to carry in their overall pockets back in Hammond Falls, John cut a tidy cube of white flesh out of the rumpled brown mass and handed it to me. It was heavier than I had expected, with a pleasant rubbery moisture, like a big art eraser. "Hen-of-the-woods. Not easy to find, and with all these oaks up here you're surrounded. Tell your missus what I showed you, and she'll be thrilled, I guarantee."

Is it my impotent hypersensitivity, or do men keep making overtures to my wife? Am I dead already?

But in truth Gloria was disgusted by the idea, and didn't even want the pieces I had nicely sliced, washed, and placed in a bowl, covered by Saran Wrap, in the refrigerator. To her, this piece of nature, grown beyond the realm of her garden, was impudent if not poisonous. I tasted a raw piece—it was bland at first, like a firmer tofu or a coconut meat less sweet and crisp, but then the aftertaste had a caustic kick that stayed with me, even after I washed it down with a glass of orange juice. "John says to sauté them in a little butter," I said, but Gloria forbade it; she didn't want her kitchen stunk up. Forbidding comes easier and easier to her. It is becoming her métier.

When I venture outside, the sky rushes down at me through the oaks, which have blanketed the lawn and driveway with their leaves. In the woods and along 128, entirely bare trees are appearing: silvery sea-fans—dead or merely asleep, it is not easy to tell. Naked, they reveal their beseeching, striving shapes. The oak trees reach sideways, and the hickories up and down. The ashes are especially tragic in their clustered end-twigs, like snatching, clutching fingers, and the birches in their windswept huddled curves. The leaves were just a cover-up; these colorless warped skeletons are the truth.

In my seaward view, as the sun nears noon, it transforms the sea into a sheet of unalloyed light, cruel to see. The line of the beach is visible through the trees. The autumn's polychrome sinks toward a brittle rust, broken into a thousand dry facets of reflected sun. My eyes keep going to the charred scar where Mrs. Lubbetts' beach house had been, like a tongue to a missing tooth. In the other direction, at night, the lights of Haskells Crossing come closer through the stripped trees, like the flashlights of a hunting party. The poor Lynn boys, if the metallobioforms had not shredded them, would have been exposed by this time of year like wood lice when a rotten log is overturned.

On Halloween night, a new intensity of cold has swollen

the stars overhead. No child comes to the house. It is too far off the beaten track; the driveway is too forbiddingly long. Gloria and I, faintly disconsolate, make ourselves sick by eating the candy corn and Reese's Peanut Butter Cups we had laid in. Side by side on the green sofa, we watch a television documentary on the Old West. Still photos of vast stony vistas and of impassive bronze faces: Indian chiefs hounded to a humiliating surrender, after creekside massacres and epic marches through Dakota blizzards to a Canadian sanctuary where the distant queen's providence declines to forestall starvation; they are driven back to a bitter treaty with the bearded Great White Father in Washington and the barren haven of the reservation. A heap of broken promises, and a pyramidal mountain of the skulls of bison spitefully slaughtered to cut the red man's ground out from under him. Modern descendants of these routed Native Americans are interviewed in living color. With their ethnically correct long black hair and slow professorial voices, they expound their historical grievances expertly but less affectingly than the witness borne by the silent bronze faces which the triumphant republic, in token apology, placed on its coinage and postage stamps. The Sino-American Conflict, it came to me, could be seen as revenge administered by the Mongolian superpower of that Asian continent from which the North American aborigines had crossed the Bering land-bridge.

We went to bed sickeningly awash with candy and guilt. I followed Gloria into the bedroom that was ours and has become hers. Shyly I watched her make her methodical way through the rites of flossing, toothbrushing, mouthwashing, and applying face cream. She inserted the gel-loaded plastic tooth-guards with which she keeps her teeth the valuable white that my mother had once, not insincerely, appraised as

The Deaths

worth investing in. These plastic insertions, though transparent, push her lips out and give her a speech impediment that arouses me, the fraction of me that can still be aroused. A desolate helpless love, as for a child, came over me as she tidily inserted herself into the bed, preparing, with the uncapping of a small bottle smelling powerfully of banana, to replace the paint on her nails. All these rites, I see, are her way of trying to freeze and defeat time, as mine is the writing of these scattered sad paragraphs. Futile, both exercises, but only in the long run. "Shall I stay?" I asked.

"Why?"

"Oh, for coziness. Because we both feel bad and embarrassed about the Indians."

"I do," she conceded, "but realistically we just couldn't let them have the entire country to run around in with their bows and arrows."

"They had learned to use guns. They were trying to learn our ways. Farming, going to church." I was stalling, saying anything to postpone the moment of our parting.

She had become intent upon her nails. She is her own innermost garden, needing incessant tending. I was intruding upon a precious moment of peaceful concentration; her pale eyebrows were knit in a small frown of unvoiced irritation.

"I need a hug," I said.

"Ben. I am doing my nails. You're making me make mistakes."

"I miss *us*," I told her.

She knew what I meant, but did not look or speak. The tiny brush of chemical solvent made its way around the oval nail of her lefthand ring finger with its slim gold band. What would an interplanetary voyager understand of our little symbolic shackles and their invisible chains?

"I can't do the main thing," I apologized, "but—"

"You'll get me and the bed all wet," she said.

Blushing, I finished, "I need to be touched. Somehow that show frightened me. That whole dreadful century, all that imperialism, and now everybody dead—the winners and losers, the cowboys and Indians, North, South, everybody. And no children in costume coming to the house. I was talking to Roberta today; Jennifer was going out trick-or-treating with Keith dressed as a bug, with those caps with bouncy antennae on springs. Irene told me that Olympe and Étienne got the idea of painting their faces white, that was their only disguise. A sort of portent in that, no? A few more years, they'll hate me. The white grandfather."

"Nobody hates you," Gloria said, concentrating downward on her hands. "Everybody knows you can't help what you are."

Hands—how I used to love my own hands. At the ages of twelve or thirteen, sexuality just beginning, and narcissism. Lying on my bed in my tiny dormered room in Hammond Falls, with its slant ceiling and Joe Namath poster, I would stare at my hands and flutter my fingers, and slowly twirl them in the dust-spangled air, the creased palms and freckled backs, and dive-bomb with them and soar, flaring one upward like a space rocket flattening into the stratosphere for its toss to the moon. I would ponder their articulation, their involuntary grace, their jointed sensitivity and prehensile strength. My fingerprints, unique in the world, in all those billions living and dying. When I asked—when that imperious voice enthroned at the back of my skull asked—my hands obediently became little dancing men, or firing pistols, or butterflies, or fists. They were always with me, the closest me I could see at will, without a mirror—emissaries my inner monarch would some day send out to grip and mold the world.

"You won't get wet," I promised Gloria. "I'll put on a fresh Depends—they're quite well designed, actually. I've been doing the Kegel exercises, I can feel a difference, and sometime soon—"

"Exactly," Gloria said. "Sometime soon." She held her face—shining with unabsorbed grease and protruding around the mouth like that of a beautiful buck-toothed ape—up to be kissed. Her eyes were shut; a little smile of expectancy on her pale lips anticipated my kiss, which descended upon her mouth like a hawk gliding down to take up a songbird or vole in its claws. Her face was a cold lake of grease, smelling medicinal.

"Sometime soon," she promised, "we'll do something. It's good you want to; you're getting better. But now go to your room, please. Take a pill if you don't think you can sleep."

I obeyed. It was pleasant enough in the guest room. The bed sheets were clean and cool, and the odd-angled shape in the far corner of the ceiling had acquired by now a guardian-angel quality, a boxed numen. I fell asleep upon the rumble of the eleven-ten train making the whole house quiver, woke once wet, and woke for good when the *Times* man swerved around the driveway. Dawn had yet to break, but a plump moon in the west bleached the bare November earth the white of a saint's bone, a knuckle or splinter of scapula in its reliquary of chased electrum, burnished at the base by the hungry kisses of the worshipful.

v. *The Dahlia*

THIS PLANET supports but two life-forms—
myself, and an immense fungus that has covered all
but the stoniest of available land. The brownish,
writhing, mounting formations aboveground are but a fraction of its mass, made up of microscopic hyphae that extend
their network in all directions, knotting and interweaving
into the mycelium that makes up the thallus, or undifferen-
tiated body, of my immense companion in vitality. It does
not speak, or visibly move, but it does undergo change, the
telltale mark of an organism. Its protoplasm is in constant
motion, streaming into the tips of the newer hyphae, draining from the older, which become vacuolated and turn pulpy
and a darker, more velvety brown. Though the fungus is ultimately one substance, consistent and immortal, its hyphae
do organize at times into compact masses that perform var-
ious functions—stromata, for instance, cushionlike forms
that bear spores, and rhizoids, anchoring the thallus to the
substrate, and septa, which more or less elaborately function
as valves controlling the flow of enzyme-liquefied starches,
sugars, celluloses, and lignins. Since the fungus possesses no

chlorophyll, it depends for nutrition entirely upon the rotting organic matter in the substrate. Whence came this matter? Its particulars are a mystery, but one that certainly testifies to a deep prehistory upon the planet, deeper than the imagination can grasp. The ground beneath my feet is an abysmal well of time.

I move about and eat of the fungus, tearing it with my hands. Its white, tan-skinned, at places freckled flesh is generally bland, sometimes sweet, rarely bitter. When it is bitter, or sour, I spit it out, and rinse my mouth with a cupped handful of the H_2O that is mercifully abundant. *Thank God for pure water,* I think; but are such thanks tautological, since without water I would not be here to offer them? Life exists amid benign conditions, inevitably, since conditions elsewhere, malign, would never have spawned it.

The fungus is everywhere, but not everywhere the same—far from it. In especially nutrition-rich stretches, it is mountainous, the hyphae so thickly interwoven as to have a leathery, though resilient, hardness underfoot, like a springy turf. In other, barer, colder regions, the fungus exists itself as a thin dry film across the rocks, in spots a mere stain, which a finger rubs off. I lick my finger then, for the fungus in this attenuated state is oddly tasty. There are grottoes, splotched and shadowy, where curved gills of a sweet, crisp mycelium form a cave of easeful comfort, and there are wind-troughed plains where rare upright conidiophores, brightly beaded with conidia, reward the wanderer with a pungent meat. A growth so vast and essentially amorphous at some point on its great surface folds and crests into every possible form—the stalked cauliflower of a tree, the flowing curves and protuberances of a reclining woman, the glimmering flatness of the sea. Everywhere, as I have said, it is edible, though my hands come away with broken fingernails from harvesting the stubborn delicacies in the crevices of rocks. The particularly delectable patches, wherein some secreted chemical such as lysergic acid induces a visionary sense of well-being, are maddeningly hard to distinguish, by outward appearance, from patches of the bland, somewhat rubbery daily fare. In general, one must either eat a great deal to arrive at a strikingly pleasurable mouthful, or else altogether refrain from eating until hunger renders any random handful delicious. The one promise the fungus makes is to be, however monotonously, *there*, day after day. Its evolution—the organic predecessors upon which its rhizoids feed—is mysterious, but not so basic a mystery, I dare say, as my own existence here, on this planet of all planets.

I often wonder if the fungus has a consciousness. Not like mine, of course (I am clearly more elaborately differentiated, from toenails to eyelashes), but in some diffuse way comparable, compatible with its endlessly repetitive structure—a dim awareness, like the light-sensors of blue-eyed scallops, that exists at the probing, searching tips of the tireless hyphae. Does it, moreover, *like* me, or is its patient feeding of me, day after day, an indifferent accident, a heartless largesse spilled from its own blind, entirely self-absorbed life? At times, curled beneath its soft beige gills of thallic matter, I feel a kind of vaporous breath that hints of love. The perpetual silence seems to develop an almost audible node in which an urgent benevolence is held as in a clenched fist. Sometimes I find in the convolutions of a folded outcropping some strikingly anthropomorphic set of ridges and vesicles—another man, about to stand forth!—and sense a joke, a thinking comment, a wry salute from my ubiquitous co-inhabitant. Certainly its vast body is warmer in some spots than others, and exudes a language of smells—punky, pungent, musty, faintly fruity—that is inflected as if by an inner consideration, a hope of achieving communion. At moments it even gives me back, as if out of an armpit or a groin, my own odor of stale male sweat.

John appeared today, in mid-afternoon in his green truck, to take his stand in the woods for a few hours. Hunting season has begun. Gloria was outside raking leaves. In my infirmity, she has to do it all herself this fall, except for the Saturdays when Jeremy can tear himself away from his computer classes and the aftermath of frat parties, including, he resentfully hints, a hungover and irritable girl in his bed. Gloria rakes up heaps of leaves and totes them off in bulging sheetfuls so heavy she staggers and stumbles in her slick-soled Wellingtons. She wears a red bandana and, when John pulled up, she put on a toothy smile that telegraphed happiness through the November drizzle even from my distant vantage at the guest-room window. Her face has a glow, from the vigorous exercise, as she puts down her burden and walks across the driveway to greet the gallant deerslayer. To me he seems, white-haired and stooped, with trembling hands, too old to warrant such a girlish greeting, but then I reflect that he is my age, if not—can it be?—a few years younger. Despite my post-prostatic discomfort, I put on trousers and shoes and a shirt and make my way downstairs. Steps down, I have discovered, are more painful than steps up.

I go outdoors, inhaling the heady liquor of oxygen and mist-filtered afternoon light. Only the ornamental bushes—forsythia, lilac—still cling to their leaves. John has a beautiful, unhurried grin, for all the defects of his lower teeth. His saintly patience slows all his facial movements, including the tongue and lip exertions of his careful, explanatory speech.

Proudly he shows us the absurd panoply of his camouflage gear. He owns, stacked on the driver's side of the truck, a variety of patterns and weights of costume. The splotches on one canvas jacket imitate the greenery of pine forest, and on another are painted the branches and coloring of deciduous trees in the fall. For today, he chooses a water-repellent Gore-Tex suit with a life-sized tree trunk prominent on the front. But before he puts it on, he shows us his bow—of gray metal, notched and calibrated like a gun, with a set of candy-colored sights embedded above the flat-faced grip, including a small tube that, when tightened, as he demonstrates, lights a tiny red light, for aiming in darkness. The string of the bow, as dark and plangent-looking as a harp string from Hell, has an incongruous tangle of fluff, like a gauzy pipe-cleaner, tied to it. "What's the purpose of that?" I ask.

"You know what they call that?" he asks in turn, chuckling. "A tarantula. It deadens the sound," he explains. "If a deer hears the twang, it'll drop down lower, as much as ten inches." Dramatically, he illustrates the sudden defensive action with his own body. "It'll 'jump the string,' as hunters say. Throws the shot totally off. The deer's instinct, you see, when it hears anything, is to crouch down ready to spring."

From Gloria's beaming expression she expected him, her miraculous savior, to complete the lesson by levitating into the air. "You're aiming at a seven-inch circle," John went on, equably addressing the two of us, though we stood some feet apart, estranged by my illness. His half-gloved fingers and thumbs described the imaginary target. "So you can imagine it throws you off if they hear the string."

In the interests of clarity, he bent his knees and became a

deer, about to leap. It seemed a kind of courting dance he was doing. An arrow of pain pierced me down below, on the dark side of my abdominal depths, as I murmured, "Interesting."

He showed us his arrows—again, metallic and machined. "Grooved," he explained, a finger lovingly tracing the groove. "For rigidity. Slow-motion movies show how a wood arrow, you can imagine with all that sudden pressure of release at the end, bends this way and that in flight, maybe six or seven times before it straightens out." His hands showed how, flexing in and then out. "By the time it reaches its target it's expended a lot of energy."

"But not these arrows," Gloria prompted, eagerly.

"No, ma'am," he said, the "ma'am" conveying, in its odd formality, an ironic intimacy. "These fly true."

The drizzle was making the driveway asphalt shine and gave a film-noirish intensity to our conference. The sun was a golden smear in a coarse gray sky washed by blue stripes of watercolor. As I made feeble motions toward helping Gloria with the leaves, John set about dressing, first in the large green-and-brown mock-arboreal pants, then a jacket, and last an olive wool hat stiffened in front like the cap of a Swiss yodeler. You would think he would have looked absurd, a walking tree, but in truth he looked distinguished, younger than his years—a gentlemanly shaman off to blend with the forest.

The light failed within an hour. Back in bed, I must have been napping when his truck drove off loudly into the darkness. As she set my dinner on a tray before me, Gloria moved with an abstracted grace, smiling to herself.

"Did he get a deer?" I asked.

"Of course not, not so soon. Not im*me*diately. But he said he'll be back in a few days. He'll bring a fawn blat."

"A fawn what?"

"*Blat*, apparently. It imitates the sound a fawn makes, so the mother comes."

"My God, how cruel. This is the cruellest guy I've ever met, and you seem to think he's great."

"I don't think that." Yet the inward-directed smile could not be erased from her tense cheeks, the tucked corners of her lips. "He's hopeful. He says that the signs are good."

"Signs."

"You know, darling. *Signs*. Intimations. He *feels* things."

"And I don't, huh?"

"Oh, Ben, you do, but everything you feel has to do with yourself. John feels things about *others*."

———

Where are the stars? The ancient legends describe the sky as full of stars, congregations of bright points that to unsophisticated eyes took on the forms of gods and godlike creatures—a centaur, a dragon, a bear, a whale. Our ancestors watched their sheep by starlight, and mariners steered their fragile ships upon the teeming sea by stars they knew by name and faithful location. Now the night sky presents a hazy slate, whose faint points of light can be confused with the small coagulations that float in the vitreous humor within the eyeball. Scientific apparatus less subjective than human sight reports that there is still a universe of mass and momentum out there in the dark, behind the closed closet door, so to speak, and science, though reluctant to admit the dimness, or visual negligibility, of the stars relative to their reported presence in their past, has tried to produce theories as to why this should be so.

A general muffling of signals has been proposed, due to

a cosmic moment of stasis. The universe after twenty-five billion years of inflation has reached the point where the Big Bang's initial momentum is exactly equal to the total amount of matter and, like a ball at the apogee of its toss, it is momentarily at rest, a pause reflected in a heavenly brownout before a future surge in the other direction. The bloated, feeble state of our sun—the muddy color of brick and so swollen its arc subtends a third of the horizon— would seem to offer confirmation. We have entered, on the cosmic scale, a dull, declining time.

Another proposal is that, through an unforeseen but per- fectly well understood effect of quantum mechanics and its uncertainty principle, "virtual" particles, called into "being" with their anti-particles, for titanically small periods of time, are multiplying in the gravitational and electromagnetic fields that permeate "empty" space, exciting each other into existence in such numbers that space is becoming a semi- transparent gel, occluding protons from afar. The condition may be restricted to our galaxy, or the nearer portion of it. A third school of scientific thought holds simply that indus- trial pollution and the dust raised by the last war have thick- ened our planet's atmosphere. But the war ended ten thousand revolutions of this planet ago, time for most dust to settle, and industrial production is still far from regaining pre-war levels. A fourth theory is that the ancients simply had better eyesight than we, or (a fifth theory) their astro- nomical descriptions were grossly exaggerated, to benefit the priestly hierarchy and its imbecilic royal puppets.

Coming back in the late-afternoon dark from a visit to the dazzlingly lit spaces of the Beverly Hospital (the doctors say

I am doing fine: my impotence, incontinence, pain, para-
noia, depression, and sense of dislocation are all on track in
the normal course of healing), we picked up in our headlights, to one side of the driveway, a man disguised as a tree.
It was John, walking back to his truck after two hours of remaining motionless in his stand. Gloria push-buttoned the
Infiniti window down and asked in a musical, sprightly, loving voice, "How did it go?"

"It was quiet," he admitted, with no hint of discourage-
ment.

"Our neighbor, Mrs. Lubbetts, told me on the phone she
saw four of them, feasting on her junipers."

"Oh, they're around," he chimed back. "It's just a question of time."

And what isn't? I sullenly thought.

The quiver of four aligned arrows on his back made him
look like an anti-aircraft battery draped in camouflage cloth.
His wire-frame glasses seemed still to hold the light from our
headlights. To make him aware of my presence, as I huddled
there beside Gloria, desperate for a diaper change, I cleared
my throat and asked, "Do the trinkets ever bother you? These
bigger new ones can do a job on human beings, I hear."

He straightened, so his saintly smile was all I could see
through Gloria's rolled-down window. "I carry a spray; they
mix it of sand and glue. One squirt of that and those darn
critters don't come near your feet again."

Gloria made the car seat bounce, this expertise excited
her so. Her radiant hair, cut and tinted while I was suffering my hospital checkup, blazed filament by filament in the
ambient glow of our headlights. Or was some cunning part of
John's armory giving off a secondary glow?

"Smell that?" he said suddenly.

"What?" she asked, breathless.

"A buck. Right about here."

We were parked, our engine idling, at a spot on the drive-way beside the sourwood tree, whose fallen leaves gave off, I had noticed, a rich, lusty smell of decay. But I didn't want to argue. I wanted only to get back to the house and get out of my wet Depends.

"There could be a *buck*?" Gloria asked, with a rising in-flection.

"Why not?" John asked in his slow voice. "This is the season. Fella I was shooting with over on Plum Island got a six-pointer whose nose was to the ground, following the scent of a doe. That's what they do. Buck smells a doe, his brain can't take in much else."

"How exciting!" Gloria exclaimed.

"Wasn't paying attention, that's how he got shot," John said, as if his nature lesson needed recapitulation.

"I'm soaked," I muttered at her side. "I'm miserable." Re-luctantly she moved the car up the driveway, nudging it along as if keeping step with the hunter walking up alone.

Next morning, shuffling down to pick up the *Globe*, I stopped by the sourwood to consider the odor in its vicinity. It was rank but, like the smell your finger brings away from probing the folds of your navel, or that your socks deliver when held beneath your nose at the end of a long day, not exactly unpleasant, because it is *you*.

It happened in my sleep, at dawn, when tender-faced rumi-nants inquisitively tread—nose extended like a fending hand in the dark—through the frost-whitened leaf mulch of the forest floor scarcely expecting, in the morning's innocence, an enemy to be awake. But John had gone three weeks without his kill and had set his alarm to ring in the dark, in the middle of his faithful wife's dreams. She rolled over, hearing him clump into his hunting boots, and fell back into a vision of venison.

I myself awoke to the sound of John and Gloria jubilating in mutually congratulatory murmurs down on the driveway. He had driven his green truck down the dirt road to collect the gutted carcass, then he had brought it back up to the house to show my wife his prize, the obscene fruit of their joint conspiracy. From my window I could see the deer's body like a taut russet sack tossed into the square-ribbed flatbed along with the metal lattice of his treestand and some stray planks of lumber. The white of the throat couldn't at first glance be distinguished from the big white-undersided tail. Heart thudding, I fumbled out of my sweated pajamas— never mind the soaked diaper, whose ammonia stung my eyes—and into yesterday's corduroy trousers and moth-eaten wool sweater. Without the patience for socks, I stuck my naked feet into loafers and, moving faster than I had for months, grabbed the old parka, with its seams leaking down, hung on the hook nearest the kitchen door downstairs. The cold outside was misty, and felt like shackles on my bare ankles. The day was still too young to have acquired horizons.

Scarcely since our wedding day have I seen Gloria's face aglow as it was beside the dusty, dented truck, with its lowered tailgate. Her bathrobe of purple chenille was clutched so tightly about her I knew she was wearing only a thin cotton nightie beneath. "He was crossing the old dirt road," she burst out proudly to me, "right where *John*"—it made me shiver, the juices of affection and respect she managed to squeeze into the monosyllable—"had figured out the route up to our yard was."

"She," I said. "It's a doe. It was a doe."

"Right across beneath my stand," John joined in. "A clean shot, the little downward angle suited me just fine, at about twenty feet." His saintly face, with its shambly brown teeth and washed-out blue eyes, was unable to conceal, quite, his murderous pride. "Maybe she sensed my pulling the bow," he went on. "She turned her head, to give me that seven-inch circle I spoke about. Zing! Right into the lungs. She didn't get more than a hundred yards, and stopped breathing where she bedded down. She gave me this one long look, like I was coming to her assistance, and then lay down her pretty little head on the leaves. I didn't have to use a second arrow. Depending on what gristle they pierce, they can be the devil to work out."

I saw the wound now, a messy matted X. The dried blood blended in with her reddish-brown coat, its hairs glinting silver in the rising sun. From my angle the deer's body stretched long as a lover's beside you in bed. "How'd you get her up in the truck?" I asked.

"The old fireman's squat-and-hoist," he boasted, unable to control his grin. "Once you've removed the entrails, that cuts out a lot of the water and slop. Still, she weighs something over a hundred pounds, I can tell you. Luckily, it was near the road. Sometimes you wind up with a mile or so to drag out the carcass. I backed in the truck and hoisted. You try to take the weight on your legs and give a grunt out loud. That's something we've learned from the Japanese, giving the power grunt."

The deer's head was toward me, on the lowered tailgate, as if to be fed something, her lips slightly drawn back, a lavender sliver of tongue visible. There were little crusts of blood around her black nostrils, relic of the bloody foam she breathed in her last minute. Her eyes were open, long-lashed, coffee-brown globules in which our oaks and tall white house set vertical reflections like tiny submerged fins. The short-haired barrel of her body, dented by the removal of its intestines and multiple stomachs and liver and lungs and heart, emitted in the frosty morning a vapor of relative warmth, like the winter sea, and a helpless strong animal smell, of dry hair and damp hide and the pellets released from her tidy anus in the sorry unravelling of death. From the inner corners of the deer's eyes flowed two dark markings, like tear trails. But the consciousness that had protruded into the two bright, snuff-flecked eyes had moved on, into another cosmic space.

John stepped toward me, exuding his own scent, of patiently absorbed woods and a hint of bad breath—he must have been a pipe-smoker, once, to wear down those teeth like that—as if to claim my congratulations. Gloria beamed in a happy daze behind his mottled shoulders. In his bulky camouflage outfit, and his intricately shaped knit cap, with its stump of a bill, he seemed princely, a groom at a pre-Christian wedding. The deer was his bride. Or was she mine, and he and Gloria the blessed pair on this gala day? It seemed plain enough that among the four of us my affinity was with the deer. Her conical slender face, with its coarse rubbery muzzle and indelible tear trails, gazed toward me; I could see myself move, a reflected splinter in parka and pajama bottoms, in the orb of dulling gel.

With a woman in love, for a time, you can do no wrong; then you reach a point where nothing you do is right. I had reached that point with Gloria a while ago and felt hardly a flicker of jealousy as she with grave sweetness—North Shore Lady Bountiful clad in naught but thin cotton beneath her regal purple robe—thanked the hunter over and over, pressing his trembling hands in both of hers.

Uneasily including me, John told us, "After I do the

butchering, I'd like to present you folks with a fine venison
steak. You choose the cut."

Class lines reasserted themselves. We both stiffened at the
offer. Did he mean for us to point out our preferred slice
right on the still-steaming corpse? It would be like eating a
large rat. Jointly we covered our refusal with the sauce of
insistent mannerly gratitude, but we had refused his, in a
sense, flesh. As he stepped out of his hunting gear and tree
costume, he seemed shrunken, smaller in size and in mystery. He put up the trunk tailgate, bending the deer's head
back so that I winced. *Ow.*

For a million years (or so), we didn't know what the stars
were. Witnessed primarily by the sleepless, by watchful
shepherds and sailors and the madmen who became the
tribal seers, the slowly spinning spatter of lights reappeared
overhead at sunset by we knew not what necessity; we gave
the most prominent of them names, and wove stories to
bind them together, but such exercise of our fancies drew us
no closer to the astonishing truth of their gigantic circum-
ferences, their unthinkable mass, their unbearable heat, their
ghastly distance from us, and their lives of atomic turmoil,
of incessant explosions and elemental mutations, fusing hy-
drogen nuclei to form the two-proton, two-neutron nuclei
of helium, and then in the convulsions of a supernova pressing helium into carbon, oxygen, neon, and ultimately iron.

Discovery of the stars' nature had to await the invention
of telescopes and spectrographs, which came about only after the rise and fall of many barbaric empires, led by kings
proclaimed by their priests to be earthly embodiments of
God. Their warfare, and the erection of monuments suit-

able in their grandeur to God-men, sluggishly propelled technology forward, through the invention of wheeled chariots, stirrups and saddles, catapults and rams, moats and portcullises, pulleys and booms, gunpowder, steam engines, radios, telephones, hydrocarbon-burning engines that could propel vehicles along the ground and even into the air, and so forth to the point where, a hundred years ago, it was understood that beyond the stars that a shepherd or sailor sees at night lie, across vast deeps of emptiness, conglomerations of more stars. These, fuzzy in their first sightings, were first called nebulae, and then island universes, and now galaxies. The numbers are so grand and round as to seem mere fabulations: a hundred billion stars in our own galaxy, a flattened spiral which is a hundred thousand light-years in diameter, and then a hundred billion galaxies beyond, of more or less the same size as our own. Such numbers numb us, else we would continually scream.

Scarcely fifty years ago—a mere wink in the history of our planet, a mere smothered yawn within the saga of our species—was it discovered that all the galaxies are rushing toward us at titanic speeds. Well, not all, for those the farthest away, at a distance of more than twenty-five billion years, are moving away, as a so-called "red shift" in their spectra inarguably reveals—which is to say, twenty-five billion years ago they were moving away. Now—but "now" makes no sense in cosmic terms. The farther we look, the more ancient is what we see. Inside this remote and ruddy ring of apparent recession there is a ring of stasis—of pause, of hesitation—twenty-four billion or so light-years away, and inside that the stars begin to scream blue. At first they murmur, but the nearer they are, the more distinctly and uniformly blue they are, since within a radius of five billion light-years we are looking into the relatively recent past. Some are rushing toward us at a considerable fraction of the speed of light.

It is clear what is happening: the universe is collapsing. The red shift on the periphery is very old news, testifying to a former expansion. There is much scientific speculation about the expansion. How did it happen? The collapse seems normal and inevitable: gravitational attraction, the most feeble but most relentless of the basic forces, is pulling everything home, to a singular core—a point, infinitely small and dense, of nothingness. But why did nothingness ever leave home, as it were? What placed the stars and galaxies, the quasars and black holes and oceans of neutrinos out there? Whence this inordinate amount of sparkling dust?

Out there—down there, up there—there must be or must have been, in the concentric rings of time, other souls. Indeed, the virtually infinite numerousness of heavenly bodies argues that somewhere, somewhen, I had or have an identical twin, amid a galaxy of brothers who resemble me closely. The odds are gigantically for it. Yet no proof has ever arrived. The distances have stifled with delay whatever radio signals or spaceships other populations might have launched. An impeccable silence hangs as answer to the great *Who?* Not that my twin would be any less puzzled than I—else he would not be my twin.

The long-range prospect appears clear. If the red-to-blue shift can be dated to plus or minus twenty-five billion years ago, the collapse will continue nearly that long before local effects can be observed. The background cosmic radiation of $2K°$ will rise to $3K°$, it is estimated, in ten billion years. From this point the universe will halve its dimensions in three and a half billion years and keep accelerating. In ten billion more years, the background radiation will have risen to 300K°. This is still cold, too cold for even the toughest life forms, but our planet will slowly become unable to divest itself of heat. Our glaciers will melt, and then our oceans will evaporate. A mere forty million years later, the background radiation will match the temperature needed for the creation and sustenance of life; but life will have vanished on our scorched planet, if it has not already been engulfed by the expansion of the local sun into a red giant. The background radiation—the temperature of space—has risen to 300C°, or 572F°, and will continue to rise as the universe halves in dimension every few millions of years. The galaxies will have merged, but star collisions will still be rare, there is so much empty space to eat up. The night sky will begin to glow a dull red. In time it will turn yellow, then white. The universe will be a furnace, an oubliette with white-hot walls. All planetary atmospheres will have been stripped; all life-forms, however ingeniously evolved in their crannies and lightless depths, will be remorselessly incinerated. Unable to radiate their heat away, the stars will explode; space will become a hot plasma of compressing gas. The rate of change will enter a scale of hundreds of thousands of years, then mere thousands, then centuries, days, minutes, seconds, split-seconds. As the temperature climbs to billions of degrees, atomic nuclei will disintegrate. In the compression of matter, protons and neutrons will no longer exist; the thick soup of unbound quarks will weigh trillions of tons per thimbleful. Black holes, those hells of absolute density, will merge with one another. Not just matter but space itself, taking with it time, will be crushed out of existence, and I and my soulmate, my certain twin in the expanding dust of aeons and aeons ago, will be one or, to be exact, no one.

But *can* time end? Space can be obliterated with the matter that measures it, but can time excuse itself from the grammar of sequence? *It was* implies a present that still *is*. Can the fact of something—especially an entire universe, all 10^{87} particles of it, all 10^{50} tons of it—having existed be ever obliterated? Time, having taken the imprint of being, must endure like a sheet of paper that, though blank, bears a watermark in its fibers. The priests who, in their conical hats configured with stars and moons, continue to practice their grotesque trade on this doomed planet even into this age of scientific enlightenment have a saying in their archaic language: *Our minds harry God from every covert, and yet he lives within. He is killed, and killed, and yet not.*

My own mind quails. The blue shift is tens of billions of years from heating the interstellar space by so much as a degree Fahrenheit. I am safe in my nest of local conditions, on my hilltop in sight of the still-unevaporated ocean. Nevertheless, I am uneasy. All the vegetation in my view is gray, leafless. The sea has no color; its uniformity of surface, scarcely rippled, offers the very image of entropy. The firmament is heavy, a mere webbing of lambent mortar between giant clouds as shapeless and motionless as paving stones. Plagues stalk the scabs of land, perpetuated by microörganisms that understand only annihilation; and nations, too, all illusions of *gloire* and civilizing mission hopelessly decayed, compete like animals in a cage where food for only half of them is supplied. The very short view alone is bearable.

The woods between here and the beach are a solid leafless brown, a kind of giant moss. Morning engenders beneath its surface a thousand forked glints of illumined bare twigs, an electric crackle of white sunlight. The flat roof of Mrs. Lubbetts' beach house forms the only note, a jarring one, of human habitation in the view.

Yesterday, or the day before—they do run together, the days—the air for the first time since last winter was so much colder than the sea that the water smoked: little cloudlets of vapor, in strips and vague zigzags, adhered to its surface until the sun warmed them out of existence. On such sunny dry days shrivelled leaves scrape and scutter almost deafeningly across the black asphalt of the driveway.

The world still holds leaves. Along 128, as Gloria drove me, "to get me out of myself," on some errands of hers (sizing up the competition in the gifts trade, mostly) to the so-called North Shore Shopping Plaza—an inferno of tacky consumerism that I once visited with Deirdre, she looking like my young nurse, I looking like every other retired parasite upon the shattered economy—I noticed that among the mostly bare trees the willows still have kept lemonade-yellow tops, the lower, shaded leaves having fallen but these top leaves still sucking vitality from the ever more obliquely angled sun. I also saw along the highway that some strange trees (oaks, I think, of a special sort) have bleached almost white in turning and yet do not drop their leaves, rather like trees abruptly killed by lightning.

A strange hallucination: in walking down to pick up the *Globe*, with my gradually more vigorous stride, I made a mental note, rounding the first curve, to pick up the sizable branch that I had seen fall off the hickory tree. But no branch was there, and then I remembered that I had seen it fall in a dream, this morning before awaking. In my dream, I was looking out this window beside which I so often sit writing and saw the branch that most conspicuously hangs down slowly break away and fall. The sight made me happy, because the branch had long bothered me and now I had a less obstructed view of the sea, and of Misery Island and, beyond it, Baker's, with its lighthouse and Methodist summer houses. The dream had been so vivid, and yet so modestly plausible, that I caught myself trying to act upon it in the "real" world of three dimensions and Greenwich time.

As the day that had begun so cold continued, the sea became absolutely silken, the same delicately rippling blue from shore to horizon, as if in two dimensions. It had perceptible threads in it—tiny "floats," as textile manufacturers say—in diagonal rows, as in gabardine. The blue line of the South Shore also floated, admitting beneath itself a thin pale line of air the same faintly tawny color as the sky.

Coming back up the driveway, annoyed with the lilac and the forsythia for still being green, I touched a forsythia branch, and several of the leaves, narrow and pointed, fluttered to the ground. They came off at the lightest tug, twirling down to join the gaudier leaves of the sourwood, already matted in a mulch, compounded like chipwood, of scarlet and gold. I withdrew my hand in distaste. I had no wish to take Nature's place, to usurp her lethal, cyclical prerogatives.

The Kegel exercises are coming well. I stand above the toilet bowl and think of all the oval toilet bowls I have gazed into since first learning to go pee-pee in that narrow country house shaken by the traffic on the road heading down into the chimneyed brick heart of Hammond Falls. Imagining myself a child again, I try to remind my puzzled, wounded body how to release the urethral sphincter and make a golden arc. There is a ghost in my machine that controls the valves. Ever more, I seem to locate him, somehow. Mind over matter: I feel such triumph, to be regaining this bit of my animal self. But I can brag about it only to Gloria, and not too often; her face shows impatience with my body.

Christmas looms a month away, and she spends more time at her gift shop, leaving me to roam, cautiously, in the house.

One day I went looking for the dahlia. The ugly white tubers, the black dirt slowly drying and crumbling off their wrinkled skins, lay for a week on a green garbage bag spread on the laundry-room counter, and then vanished. I knew she was going to pack them in plastic peanuts, in a ten-inch square cardboard box she had brought from the shop, and store them in either the cellar for coolness or the attic for dryness, but I did not know which. I dared the sinister dank cellar, where in my absence the spiders have been free to multiply their webs, and checked all the closets on the third floor, yet could not find the cardboard cube. I wanted simply to gaze at it for a few seconds, even if it was taped shut, and to hoist its weight in my hands. It would be lighter, I imagined, than I expected. It would be Egyptian only in its severe shape and sealed pledge.

I could ask her where she had stored it, but fear she would take this as an intrusion. Since I can no longer insert myself into her flesh, any other form of intrusion has become offensive to her. She does not know this herself, but her face and voice tell me, and the impatient quickness with which she moves around me. The dahlia was the unforeseen triumph of her summer. She loves it; it is hers; any attempt of mine to draw consolation from it would be an affront. She is afraid, perhaps, that I will open the box before it is ready, before spring is here. She sees me, it dawningly becomes clear, as a brute, clumsy and impulsive and unpredictable, apt to tear open everything sealed and to crush everything fragile.

Another hallucination: walking down to pick up the *Globe*, I distinctly heard the gurgle of a mountain stream, purling and twisting unseen through a narrow rock-lined gorge. But my little hill is no mountain, and though the November day was misty, no rain had fallen for days. Yet the sound was unignorable, arising from the swampy valley between the driveway and the beach, yet close to my ear—a huge invisible angel murmuring.

There had to be a rational explanation, and bit by bit, like a coded message assembling itself in mid-air, it came to me. Dark birds were flicking, I saw, from branch to branch in the veil of trees on the slope toward the sea; I realized that a great flock of migrating starlings had settled momentarily in my woods, and that the birds' massed chirping, their merry-sounding signals one to another, had uncannily imitated the sound of a gurgling stream, even to its tinny and pulsating undertones. As if flushed by my reasoning, percipient mind from their camouflage, hundreds of birds arose with a soft thunder of wings and roosted, still twittering, in the great solitary oak on the boundary between our property and the Kellys'. Thick as leaves, the starlings blackened the bare branches so that there was only a shuffle of sparks of daylight between them.

What do the little black-and-white birds that stay with us all winter live on? Plump, uncomplaining, they hop from twig to twig of the thickets visible from the driveway and yet one never sees them peck a berry from the goosefoot maple or a seed from beneath the euonymus.

The lilac has quite lost its leaves suddenly; but next year's buds are already in place. When I pinch them, they yield, as living matter does.

There are voices downstairs. Gloria's children have come for the holiday. I should be down there with them, answering to the name of "Pop." Since they will be joining their real father in Mexico for Christmas, they are giving thanks with us tomorrow. Divorce and remarriage impose fair-mindedness, with its strict mathematics, upon the children.

They have added a voice—a baby's squawk and much-tended-to cry. Roger and Marcia in the year past have produced a male child, named Adam. He is brick-red. Marcia talks to him incessantly in that baby voice of hers, while the tiny person, three months old, still stunned by the world, stares unfocusedly up into the outpour of what is to be had on this planet—light, milk, voices, danger, love. Beatrice will be having her child, my eleventh grandchild, in January of 2021.

Gloria has expanded thrillingly into the role of grandmotherhood; it gives her yet another dimension, with, impotent though I am, a stirring element of perverse fantasy. My mental apparatus of lust, constructed mainly of images from popular culture, remains inconveniently intact. In her grandmotherhood she is like an actress in a blue movie whom we discover, before her preordained nudity, dressed in the habit of a nun, or as a little girl, with rouged cheeks, sucking on a lollipop.

She says the weathermen are talking snow tomorrow. Last year this time we were wallowing in the stuff, but today, under an indeterminate sky, is unseasonably warm. She cannot mound up the roses until the ground freezes; otherwise, mice burrow and nest in the tilth beneath the mulch and eat the rose roots. The weather is so warm a multitude of small pale moths have mistakenly hatched. In the early dark they flip and flutter a foot or two above the asphalt, as if trapped in a narrow wedge of space-time beneath the obliterating imminence of winter.

A Note About the Author

John Updike was born in 1932, in Shillington, Pennsylvania. He graduated from Harvard College in 1954, and spent a year in Oxford, England, at the Ruskin School of Drawing and Fine Art. From 1955 to 1957 he was a member of the staff of *The New Yorker*, and since 1957 has lived in Massachusetts. He is the father of four children and the author of some forty books, including collections of short stories, poems, and criticism. His novels have won the Pulitzer Prize, the National Book Award, the American Book Award, the National Book Critics Circle Award, the Rosenthal Award, and the Howells Medal.

A Note on the Type

The text of this book was set in a digitized version of Janson, a typeface long thought to have been made by the Dutchman Anton Janson, who was a practicing type founder in Leipzig during the years 1668–1687. However, it has been conclusively demonstrated that these types are actually the work of Nicholas Kis (1650–1702), a Hungarian, who most probably learned his trade from the master Dutch type founder Dirk Voskens. The type is an excellent example of the influential and sturdy Dutch types that prevailed in England up to the time William Caslon developed his own incomparable designs from them.

Composed by N.K. Graphics,
Keene, New Hampshire
Printed and bound by R. R. Donnelley,
Harrisonburg, Virginia